10/03

this

SIDE

of the

SKY

this

SIDE

of the

SKY

A   NOVEL

ELYSE   SINGLETON

BLUEHEN BOOKS

a member of

Penguin Putnam Inc.

New York

This is a work of fiction. Names, characters, places, and incidents either are
the product of the author's imagination or are used fictitiously, and any
resemblance to actual persons, living or dead, business establishments,
events, or locales is entirely coincidental.

BLUEHEN BOOKS
a member of
Penguin Putnam Inc.
375 Hudson Street
New York, NY 10014

Copyright © 2002 by Janet Elise Singleton

Published simultaneously in Canada

Library of Congress Cataloging-in-Publication Data

Singleton, Elyse.
This side of the sky : a novel / by Elyse Singleton.
    p. cm.
ISBN 0-399-14920-1 (acid-free paper)
1. African American women—Fiction.   2. World War, 1939–1945—Fiction.
3. Female friendship—Fiction.   4. Mississippi—Fiction.   I. Title.
    PS3619.I575T48   2002   2002018620
            813'.6—dc21

Printed in the United States of America
1   3   5   7   9   10   8   6   4   2

This book is printed on acid-free paper. ∞

Book design by Marysarah Quinn

This book is dedicated to the staff of the downtown Denver Public Library for all the assistance they have given me with my research, for my work in journalism and fiction, over the years. And it is dedicated to libraries and librarians all over the world for so well representing the better side of human nature.

I have found powers in the mysteries of thought,
exaltation in the chanting of the Muses;
I have been versed in the reasoning of men;
but Fate is stronger than anything I have ever known.

EURIPIDES
c. 484–406 B.C.

We will learn to live together as brothers
or die together as fools.

—Dr. Martin Luther King Jr.

ONE

KELLNER

Russia

1951

Long in suffering, quick in losing—seven years. Every day, another season of winter whisked by, just like that. Did she think he had been killed? Or did she assume he had married someone who looked more like him?

He knew that to her he had become a man of dead promises. Yet, he remembered her elegant mind, the deep blackness of her hair, the liquid brown of her eyes, and the way her pearl earrings drew his eyes to the curve of her neck.

He did not know whether he would live out the day. And he had only one reason to care. The single thing that redeemed the world was that somewhere, she lived. Even now, in this endless winter, he could feel the warmth of her hand.

LILIAN

Mississippi

1930

. . . a flight of unsung hearts . . .

As a girl, I loved anything with wheels or wings—
including Pontiacs, trains, bread trucks and hummingbirds—because
they all had the power to get out of Mississippi. This is what I wanted to
do, and couldn't do on the authority of my underage feet alone. But I
swore to myself that once grown, I'd do anything to leave. If my legs
were broken, I'd hobble. If my eyes were blind, I'd grope and stumble.
If a cement wall stood at the state line, I'd defy natural laws, sprout great
wings that flailed the thick air and beat the mighty odds so I could soar
away—anything. I didn't know then that the highest fence might be my
own mind. I did know, though, that in Mississippi, I was just killing time
and mourning its passing. Away I could have adventures, cross oceans,
sample cities and get a glamorous job. I could fall in love, resolve my
deepest hurts, author my own life and write it as a gleaming epoch so
that for one perpetual moment, I'd feel joy.

One thing was certain: I'd go with Myraleen when I left. She felt as
dead as I did in Mississippi and came to share my determination to escape a place where we'd been mismatched with our own lives.

Miz Herdie was the first to get an inkling of it. She took care of us
when we were little. When we first started walking, we walked with

purpose, she said. Our stumbling steps weren't roundabout and near-sighted like the other babies'. We waddled out the door in a northeast-erly direction, past the chickens, toward the mustard and turnip greens that thrived along the gate, and we probably would have left the prop-erty altogether if she'd let us. It was as if we were being pulled by a gos-samer string.

She knew it, she'd say later. One day we'd fly away, and it would be a flight of unsung hearts and untried legs, and if we smacked the ground and shed our lives in the attempt at living, well, that's just how things went sometimes.

Myraleen and I stayed with Miz Herdie while our mothers worked. Myraleen's mother worked in a white lady's kitchen. Mine shucked oys-ters down near Gulfport. A wagon burdening two horses for one hour hauled her and some others to a house on the pier packed with wet buck-ets of grimy brown shellfish. What I remember most clearly from the earliest days was riding up to Miz Herdie's porch in Mudear's arms, and my face being pushed into the old woman's bosom. I knew better than to cry.

Miz Herdie placed me on the floor beside a little girl with no color, who bit and scratched. People who came around looked at that child, reared back their chests and said, "Yeah, daylight done broke on that one all right, damn near white!"

Myraleen had no clear reason to fight me. I'd be over in a corner, playing with a shoe box, and suddenly she'd be at my side, with those paper-thin nails poised for combat. This went on for a long time, it seemed, until I came to think Myraleen was punishing me for some un-known wrong. Mudear would get mad, and tell me I'd better learn to pick up my feet, instead of falling so much and getting all scratched up or she'd add a whipping to the scratches.

Then one time Miz Herdie saw Myraleen race her nails down my bare arm. We were in the yard, and Miz Herdie was stepping fast behind a dirty-feathered chicken wise enough to run. As she grabbed it, she saw the mischief out of the corner of her eye. Suddenly, her coal-colored free hand came down to snatch up Myraleen's arm like a great hook from heaven, and she dragged her and the chicken to the porch steps. Dangling them both in front of her, she sat down.

Her big black face butted up against the little white one. "Don't you ever let me catch you doing dat again, or I'm gon take dat belt and tear your li'l sun-kissed tail up." Myraleen turned a deep shade of pink. Then Miz Herdie looked behind her toward me, and seemed to get even madder. "Why didn't you say somepum? You old nuf to talk for yourself. Don't let people mistreat you like dat. Next time . . ." She tightened her grip on the chicken's head, twirled it around, flicked her wrist to give his body a twisted flip through the air, and he flopped dead on the porch. "Next time, I'm gon whip de two of you." Myraleen stopped scratching me and started playing with me.

Miz Herdie had us weekdays and Saturdays until we were six and went off to school. Each morning, I'd wait for Myraleen at her gate. Within a minute, she'd come out of the splintery oak door that groaned when she opened it. She'd always wear outfits that featured pleats or a sailor collar or suspenders or a combination. They'd be erected in rock starch, transformed from weak-willed cotton to the militancy of timber.

At lunchtime we pulled apart our sandwiches or chicken wings or whatever we had. Then we'd trade half for half to double the variety of our meals. Her oil-splotched bag always hosted butterscotch-colored planks of peanut brittle too, which she split with me though I had no sweets to offer her in return.

We both were only children, the sole brotherless, sisterless youngsters in the colored part of town. "Play cousins" is what we told people we were. But we never said this in front of our mothers.

"I don't know why you want to put yourself on people who don't like you," Mudear said. "You know that woman don't like you being up under her precious piss-colored child." It was true. Whenever I'd play in Myraleen's yard, her mother peered at me with a hard sideways glance, as if she'd just as soon stomp me as look at me.

Mercy Chadham was a big haunted house of a woman. Her mouth didn't seem like other people's. A scar cut across the right side of her lips like a nowhere road on a map. Two gold teeth stabbed my eyes with an unexpected flash whenever she opened her mouth. When she smiled, it looked like two long pink worms lay curled and dead upon her face. Much of the time, though, her lips bore into each other in anger. Even her size was intimidating; she seemed as big and wide as bed linen and she was so light she had freckles. The way her mother saw the world didn't seem to have a big impact on Myraleen—at least not at first. Then, when we were thirteen, everything changed.

One morning, I waited through the first promising minutes at the gate without seeing her. After fifteen minutes, the door still hadn't groaned. Maybe she was sick. From where I stood, I couldn't see inside the windows. And I certainly wasn't going to get caught peeping through Mrs. Chadham's curtains.

I finally left. I ran, my thick underbraids spanking my shoulders as if to spur me, and made it to the schoolhouse only a half second before Mrs. Marsh's hand-slapping ruler was out for latecomers. Chairs and desks stood in straight rows she had realigned from the previous day's shifting. October 22, 1930, was written on the blackboard in fresh white chalk. Long after class had begun, my eyes kept drifting toward the door. "Better stop worrying about that door, and start worrying about your lesson, little Miss Lily Mayfield," Mrs. Marsh said. Playground talk solemnly swore that hidden in a secret closet, she had a "whipping machine," a contraption with a strap to batten down wrongdoers so an electric paddle could beat them for hours. A pupil blurted this out once, and it was the only time I ever saw Mrs. Marsh laugh. We were going into a whipping machine of a world, she'd taught us. If we learned to do everything correctly, that would lessen our licks. About every other day, she'd say to us, "As a rule, always be the exception." And once, she'd pulled me aside at the door as the rest of the children ran to catch the waning after-school part of the day. "You're a dark one," she said. "So at least you better be a smart one."

I had no one to walk home with that October afternoon. Sometimes other girls would stroll along with us, listening to Myraleen make fun of everybody out of hearing range. "That Zelma got feet as big as baby caskets," she'd say, or "Miz Marsh's butt stick out so much you could set a table on it and serve Christmas dinner." But I had no sassy talk to attract the girls. So I walked along the red dirt road alone. Myraleen was the only person who'd listen to what I had to say. Where was she?

Odd that I would think back to then, when yesterday was now. Old people used to say there comes a time when you remember fifty, sixty years ago as if it were last week, but damn if you can remember last week at all. They were right. Every generation thinks their time is the *time and talks about the present as if it's some stable territory they can occupy indefinitely. Yet when we say* now, *by the time we get to the* w *sound, the* n *is in the past.*

Pallbearers haul the casket from the church into the damp day, and we stand watching and waiting for the car. A familiar shoulder rubs against mine in a by-now ancient gesture of comfort between two intimates, a touchstone to the moment. Still, my mind zigzags, traversing a century, two continents and four lives.

MYRALEEN

. . . Mr. Cheevers was getting married . . .

MY MAMA USED TO SAY, "I DON'T KNOW WHY YOU WANT TO be around that li'l tar baby. Her and her mammy's as black as a hopeless midnight." But Lily never got bold in my chest, like some of the other girls did and said, "You think you cute!" And I'd have to set 'em straight and say, "Naw, monkey face, I *know* I'm cute!" Lily's talk stayed sting-less and nicey-nice. Plus she knew things in a town where folks didn't know pee from perfume and were proud of it. Strange, dark as she was, Lily was my only snatch of light. You could ask that girl anything, I swear. When God was handing out brains and everybody else was off picking their noses, Lilian with that polite look of hers stood holding out a bushel basket for extras.

On the way home from school one day when we were about twelve or so, Edna Crawford told us how her cousin was eighteen before she got her period. "So my auntie took her to this lady who was like a nurse and the lady stuck a long needle up her you-know-what and made her period come down."

The thought made my steps come to a stop in the red dirt and my thighs clap together to shut out evil. "Oooh, girl, no!" Edna and Lilian stopped when I did, in sympathy. Edna wasn't afraid of anything, and for some reason Lilian didn't look too concerned.

"I should know. It happened to my own cousin."

My knees moved forward again but my shoulders slouched in disgust. Periods were a secret only a few of us knew. Edna's older sister Johnnie started that year and thought the red pop she'd been drinking had leaked through. That's how we got a little of the lowdown about it. Why did such a nasty thing have to happen at all? I'd made up my mind I wouldn't start until I was at least nineteen. "I hate needles," I said. "That would be the worst thing in the worst place. But I don't want to get a period either."

"I guess you damned if you do and damned if you don't then," Edna said.

"Girl, damned-if-you-do-and-damned-if-you-don't is the house where I live."

About this time, Lilian, usually too shy to buck anybody, put her two cents in. "That doesn't sound right, Edna. Maybe you misunderstood."

"And who was talking to you anyway, blacky?"

I laughed. Generally, I enjoyed any bad-mouthing that wasn't aimed in my direction.

"Well, I ain't no liar. That's what happened."

"Look, I can't listen to no arguing. All that talk about needles gave me a nervous headache. I hate needles."

Edna's mother was waiting at the gate with a list of chores long enough for Job and a what-took-you-so-long-you-always-lollygagging speech. Lilian and I had a ways more to walk.

"Still got a headache?" Lilian asked down the road.

"Yes indeedy."

"Let's go to the library."

I didn't see how that could possibly help a headache, only make me late enough so my mama would double my misery.

"We'll be quick."

" 'Sides, that lady might not let me in."

"We'll see. If not, I'll go in and you won't have to wait but a little while."

Lilian had told me she walked into the white library when she was nine years old. Instead of getting her butt beat by both the lady in charge and her own mama, she got to stay. At first, the lady put the palm of her hand on top of Lilian's head, turned her in the direction of the door and pushed her until her little chin almost bumped the knob. She took her outside and pointed to the colored library that owned a used-up, old-fashioned pile of not-much and at least four *Little Black Sambo* books.

But when Lilian was halfway down the street, the lady called her back. Only one of two folks showed up on weekdays, anyway. Lilian could come, she said, but never on Saturday and always through the back door. "If anybody's here and says anything, you beg their pardon and pity and then scat." Lilian said, "Yes, ma'am," and she's been going to the white library ever since.

All books having anything to do with ladies' problems she swept off the shelves. She hauled them to a back table where the librarian couldn't see what we were doing. Her forefinger rode down the index of each book looking for the words *needle, menstruation,* or *amenorrhea*—whatever in the heck that meant. It sounded like somebody got the Holy Spirit and couldn't stop saying amen.

She didn't find a paragraph or page (Lilian read bullet fast) that paired *needle* and *menstruation* or *needle* and *amenorrhea.*

"Edna misheard something, that's all. When grown people are talking, they're half whispering, anyway. She just put wrong words in the empty spaces."

My headache left. Lord, this girl had magic.

EVEN THOUGH I prayed every night to keep it away, one morning when I was thirteen, I woke up with reddish brown stains in my underpants. After that, Mama complained more about the time I spent with Lilian, and any other children for that matter. "You don't need to be doing all that ripping and playing and foolishness. You too old for that mess."

"Yes'um," I said and out of her eyeshot, I ripped, ran and hopscotched as much as I pleased. But all that soon stopped.

When I got home from school one Thursday, Mr. Cheevers was sitting in the front room. He was a man with big, old, piano-key teeth, who worked as a house and barn painter in our county and the next. I figured he was waiting for my daddy to get home from work, so I passed right by him, headed for the kitchen. "Hidy," I said to my mama. She was making ham sandwiches. She stared at me in that knocking but steady way that made her eyeballs seem like fists bouncing off my face. That's the way it was with Mercy. With her, you never knew whether it was going to be the picnic or the flies. More and more, it was getting to be the flies.

"Cain't you speak?"

"Yes, ma'am. I spoke."

"You ain't spoke to Mr. Cheevers."

"Hello, Mr. Cheevers," I called. "Hiya doing this afternoon?"

"Girl, go on in there and talk to the man like you got some sense."

How to act around grown-ups could be tricky. I hadn't spoken to Mr. Cheevers in the first place because sometimes if girls spoke too easily to men, their mamas would say, "Shut yo' fast ass up. He grown; you ain't got no business talking to him." Mama had never before told me to talk to a man other than my father.

Mr. Cheevers flashed those old piano keys in a wide grin. He was a long skinny man whose walk was wide legged and hard as if he was stomping a snake with each step. His voice was so deep it sounded as if it was coming from hell. He was maybe about thirty years old.

"Come over here, girl, and sit down." He patted a spot on the couch right beside him. I sat three or four feet left of where he patted. "You still in school?"

"Yes sir. I'm in the eighth grade." At this point I expected him to say I was smart, as most grown folks did when you told them you were in your right grade. He said nothing, though, so I went on. "I'm good at mathematics, history and geography, but I'm not that good at English." This is when adults would give advice on how to do better, even if they'd never gone to school themselves. "After you finish studying, sleep wit yo' books under yo' pillow at night," they'd say.

Mr. Cheevers said a funny-sounding thing, though. "You don't have to worry about that no mo'," he said.

Then my mother was bending over him, draping a starched cloth napkin over his lap, giving him a plate with a sandwich on it. "Here, William. Hope this'll hold you till supper time. We'll be eating as soon as Luther gets home."

Talk around the dinner table that evening had a Sunday ring to it. Voices clanged against each other. Laughing rang through it all. Something special was going on. But I didn't know what, and if I asked, Mama might have told me not to mess in grown folks' business. "Yeah," she said to Mr. Cheevers, "I think she gonna be a pretty good old helpmate."

She! She! Who was this "she" they were talking about? Most of the time I had no problem understanding adult conversations. It was pretty simple once you figured out the signal words they had for secret things like man-and-woman stuff, dying and sickness. I could understand the gist of it: Mr. Cheevers was getting married. But who in the hell would want him? Mama kept saying how well he'd be able to take care of the lady because his painting business was "in demand and up and coming."

On the way out the door, Mr. Cheevers shook Daddy's hand. "I think we done made a square deal here, and thank you kindly, Mercy, for the nice dinner.

"And you," he said to me. "I'll see you on Sunday."

You old ugly-mouthed son-of-a-bitch, I thought. Who'd want to see your tail on the Lord's Day? What was in my mind must have shown on my face.

Mr. Cheevers's head flew back in a laugh. "Don't you be frowning up at me, gal," he said and laughed again, closing the door.

Mama hit me hard on my left shoulder. "Did you roll your eyes at him?" she said.

"No, Mama. I just didn't know what he was talking about, that's all."

"Ain't you got a nickel's worth of sense?"

I knew there were two kinds of knowledge a child could have: too much and not enough. If you knew too much, you were a fast ass; not enough, and you were a stupid ass.

Daddy drifted into the back room, as he always did when Mama was about to light into me. He was a "house-is-hers" man. Children came under the category of the house business, like cooking or deciding what kind of curtains to make, which came under the category of nothing he wanted to be bothered with.

"Damn," Mama said, her face moving closer to mine. "You lucky we got somebody willing to marry your stupid ass."

"Marry?" I looked at her harder than it was safe to do, searching for some sign she was just playing, messing with me.

Her face said she wasn't kidding. Maybe I had known all along, and hoped that if I didn't think it, it wouldn't be true.

"Mama, Mama. I'll be good. I'll do more work around here, and stop lollygagging on the way home from school. I promise. I promise. Please, Mama, I don't want to get married."

"You don't want . . . ," she said slowly. "You don't want." Then that line came across her face that was the opposite of what a smile should be, hatred happy with itself.

Every time she said those words, her chest got bigger with strength to beat my ass. "You don't want? Who gives a damn what you want. You don't rule nobody here!" Then her hand sailed to my temple where she grabbed a handful of hair. She used it as a handle to yank me around the living room. "I try to make a way for you, and you got the nerve to come talking about what you want." She stressed each syllable with a short hard jerk of my head. "I know what you want, all right. You want to lie around here till one of these tail-sniffers notices you. So you'll end up with a bellyful of niggah and a cupboardful of nothing. FOO-OOL! IS THAT WHAT YOU WANT?"

"No, ma'am, Mama. No, ma'am, Mama." Tears met snot above my lips. Tiny streams blended at my gasping mouth, and droplets flew into the air. The room swirled and rocked. Floorboards, chair legs, my own legs and feet swept in and out of my view. The white blouse I was wearing lost its backbone, got damp and limp. "No, ma'am," I said, as she let me fall to the floor, wet and red and shaking.

I WAS GOING to go to school the next morning. Mercy said there was no reason to—and no time to, either. "Girl, you don't know how much got to be done 'round here before Sunday. If you get a chance to scratch your butt, you be lucky."

LILIAN

. . . *"too young" . . .*

WOMEN CHASED BY THEIR TROUBLES SOMETIMES RAN INTO
our house under the discretion of darkness to see what Mudear could do
for them. The fast pounding of their desperate steps jarred my sleep and
made me dream of Cinderella fleeing the night.

Mudear would fix what bothered them or at least part of it. I didn't
know exactly how she did it. I'd wake perhaps for a moment and hold
my head up, stir audibly in my cot, lean my ear toward the sounds. But I
found it easy to obey Mudear's gruff "Go back to sleep." So I never saw
what went on until the very last time. And that would never have happened had it not been for a story. I'd read it to Myraleen a few days before she'd disappeared from school. In the yard at lunchtime, after we'd
eaten our divided sandwiches, I slid a sheet of folded paper from my
dress pocket.

I read softly so no one else could hear and make fun. I'd written a
story about a princess who sat on her throne in front of her castle, which
was made of gold. Many men asked for her hand, but they never looked
into her eyes. All the time they were proposing, their eyes were on the
castle. One day a man appeared who looked into her eyes. He saw so far,
he saw her heart for the good, true thing that it was. It, too, was gold.

"You are the one I will marry," she said. "And she kissed him."

"You made up all that by yourself? It sounds like it came from the Bible," Myraleen said. "Save it and when you get grown, maybe they'll put in a fairy-tale book."

I took it home to Mudear and waited expectantly as she read it. When I brought a test paper with an A, she'd give a weak nod and say "yeah." That was as lavish as her approval got, and I cherished it. This was one better than a good grade on a school paper because no one even told me to do it.

She put the paper down. No nod. No "yeah." "What do you mean she kissed him? What do you know about kissing?"

"Nothing, Mudear."

"Then why you writing something about people kissing all over each other."

"I don't know, Mudear."

Deep into that night when trouble knocked, Mudear told me to wake up and answer the door. It was Mrs. Wright in a long black chenille housecoat and leather work boots.

Quick breaths told me she'd run most of the way from the far rim of the colored wedge of town, where she lived with her husband and five children.

"Ready for you, Lucy," Mudear said from the kitchen. Mrs. Wright brushed past me, and I turned in the direction of my bed. Our house was more shack than sanctuary, and I always felt a little ashamed when people came around for any reason. It was composed of just a kitchen where we ate and a main room where Mudear and I slept in two roll-away beds at night.

"Got something for you to do, Lilian," Mudear said. "Come here." At her feet was a stack of at least three blankets spread on the floor and topped with an abundant feathering of newspaper pages with headlines crying of bank failures, crop failures and foreclosures. Mudear told me to get the clean white sheet she'd set aside on the table in the main room. Stooping, she took both ends and she cast it in the air above the newspaper. It hovered in the air for a second, giving off a scent of bleach, before it settled on the flat bed beneath us.

On the kitchen table lay a stack of white towels. A flashlight, a bottle of iodine, a wide piece of coil and a box of Kotex were next to them. Then I saw three metal rods: a thin one made of chicken-coop wire; a thicker one that looked liked a straightened mattress spring; and the thickest reminded me of a lightning rod, miniaturized and flattened, with the ends melted down to smooth sharpness.

Next to it lay a rod of the same circumference, but the upper tip of it was shaped like a narrow spoon tiny enough to feed a bird.

Metals glowed. Linens gleamed as if they had been cleansed by the sort of washing that hurts the hands. Mrs. Wright took off her robe and hung it on a chair. She put her hands under her nightgown and maneuvered her underpants off and placed them in the pocket. Then she lay down.

When I turned to go, I felt Mudear's grip pinch my shoulder. "I want you to hand me some things when I tell you." First, she wanted the iodine, then the flashlight.

I tried to look only at the table. Though her work boots remained on, Mrs. Wright had rolled her nightgown above her waist. As I turned to give each thing requested, I couldn't avoid seeing. Mudear used the rods, the thinnest one followed the thicker one and then the thickest, to open someplace up inside of Mrs. Wright. There was a scream muffled by her hand clapped over her mouth. It hit me: Those were the "needles" that were the source of Edna's confusion. Her cousin must have . . . The sight of blood rushing to pool at naked thighs made me dizzy.

My mother worked inside Mrs. Wright through the coil-expanded opening, with the tiny spoon. "I'm almost done, Lucy," she said.

From the floor, a cry mixed with a moan: "Thank the Lord."

When it was over, Mudear told Mrs. Wright to rest before the walk home, and she dismissed me to bed. But she shadowed my steps, and just before I climbed into the cot, I heard a rough angry whisper. "See, some things are a lot easier going in than they are coming out."

THE NEXT TIME I saw Myraleen I was sitting under the dying Carolina hemlock, near my house, reading *Slow Train to Arkansas*. Above, thrumming a tune produced by flight, a hummingbird sang to the sick tree as if to lend it hope. The book had kidnapped my attention when I first withdrew it from the library. I had taken it to school to read at recess, and when it dropped from my satchel, Mrs. Marsh turned her mouth down farther than usual and said, "Miss Lily Mayfield, your only concern should be taking the fast train out of the eighth grade." But the story fascinated me. Why the devil would anyone want to go to Arkansas, anyway—and on a slow train at that? If I kept my mind filled with a distant riddle, maybe there would be no space to revisit the puddle of Mrs. Wright's blood. But visions of crimson and secret orifices kept reopening in my head.

Myraleen called and I felt saved for a moment. But she was about a dozen yards away, and her walk made me uneasy. It was slower than I'd ever seen her walk before; seemed till that day she was always running and racing, no matter how unurgent the destination. Had someone died? I scooted over to make a place for her. "Careful, don't sit on those cones," I said of the hemlock's dry, scratchy castoffs.

"A cone sticking in my tail is the least I got to worry over." When she told me what had happened, I felt sick, as if I'd eaten bad food.

"It's not that I don't want to ever get married," she said. "I don't wanna be an old maid or nothing. When I'm eighteen, I'm sure not going to be still sitting up under Mercy with no husband. But I always wanted to get in love the way they do on the radio stories.

"And the man I'm gonna like will be one with wavy hair, not some old knot-headed, giant-tooth fool like William Cheevers. He only want me 'cause I'm light, anyway. He's not looking at nothing else. If I had two heads, he'd just think I was twice as cute."

"Why are people like that?"

Myraleen gave me a funny look, somewhere between an annoyed frown and an indulgent smile. I might as well have asked why people liked money.

"You always got to make a big philosophy out of everything. I'm not saying I cain't understand what he see in me, I just don't see nothing in him."

"This must be against the law," I said. "Thirteen is too young."

"Not if my mama and daddy sign. Besides, what law you know would care about whether a colored girl get married, go crazy or drop dead?"

I stood up on my knees, and the book dropped to the grass. "You just have to refuse to, that's all! I know we're supposed to do what our mamas tell us, but the only person who's never wrong is God. You can't just let yourself be ruined cause of somebody's stupid notions."

"Girl, you don't understand a word I done said. How I'm sposed to 'refuse' anything, when Mercy done played my head for a yo-yo as it is?"

"Well, what's worse? Getting a whippin for a little while, or spending the rest of your life with Mr. Cheevers?"

"Oh yeah, you can say that 'cause you don't get your behind beat every time a good breeze blows."

"I've gotten some whippins." Remembering them, I was close to whining. There was no behavior so perpetually perfect it would save a child in Nadir from being beaten.

"You call them whippins? Half the time you say your mama just give you one good lick. If Mercy hit me just once, it would be with a train."

"Anyway, we shouldn't be picking at each other. We should be trying to solve your problem."

"You right," Myraleen said. She let her back slump against the tree's wart-plagued trunk, and sank farther down into the grass. She'd given up. "I got to get going now. I'm sposed to be at the store getting some things for tomorrow." I watched her walk away from me as slowly as she had walked to me.

Next to what Myraleen faced, the shame of having to watch Mrs. Wright's most personal moments seemed small. My mind ransacked possible escapes: She could pretend to be sick, deathly ill. That would at least postpone the marriage. She could run away. But where would she go? With no place to live, she'd be in worse trouble than she's in now. Maybe she could live with us. I was glad it was Saturday and Mudear would be home early from Mrs. Larkins's. Maybe she could help.

From books I'd read, like *Little Women*, I'd gotten the impression parents were there to help children, not just feed and clothe them, but guide them when it wasn't clear what direction to take. I had no father; he was dead. He liked cigars. Mudear didn't. "I used to tell him, them cigars going to be the handbasket you ride to hell in," she'd say. "His throat and lungs already had a tendency to clog up on him. Wouldn't listen, though. Would be too much like right." Chest pains ushered in the pneumonia that killed him a few days after I was born. "Guess he liked his cigars more than he liked us," she'd said. But he'd scared up a bundle of wooden planks when Mudear first told him a baby was coming. He hammered together a swing for the porch that I always thought of as his present to me.

Mudear's father had bought the house when whites still lived in this leg of Nadir. It was a square, bare shack. Bad ladies who did bad things in it sold it to him for a good price—for them, that is. They'd traveled from Nevada—a wild state in the West, I'd heard Mudear say. Out there, people called the shanties "cribs," and one or two women worked out of them. My grandfather had nailed clapboard to the outside and slapped plaster on the naked wood walls inside. And he built a kitchen onto the back, pieced together a porch, dug a fireplace and chopped a hole in the roof, around which he laid bricks for a chimney. Big Mudear cleaned the inside, and what she found became family legend: hair. White folks' hair, blond, brown, red, and dyed, from a hundred different white folks: It lay in corners and between planks on the floor, even stuck to the scurrying bodies of oblivious bugs. Most of it came in long lone strands. Some of it came clumped together in nasty swatches. The worst, though, were "the hairs," short and coarse. Big Mudear threw scalding water on them and mopped them out of the house into the dirt without touching them with her hands.

As my mother grew up, the two women—now respectable married ladies on the other side of town—showed up every Saturday morning for a payment. At least one husband stood by for protection. "You woulda thought they'd come from royalty," Mudear said. My grandfather died two days after he made the last payment, fifteen years after he had bought the place.

When Big Mudear died, I had to be handed over to Miz Herdie for safekeeping during the day. I remember assuming Big Mudear was my mother. She handled me with such authority, whether it was to rag-clean a dirty nose or firmly spoon-feed me a part of my meal I'd rejected, I knew she was the one in charge. After she died and left us, it felt like I'd been shoved off on a nervous older sister.

Mudear was the only parent I had, and my one way to help Myraleen. I had dinner cooking when she walked in, and let her settle in before I bothered her. After we ate and were working together on the dishes, I brought it up. Her eyes never left my face the whole time I spoke. I couldn't remember another time when she listened to me so intently. My body swelled with hope that poured into my words. ". . . See, Mudear, that's why I think we've got to do something. Myraleen *can't* get married."

"You crazy?" she said. "That's they business, not ours."

I breathed out, my body deflated. "But, Mudear, she's my friend."

"Friend is as friend does. I don't see her doing nothing for you. All she doing is using you for contrast."

Mama's eyes deserted mine, and she seemed to be talking to air. "Just wait till I tell Esther. Well, well, well. That old hincty Mercy. She may be high yella, but she sho low down. Pimpin that girl off at thirteen. Ump, ump, ump. She oughta be shot with a shit pistol."

Then her eyes locked into mine again. "And I don't want to catch you 'round that Myraleen no mo'. I mean that. She ain't no little girl like you no mo'. Her girlhood about to be taken away."

I bit my lip to keep from crying. Tears tumbled anyway. I turned away, busying myself putting dishes in the cabinet, so Mudear wouldn't see.

Later, when chores and obligations ceased to call and quiet led in the night, I picked up *Slow Train to Arkansas,* which rested by my cot on the unbothered piece of the floor where I stacked library withdrawals. I opened it and sat on the bed. Books had the power to set my mind adrift. When I first learned to read, I'd discovered my soul within the sheltering depths of paragraphs. To read was to be lost and found at the same time. But thoughts of Myraleen and Mr. Cheevers interrupted the flow of words. And Mrs. Wright leaped in for good measure. They swirled around in my head as if they were all part of the same bad brew.

I thought of what Myraleen had said about whippins. Truth was I hadn't been hit for two years. This was not something I'd tell anyone, though. It would have been like revealing an extra thumb.

What finally stopped Mudear from hitting me was a white, porcelain, gold-rimmed cup she bought before I was born. It had been part of an expensive dinner set and sold off piecemeal after sitting in the store too long. She paid a whole two dollars for it. "I would rather heard the devil belch than heard what your daddy woulda had to say about that," she once told me. "But I wanted something really nice for once, even if it was just a tiny piece of something nice. I was about to become a mother.

Seemed like I was due it. He didn't even notice that cup, though, thank-the-Lord."

Mudear wouldn't use the gold-rimmed cup—real gold plating, she said—to drink from. Instead, she made it a centerpiece on the table in front of the couch. In it, she collected the pennies she could spare. They had to be new pennies so the shiny copper would come close to matching the gold on the rim. It was one of those things in the house I knew not to touch.

The problem was Mrs. Houser's cat, Teeny, from down the road. It was the only cat on our side of town. Colored people didn't like cats much. They weren't down-to-earth animals like dogs, but back-curling creatures that looked haunted. Maybe loneliness had driven Teeny crazy. He never cared whether he was in the right house.

Teeny would shoot in between our legs sometimes when we opened the door. Though he wasn't that old, he had thinning gray fur and a shrunken look that made me afraid he would die at any moment. What surprised me was that Mudear would let him stay for a while. She'd even put a little milk for him in a tin can. I knew he was an odd cat when he let her gently hug him, something I never remember her doing to me. She was holding him, stroking him and cooing. She must have done this with me when I was a baby, because I'd seen her with other babies. I strained painfully to remember, but couldn't. "That stupid cat doesn't even know who he is, thinks he's a puppy or something," I said. "What a dunce!"

The cat's liquid gray eyes and Mudear's liquid brown ones shot to my face. "Who you think you are? Miss Important Opinion? Don't you be calling nothing stupid in this house. The floor going to end up wearing your teeth."

So I endured the cat, even when Mudear wasn't there. I'd get home from school an hour before she'd get home from work, and when he felt like it, Teeny would whoosh through the door as soon as I'd open it. He'd run around and around like a furry tornado. When he did sit down, it was always on the wrong place, like the table or a chair. Then I'd have to grab his gray fuzzy body, put it on the floor and hold it down as if I were fixing it there forever. After he seemed still, I'd go pull my books out on the kitchen table and study my lessons.

I had just parted the first pages of my book one afternoon, when I heard a few small, echoing, tinkle sounds. I dashed to the room and saw the gold-rimmed cup on the floor in front of the table, surrounded by five pennies. It was in two pieces, almost equal halves.

I wanted to scream and wail. "You teeny tiny-brained devil of a bastard cat," I said. "Now I'm going to get in trouble for what *you've* done." That was the first time I'd cursed, and I felt that sealed the catastrophe.

Other children I knew, especially Myraleen, cursed with impunity, as long as it was out of an adult's earshot. But I assumed I'd better not, even when there was only a cat to hear. I felt I couldn't do the slightest wrong without punishment, that I had to anticipate and obey even rules that were yet to be made. Because I was barely tolerated as it was.

In fact, Mudear didn't believe the cat had done it in the first place. She stood, arms folded, with a leather belt as wide as the Bible doubled and dangling from her right hand, which was nestled in the crook of her left elbow. "Now you gon get double the whippin, once for breaking my cup and once for lying. I ain't never seen that cat get up on a table. What do you think I am, popcorn or peanuts?"

"Please, Mudear," I said. "I didn't do it. Really, I didn't do it." Her face changed at these times from that familiar soft brown moon with large crater eyes to a scowling knot. "Shut up, ain't nobody asked to hear your mouth. You don't tell me what you did and didn't do," she said. "Period." Unlike other Nadir mothers, she hit in silence. Mudear wasn't one of those who combined the rhythm of the beating with a berating chant such as, "A hard head," swish . . . pop . . . "make for a hurt behind" . . . swish . . . pop . . . I had sat on the porch on hot days watching mothers compose entire poems as they walked down the road beating their children. Though she had said it would be two this time, she gave a single stinging slap of the belt, and walked away.

After a whipping, I always treaded carefully. It was so unfair, I thought, knowing that if Mudear could read my mind, she'd hit me for assuming a right to fairness. I made sure never to let the cat in when she wasn't there, praying she wouldn't be offended when she arrived home some days and found him scratching to get in.

Two days after it happened, she walked through the front room and into the kitchen and reminded me. "See, that cat's just sittin out there, ain't bothering nothing."

"Yes, ma'am," I said.

Funniest thing: Within two minutes of her saying that, the cat began darting around the room, as if chasing something invisible. He finally landed messily on the table, and the newly cemented cup tumbled to the floor, two pieces once again.

For one moment I loved that cat. But I was very still, and slid my eyes away from the crime, and back to my book. I could feel Mudear looking at me.

She stood in one place for a long time before I could hear her walking around the room. Her steps sounded as if she were looking for something. I heard the clanging of copper as she gathered the few pennies, spread near the cup, in her hand. Suddenly, it sounded as though she was crawling around on the floor. I moved my head slightly and sneaked a look and saw her sweeping her arms under her cot, netting more pennies. Underneath the bed was Mudear's equivalent of a bank. It was good luck, she claimed: "Money on the floor means money at the door." Actually, she was much too embarrassed to take the most she'd ever saved, which was about ten dollars, and have white people look with contempt upon all she had in the world.

The Depression sweetly vindicated her, though. Now you could hear even white people crying poor. One man in town would pass another, and say, "How you doin'?" The other would say, "Without." And the first man would nod that it was the same for him.

"See, them jackasses drop they money in a bank, and end up dropping out the window," Mudear would say. For us, the Depression was just a dent in a canyon. They'd needed fewer people at the Gulfport pier. Mudear went to work keeping house for a family in town. It was a bit less money, but an end to the twelve-hour oyster-shucking days. She swept her arm underneath the bed maybe an extra time a month these days. Still, probably only a few cents remained. Especially today, "poor day," right before payday, when we had rice with milk and sugar for breakfast, and dinner would be salted rice with a few neck bones. We always had food. Being poor in Nadir didn't mean being starved to death; it meant being worried to death.

I still pretended to study when she sat down beside me with a fistful of coins. She had her black pocketbook in her lap, and she was mining it for money.

"All right," she said, "take this and go down to Mr. Stokes and get three sweet potatoes, Pet Milk, three eggs—just three now. That's all we need. I'm going to make a pie."

After rice and neck bones, we had sweet-potato pie that evening, which was my very favorite thing to eat in the whole world. It was more a Sunday than a poor day, or a kind of rich poor day. In the morning, Mudear left forty-five minutes early. From the kitchen window, I watched her walk up the road, passing the place where a morning bus would stop and pick up a cluster of domestics at seven A.M., straight up. She had spent the nickel that was to be her car fare on three sweet potatoes. She walked alone as if it were nothing. I noticed she wasn't as skinny as she used to be. She'd always loved food. Now it appeared food had loved her back and embraced her with a modicum of padding.

My mother never had been strong, only burdened and couldn't afford to collapse. I then knew she had feelings, and I'd started to cry.

Now words in the Arkansas book blurred. Tears from two years ago had paid an unwelcome visit. I put the book back and undressed for bed. Anyway, I'd been staring at the third page for an hour. I was too weighed down to accomplish that light leap into escape which, until tonight, was guaranteed to soothe me with its magic.

MYRALEEN

. . . kill it fo it slide under yo' dress . . .

THAT HORSE'S ASS WILLIAM CHEEVERS WAS COMING OVER TO
marry me at three o'clock. Reverend Matthews was set to meet us back
at the house, where a few of our kin and a couple of my mother's friends
would gather. And I guessed Lilian was right: the only way I could get
out of this mess was to stand up and say no. I was going to have to show
my tail in front of all those people.

In church, I fanned my face to the beat of my panicked heart with a
cardboard, wood-handled fan, though it was early October and not hot
anymore. I looked as pretty as a package from heaven. My hair was done
up in curls. The top portion was pinned up in a swirly crown, while the
rest ran down my back like a waterfall. I had on my white taffeta dress
with its long toothpick sleeves that ended in lace at my wrists. Below the
waist, it ballooned into a full sweep skirt that was puffed up by a petti-
coat. My favorite dress and it might as well be used to clean pigs.

At the house, it was the way dinner had been Thursday night. People
were talking about me, but no one was talking *to* me.

"You sho fixed her hair nice," my oldest cousin, Mammie, said to Mama.

"I bet we gonna have to call you 'Grandma Mercy' in a year or two,"
her mother, Aunt Sylvia, added.

My stomach got an upset, bubbly feeling as if fussing back at trouble. Suddenly, I felt Mama's hand pulling on my arm. She drew me into her bedroom. "Look," she said, "you better stop looking all down in the mouth. You not going to ruin this day for me. 'Cause I'll give you something to be sad about. I'll slap you till your ears ring like bells, swear to God."

I came out of the bedroom smiling. Anyone might have thought Mama had told me how nice I looked.

Cheevers was late. For a whole ten minutes I clutched the hope that he had changed his mind. Then his face was at the door grinning like he had two sets of teeth. We were in front of the minister pretty soon after that, and I knew what I had to do.

"Do you take this man to be your lawfully wedded husband?" Reverend Matthews asked.

I said nothing. After three or four seconds, the reverend looked up from his Bible and at my mouth, watching to see if something was coming from it. Everyone in the room was in a dead hush. I never knew quiet could feel like a scream. Then I heard Mercy's hard footsteps. She'd been standing behind me. Now she walked around so she could pose in front of me, just behind the Reverend. Her eyes locked into mine, and held them and stretched out that twisted smile. It was like being licked in the face by a flame.

"Yessir," I finally said.

When Cheevers kissed me, I sealed my lips as tight as I could. For the rest of the afternoon, folks talked and ate. We had fixed enough food for twice the guests we had. Why wasn't I eating, they kept asking. Then Daddy answered, "She's too excited about being a new bride."

It was nine at night before the last guest left. Mama handed me a purse with a nightgown in it. She said I could come get my other clothes in the morning. When Cheevers and I walked to his house, a mile south of ours, I was still wearing my white dress.

His house was smaller than ours, just two dusty rooms. "You don't have to worry about cleaning up nothing till tomorrow," he said. "Your mama put out a real good spread, but my only complaint was she didn't have no liquor. I can understand, it being Sunday, but I likes me a little juke juice every evening. I'm going to go down the road to Manny Fields's house and get me a little taste. He always got some.

"You go on and get dressed for bed, but don't go to sleep, now. And don't look at me so scared like that, I ain't gon bite." He laughed. "But then again maybe I will. After all, I am your new husband," he said, chuckling as he walked out the door.

I breathed with a bit of ease for the first time that day.

Then he poked his head back in the door. "I be back inside a half hour."

I fell to my knees and started to cry, me and my dress, a white heap on the floor. Then a voice inside me, one I hadn't heard till that night, told me I'd better quit watering the floor and do something about my situation. Run, that's what I could do. A good run was better than a bad stand. But it was dark and chilly outside, and I would surely trip, running in this dress.

I searched through Cheevers's drawers. Had to find something. Quick. When I ran out the door, I had on a pair of his pants, rolled up at the cuffs and held up with a belt made of two tied-together socks. I wore one of his short-sleeved shirts under his wool jacket. The only direction I knew to go was north. That way I wouldn't run into Cheevers as he returned. My skinny legs flew until I got back to my house. I stopped for a second. Uh-uh. They would only send me back.

I ran some more until Lilian's house appeared. Uh-uh. Mrs. Mayfield would rather see five years of locusts than me at her door. I set off again, and ran and ran until it was clear I had no place to run.

I walked back slowly, thinking. If I could only hold out . . . hide someplace . . . maybe. Light still glowed from Cheevers's windows. I could see him in there walking around. What was that simpleminded fool thinking right now? That I was up under the bed, just being a playful child bride?

"Where you been?" he said when I walked through the door. "And why'd you put my clothes on? Girl, you a crazy li'l thing." He chuckled. He didn't know I'd cut his good pants off at the legs to lessen the material I'd need to roll.

"I was going to go home, and I was cold."

"And they sent you back, did they?" he said, rocking his head back to laugh.

I didn't answer.

"Well, I guess you trapped with me then," he said, still laughing.

I had come close to deciding I would go along with everything— until he said that. It made me think of some old mouse with his body crunched up between wire and wood. I just wasn't going to be that pitiful. So all the time I was standing there, I kept thinking what I could do to make Cheevers want me less than head lice.

"Get that nightgown your mammy give you, and get ready for bed, now."

I picked up my purse and headed toward the kitchen, the house's only other room.

"Where you going? You can change in here," Cheevers said.

I shook my head.

"Girl, you starting to swing on my nerves, now. I'm tired," he said, his laughter gone. "I got to get some rest so I can get up early to meet that job in the morning."

I stood fast, holding the purse to my chest.

"Look here," he said, stepping toward the dresser near the bed. As he walked, his body swayed to the right. The little taste had him walking crooked. "That kitchen ain't got no 'lectricity," he said. "Mostly use it in daylight, so it don't need any." Cheevers reached in his pants pocket to scoop out a book of matches and walked over to the dresser by the bed. He lit the wick of a half-melted lump of wax in an ashtray. I came over and took it from him. He still had on his good Sunday pants, black and cuffed at the bottom. The candle made the space between us glow. My hands looked milky and ghostlike. I thought about pictures of candle-toting angels, taped to store windows at Christmas. Something from a Sunday-school lesson shined in my mind: The devil was once an angel.

I looked at him straight. "I'm going to tell you honest, Mr. Cheevers. I don't want to be married to you 'cause I ain't ready yet to be married to nobody. I'm just but thirteen; I want to wait till I'm about seventeen."

"Girl, you ain't no baby. You beginning to develop," he said, his eyes on my chest.

His right hand crept toward me like a big nasty animal claw, like evil looking to grab ahold of something new. I threw the candle at him just to get him out of my way. "WHAT IN THE HE . . ." Cheevers hollered, reaching out to grab the candle. He just barely nabbed it with the tips of his thumb and forefinger, but before he could get a better grip, it tumbled again.

The candle's burning head dove into his right pants-leg cuff, and he looked down as if a hand from the grave were tugging at his leg. He kicked and kicked when all he had to do was reach, snatch it fast and burn his fingers a little. I knew then he was deathly afraid of fire. He'd lived long enough to see a couple of shacks turn into funeral pyres for the folks inside. And he'd seen a few mean blazes tearing at barns and put himself in the place of the yowling, crying, cooked-alive horses. He kicked and kicked, only waving the weak flame to strength. It spread its yellow fire to the black fabric, and Cheevers started stomping with his flaming leg as if that would help. I ran outside to the pump to get water. But it was dark, and the moonlight wouldn't show me the bucket.

I came back, empty-handed, and saw the drunk fool finally had the sense to roll around on the floor. He looked like one of those men in church who "got the spirit"—hollering and rolling, whooping and wagging his arms.

Only when he was no longer burning but still smoking did I get scared. Stretched out on the floor, he coughed and groaned. Through sighs and moans, he said I was a dirty wench (or was it witch?), and he was going to kill me. My welcome worn to threads, I ran out the door and up the road, so if he looked, he would think I had gotten a ways away. When I came to the third house on the street, I sat on its lowest porch step. It was dark. People inside were asleep. No one would notice. But after about forty or fifty minutes, I doubled back to Cheevers. The light was still on. I ducked under the windows and headed to the back.

About an hour had passed since I had left. Maybe this was the first place he'd looked. Still, what if he needed to come out here? Tired, I slumped to the floor, letting my bottom rest on a thinned-out Sears catalog. I breathed in the smell of pine salt mixed with a little pee. It was a good thing for me Cheevers kept a clean outhouse.

I MUST HAVE fallen asleep, after hours of worrying in the dark. A while of forgetting followed, and suddenly I blinked and saw it was light outside. I'd been given new eyes in the past few days. Everything looked different. People were jealous rascals, I decided, and were willing to do wrong, no matter how much it hurt someone else.

All this time, I'd been thinking I was the prettiest little thing around. And everybody knew it. How could they not? I was the center of everything—yeah, just like the Thanksgiving turkey on the table. Being light skinned was the ace I threw at any child with the nerve to go against me. It meant I was right in every argument, first in every game, and best in almost everybody's sight. High-high yellow was the hand that I fanned with. But having things turn on me like this, it was as if that hand had slapped me in the face. And it woke me up.

I jumped. Footsteps. They were coming this way. In a lightning second, the outhouse door flew open, and there stood the common clown I had lawfully wed. He wore a tattered old coat as a robe. It drifted apart at the opening, and his boxer shorts showed. His eyes grew wide as gopher holes. "WHAT!" he said. "WHAT! I was looking for you and looking for you last night! Thought you got so scared you ran on back to yo' mammy's." He stepped forward.

"Leave me alone!" I screamed and ran right past him, not stopping until I was a few yards away.

"Girl, you don't have to worry!" he turned and called. "CAUSE YOU DONE RIPPED YOUR DRAWERS WIT ME, BIG TIME! You just as crazy as a Betsy bug. I be more than glad to take your nutty almond ass back to your folks, then you be they problem. And you can dress up funny in *they* clothes and sleep in *they* outhouse!

"You just wait right here while I relieve myself. Then I take you home."

Cheevers didn't bother to change. He just wrapped the coat around him and belted it tight, and put on some house shoes. He said he'd be late for work, but he'd make something up. We both looked a sight. I was glad it was so early that no one was on the road.

MERCY WAS STILL in curlers when she opened the door. The twisted strips of brown paper bag always became partly undone overnight and snaked out of her hair, each piece going its own way. She walked backwards several steps to let us in. Her eyes were fixed in a hard stare, trying to take in what was happening. Cheevers explained. While he was there, her expression never changed. "I'm sorry bout all this mess," she said as he was leaving. The door closed and I felt faint. She stood in front of me, saying nothing for a minute. Then she laughed. With Mercy you never knew whether it was going to be the lace ribbon or the thick rope. "Ha, ha, ha—crouching in somebody's outhouse. You almost as crazy as I am."

Suddenly the wide laughing eyes turned into the narrow lead eyes. "Why, you little hateful whore," she said slowly. Her arm swung back and flew forward to slap my face. The blow knocked me back yards, and I tumbled to the floor. She walked and stood over me. Bending my head down, I covered my face and head with my arms and hands. I peeped up at her, but she didn't look as fiery as a minute ago. She'd let some of that fire go, and it was now burning my face where her fingers slammed across it. Paper snakes drooped past her eyes, and her chin hung close to her neck.

"I'm not going to hit you," she said. "You ain't worth the bother; you ain't worth a thing," she said and walked away. I went to my room, closed the door, wondered if I was safe at last. For the time being, I pushed Cheevers's clothes under my bed. After that, I changed into my school clothes. Grabbing my book satchel, I opened the door to find Mercy standing there like a guard. "Where you think you going?"

"To school, Mama."

"School, my ass. You not going to just do like you please 'round here, not as long as you living under my hard-paid-for roof."

I went back into my room. I could still hear her and Daddy talking, and I strained to make out what they were saying. "What you going to do wit that girl?" he said. "And all that trouble you went to—wasted. Well, I'll be."

There was a knock on the door. I couldn't hear what Mercy said to the person, but in a second, she closed the door. I peeped out. Just catching sight of a small slice of my face made Mercy holler. "Don't you worry about who's at this door 'cause it ain't nobody you ever gon see again!"

After they left for work, I came out of my room again. I was glad Mercy had left some of the dishes guests had dirtied in the sink. I put a kettle on the stove and washed them in steaming water as hot as I could stand it. My hands were flaming red for the next few hours as I worked polishing floors and cabinets, cleaning cracks and corners. Around noon, I picked four or five things for dinner, and started peeling peaches for a cobbler. By the time Mercy walked through the door, the house was cleaner than any in the county, and smelled like Christmas dinner. She didn't say anything about that, but she would have whooped and hollered up a storm if it hadn't been that way. "I got something for you today," she said. From a burlap sack, Mama pulled out some kind of big knife that was about two feet long. Its blade fanned out in a lopsided V-shape that narrowed into a long wooden handle. I stopped breathing for a few seconds. Maybe she'd decided to just out-and-out do away with me. "This is what you going to be using tomorrow."

"For what, Mama?"

"It's grinding season. Got you a job chopping cane, over cross state line in Louisiana. Truck pick you up, take you across, and bring you back every day but Sunday. Since you don't want an easy life with a decent man taking care of you, guess you must want the hard life. So I'm going make sho you get it."

I stood outside at five the next morning, waiting until four nasty gray horses stopped in front of me. A big wagon rolled tied to the animals. A white driver perched high, topped by a straw hat, squinted at the horses, and paid no mind to his cargo. About five ladies sat on rough wooden planks on each side. They all wore red or blue bandannas. The two rows of heads reminded me of the brightly colored pieces of a flag I'd seen in a schoolbook. They looked at me. I didn't have a bandanna. You could barely tell them from men because they all had overalls or dungarees and flannel shirts on. I wore an old dress I used for housecleaning. When I climbed aboard, only a tiny bit of space cracked open for me to sit. The woman next to me scooted over as much as she could, and said, "Where you going, Cinderella? To da ball?" The ladies all laughed. After that, quiet held till we got to the fields.

With the little might in it, my arm was swinging a hatchet at some damn die-hard stalk of brown cane, when three inches from my feet, I saw a tan-gold flash of color—a rattlesnake. "What's de matta wit you, chile?" the lady working next to me said. "You betta kill it fo it slide under yo' dress." She slammed the blade of her cane knife below the snake's eyes, cutting off its head.

I'd been so scared I couldn't move. Then I hustled away from the dead snake to find another spot to work, hollering, "Thank you, ma'am" as I ran. "You betta come back here," said the lady. "You cain't work where you wanna. You gotta work where dey put you." I dragged on back. "If you was gon run, you shoulda run while it was alive. It cain't do nutin to you now. You kina backward, ain't you? Lemme show you something." She raised the cane knife over her head and brought it down fast at an angle. "You cuttin' like you cuttin' tulips."

She said her name was Willamae. She was a brown-skinned woman who was about thirty and as teeny as a minute. Cane soared past her head, and seeing her chopping it, she was like David beating the heck out of Goliath. "You come tomorrow wit de right clothes, you hear? Cain't wear no dress around here. You get your ankles all scratched up." Willamae said she'd been working grinding seasons for fifteen years. How could anybody stand it that long? When I first climbed off the truck, my mouth dropped open to my knees. The cane was as long as lightning, and the field stretched so far I couldn't see where it ended. We followed the boss man where he led us: deep in high cane on all sides. Only when I threw my head back could I see a patch of gray sky. It was like being in a deep, chilly barrel. Now my hands were freezing from handling cold stalks and my toes were numb. Willimae shook her head. "Girl, you oughta be shamed of yourself, coming out here wit dem puny ankle socks and no gloves." Then she disappeared for a little while. She came back with a fistful of clean white rags in each hand. "Got dez from de boss man. Dat man sho don't like to give up nutin." I sat on the ground while she wrapped my feet and hands, wrapping each finger apart so I could move them. I felt like a mummy in a picture show. "You too ol' for dis," she said. "Oughta be shamed."

"Thank you, ma'am," I said rising.

"Now member what I told you about swingin high," she said.

Sweat and scars covered the arms and legs of the folks who worked beside me. I thought of old folks talking about slaves being laid into with whips. Did they give beatings here? No, Willamae said. But sharp edges of the cane will cut into your skin. On the side of her right forearm, a line stretched from the wrist to the elbow like a natural divide. "That's why you got to be careful," she said. "Swing fast but not as fast as they want you to."

The next few weeks, I stayed close to Willamae. The boss man seemed to think it was all right because he knew I'd cut better under her fault-finding eyes.

When I got home every evening, I never said a sad word. That would only have given that old bat out of hell more satisfaction, and the more satisfaction Mercy got from the way things were, the longer I'd be chopping cane.

Meantime, that old piano-mouthed Cheevers was going around telling everybody I was crazy. He said I ripped his clothes and shoes up with a knife and set him on fire as I hollered, "Bless you, Satan." When he found me in the outhouse, he claimed, I was dressed in a full suit of men's clothes, including a hat and a necktie. And, to have him tell it, I was smoking a corncob pipe, too.

Why'd he have to lie like that? I could have kicked that man square in the butt with a righteous heart. People could have understood if it was an old husband I had set fire to, someone I had come to know for no good. But to torch a brand-new husband, that proved I was out of my mind. Being caught in a man's clothes: they didn't completely know what to make of it. Nadir had seen no other cases of girls and men taking on each other's ways. A bride who hopped in the groom's clothes, well, that just went to show I was nuttier than a pecan tree. Girls I'd gone to school with didn't talk to me anymore. As I walked by, they'd start lollygagging about me without bothering to speak low.

"They say she's off in the head," big-footed Zelma said, amidst a group of girls on their way to church on Sunday.

"I'm sho glad I got all my good senses," she said.

"Me too, girl," the others threw in.

"Yeah, she so crazy," Zelma said, "she sleep in the outhouse every night. . . ."

I sorely wished Lilian didn't go to a different church. The fact that I walked alone made it look like not even one soul was on my side.

I moved faster past their voices. They all had on pastel crinoline dresses. It was almost a shame that to keep the cold out, they had to cover them up with droopy sweaters that didn't match. If it wasn't for that and the nasty way they talked, they would have seemed like a fistful of different-colored flowers. My pink wool jacket matched my dress to the tee, plus it had a sailor collar. I was dressed way better than those heifers. But how I looked didn't matter anymore.

Little boys would throw rocks at me as I walked to the store, saying, "Get away from us, you old fruitcake head." Then they would run, pretending I was trying to chase them. All the parents had told their children to stay away from me.

That was the way folks dealt with crazy people. They treated dummies that way, too. I mean, the couple of people who were dumb enough to stick out in Nadir, like Slow Willy and Fool-Headed Bertha.

Willy was about fifteen. His head was big and his face was flat with funny slitlike eyes. This told you something was wrong with him before he even opened his mouth and stuttered something you probably didn't understand. He couldn't go to school. So he'd walk around all day looking for bottles he could get one cent for at the store.

Sometimes he'd even ask people if they had any. If the person was feeling good that day, he'd get bottles. If not, she might say, "You old grits-in-the-head fool. Boy, I ain't got time to be messin with you." I never understood why he went to all that trouble to get bottles. He never could keep the money. When other boys saw he had something, they'd get him to pitch pennies with them on the road. He would grin so big when they said he could play with them. But no matter where the pennies landed, he'd always lose.

Bertha had it worse. Boys would save up nasty copper-colored flying roaches in paper bags. When they were soft-toeing up on her, it seemed she'd be able to hear them nevertheless. Showboating, they'd step toward her like silly old circus horses, raising their legs so high their feet made pounding noises landing on the ground. Still didn't hear a thing.

One boy would sneak up from behind, and hold her by the shoulders. The one with the bag would jump on her and empty roaches all down her back and even inside the collar of her blouse. They did it to hear her holler—the only sound she ever made. You couldn't go up to her and knock the damn things off and say something to make her feel better or the boys would turn against you, saying you'd caught her dumbness by touching her.

Bertha died a couple of years ago from something no one bothered to figure out. I guess I'd taken her place.

LILIAN

. . . we'd exchanged costumes . . .

THAT MORNING I KNOCKED, MRS. CHADHAM THREW OPEN THE door, looking like Medusa. Paper curlers were going every which way on her head and she didn't care. Her eyes were so red and angry, they were flames. Still, I had to know what had happened to Myraleen. But I could see only that her mother wasn't pleased with the way things had gone.

"Myraleen ain't in school no mo'," she said, and with a single powerful push of her right hand, she slammed the door shut.

It was under the hemlock days later that I saw Myraleen walking toward me with overalls on. I sucked my breath in, shocked because I figured her mother had sent her to reform school, where I imagined they dressed children in unsightly uniforms. Certainly nothing but the law itself could have made Myraleen put on a pair of overalls.

She fell beside me more than sat. "Oooh, girl, have I a got a story to tell you." So what actually happened was worse than reform school but better than marrying Mr. Cheevers. It struck me then that there was always something worse, that worse stretched into infinity before it became worst. "Only good thing about it is she don't bother me when I get home, and don't keep track of me as much. As long as I put the money on the kitchen table. Get paid every day but don't get to keep none of it."

As months rambled by, Myraleen and I met under the hemlock every weekday after she returned from work. Sitting in the grass, we looked like a mismatched pair. I'd have on smart homemade jumpers and white flour-starched blouses. She'd be wearing brown-smudged overalls over old plaid shirts. She smelled both sweaty and sickly sweet.

Each time I'd bring notebooks and textbooks, and go over what had been taught at school that day. She never asked me if I wanted to do this. I never asked if she'd be interested. It was just something we did. I read and she repeated. I drilled and she recited. She yawned on occasion and sighed more and more as the day's lesson was crawling to a close. Her hands were achy from chopping, so she'd prop open a book in her lap to keep from having to hold it.

It was as if we'd exchanged costumes. She was wearing misfortune these days and I, only by comparison, was wearing good fortune. From the time she was little, I thought she'd been favored by God. Now she seemed godforsaken. This girl, a girl so high-toned she made the sun look dim. Her face was shadowed with exhaustion and sadness. She sometimes gave wrong sleepy answers when I drilled her, yet she insisted we go back over the lesson, forcing her eyes open wide during the review. This girl, who was no longer the sunny, lucky one, now shined brighter to me than ever.

DAYS I CAME BACK from the hemlock, more often than not, Mudear looked at me, shoved her mouth to one side and contorted her face in disgust. Usually, she said nothing. I was grateful. We both knew if she told me not to, I'd find some way of doing it nevertheless. For the first time, I was willing to defy her, and it made us both nervous. This juncture came up between mother and daughter routinely in Nadir. Usually the girl was about fifteen or sixteen, and the object of defiance was some trifling boy with a fresh fever in his pants and not sufficient resources to get through yesterday. He'd come to claim the daughter as if she'd been incidentally his all along, like lint in his fist when he was born. Ugly words and predictions shot back and forth. The girl naturally ran off. Her boy got a job. The two families anted what they could afford when babies fell out like a bloody procession of reproach. Mother and father now, the boy and girl found there were never enough dollars and cents to cover the month, but blame and scorn to smother a lifetime. After fifteen or sixteen years, life settled into a tamed disaster. Then another pepper-tail boy came to the door, deaf to reason, dead dreams in his groin, to claim another daughter. In Nadir, disaster was never a deterrent to repetition.

Compared to that, Mudear and I were sitting pretty. Studying some books under a sickly tree with a raggedy yellow girl was my only wayward motion. After dinner once, Mudear did say something, though. I was scrubbing a pot in the tin basin we used for washing dishes. She was mopping the small strip of splintery wooden floor around me. She suddenly stopped swabbing and stood straight at my side, looking at me: "Girl, how you going to be giving somebody else so much, and you ain't got a damn thing yourself? Don't you know, despite everything done gone on, that yella mongrel can marry somebody thinks she the Queen of Sheba, and do much better than you, all the way around?

"If you were out of school and needed somebody to teach you your lessons, think she'd do the same for you?"

Mudear's questions to me, unless she wanted to know the whereabouts of a kitchen utensil or something, were always rhetorical. But this time she wanted an answer, not just an apology or a "yes, ma'am."

"Well," she said. "Do you?"

I looked down at the floor, at the grisly gray head of the mop and inhaled its sour smell. I thought for a moment. She was strangely patient.

"I don't know."

A LIGHT DRIZZLE dampened us the next time we sprawled under the hemlock. Papers grew moist and soft, and I shielded the books against wetness by covering them with my skirt tail, which fanned out in a circle as I sat.

Grass keeps sound a secret. I looked over and saw Mudear's feet planted next to my lap. Tiny pearls of rain dotted her almost-worn-out shoes.

"What is the matter with y'all!" she said. "If you don't come in from this rain, you better." As we followed her to the house, clutching books and work papers to our chests, she said, "I oughta beat both your tails."

She pointed to the kitchen table. "You can study over there till it's time to eat. Myraleen, you staying for dinner?"

"If it don't put you out, Miz Mayfield."

"What put me out is two big old girls like you don't have sense enough to come in from the rain. Act like nobody ever taught you anything . . ."

Even if I delivered every lesson through the end of high school, Myraleen would have nothing to prove that she knew anything. And colored people always had to prove themselves. She needed to be back in school. I thought of a way and prayed it worked better than my advice for stopping her wedding. I went to see Miz Herdie Sunday afternoon when I knew she'd be less busy with other people's children, her own chickens and chores around the house.

"Well," she said, snatching the screen door open. "I done thought you got too big to come see old Miz Herdie."

It had never occurred to me to visit. When she used to keep us, she was always fussing as if we children were just necessary annoyances.

Now I realized she was probably fussing about things in general more than us in particular.

She sat me down at the kitchen table. "I got somepum you might like in the icebox," she said with a wink of an age-glazed eye. "Root beer." She set a cold, sweating bottle down before me. "I keeps it for the young'uns when they good. Pour a little cup of some for each of 'em. But you can have that whole bottle. You a young lady, now."

"Thank you, Miz Herdie."

"How's dat li'l light-skinned gal doing?"

Good. That made my work easier.

"Yep, yep, I heard," she said when I told her about Myraleen's having to marry Mr. Cheevers. "Been bout a year ago now. How'd dat go exactly? I done heard bout four different stories on it."

She slapped her thigh and gave a laugh that bounced through her house when I told her about Myraleen's harrowing escape. "I know I got it right dis time. 'Cause it's only one gal removed from straight from the horse's mouth."

I talked about Myraleen working in the cane field, and having to catch her lessons with me on the sly. "Didn't know bout dat," she said. "Just thought she didn't want no mo' schoolin. Ump," she grunted, "a shame."

Miz Herdie left her house only on special missions, funerals mostly. But every now and then, someone would appear at her door with a troubled face, and ask her to "go talk some sense" to so-and-so. It could be a man who was drinking too much and mistreating his wife to a potentially deadly degree. It might be a woman who'd fallen so deeply into mourning over burying a child, her family feared they might have to bury her too. Miz Herdie would put shoes on her usually bare feet, take her little straw purse and walk down the road to Mr. or Mrs. So-and-so's house. In an hour, her squeezed feet already threatening bunions, she stepped back over the threshold headed for home. Who knows what she said once the door was shut, but it always made a difference.

HIGH-SCHOOL GRADUATION was held in Reverend Matthews's church. It was late May, and Easter clothes made a reappearance. So the mothers looked colorful and light like bright pink tissue paper springing from fancy gift boxes.

I was one of sixteen others in black gowns and box caps, handed down from one class to another and returned to the church basement closet between graduations. We all sat in a shimmery black cluster in the front right corner of the church. Mrs. Brown, the twelfth-grade teacher and school principal, sang names out alphabetically in her contralto voice. White cotton gloves I feared I'd lose before the day was over were squeezed into a tight ball in my right hand.

My first corsage—a configuration of daffodils—bloomed above my breast. Mudear bought it. I wasn't sure how she managed to link the dollars together, but she bought me a bounty of presents, including a set of seven underpants, each with a day of the week written on it in cursive, a bottle of green cologne and two lace handkerchiefs. She'd made today's white party dress, beneath which I donned underpants that read "Saturday" and above which floated the romantic scent of the cologne.

With two yards of crinoline and a big silk swatch from the woman she worked for, she'd worked on my dress a week straight. When I tried it on, she stood back, her eyes inspecting every detail. Suddenly, she appeared disturbed.

"Doesn't look good, Mudear?"

"Looks too good. You got a perfect hourglass, girl. You must have gotten that bosom from your daddy's ma. Ump, ump, here I was thinking you were just a little string of a thing. Guess eyes don't always see." She walked back over. "Take it off so I can let it out a touch. Perfect hourglass, ump, ump. But everybody doesn't need to know that, do they?" She lightly pushed my upper arm and gave that rare little laugh.

I'd noticed the wavy symmetry back when breasts started to push beyond my chest introducing themselves to the world without my permission. Unrequested bumps, the growth of intimate hair and blood rushing from a place with no unashamed name made trading a little girl's body for a woman's a bad bargain. Yet sometimes now, glimpsing myself in the mirror in the wake of the upheaval, I saw a bit of grace, even loveliness. And though for a dark-skinned girl to feel lovely was treason, during some wayward moments, I saw poetry in my flesh.

Three years had passed since Miz Herdie visited Mrs. Chadham. Myraleen had listened from her bedroom. Her mother didn't know why Miz. Herdie had come gunning for her, but she wanted to disarm her. "That certainly is a pretty dress," Mrs. Chadham said in her good-hostess voice. "Store-bought?"

"No, no, no," Miz Herdie declared as if accused of blasphemy. "Never plunked down money on no dress in my life. I made it." She was cranky because she didn't like having to wear shoes when nobody had died.

"Well, you sure are a seamstress. With all your talents I'm sure you would have made some man happy to be a man. Why didn't you ever marry, Miz. Herdie—not that it's too late."

Miz. Herdie must have frowned as if she had to explain the obvious to an idiot. "Men are dogs. If anybody should know, you should."

I don't know why Miz. Herdie said that. But at that point, I bet the smile on Mrs. Chadham's face froze.

Why would she want some leftover fool with his head blooming for the grave? Miz Herdie said. "When a man old enough to done run de dog out of him, likely he's run de life out of him, too. And I don't want to be a nursemaid anymore dan I want to be a kennel keeper. Men are a danger when you're young and a disappointment when you're old. If anybody should know, you should."

Before Mrs. Chadham's mind finished chewing on that, Miz Herdie served some more spinach. She said it was a shame Myraleen would be the first of the Bakers, on her mother's side, not to finish school in who could remember how many years. "A terrible, terrible shame," she said.

"She laid out her bed," Mrs. Chadham said.

"And got you lyin in it right next to her. A woman done as much wid herself as you, live in dis nice house, and her one and only child don't get de rest of her schoolin? Young'uns these days, getting educations like it's nutin but getting a drink of water. Now you take dat li'l Lilian, why she doin just fine. And her mama, bless her strugglin soul, is a widow as poor as Job's turkey. Ain't it mysterious how God can work? Her child turned out one way, your child another."

Myraleen was in school the next day.

Today Mr. and Mrs. Chadham sat in the front pew. Miz Herdie sat behind them, wearing a white straw hat to match her purse. She wore her black funeral dress, but on this day made it smile with two strings of pearls draped around her neck.

"Myraleen Chadham," Mrs. Brown sang out. I jumped slightly as if it were my name.

Myraleen strolled up on the stage wearing the most beautiful shoes anyone in Nadir had ever seen. They would be talked about for years to come: "Ya remember those shoes that gal had on when she gadjated? Those sho was some purty shoes," people would say. They were silvery high heels summoned from a New York mail-order house. The tips of their toes were highlighted in cones of gold silk, and each tip was dotted by a triangle of three discreet rhinestones people thought were real diamonds.

A little lady in back sitting with a congregation of children clapped loudest. "Hallelujah! All right, all right, go on, girl, and get that piece of paper! All right!" the lady said. Mrs. Chadham looked back and gave the shouter a sharp glance.

No such commotion exploded when it was my turn. In fact, it felt no less ordinary than being handed an envelope by the mailman until Mrs.

Brown said, "This too." She turned around and lifted a brilliant yellow bouquet of roses from the back table, and handed them to me. (The class's highest-ranking pupil always got flowers, or supposedly something more masculine, if it were a boy, but it was always a girl.) A sudden holler came up from the crowd: "Hallelujah." I thought it was the shouting lady. But I looked down and saw it was Mudear.

MYRALEEN

. . . roses . . .

IN OUR SCHOOL DAYS, I NEVER THOUGHT MUCH ABOUT LILIAN.
She was my friend. Everybody had a special friend. Lilian was always
around. She was like a surprise stretch of pavement, on gravel, that
made a hard road a little easier.

Still, something about her tended to scratch at me. Out of our caps
and gowns at the reception, I could see she had on the prettiest dress by
a leap and a jump. Folks got big eyed and ran their fingers down the silk
sleeves that tapered to an end just past the elbow. Meanness ran through
my mind. I was going to be spitting mad if her mammy-made outfit up-
staged my high-priced high heels.

At the very moment I was thinking that, we were standing around talking to Willamae and her playground-load of children, and Lilian gasped
a bit as if she'd forgotten something. "Hold out your arms," she said.

"What?"

"Just hold out your arms." She gave me her roses. "You deserve
them more."

I shoved them back, but she folded her arms and grinned. What was
different about Lilian finally dawned on me: what had scratched at me almost since the first day I scratched at her was that she was better than I.

LILIAN

. . . life unlocking . . .

AT THE RECEPTION, IN THE BALLOONS-ON-LAUNDRY-LINE-
decorated basement, Myraleen introduced me to the shouting lady.
"This is Willamae."

A few times Mrs. Chadham cut Willamae a dirty look, but mostly she
stood with her back to her, talking to Miz Herdie about how proud she
was yet another Baker had achieved a diploma.

"These my kids," Willamae said. "Amos, Vivian, Louise, Charles,
Elbert, Leatrice and Herman." Each held a paper cup of red punch.
"Wouldn't give a nickel for another one, but wouldn't take a million for
the ones I got," she said. "You gon graduate in two years yourself, ain't
you Amos?

"You sho got yourself way from that cane field," she said to Myraleen.
"I gon do the same soon. What was you doin out there anyway?" she asked
with faked ignorance. "Yeah, in the cane fields, a girl like you whose folks
doin all right for themselves and can buy you such boo-ootiful shoes."

Mrs. Chadham didn't turn around, but I saw her shoulder quiver, as
if from a tiny stab she felt in her back. I whispered to Myraleen that I
was wearing all of my graduation presents, including "Saturday." The
last of the little-girl giggles bubbled out.

After the reception, parents left, and the same basement was used for the graduation dance—partially in vain. After all, the close-shaved heads of only five boys dotted our graduation class. So Mrs. Brown made sure the boys asked all the girls to dance, not just their girlfriends. She also made sure any dancing was confined to tame two-step glides across the room. "This is still a church. I better not see so much as one hip a-shaking."

It didn't matter. At that moment, we felt we could do anything. Earlier we'd seized our diplomas with our fists. People applauded, and it meant they knew we were grown now. For one magic day, we could hear the click of life unlocking and feel the emancipating breeze from all those impossible doors flinging open just for us.

TWO

LILIAN

. . . the sad thing about it . . .

FOR TWO WEEKS THE SUN HAD BLAZED ON AND ON. WE were captive to the kind of hot spell that lent evidence to the suspicion Mississippi was just the slow, painful way of spelling hell. Myraleen was about to go crazy. Moisture in the air colluded with the sweat on our bodies to shrivel our hair and drench our clothes. That was tough for Myraleen who liked to look so crisp she'd crack if you pinched her.

We sat on my porch swing desperately fanning ourselves, not knowing whether it was hotter inside or out. Nadir heat was a killing hand. Like the town itself, it gave you every reason to run for your life but drained the energy you'd need for flight. "Damn," Myraleen said. This was our Saturday afternoon off, and we would spend it beating hot air with wooden-handled cardboard squares decorated with white praying hands.

After graduation we found jobs working at the same place, the Humphreys'. We were maids.

I'd winced when I heard Mudear bragging to her friends. Her high-school-educated daughter, she boasted, had a job working for the richest people in Mississippi. Who knew if they were the richest, but they were rich. They lived in a mansion glorified by great white pillars in front. Rooms were vast galleries with satin couches and cherry-wood tables.

Mr. and Mrs. Humphreys had the most intelligent pool of colored domestics in the state, people said. "There's no dis'un and dat'un in this house," we were told by the male cook on our first day. Rita Mae Peel, class valedictorian the year before me, also worked for the Humphreys. The family's maids, butlers, chauffeurs and cooks considered themselves an elite group, like President Roosevelt's cabinet. They'd say "the Humphreys' home," never "the Humphreys' house." You would think it was the White House.

The couple was originally from Connecticut. They'd come south with their two baby boys ten years ago to save a family-owned, Depression-ailing factory outside of Hattiesburg. Their ways were nicely foreign. There were always an extra few dollars at Christmastime. They never raised their voices, and they said their servants' names with gentleness. "Mary . . . Rita Mae . . . Samuel," they'd call at moderate pitch when they needed us. They didn't spit our names out as if they were spewing nasty chewing tobacco.

"Well, at least they're nice," I'd said to Myraleen as we stood waiting for the bus home, after the first day.

"People with money should be nice," she said. "They should be the nicest, grinningest people in the whole world. If I were rich, I'd be nice, too."

"But you're nice anyway, Myraleen."

"Yeah," she'd said, "and that's the sad thing about it."

People these days said Myraleen looked like our colored singer Lena Horne. But Myraleen's skin was touched by a pinkish tinge, and she had a mass of velvet black hair. After I saw the picture *Show Boat*, I decided Myraleen could be Ava Gardner's better-looking twin. Even damp and discontent, she possessed a movie-actress quality. The ends of her hair shrank to cascades of wavy curls. She looked as if she'd gone to the beauty parlor, though she hadn't left the porch.

"We might as well go on up to the lake," she said. "But first I've got to stop home and change. You could ring this dress out and get a pitcher of water."

Her changing would take a good half hour. She had to wash up, find the right clothes, and then match everything up perfectly.

I excused myself from changing, reasoning that I was going to wade and get wet. Besides, there was no one to appreciate a willowy skirt or the bow on the bodice of a sundress. Most of the boys we'd gone to school with were by now good and married, just plain no good or some rough combination.

We'd been working at the Humphreys' for seven years and were now twenty-six—officially a year past hopeless by Nadir standards. Sure, there was a social straggler or two, somebody's cousin just moved here from somewhere or the couple of Slow Moes, just starting to make their serious moves. Every year one or two would drag-tail Myraleen's way, only to be told to drag his tail on back to where he came from.

I naturally didn't get much attention. Most colored men in Nadir had a skin-tone cutoff point for women and wouldn't court anyone whose skin deepened into the regions of dark brown. Some were silent about it; others bragged they didn't "haul no coal."

Still, two or three times, an interested male did sidle my way. Just that past winter Homer Wilkins stood before me outside church, asking if I wanted to go with him to a meeting about the Christmas program that night. I knew the invitation had nothing to do with my opinion about how the manger scene should be done. Homer, for reasons mysterious to me, had made a choice to pick a partner. A medium-sized, brown-skinned man, he clutched his hat to the front of his coat, though it was chilly out, as a pronouncement of his sterling intentions. It was in his eyes for anyone to see: We could make a home together, make poverty-crippled babies for the world to smash under its hungry heels, make years of companionship and evening conversations. And of course, on occasion, when my end of the conversation met with his disapproval, the palm of his hand might meet with my wayward face. Men in Nadir had a tendency to do that.

"I don't think so," I said when he suggested, "You reckon you can come, Lilian?" Then I muttered some false excuse—lying in front of the Lord's house—for which I felt guilty.

I waited in her yard until I could hear Myraleen's movements getting closer to the door. Many times I'd been invited in, but I avoided the other side of the Chadhams' threshold whenever possible. My child-hood discomfort about being in her house endured even though much had changed since then.

Myraleen came out in her pink floral-print sundress. Sleeveless and light, it gave her body the benefit of whatever bit of air was drifting. Her feet were swathed in laced pink linen espadrilles to match, of course.

Ostrich Lake was a mile up from Myraleen's, across the road from the Taylors' property and down a grassy slope. As we approached, I could see the Germans weeding the field. Every Saturday, the Taylors' nephew Toby drove a couple of towns away to the military installation to pick up two of the captured Germans incarcerated in the prison camp. Uncle Sam rented them out to farmers, even colored farmers, for a cheap price.

Mabel and Joseph Taylor were among colored Nadir's better-off, maybe best-off, folks—but they never acted like it. They had a wide parcel of land, more schooling than most whites and more ambitions than most people. They had done as well as the world would allow them to. If you happened to be coming up the road at the right time, you could see Toby driving the Taylors' green pickup truck, with the two long-limbed and light-haired Germans sitting beside him. He was a scant boy of twelve, the height of a picket fence, the color of a penny. His small head would bob up and down so freely as he drove that it looked like it wasn't completely attached to his neck. Farm boys drove tractors at eleven. Most families couldn't afford a car, but if they had one, any boy in the house older than nine knew how to drive it.

The short black child driving the tall European men was an unearthly sight in Nadir, where even someone from Atlanta had never been spotted. Before he first started going back and forth with them in the autumn, Toby, who lived with his aunt and uncle, was invisible. Now he was an object of curious attention. When people asked him about the Germans, he'd say, "They's okay," without a word of elaboration.

We could see him today working in Mrs. Taylor's big tomato patch, several yards behind the men. All disappeared from view as we crossed the road and made it down the slope.

A foot from the water, Myraleen spread a blanket and opened up an umbrella on it for shade. She wasn't going in. To her, publicly flapping around in the water was unworthy of a lady. But she didn't begrudge me the experience because she saw me more as a little girl. In some ways that was true. I didn't care about being seen wet. My only worry was that the hair around my temples would pull away from the two tight plaits I'd entwined and pinned at the top of my head and rebel into kinky beads. I never did know exactly what to do with my hair.

Looks weren't a concern here, though. At a bigger lake outside of town, where the whites went, people wore bathing suits. It was said the wilder ones swam at night in nothing at all. People who used our lake weren't fancy enough to own a bathing suit. Those who wanted to swim, male or female, wore cut-off pants and old shirts. Today I wore an unpampered blue dress I'd had since high school.

Because at our tiny lake there were no trees for shade, the hottest days drew the fewest swimmers. The only way to feel a touch cooler was to stay in the water, and even it was warm. Most folks found it more comfortable indoors. So Myraleen and I were the only two there. Right away I jumped in the water, got my fists wet, ran up to her and flicked her face. "You heifer," she said. Actually, it felt good and the tacit agreement between us was that I'd do it intermittently.

We could hear a car stopping slowly above the incline. More people had come, maybe. Down the slope came Red Briggs, a white boy in his mid-twenties. We'd known him since we were all small and had played with him a few times in unattended fields until a grown person felt the sting of propriety and called us away. I think it took Red a long time to realize Myraleen was colored. Whenever they'd cross paths, he'd chase her and tease her, until she was about eight and he understood.

We hadn't talked to that boy since then. As he got older he was always picking fights and not getting along with the white kids or the colored. It seemed he was born with a butt molded to be kicked.

As he negotiated the slope, Red stumbled on a few obvious rocks. "That boy so dumb," Myraleen whispered, "his head has fewer brains than a head of lettuce."

Sad but true. Red was widely known as a discredit to his county and a rain cloud above his mama's head. In fact, as the tongue waggers told it, his mother had fled Red and his fool father in disgust and relocated somewhere in Pennsylvania. Another story was that she got a chance to marry money, and she cashed it in. Red was one of those people who was such an irredeemable imbecile that even being white didn't help him much.

"How you ladies today? My car done stop running," he said. It was his explanation for being at the lake.

"Fine, thank you," we said. Whites did occasionally appear down the slope to take a swim, but we knew better than to show up at their lake.

"Damn, it's hotter than the devil's piss," he said kicking the ground. "You know any boys down here who can help me get it moving?" Red asked. His hair was the color of a baked sweet potato left out too long, making his head appear as if it had gone rancid. "I pay 'em."

"No," we said. We had no intention of getting involved in his business.

He hunched down and got seated several yards to the right of us. I went farther into the lake and splashed around. Red looked my way and crowed, "Oooh wee, that girl sure be liking that water!" A true statement until he said it. I let my hands float to my sides and tried to be less engaging to his glance. Red struck me as someone itchy with the longing for something he could not name.

"Why ain't you wriggling around in that water?" he called toward Myraleen. She ignored him.

For a while, he said nothing and I relaxed a bit. A few minutes passed. "Girl, you can talk to me. You think I'll bite?"

"You have teeth, don't you?" Myraleen said.

"Just tryin to be friendly. Some people always think folks tryin to insult 'em, when I's just tryin to be friendly." He got up, walked over and sat just a couple of feet away from Myraleen.

"With the war, and everything thas happening, I think we should stick together. Besides the negra getting more like the white man as time goes by. Take you for instance," he said turning to Myraleen. "You almost as light as me."

"I'm lighter," Myraleen said.

"Yeah, guess you are. That just goes to show you what I say. We gettin to be almost the same. Every generation, jus a li'l closer to the same. I don't care what other folks say, as far as I'm concerned that means things is progressin." He placed a forefinger on the tip of his chin, and paused a while. "Why there used to be a time . . . I'd say right bout at the beginnin of slav'ry . . . when negras had tails."

I looked at the sky, but Myraleen just burst out laughing.

"No really, I mean . . ." Red said, nodding his head in sincere affirmation. "I know it seems strange to think bout it in these modern times. But I done seen pictures, you'd be surprised, negras wit tails as long as you please. I betcha your ma never told you that."

Myraleen laughed harder. Her shoulders shook, and tears ran down her cheeks. Suddenly the water felt cold and bumps rose on my skin.

Red's face brightened with anger. His eyes—corpse blue things that looked like cheap plastic beads—bulged. He jumped up and glared down at Myraleen. "Here I am tryin to talk to you like one person to another, gal . . . and you act like you take me for a fool."

Myraleen's big laugh diminished to a few chuckles, and she shook her head. "No, I don't take you for anything, Red. I wouldn't take you if you had a brick of gold strapped to your chin."

I knew the good-sense thing to do would be to leave matter-of-factly before lightning struck. But my steps through the heavy water were slow, and Red's moves were fast.

"Nigger, you must done lost your mind, talking to me like that," he said, grabbing her elbow and pulling it toward him. "You going swim-min 'cause I say you goin swimmin! You need to be reminded of who you are before somebody really hurt you."

"Stop!" Myraleen said, jerking back.

He snatched her up from behind, by her arms, and threw her forward with such hateful power that she was, for a second, airborne before she slammed face first into the lake and water exploded all around me.

After gaining her balance in the water she had two choices: she could say nothing and be safer and let stand the implication that she deserved what he did—or she could cuss him out.

"You evil . . . peckerwood . . . no-dick peckerwood DAWG," Myraleen hissed. "Never been no good, never will be. Nothing but TRA-ASH! When you were born yo' papa shoulda shot yo' mama. You just hate niggahs cause it distract you from the hate you have for yourself."

Red leaped into the water and yanked her off her feet with a hand that gripped the back of her neck, which he held until her face reached the water, and he pushed it in. I screamed and jumped on his back, which only pushed his hand and her head deeper into the water. I jumped off. He was a big man.

I clawed at Red's scalp and pulled two fiery fistfuls of his hideous hair out by its roots. He was unaffected. "Let her go!" I screamed loud enough for God to hear me.

Riding his back again, this time I reached around to gouge his eyes, my blind fingernails raking between his cheeks and his eyebrows. Before I reached the blue targets, he let go. She sprang up coughing and crying. He reached around for me, and in a second I was being held underwater and fell limp with acceptance. It was all right. I was too tired to struggle. Then I felt someone else's legs in the water. I was being pulled up and dragged onto the grass.

The man who helped me was saying something I couldn't understand. I could see him clearly now, and get the scent of his wet, brown hair that smelled like damp paper. He was one of the Germans. Myraleen sat on one side of me patting my back the way you do to make a baby burp. He sat on the other, dropping his head and pretending to cough to show me what I should do to expel water. But I hadn't taken any of the lake into my lungs. I'd just stopped breathing, and now inhaled violently and felt dizzy.

"Dammit to hell, I was just tryin to be friendly to them gals," I could hear Red saying to himself in the distance. "That's what a man get for tryin to be friendly. I swear, cain't be friendly to no negras."

I looked at the German, and felt pain because there was nothing I could say that I thought he could understand. His eyes were an alien green. We looked at each other, neither knowing what the looks meant.

Joseph and Mabel Taylor were standing beside us soon. Him, with the pick he'd been using, and her in a paisley apron. They were what was considered old, in their fifties or so. "You young ladies all right?" he said. Clouds had sneaked in and it was raining. The sun had finally burned out and the sky cried in exhaustion, adding to the tears of my own.

"Trouble here?" Mabel Taylor said, smiling slightly and gritting her teeth, bracing for the answer.

"Trouble's everywhere," Joseph Taylor said.

IT SOMETIMES SHOCKED ME that I was alive. What throw of the cold dice, blink of an unseeing eye, fancy of an unthinking mind produced me, I wondered. And although I said I was a Christian, I couldn't imagine God gave anyone specific instructions to plant me upon this earth.

The Monday after the lake incident, I tried to say this to Myraleen during our sundown stroll. At dusk in the summer we'd take walks on the stretch of road between my house and hers. We'd go back and forth in a loop until the horizon was gray and one more circle would send Mudear out to the road complaining. Then we'd alternate which one was dropped off and stood out on the porch squinting to watch the other one walking home.

"Myraleen," I said. "Do you ever wonder why we're here?"

"Here? Here, where?"

"Here on earth, alive."

"No. Must be some reason or we wouldn't be here."

"Like what?" I said and heard the punch in my tone before I could stop it from breaking through.

"I don't know. Don't get mad at me. I didn't put you here. And don't let anybody hear you saying something like that. 'What am I here for?'—people'll think you're crazy."

"I used to think there was a reason. I thought things would happen, things I wouldn't want to miss for the world."

"Hell," Myraleen said. "Most of this shit, I *wish* I'd missed. Fact,

66

sometimes I wish Mercy had stayed on her side of the bed. But we're not supposed to say things like that either, so be quiet . . . Dice!" She shook her head and laughed.

That night I dreamed of dice. Odd, I'd never even held them. In Nadir, dice were the toys of bad men who made their hands into limp and reckless cradles rattling the cubes defiantly as they walked down the road looking for other players. The looks on their faces said it all had something to do with romance, but my dream was not romantic. It was a vision of being in a strange room dotted with dice in the oddest places: stuck on walls, sprinkled on chairs, trimming doorways. Jarred awake, I faced another day in Nadir, two hours early.

On Saturdays, I worked half days and returned home from the Humphreys' air-conditioned rooms when the sun was staring down mercilessly at my own defenseless house. I got in the door at about noon, headed for the already hot kitchen and turned on the oven.

About an hour later, three apple pies sat cooling on the table. Apple was a safe choice. Sweet potato might be too strange to him. I couldn't imagine they'd have sweet potatoes where he came from.

Making them in the cool of the morning before going to work wasn't advisable. "Why you making three?" Mudear would have asked, before she left for the Pattersons'. It was my way to make us two pies of some kind each weekend. The third would have steamed with questions, the answers of which Mudear didn't need to know. Telling her about what happened last Saturday would scare her into expecting that stupid Red to show up at our door enforced by a pale, murderous mob. Nightmares like that happened when she was younger and did occasionally even these days. But Myraleen, Red Briggs and I were a different generation. If he wasn't as embarrassed about how far things went as we were, he certainly couldn't be proud enough of what happened to inform the local lynch mob.

Red Briggs never intended to drown either of us, but unfortunately he probably thought it took a full fifteen minutes to drown. All he'd wanted to hear was "Yessir, sounds like you got a point." He needed nothing more, and he would have gone back up to finish the fight with his automobile, saying, "You girls, you be good now. See y'all." Keeping peace in Nadir required only the routine concessions and the occasional quiet acknowledgment of one's own inferiority. But that day Myraleen and I didn't have that much to give. Shortly after, Myraleen made her summary pronouncement on the incident. "I hate that son of a bitch Red Briggs," she'd said. "And once I hate a bastard, I hate him forever. I guess I'm just loyal that way."

I took the third pie and walked down the road toward the Taylors', thinking that maybe Mudear would have approved and even accompanied me. The extra pie was partly a product of what she'd taught me: If someone does you a good turn, you do him one.

Four colored families owned farms in Nadir—and about two dozen white ones. Cows grazed and cucumber patches grew all around, but I knew almost nothing about farming. The only book I'd read touching on it was *Animal Farm*, by George Orwell, in which the wild stock talked to each other, held meetings and launched a revolt. This was certainly no Mississippi farm Mr. Orwell was writing about, because here people hadn't come nearly as far as his pigs and horses. And, from the grisly accident stories I'd heard, real farms were bloodier: people falling from silos and dying; wild barn fires lashing out to the main house; farmers on tractors running over their own children—Death Farm.

Seeing Toby's peaceful face inspecting half-grown roadside cornstalks contradicted that thought.

"Hi. Your aunt and uncle home? Do you think they'd like some pie?"

"Well ma'am, Miss Mayfield. They in Jackson till tomorrow. We got kin that's sick. They gone to see about him."

I could see the Germans working in the back acres of corn.

"Well, this is for you and those two gentlemen back there."

I turned into the break in the cornfield, a strip of dirt that led to the Taylors' gray clapboard house. Toby zigzagged through several rows of green stalks, and met me at the bottom of the porch steps.

I held out the pie to him.

"This just for us, Miss Mayfield? Well, I'll buy ten tickets to that! Thank ya."

The pie secure in his hands, he rumbled up the steps. On the porch, he felt his upbringing tugging at him, and he turned around.

"Will you please stay and have some with us, Miss Mayfield?" I would have said no-thank-you but for the hope in his eyes. All alone all day with those harmless but strange men, he sought the more familiar for a moment. "I bring down some water, too."

"Maybe just some water. No thank you on the pie."

Seconds later he was two-stepping from behind the door, his arms wrapping around the back of a kitchen chair. He angled down the steps and placed it by my feet, facing the porch. "This is for you Miss Mayfield. Have a seat, please."

Next he brought a big metal pitcher of ice water and a glass trimmed in the middle with a circle of painted daisies. I sat, thanking him for the water, letting my free hand lie delicately on my lap, and trying to act like the adult he took me for.

In the distance, I could see the taller German's head was turned my way, and his movements in the corn had slowed. He was the one who'd helped me last week.

Toby ran toward the two men in the field. "Mister!" he said, turning to one. "Mister," he said, looking at the other. "The lady done brought us some pie. Come on," he said sweeping his arm toward the house. They followed.

He made a last trip into the house and emerged with the pie sliced three ways, and three tin cups and plates in the crook of his arm. He passed out the plates to the Germans, who'd made a place for themselves on the lower step. Then he motioned for each to grab a piece of pie. He sat on an upper step. They all were facing me, which gave me three degrees more male attention than I was accustomed to receiving. I felt awkward.

"Excuse our fingers, Miss Mayfield. But we don't need no forks cause we's men," Toby said, sliding a scoop of crust and apples off the plate with his hand.

From where I sat I could see the Taylors also grew big patches of tomatoes, cabbages and greens, and to the far right . . . lots of cucumbers, it appeared. And I smelled the scent of pigs and chickens, probably behind the house. They also owned a white goat that seemed to have the mind-set of a dog, and was resting in the triangular shade underneath the steps. He drifted out once to see what was going on, and then slinked back to his comfort.

The German who appeared a little younger than the other, about nineteen, nodded his head at me. *"Gut, "*he said. *"Gut."* He was blond, but the older one wasn't. His hair was the color of lightly baked bread crust.

He looked up from his plate, smiled at me and said something about dunking. No, he meant thank you.

"It's nothing," I said slowly. "Thank you for what you did last week."

He gave me another smile as if he actually understood. But maybe he guessed. What I said was logical, and the basis of any language, I imagined, was logic.

His eyes turned back toward his plate, leaving me a bit reassured. A breeze broke into the still air, and I looked up to see clouds tumbling through the sky like huge white spools of yarn. *Where were they going?* I thought. Wouldn't it be nice if they had passenger seats? As Toby said, I'd buy ten tickets to that.

As my eyes fell back down to earth, they met the German's again, his also in mid-descent from the clouds. My glance shifted quickly to my feet, in embarrassment. Still, I wondered if we'd been thinking the same thing.

KELLNER
. . . the Black Forest . . .

IT BOTHERED HIM. HE HAD NOT TOLD THE BLACK GIRL thank you. *Danke schön*, how was she to understand? Likely she made the pastry herself. He knew she did not have a servant who made it. In fact, she probably was somebody's servant. Seventeen or eighteen, he figured her age. At least he should have met her partway, thanked her in her own language. But the Americans should not know of his English. The less they knew, the better for him.

He rolled over and almost spun off the bunk. The poverty of sleeping on cots still shocked him. Usually, he woke up three times before morning. This was the second time.

Struggling through a translator had made him feel silly, he recalled. But it was necessary. The treaty mandated that officers never be ordered to work. Yet what else was there? He could go to the prison library and be depressed by its simpleton books and outdated newspapers that read as if written by people who had been asleep for several months. (Current news was not allowed.)

He had noticed a green rectangle of ground with a net across it. A low gate on the east side of the camp cordoned it off. Initially he assumed it an accommodation for the American officers. No, it was for the

Germans, he heard. He could not see himself as a tennis-playing prisoner of war. It was an absurd incongruity, like a ball-juggling seal.

"Ich will arbeiten." I want to work. First one sergeant listened. It had to be repeated in front of another as well. The Americans brought papers for their protection. "Tell him to sign," they told the German soldier who translated. Odd. Was he a prisoner or a boarding school charge? He lived surrounded by armed guards and high wire fences. They could kill him and call it a mishap. Yet, letting him toil to pave some road or such, that was a delicate decision.

He got up and tiptoed so Urs, a perfect fit in an adjacent bunk, would not wake. A glance out the tiny window (no bars on it as one might think), in front of the beds, showed dawn was hours away. It was hard to believe sometimes. The sky over America was the same one over Germany.

Sky is half the world at sea; the other half water and nothing else. He thought of the last morning on the submarine: He, Knut Hazelhoff and two crewmen came off the watch after sunrise. Nothing had appeared on the water. The enemy had been great flying waves slapping his face like an insulted woman. And the cold; every time he put the binoculars to his face, it felt as though he was plugging his eyes with ice.

On a drenched surface as slick as a frozen lake, the men slid around, undefended but for the safety belts around their waists that hooked them to the railing. Knut feared the belts were going to break and they would all be flipped overboard. So many fears. Kellner wondered about the man's childhood.

Trading the clawing cold for the pinched confinement inside the *Unterseeboot*, Kellner descended the tower shaft, feet blundering blindly down the stairs. He would not have to face the water again until midnight. The interior of the submarine looked almost black until their eyes adjusted.

Kellner could hear the clang of Knut knocking his head against the same dangling lamp he always banged it against. The man's frame was not meant for a submarine. His body unnaturally long and wiry, Knut possessed a bit of a monstrous appearance. He was only twenty-four, but his receding hairline made it look as though his skull had grown too big for his modest cap of hair. Though Knut was an enlisted man, Kellner stuck close to him. It was the man's first tour. A day after the ship left the dock, Knut, deathly pale from the beginning, went into convulsions, his body jerking as if responding to machine-gun fire. Undiagnosed epilepsy? As the other men held him down, Kellner stabbed his arm with enough barbiturate to kill the fit.

As Knut lay groggy in his bunk, Kellner asked questions. The answers were not good. He was a full-blown claustrophobic who had kept it a secret even from himself. Now he was on what was spatially no more than a narrow floating cave crammed with pipes, gauges, supplies, equipment and men. Who knew how long the tour would last! Knut's mental defense mechanisms and the Navy's appetite for recruits had delivered him as a bound prisoner into the cold heart of his worst fear. The ship required a grim adjustment for even the healthiest. Seventy odd men in the belly of a swimming boa constrictor. The air was cold, wet, smelly, and there was not enough of it. At each boarding, Kellner's breathing had become shallow, recoiling from the compounded odors of spoiled food and mass perspiration.

With permission, Knut remained in his bunk the next day. Kellner came to him late at night. The bunks and hammocks above them were heavy with overworked bodies and labored snoring. "I need to talk to you," Kellner said. "Give me all of your attention. It is very important."

The medicine had worn off hours ago. Knut looked like a toppled statue, stiff and pale, his eyes clamped open by insomnia that courted eternity. "See that tie rope hanging from the hammock straight above," Kellner asked, his voice slowed, deliberate, almost grave. "The longest one, the odd one, look at it. Keep your eyes on it." Knut did as told.

"Watch it for a while, the way it's limp, the way it bends a little in the middle.

"I am going to tell you something. You are not going to be afraid here because this ship is a very strong vessel. You saw it sitting at port. It was the most powerful thing you had ever seen. Much larger than the house you were a boy in. Big enough for seventy men. Think of it. Every time you look at all the tiny dangling ropes in this huge place, you will think how safe you are in this ship. You are going to do a fine job tomorrow. On this strong, big ship, you will be a good sailor."

Kellner sat there, on the wooden bench between the lower bunks, fifteen minutes after the man fell asleep. He would take the upper bunk tonight, give up his place in the officers' compartment and sleep here until he got Knut through the tour. As he got up, he noticed Beckmann, one of the ship's youngest, looking down at him from the upper opposite bunk. Though in his long johns, he hopped to the floor and stood straight. "Lieutenant, sir, could you please teach me how to do what you just did, so I can get girls?"

"If you need to do this to get a girl, you do not deserve one."

"Yes, sir."

Kellner hoped Beckmann was the only man to notice what he had done. Usually, it was only bandaging machinery-carved gashes and warding off infections with iodine. Some nausea-and-diarrhea cases emerged in the beginning and subsided farther out to sea. A fall onto a carving knife caused a wound one of the kitchen crew could have bled to death from.

Unterseeboots did not have enough men to justify doctors, Navy policy decreed. But the number of ships forced to dock to get treatment for urgently ill sailors concerned a few higer-ups. As an experiment in efficiency, Kellner received U-boat duty. The men thought of him simply as a doctor. Only the commander knew he was a psychiatrist. "What good does it do to talk to crazy people?" Bautzner had asked. He was one of the few ideologues on the ship. "Better to get rid of them. But people make such a stink about it. 'What did you do with crazy Aunt Gretchen?' they say. 'Bring her back'—as if not enough of them exist. Mental defectives, racial subhumans and the sort, they're being born at higher rates than us. Every morning that I get up and put on my trousers, there are more animals in human form on the earth."

Were Kellner talking to a civilian acquaintance, he would have said, "Perhaps you should leave your trousers off." But there could be consequences for even that.

"Who knows what would happen to a man like me—healthy and sane and normal—if those kinds dominated," Bautzner had said.

Kellner had wanted to tell the commander his patients were not insane. He treated neurotics, not psychotics who, too, were treatable. Instead, he said, not knowing what demon moved his mouth, "They will eat you."

"What?"

"That's what primitives do to people like us. We taste better than Jews, and other saltier creeds."

His commander looked him up and down before he turned to leave. In a few moments, Kellner had declined in Bautzner's esteem, plunging from competent to curious.

Silly, he had risked himself for a joke, to enjoy petty revenge. His patients were no longer his responsibility. Still, worries pinched his mind about melancholia sufferers who might be punished as malingerers, agitated obsessives who might be taken away and . . . Regardless, they were only a part of that lost dimension called the past.

The *blitzkrieg*, the lightning war, had stretched into the longer-than-promised war. A flood of American and Canadian newcomers appeared and spiked the sea with fresh chances for death.

German submarines were once quick, invisible, invulnerable. A British official had said to the Germans in a speech broadcast on the radio,

"You have sent the wind. You will reap the whirlwind." The men laughed about it, saying the "whirlwind" was merely one of Winston Churchill's ample burps. "I don't know about you," a crewman had said, "but I wouldn't want to be in the path of one of that big bastard's belches. It might be better to surrender."

This year, the imbecilic enemy had risen to bright-moron level. They had cracked their code. Now allied radar could slice through the waters and find them. Higher-ups denied it, but Kellner knew it. That was the true explanation for their sudden competence, not impotent spy planes sent out at the right times to make it look as if information came through mundane means. But if he said that, he would be a defeatist. And that was a crime.

"Looks like no Swiss cheese for Father," he said to himself after each setback. It was a personal joke. What dawned as just another morning on which they came from watch soaked with sea and exhaustion would become something else. Kellner and the man he shadowed undressed and eased into their bunks. Knut's words interrupted the slide into sleep. "Lieutenant . . . Thank you."

Except for a bit of insomnia, the man now appeared no different from the others. Kellner remained watchful for bad effects since the hypnosis. Each night seemed to run into the next as if it had an urgent appointment. The sea could be like a book without a bookmark. You lost your place in life. Days of battle, those were the bookmarks.

"You are welcome." Kellner let his head fall back onto a flat sack that was a pillow in name only.

He heard a thick, blazing alarm in his dream in which he was hiking in the Black Forest. Why would anyone bomb the woods? For a half second when worlds fused, he looked up and the scowling moon over the Black Forest was Knut's panicked white face. "Lieutenant! Lieutenant!"

Then he was standing, his dumbfounded feet paused to balance his weight. A crush of men ran by them, headed to their stations. A roaring explosion shot two bodies back into them. Kellner flew through the air, limbs, organs, flesh and eyes surrendered to the harsh laws of physics. He didn't own his body then and could not protect it.

The world ended. Good. It had been too much bother. Then he was in the Black Forest, dead. But some animal began pulling at his chin and tugging at his long johns. He opened his eyes and saw Knut before him, shouting, "Up, up, out, now!"

Water was all over, up to Knut's waist and other men's chests. Sparks buzzed around electrical equipment. Knut pulled him, dragged him through every flooded compartment until he could drag himself. Dead men paved the flooded path beneath them like strange cobblestones. Knut turned to him, his face ferocious. "SAFE? SAFE?" he screamed. Under calmer conditions, Kellner would have explained that he had not meant it literally. It was only a hypnotic suggestion.

At the stairs, they climbed outside to the tower. The sea was a vast, fluid valley. Two torpedoes had awarded it half the ship. Like endless grabbing hands, the water was all over them. Knut's mouth moved, shouting something. All Kellner could hear was water crashing against his ears. With rough impatience, Knut placed Kellner's hands on an exposed piece of railing.

A high, salty crest smacked Kellner's head, hot biting teeth on his bleeding temple. Otherwise he was freezing all over. His eyes hurt. His head injury produced drunkenness. He couldn't see a thing except the water that waged a battle to drown his soaked and easy body. But Knut could see. A rubber raft with two crewmen bobbed against the waves only meters away.

"WE MUST SWIM OUT!" Knut shouted this in his face twice. And he didn't know whether the beads of water spraying him were the sea or his friend's determined spit. He slapped back at the water with arms of pain and ice. Knut swam ahead of him, head bobbing, arms fighting. Kellner would never make it to the raft. It was too hard. Foamy liquid death came in waves and waves to oppose his every movement. Each time his exhausted arms broke a current, it collapsed into more wet hopelessness. Fate's indulgence would run out a half meter before he could make it. He just knew it. The precious proximity alone would kill him. Suddenly his fingers slapped at something solid, the raft. Seamen he recognized to be Lieberman and Bittens helped him in. He fought to stay awake. But consciousness creeped away from him like one hand slipping from the grip of another. Thoughts flowed into nothingness: No Swiss cheese for . . .

He woke in a wood-paneled room with bright lights. He guessed it was an American ship. Americans liked bright lights.

Lieberman and Bittens told him they had been hauled aboard an hour ago.

"Where did they take Knut Hazelhoff?" Kellner asked.

Their faces went blank. "Hazelhoff? Did you see him make it off the ship?" Lieberman asked.

"He swam to the raft with me."

"You were alone," Lieberman said.

"No, I was not alone!" Kellner said loudly enough to make his head hurt.

"I think we were the only ones who made it," Bittens said.

Lieberman's eyes shifted back to Bittens with a look of warning. "We don't know that. It was such chaos we couldn't see where everyone went. Hazelhoff must have got on another craft." The power of his injury subsided, and Kellner felt a clear cursed consciousness.

He spent a week on the ship that rescued him. (Was it also the ship that sank them? He didn't want to know.) They gave him dry clothes and locked him up with Lieberman and Bittens in a tiny room with a toilet. He outranked the two and made sure the second morning they made up the bedding on their cots to look as neat as a brown paper package. Capture was no reason for sloth.

Two American officers with forceless voices questioned him the third day. One spoke German. They took him to a meeting room with an oak desk. Where do you come from? What Navy unit? Name? Rank? The first one's eyes darted in tiny restless movements sifting for more than the obvious; an educated man. He could see in the second one's stare sadness hardened into cruelty. His oblong face wore a smirk as a disguise. Kellner had heard American men were fundamentally a bunch of gangsters. It surprised him that they were not more surly.

"Is there anything you want to say that I haven't asked?" the first one said. "Anything at all?" The second one then offered questions in English for which he did not expect answers. "Any state secrets you'd like to give away? Tell us you're actually somebody important instead of some damned riffraff Kraut. Confess that you're actually the Führer, the jig's up and I can go back to Milwaukee."

As they walked out, Kellner said in German, "What about my comrade who was in the boat with me?" The polylingual officer stopped and gave a shrug. "No others found," he said. "You were very lucky. Maybe you got your luck and your friend's luck too. But we're still looking for survivors. I've heard of men lasting on lifeboats for many days."

The monolingual one asked what had been said. His smirk grew deeper. "Sorry, Sauerkraut." They escorted him back to his tiny room.

Thinking about such things, how was he ever to sleep? Kellner noticed the night sky had lightened a shade. Knut had bequeathed him this insomnia. He must have been staring for an hour. He thought, *One of the most frightening things about life was that a phobic's opinion is as good as anyone's.*

LILIAN

. . . luck's ladder . . .

MUDEAR LOVED THE WAR. SHE WAS THE HAPPIEST I HAD EVER
seen her. I had read newspaper articles to her about ships down and soldiers dead, and she would nod and press her mouth almost into a smile.
"Uh-humm," she'd say. "See, some got to die so some can live. That's
how God works."

Bitter times had turned to better times. With our combined sala-
ries, we bought plenty of whatever we wanted. We went into town and
picked out our first couch. I bought a real bed for myself, and we gave
my cot to Mrs. Wright, who had two leftover children at home sleeping
in one bed. Now the Sears catalog became more than just a source of toilet paper and daydreams. We picked out nice clothes and a blue throw
rug and got a big kick out of the fact they had come to us all the way
from Chicago.

Our wants were not too widemouthed, since deprivation had long
ago shrunk them. Relatively little seemed like plenty to us. Mudear said
if she ever won a contest or something and got her hands on, say, ten
thousand dollars all at once, she'd have one mind to crush it against her
bosom and never let it go and another to dance naked down the road

throwing it up in the air. "Whoever said money can't buy happiness was a fool," she said. "If you don't pay for happiness, how you going to get it?"

Even the rationing didn't get in the way. Mudear managed to get gas ration stamps, though we didn't own a car, by lying on request forms. She'd trade with a car-owning man at church: our falsely gained gas stamps for his sugar and flour stamps.

When I suggested to Mudear this was probably a bit illegal, she said, "Illegal my Aunt Fanny! Things been rationed one way or another out of my reach all my life. The Depression, then everything was cheap, but you didn't have the money to buy anything. Now there's money, and they trying to block you with ration stamps. It's always something. No, Lord, not this time."

Mudear was working for a new family, the Pattersons. She kept their three cowlick-crowned boys and did the housework. Both mother and father worked in a Hattiesburg diner frequented by servicemen. He was a cook and she a waitress. "Just think of the tips that woman must make!" Mudear was making more money waiting on the waitress than she'd ever made in her life.

News of the Pattersons' careers came to me daily through pancake and egg counts. "Mr. Patterson said they served up over fifteen hundred pancakes today," Mudear would say. "And more than two thousand eggs. Just think of that!"

For me the war imposed uncertainty about where Mudear and I stood on luck's ladder. I kept reading about people dead or displaced, mistreated or miserable because of the fighting. Did that make us lucky by comparison, or were we still unlucky by birth? Lying in bed, I would ask this question to the night air, hearing crickets scraping their confident legs as if they had the answer and I just couldn't understand.

It was better to contemplate fortune and misfortune than think of leaving Nadir at that point. If I left, Mudear would be alone with the rent and bills and no extra money to play with. Who would she have to talk to all the time or go to movie shows with? Every other week we got a ride to the theater in Hattiesburg. We would sit in the balcony, the colored section. Newsreels about the war ran before the main feature. Mudear found every Hollywood picture delightful. She came out beaming, saying how much it tickled her to see Myrna Loy or Barbara Stanwyck or whoever the plucky actress was whose skin Mudear had been able to project herself into for a couple of hours. "That girl can act her country hips off!" she'd say. I was afraid if I left, I would be taking Mudear's happiness with me—the only happiness she'd ever had.

Evenings we read the day-old Hattiesburg paper she got from the diner. Occasionally, on the first or second page, they ran a picture of the menacing German leader whose face looked like his soul turned inside out. The Allies labeled the war zones, calling them the European Theater and the Pacific Theater, as if the world were acting up and putting on a show. Sitting side by side after dinner at a new Formica table, we'd exchange a confusion of rattling pages. Mudear read aloud anything she saw about colored people. "See there," she'd say, "'Negro Holds Up Store.' That's why we can't get anywhere. We don't know how to act."

"But, Mudear," I said, "plenty of white people stick up stores, rob banks. And you don't see a headline saying 'White Man Robs Bank.'"

"Got a point," she said. "See, that's why I sent you to school, so you could think. Not too many folks can think. A lot can only talk. Better if it was the other way around."

Mudear became a geyser of criticism. She read about some physics professor at a top school who claimed that with effort and millions of dollars, America would put a man on the moon before the end of the century. "Ump, ump," she said. "White folks so rich they can throw money at the moon."

People's constant misdeeds amazed her. "Poor men think they got nothing to lose," she'd say, "and rich men think they just *can't* lose."

Reading about all this fresh enthusiasm for war, I felt as if the country had gone senile from sea to shining sea. Roosevelt had testified like a sanctified man that he would not, *would not* get the United States involved in this foreign war. The Great War had been lesson enough. Most people saw no reason Americans should jump in the brawl just because those people in Europe started fussing and fighting again. Then along came Pearl Harbor. Roosevelt had an excuse to go to war that fit like a custom-made suit. But at least Mudear was happy.

Usually, we went outside after dinner to sit on the porch swing and watch the occasional automobile pass. At least twice as many cars rolled through Nadir now as ten years before. We always waved if we knew the driver.

"Guess you ain't never gonna get married, huh?" Mudear said.

"Doesn't look like it."

"That's all right. I blame myself for that. Shouldn't have showed you what I showed you those many years ago."

My shoulders tensed. She had never spoken of that night before. "How long had you been doing that, Mudear?"

"A couple of years before you were born, after I first married your father. Your granny midwifed to make a dollar here and there . . ."

"I didn't know that."

"But sometimes people didn't want a baby. They wanted the opposite. Year she died the colored hospital opened, good thing. Still, one thing they didn't do. So I started where Mama finished. Every so often the hospital got a gal running in there cause of a stumble. The ladies' doctor told them, 'Go to Mrs. Mayfield. She'll help you.' But when it got to where I couldn't see perfectly, even with glasses, I just stopped. That's one of those things, if you don't do it exactly right, you don't do it, nothing to be playing with."

"Where do girls go now?"

"Grapevine has it that a lady in Hattiesburg'll fix things. If they can't make it that far, they just have to have it."

Another automobile drove by. We knew the man and waved. "Whew! It's hoppin tonight," Mudear said.

"Lilian," she said, "you not such bad company."

Now that I was grown, I received a rare, muted compliment, but never anything extravagant. I never heard anyone mention "love" in Nadir, unless they were talking about loving Jesus. If I had a craving to hear someone say I love you—and though I was ashamed of it, sometimes I did—I tried to satisfy it at the movies.

The show was one event to look forward to. Going to the Taylors' farm every Saturday became another. I didn't try to hide it from Mudear anymore. I just said Mrs. Taylor and I had become friends, which was mildly true.

On the Saturday after the apple pie, I baked a coconut cake, and brought it down to them. The Taylors were outdoors working in the garden that ringed their house. "Well, you could have just come round to visit," Mrs. Taylor had said. "You didn't have to bring nothing."

"Didn't want to come empty-handed," I said, citing part of the southern code of honor. The Germans were in an eastern corner of the farm, weeding tomato patches. "Do you think they'd like a piece of cake?" I asked. "The tall one was nice to me that day I almost drowned."

"Oh, don't talk about that day," Mrs. Taylor said, waving her hand toward the ground, as if to keep evil down in hell where it belonged.

I walked behind Mr. Taylor through his fields, holding two tin plates of cake, trying to step only in the grooves between crop rows.

"Did you get properly introduced?" Mr. Taylor said as we walked.

"They don't speak English, though."

"Well, we've traded a few words. Tall one held out his hand and said, 'Kellner,' first day. Now I don't be knowing whether he's giving his first or last name," Mr. Taylor said, with a little laugh. "But I just grinned and say, 'Pleased to meet you, I'm Joseph Taylor.' The second one says his name is Urs. I don't know whether that's first or last either, but least I got some kind of handle on them."

When we reached the two men, both browned from the sun, Mr. Taylor told them, "This is Miss Lilian Mayfield." One nodded and wrinkled his forehead trying to understand. The one who helped me at the lake just smiled.

"This is Urs," Mr. Taylor said. "And this is Kellner."

KELLNER

. . . cloak for madness . . .

HE WAS IN A PRISON, WHICH, WITH ITS SATURDAY-NIGHT SOFT-ball, Sunday-afternoon tennis and all the beer one could drink, seemed too amiable to be one. This was not like being captured by enemies so much as being forced on holiday by dimwits.

Urs's snore sounded like a death rattle. If a good night's sleep reflected happiness, Urs was an ecstatic individual. But if to work, to love—and to sleep—was the measure of health, Kellner fell short. Tonight like any other, he would have only a few brief respites between long intrusions of consciousness.

Some men were contented prisoners, others not. Camp life was the regimentation of emptiness. They got up at 6:30. A half hour to shower and dress. Meals heavy in starches were served in an expansive dining hall. Americans put sugar in everything. They were too weak to take things as they were. Bread equaled cake. A drink they called punch was only thin, red syrup. In the camp kitchen, German cooks heeded American recipes. It was as if they had turned into tiny children cooking to their hearts' confectionery contentment; either that or a bunch of wild, laughing drunks committing one last atrocity before collapse.

Most of the soldiers relished it. A plate heavy with an avalanche of mashed potatoes and a glacier of meat made them feel fortunate. At home, even during the war, people ate adequately. This, however, was a country where the word *enough* had been replaced by the command for more. Here to gorge was to thrive.

Regular mail delivery was the only camp benefit he valued. He marveled that they allowed prisoners to receive mail. An obligation according to the Geneva Treaty, but what did that matter if they wanted to ignore it? Each week he would get letters from his mother and sister. They were opened and a bit wrinkled, having been preread by some censor. Still, nothing was ever crossed out. The letters were imported bits of a previous life: his mother's lovely handwriting, so many flourishes it seemed a celebration of literacy; his sister's attempt at joking: "The Americans will let you go when they discover how much trouble you are." His mother never used the family name in the return address, but her mother's maiden name instead.

When he addressed the letters back, he also used the name Himmelstoss. "Do not worry, I am well," he'd say and hypocritically list all the camp's privileges: "clean quarters," "ball games" and "remarkably generous rations of food."

His father never wrote but had his mother send messages such as "endure with honor." Kellner preferred it that way. Another analyst would accuse him of having an unresolved Oedipal complex. However, suppose one's mother is likable, and one's father is not? Had Freud thought of that?

He rolled over. He remembered four years ago, the last ballet he went to at the Semper Opera House. The ballerina, in a duet with a male dancer, unwound from a spin and bowed her head with such vulnerable grace it made him want to be a brother and a lover and a gentleman all at once. Attraction was biology. As a scientist, he knew this. Still, he felt sorry for men who could not be moved by women. He missed women.

He got up. At the window, he looked into the blackness. The moon gave the darkness a shine. A firefly glided by, and sparked in the darkness a memory.

U.128 surfaced that particular night. Kellner went up the tower shaft and met the captain on deck to witness the damage to the British ship they had sunk. A rush of smoky air poured over him from above. Incredible. It was like Zeus on fire, rising from the sea before dying. Its flaming stern reached seven or eight stories into the sky, just a quarter of a kilometer in front of them. What was left of her crew huddled in two lifeboats. They were dark shadows against the darker water—ghosts already. It would have been better to burn. Subs have no room for prisoners. The angry weather front, on its way, would likely sink them. If they were less fortunate, they'd drift until they died of dehydration. And the injured, well, they might as well just toss them overboard now.

Whenever the submarine launched an attack, every man on board seemed to merge into a common body, as though they became part of the ship herself. All became still and breathless, inhaling at the sound of "tube three—fire . . . tube four—fire," exhaling when the last torpedo zoomed to its destiny. Silence reigned again until they reached their target. Would death answer with death? Seconds later, the ship would reverberate from the explosion and the crew explode into cheers, even those thrown to the floor by the echo blast of a close hit.

He seldom came up to look if the sub surfaced. But on this night he did. And through his binoculars, on one of the boats, he thought he saw someone he knew. That was impossible. In the short distance, he heard "Help . . . please" from a few different desperate mouths and shut his eyes. War is the perfect cloak for madness, he thought. War is the id masquerading as the superego. He was alone with these thoughts. No more alone than the other men were with theirs. But he felt like it.

After medical school, he'd gone to the Göring Institute in Berlin where he'd been trained as an Adlerian. His colleagues didn't talk about it, but Sigmund Freud's work was the basis for Alfred Adler's.

Kellner had read Freud's books before they were banned. Psychoanalysis, though, was like playing a Benny Goodman record or tapping your foot to a jazz tune snaking from a foreign radio station. It grew from a contaminated source. So German psychotherapists these days called themselves Adlerians, Jungians—anything but Freudians. It was better to be an admirer of Jack the Ripper.

Much of his education stemmed from contaminated sources. He remembered times when he walked and ran through the rambling grounds of Oxford on his way to class, where he'd strain to capture the approval of some black-robed professor. Noblemen in their boyhoods, wearing braided gowns, had traversed to the same gamut of letters for seven hundred years. He liked his arrogant classmates whose sense of superiority cast an abrasive challenge to his own. There was a fellow named Theodore Eddington who stood out as noncompetitive. A portrait of tweed and good posture, Eddington would interrupt his composure to bellow, "You're a spectacular chap, a spectacular chap." It was like being cheered by a crowd of one, but he liked it.

Despite all that Oxford and Berlin offered, he was happy finally to go home. He had grown up in an art museum, a baroque city heavy with statues of staid men on crazed horses, and arched doorways propped with naked angels hailed by the clangs of a forest of fine belfry towers. It was among the world's most beautiful cities.

He opened a practice. Ignoring his father's poking remarks, Kellner continued to ride his bike. Jakob, too, was a physician, but he'd floated so fast, far and silently into the upper reaches of the Reich, the family no longer knew exactly what kind of work he did.

On the way home each day, Kellner would stop at the market and search for something that would make his mother's eyes shine. Despite shortages, the merchant, a small man battered by years, hid produce for him. As Kellner feigned interest in a cart of anemic potatoes, the merchant loved to tiptoe up behind him. Anyone could hear him coming, though. His aged lungs breathed noisily and sounded like the stop and start of a ceiling fan. "Surprise for you!" He'd present some cherries, perhaps. From behind his back came another hand dangling the stems of two triangles of grapes. He'd stand back to see Kellner nod and smile. People often gave him what he wanted just to see his approval.

Small things made his mother happy. Only very big things made his father happy, like conquering Poland. When he ate the first in a case of Kielbasa sausages, a taunting merriment flared in his eyes. He jabbed it into his mouth furiously, as if it might be stolen back at any moment. After France surrendered, plates of caviar that no one wanted to eat covered the table. His sister was too young. He and his mother thought it slimy. And his father had never eaten it in the past. But Jakob Strauss had hauled big full boxes with a weary pride as if it had been his own feet that marched over Paris. In May of 1940, he brought in big rolls of Belgian wool. Then, too, he was breathless and gleeful. After all, the soldiers' needs had spawned a fabric shortage. It had been a year since either female of the house had appeared in a new dress. And a month before, it had taken two panzer-division soldiers to haul in the armoire from Denmark—even though every bedroom already had one.

All the well positioned did it; not as much as Jakob, though. The cupboards and storage rooms were full of foreign foods and neglected crates of champagne. Berta, the cook, looked confused and frightened.

The panzers would take Moscow eventually, Kellner thought. And only the pretense of propriety would keep his father from rampaging into the house drunk, clutching a bottle of vodka in one hand and dragging a Russian woman by the hair with the other.

Jakob's stout face appeared stuffed and hungry at the same time. He made Kellner think of the German proverb "Envy is the sorrow of fools."

"What I truly want is Swiss cheese," Jakob had said. "Aah yes, soon."

Urs got up and shuffled to the bathroom stalls. When he came back, Kellner heard his footsteps taking a detour. "Do I snore? Is that why you do not sleep?"

"No, it is not you."

He thought of one of the last dinners with his mother and sister. Dimmed lighting, to save electricity, yellowed the white napkins. It made the modest spaces, between him, Dorlisa and Kristel, feel greater. Jakob's chair stood vacant as usual. A draft, a pest from the coal shortage, swallowed the room's warmth. It tempted him to hunch his shoulders. The women seemed unaware. Their eyes, as usual, turned to him at the start of the meal. Was he pleased with it? If not, a better piece of meat would be requisitioned, side dishes replaced.

The color of his mother's hair matched his own. She had magnetic blue eyes, heart-shaped lips and a graceful neck above a sturdy but small body. Olive tones shaded her skin. Dorlisa's maternal grandparents had been Italian.

But, Jakob could practically trace his Germanic heritage to Aryan primates. His parents' picture hung in the front hallway. Side by side they stood, their noses as straight and sharp as their postures. His grandfather's savage temperament glinted from his aqua eyes. His grandmother's thin lips fastened together as if to keep any kind word from escaping.

Kristel was a hybrid of Dorlisa's engaging eyes and Jakob's wide face. Her big-boned body trespassed an inch or so beyond the acceptable width of the times. She feared she wasn't pretty. So before the arrival of any suitor, Kellner became dramatically suspicious. He questioned the night's itinerary as if he believed the slightest deviation would give some timid young man the opportunity to exercise the galloping desire Kellner maintained any man would have for his sister.

"Are you losing weight?" he asked Kristel that night. Suggestion was a potent plant. "You're getting as skinny as a French girl. No, in fact, you're getting as skinny as a French boy."

Kristel smirked, crookedly pulling the end of her mouth down toward her chin. "And you're getting as crazy as a French lunatic." She leaned forward and with a quick reach, plucked a deep blue grape from the fruit-choked centerpiece. She set it on the table, and flicked it swiftly with her thumb and forefinger so it caught him on his lower right jaw. He broke into a laugh and raised his napkin.

"Goodness, children," Dorlisa said. "No more." It was automatic propriety speaking. She valued everything that they did and said, every breath they breathed on earth.

Mornings when he was small, she'd come to his bed and stroke his forehead until he opened his eyes. Then her face lit with celebration as if he had done something brilliant when he had done nothing but wake up. She had given him her maiden name—Kellner—so that every time she called him she would hear in its solid syllables that he was a part of her.

She had lost her father and two brothers in the first big war. "And it is not over." Dorlisa had told Kellner this again and again from the time he was eight or nine.

Before dinnertime ended, hard footsteps thumped through the entrance hall. Jakob Strauss was a big man with a bay window of a stomach that entered rooms before the rest of him. He stood silent for a moment an arm's length from Dorlisa's chair.

She lowered her eyes. When he entered a room, some part of her left. Dorlisa was the sort of wife Jakob approved of for she was the kind upon whom he could deposit disapproval. Her softness was silliness; her concern cowardice; her attention to complexities pettiness.

"There was a crash—a plane crash." Every heart at the table beat faster. "Two from the military and two from the ministry of health, dead." Jakob would replace the health minister, moving up a rank or two. He'd leave for Berlin in two days.

Kellner received a letter a few weeks later. He knew what it said by looking at the envelope. He needed to open it only for the details. The war that had come to Europe in 1939 had come to his home in 1941. At first it sent gifts. Now it sent for him.

MYRALEEN

. . . a lawfully unwedded woman . . .

I NEVER HAD ALL THOSE TALL COTTON DREAMS, LIKE LILIAN, of doing this and that. I was just going along to get along, without knowing where I was going. My workweek was made up of five and a half days dancing with brooms and mops. On Sundays, I went to church in the morning and to the movie show in the evening. Mason Lewis drove me in his Ford.

He'd moved from Jackson a while back and gotten a job as a janitor at the Army base outside town. He was in-the-money by Nadir standards: a young man with his own car and a few lazy dollars in his pocket all the time. Almost any other Nadir woman would have been fall-on-her-knees grateful for his attention. I was grateful just to get away to the show every Sunday. Every other week we'd pick up Lilian and Miz Mayfield and take them too. He wasn't tickled about the idea at first. But they were so sweet that he got attached to them.

The Sundays we weren't alone were the better ones. Miz Mayfield always made us stop in on the way back. "Now, Mason," she'd say, "you must be crazy if you think I'm going to let you buy tickets for me and my daughter, pay for both our Pepsi-Colas and popcorns, and not at least fix you a plate of something." Then Miz Mayfield and Lilian would heat up whatever they'd had for Sunday dinner that day, and we'd all eat for a second time. Mason got the biggest chunk of cobbler or cake or bread pudding and a helping of everything else wrapped in waxed paper to ease his bachelor living.

By the time we'd get back to my house, it was late enough for me to excuse myself from a lingering good-bye. "Don't want to worry your daddy none," he'd say opening the car door for me.

My being twenty-six with not a husband anywhere in the vicinity was what worried my father. Cheevers was long gone. He headed to Chicago about two years after he learned his blessed bride would rather crouch in the outhouse than spend the night with him. Over the years, the stories about us had slacked off. Now the line of thinking wasn't so much that I'd been crazy, but that I'd broken his heart because he wasn't handsome enough for me.

When I was nineteen, we found out, through a lady at church who knew some of his kin, that he'd remarried and spit out a pile of children. He'd never legally divorced me. A lot of men did that. Daddy had said, "We can't have that from Mr. Cheevers. I know he got tricked, kicked and licked when he tried to hitch up with you, but he got to release you in the eyes of the law. That way, you can marry for real when somebody else comes along."

"*He* got tricked, kicked and licked?" Legal divorce didn't concern me. Not ever seeing his stolen-from-a-mule face again was divorce enough for me. I simply didn't want somebody who was nobody meaning something to me. I'd said it and meant it: "I'll never marry, Daddy. I swear to God, I will never marry."

"You just want to be Miss Contrary, don't you?" he'd said. "Now don't start lying to God. Everybody got to marry sooner or later."

"The only thing I have to do, Daddy, is stay black and die."

My father wrote to Cheevers and offered to pay the county fee if he'd just sign the annulment papers. A few months later, I was a lawfully unwedded woman.

Daddy tried to take care of me a little, once I was older. Maybe he was trying to make amends for not protecting me from Mercy's craziness. Maybe not. I never knew what his true thinking was on the subject of my mother and never asked.

My getting older, even graduating and getting a job had made Mercy treat me no differently. I remember the summer I was twenty-one, with Ed Matthews starting to court me, walking me to get ice cream, taking me to the social functions at the church, things like that. He was the minister's son. Common talk claimed that ministers' sons were devils. Ed was innocent as milk. I even tried to tone myself down. Didn't want to scare the poor fellow, so I tried to be less smart-mouthed.

But Mercy didn't like my going anywhere and doing anything with anybody. When I said he was coming to call, she didn't say a thing. We went to the young people's fair out in back of the church late that afternoon. Most who showed up were fourteen, fifteen or sixteen. Two hobbyhorses, one painted with tiger spots and the other zebra stripes, had been put out for decoration. But there were always girls willing to climb on them and boys willing to tease them about it. Everybody played games. They popped balloons with darts to try to win prizes and threw softballs to knock down faraway toy ducks. The balloons and ducks always seemed closer than they really were. Ed and I were the oldest people there. He was my age, the point where almost everybody was married, and not considered "young people" anymore, but grown folks with "young'uns."

He was too slow for that, and I suppose I was too swift. At my porch he said, "Myraleen, I had a very enjoyable evening. I hope you'll allow me to spend time with you again." In my new toned-down style, I said something nicey-nice to him, too.

When I walked in, Mercy was waiting, sitting in the big chair near the front window. It was dusk. Her body threw a wide shadow on the wall as if she were being watched over by her own ghost.

"So what'd you do?" she asked.

I was surprised she'd spend the spit to ask. With Mercy you never knew whether it was going to be the cotton ball or the needle. I told her about every little thing, even what he'd said at the door, thinking she'd feel it was all fine.

"What else did you do?"

"That's about it, Mama."

She rose from the chair and walked toward me. Her shadow followed as if they were going to double up on me. "Well, Miss Fast Ass, I wasn't there, so I don't know what really went on." She told me she was going to have to check something to make sure she wasn't "providing a roof for some whore."

She held out her hand. When she told me what to do, I didn't say a word. I just did it. I took off my underpants and gave them to her. She smelled them and handed them back. "Okay, this time," she said. "'Cause I can smell it if you been doing it."

What happened didn't hit me until I slid into bed that night. Even then I didn't have the words to think about it.

Ed called on me two or three more times, and each evening Mercy would be waiting at the door when I returned, her hand held out.

I started telling Ed I didn't feel well, had to get up too early for work, needed to get things done around the house. He finally stopped asking.

I didn't go out with anyone again until five years later, when I met Mason. He'd sat in the pew in front of mine one Sunday, and he kept turning around to look at me, bold as a brass band.

"Let me take you to the show," he said after church let out. The first few times, I'd catch myself grinding my teeth before he was due to pick me up. I guess that was just my nerves remembering what the price of going out had been before.

Mason wasn't anything like Ed. He had the darnedest knack of keeping up conversation without hearing much of what I was saying. Mason heard only what he thought I should say. That's how we became engaged. Or that's how he got it into his head we were engaged.

He drove a battered brown Ford that must have come off the assembly line some time in the late 20s. During the second month of our Sundays, he said we should take a detour to his house after the show.

"I don't think so," I said.

"We'll have a good time, and I'll get you back before too late."

"Naw, I'll be getting home."

"I got a little juke juice."

"If that's all, you'd just be wasting your good stuff 'cause I don't like liquor, too bitter."

He flashed a sneaky grin. "Now you more than old enough to know that's not all."

"What I know is you better take me home before I cuss you out."

His mouth turned down like a disappointed little child. "You women," he said. "You just don't know. I could be dead in a year, could get sent to France and shot fresh off the boat."

I had to bite my lip to keep from smiling at the picture in my mind of him shot fresh in the tail first thing off the boat, with his stupid self. "Thought you said the Army wouldn't take you 'cause you got a heart that gossips." I smiled and breathed in the clean night air. I was just messing with him.

"It murmurs," he said.

"Oh, thought it gossiped. Thought they were afraid if you got captured, it might tell the enemy all the secrets."

"No, it MURMURS."

"Uh huh. Reminded me of that story *The Tell-Tale Heart*. Lilian got it out of the library for me. Not bad. About a man killed somebody, thought he could get away with it, but his heart told on him. Beat real loud when the police came, and wasn't he shamed."

"MURMUR!" he barked. "What you laughing for? That ain't funny. I tell you, even that murmur won't mean nothing if things get hot over there. Then they're gonna be calling up every man ain't dead. What I'm asking you ain't but a tiny bit, cause I could be somewhere in the dirt giving my life for you."

"For me?"

"Yeah. So I don't think it's too much to ask for a little something special in return."

"I don't think it's too much, either," I said. "But since it's Mr. Roosevelt who would be sending you over there, and not me, I think you oughta go to Washington, and tell him you want something special. Maybe he'll give it to you."

His frown sank deeper. He knew this meant no.

By the time he'd pulled up on the dusty road outside my yard, his face had reclaimed that sneaky look. "You don't want me pulling no teats on a cow ain't paid for, and I can respect you for it," he said. "Guess I'll have to marry you."

"What? What would make you say that? Plus, who you calling a cow, anyway?" I thought of those tales that old people told about spiders and earwigs crawling into people's ears and making them lose their minds.

"I know this isn't your first time around," he said. "But it's okay you're not perfect."

Aggravation overtook surprise. "Sweetheart," I said, "if I had turnips growing out my armpits, I'd be too perfect for you."

He smiled as if he'd heard only the "sweetheart" part. I waved bye to him from the door. Oh, the hell with him, I thought. Try to argue with some goddamned fool-jackass and it'll only make you one too. So I just hollered, "Good night. Thank you for the show."

Inside, I moved around in the moonlight. I didn't want to turn the front-room light on. Daddy was a shallow sleeper. Even a stringy glow through the cracks of his door would be enough to wake him. My shoulders still tightened when I walked in the door at night. Yet the reason for it had ended on November nineteenth, four years before.

Daddy woke me up at about five that morning with a knock I hardly recognized to be his. It just seemed a funny noise in some wing of a dream, until I heard his voice. "Myraleen," he called, not excited or scared, but in a low, patient voice. "Myraleen, get up, honey. You've got to get up." He'd never called me, or anyone else in my earshot, "honey" before. Something had happened, and before he told me, I knew. He'd woken up and found Mama stiff as wood, staring sightless at the air.

"I'm sure she's gone," he said. "I'm going to go out, wake up Reverend Matthews and get Dr. Greene. You stay here, now. You can see her, if you want. Why don't you put her clothes on? Can you do that for me, honey?"

After he left, I stood right where he left me, in the middle of the front room for at least fifteen minutes, as stiff as Mama probably was. The door to their room was half open. At first I didn't think I could ever look inside, but I started inching toward it. Half inch by half inch, I made myself go inside.

I breathed out a heavy breath. It wasn't so bad. It was just Mama lying there. Daddy had closed her eyes.

With quick, worklike steps, I gathered all her clothes, sweeping them out of the dresser as if they were garbage in a clean house. She was a trial and tribulation to dress. But that didn't slow me. I struggled with one shoulder, one arm, and one leg at a time. Her left arm complained with a short, cracking noise. I looked at her face. "As if I give a damn." She wore a deep-sleep expression. It lacked peace, though. The hardness stayed. She still guarded herself against something. I left her nightgown on, put her dress over it, pulled up her stockings under it.

All done, I sat in the chair across from the bed and studied her. I got up and took off my underpants. I placed them nicely on her head like a lacy, pink nylon bonnet. They stretched across her wavy black hair and covered both ears. "That's it, take one last smell, Mama," I said, and went to make breakfast.

Just as I started to fry some eggs, a gust of people rolled into the house: the reverend, his wife, the deacon, the colored doctor, Miz Herdie and another older lady, from the church, I didn't know well. Miz Matthews put her arm around me. "Are you all right?" she said. "Aw, I shouldn't even ask. How could you be?"

I smiled, trying to look grateful for her kindness. I was still thinking: Whelp, Mercy is dead. Chicken today; feathers tomorrow.

Miz Herdie came around to my other side. "Myraleen, your mama's holding God's hand now, and she gon be just fine."

People went and looked at Mercy, had breakfast. More folks came and left.

No one said anything about the pair of drawers sitting on her head. Someone must have removed them, but I didn't know when. I just remember the men from the funeral home came and took her at about noon. By then she was bareheaded.

No one ever said anything about it. It was one of those things folks needed to pretend they didn't see, because who could have explained what a pair of drawers was doing on a dead woman's head? Maybe a couple of the ladies thought about it and decided that in my awful grief I confused Mercy's head with her ass.

Then they probably pushed it out of their minds.

KELLNER

. . . if that don't beat all . . .

ON THE FIRST SATURDAY IN JUNE HE GOT OUT OF THE TRUCK
to see Herr Taylor standing by a ladder with open white buckets of paint
at his feet. *"Guten Morgen,"* he and Urs said.

The farmer imitated them. *"Gooden Morging,"* he said and pointed to
the gray slats covering the side of his house. "Sorry to put you boys up
this ladder on this doggoned hot day. Ain't but eight, and it's warm already. But May been burning my ears up about how this house needs
painting. I use to could do it all by myself, but I'm fifty-seven now, and
I need a bit of help.

"Toby and I are going to take the front. One of you do the high
painting," he said pointing up. "And the other do the low job," he said
pointing down. He picked up two large paintbrushes from the ground.
"You understand? Understand?"

They nodded. Kellner climbed up on the ladder toward the edge of
the roof. Up there, he could see the lake to the west. About two kilometers to the south began a row of tiny primitive houses set a couple of
hectometers apart. If he turned his head around and looked north, he
could see the bigger houses on the other side of the town. For someone
from a gray barracks, it was generous scenery.

The heat aggravated the smell of the paint. Oily malevolent fumes harassed his nostrils. He had never done this before but as with everything he did around the farm, he didn't want his inexperience to show. He assailed the wood with quick, strong brush strokes, neither hesitant nor reckless. Ever vigilant for a pinpoint absent of paint, he watched the ridges left by the bristles settle into smoothness. The quality of the man was in the quality of the work, no matter what kind.

He worked for hours he didn't count, until Frau Taylor's voice intervened from below. She was a medium-sized, yellowish-brown woman, a little darker than a Chinaman.

"Mr. Kellner," she called. She held up a white cloth. "Don't mean to disturb you. But why don't you take this clean rag in case you need to wipe your face. It's getting so sweaty out here."

He climbed down. Urs was wiping his soaked face with an aged handkerchief she had provided. "I'm going to bring out lunch to you in a few minutes. So you might as well stay down, and get a rest, then I'll be back with a couple of chicken sandwiches and some orangeade."

Kellner ate, the poultry good, the drink luxuriously cold though too sweet. Then he took his place back on the ladder, which he moved to the east to tackle more gray neglected slats. He worked facing south. He saw her when she came walking up the road at two o'clock. His brush strokes grew wider.

He watched her, surrounded by corn, strolling down the walk that led to the house. She wore a pink dress, fitted at the waist and flowing out at the hips. The blacks dressed differently than he would have guessed. Before coming here, his mind held pictures of dark-skinned serfs in slave clothes. She was carrying something, of course, the palms of her hands supporting the bottom of it, the top of it covered by brown paper. Down the ladder he went.

Toby was working on the lower front of the house, his clear brown eyes searching out missed crevices. "Hey, Miss Mayfield," Toby said and waved his paintbrush, sending more of the white flecks that already freckled his face flying through the air. She was about to go up the steps.

Kellner walked up to her. "Hello . . . how are you doing today?"

Her eyes widened and she almost dropped what she was carrying. He didn't mean to scare her. "Auntie! Uncle!" Toby screamed. "Mister Kellner done learned to speak English!" Herr Taylor came running to the front of the house. Frau Taylor flung the screen door open and emerged with grainy yellow batter dripping from one hand and a square pan in the other. Urs came around to see what was going on. Even the goat came out from under the steps.

"You know English?" Herr Taylor said.

Kellner nodded.

Herr Taylor swung his foot up off the ground a few inches and slapped his thigh. "Well if that don't beat all!"

Kellner was deeply embarrassed. He saw himself as a discrete man. How could he have caused such commotion?

"Yes, my English is not very perfect. I did not want to exasperate you with it."

Herr Taylor cocked his head and squinted his eyes, as if to get a better picture of Kellner. "Boy, what? What you mean your English ain't good? You don't want to 'exasperate' us? Why I don't even know what exasperate means! You probably speak better English than anybody in this town!"

He bent his head toward the steps. "Come on over here and talk to me for a while."

As he moved toward the steps, Herr Taylor noticed his newly arrived guest. "Oh, my goodness, Lilian. My manners left me completely 'cause this boy started speaking English!"

The girl backed away from Kellner. She looked at him as if he were something once thought harmless that had suddenly exploded. She went inside with Frau Taylor.

"All right," Herr Taylor said, sitting down on a step, motioning for him to do the same. "Now tell me, what town in Germany do you come from? I might have heard of it 'cause I had a brother over there in France in the Great War. And is Kellner your first name or your last?"

PERHAPS EIGHT HOURS at the heel of the constant conflagration thought of as sunshine in this strange place had consumed his resistance to sleep. In his cot, he turned from his right side, where his arm still burned from the day, to the left. He gave himself up to the realm of forgetting and forgiving—until about four A.M.

He woke up grateful still. He hadn't achieved five hours sleep since the *Unterseeboot*. None of this would have happened had he not closed his ears to his father. Jakob had looked at the draft notice and said, "I can fix this, or delay it at least."

If the boys from the trade school and the one-barn farms could serve, then he should serve, Keller said. If those who had gotten the least out of Germany should go, those who had gotten the most should go.

Jakob's voice became thunder. "What would you know about a war? It is not a game with boys shooting imaginary bullets from their forefingers until they get bored, then going home to play with their tiny dicks when their mothers are not watching."

Wrestling against his father's will rattled him. Yet defiance had usually yielded good results. He had relished going to school in England. He thrived in psychiatry, a field Jokob called subversive. Until her family went into exhile, he had courted a brilliant girl whose father was a communist. Jakob had accused him of being impulsive, subnormal, capable of anything. Maybe he was.

Looking out, he could see the windows from the dining room kitchen now shined like a lighthouse beacon. The cooks were at work (or more likely, at mischief). Such bright lights: Was everybody in this nation nearsighted? Haugh, an officer who had bunked across from him his first time out, said hitting an American ship two years before then was like shooting a retarded rabbit. The U.S. claimed neutrality at that point but it ferried supplies to the English coast. They sailed with their lights blazing. "Did they think were we having a yachting festival out here?" Haugh had said.

Reich subs lunged quick and nasty knives into the enemy's back. One powerful night they downed seventeen Allied merchant ships, half a convoy, without any losses.

Kellner served on *U.48* initally. Out of respect for his father, the Navy assigned him the best submarine. She had the record. *U.48* had destroyed fifty-one ships—thousands of tons in metal; hundreds of tons of men—in twenty-one months. After forty-nine days at sea, they returned to the dock at Cuxhaven, their kill rate as high and proud as ever. In a short ceremony, the commander pinned an Iron Cross on Kellner's jacket and on those of four other officers. At home on leave, he abandoned the medal in a drawer beneath his undershirts and never looked at it again.

By the next time out at sea, Kellner felt less of that churning nausea—his stomach attempting to flee when his body couldn't—that haunted him the first time. But *48* already had a medic onboard. A doctor was needed on *U.128*, the commander told him after the second mission. The knives turned.

Dark paper covered the windows of the train on which he and the others were transported. Had he not been such a good geography student, he wouldn't have remembered the single obscure lesson that included this province. In the first days, those with less illustrious grammar-school careers would come to him. They heard he could explain. "Mississippi?" they would say, pronouncing it tentatively with a heavy German influence. "What?" "Where?" "Where in hell are we?"

Most of the men asked little of one another beyond mild friendliness. Only a handful of them, the head-to-toe Nazis, required avoiding.

He knew a colleague at home who had sat in the back of the meetings and scrawled a small signature on the right papers. He trusted Kellner enough to say he did not really care. Didn't agree. Didn't disagree. He joined for the security the party provided and the discrimination it prevented. Some others did the same.

On the American ship, every day two irritable, white-suited sailors escorted Kellner and the two seamen to the upper deck for exercise. "You goddamned Nazis," they would say. Kellner wanted to laugh. Not only were not all Germans Nazis; not all Nazis were Nazis.

LILIAN

. . . well, shut my mouth . . .

USUALLY, I VISITED WITH MRS. TAYLOR FOR NO MORE THAN an hour. But today when she invited me to stay longer, I did. I was ashamed to go back outside because I'd see that man. He'd gone out of his way to speak to me, and I hadn't even said hello.

"Well, do Jesus," Mrs. Taylor said. "Ain't it something that boy can speak English!"

Running water over the vegetables and checking on simmering pots, I helped while she prepared corn bread and ham hocks. The Taylors were the first colored people in Nadir to have full indoor plumbing. It had been installed just a few months before. When her girlfriends came to Sunday dinner they fought each other to do the dishes, so they could dip their hands into the sudsy warm water of that new porcelain sink, Mrs. Taylor said. People loved it. Like water from nowhere, they said. I placed my hands under the head of the silver faucet, noticing how long and perfectly brown my fingers looked. Cold water splashed on my skin and I felt a shiver, not due to chill, but pleasure. I stayed until I heard the truck with the Germans pull away.

Walking down the road back home, I vowed to say hello next time. Even if I had to go find him out in the field or in the pigpen or wherever he was, I was going to say hello. That thought stayed with me all week as I was pouring Oxydol in the Humphreys' washing machine, listening to the radio with my mother, reading by myself. But if he wasn't at the farm next Saturday? Who knows? Maybe Germany would surrender. I hoped the war go on for one more week, just so I could say hello to this man. I'd been so impolite.

In Nadir everybody spoke. Even colored people and whites passing each other would give a "Hey, Fred" or "Hey, Mr. Lee." Not to speak to somebody was worse than to cuss him out.

I was perspiring a bit as I walked up the road to the Taylors', though it was an exceptionally cool day for August in the Deep South. The man was in the front cornfield today, checking the stalks for bugs. Through the stalks and high grass, I walked up to him. The brush was scratching my legs as if to discourage me. "Hello," I said, then felt panic, thinking "hello" had shot from my mouth with such a determined sound, it came across like "go to hell." A little softer, again I said, "Hello."

"Good afternoon, Lilian. How are you?"

It was a little tentative and followed by a slow, cautious upturn of his lips. His speech wasn't as accent-clotted as I would have thought. It was as if there were a radio inside him and somebody I couldn't see was talking.

"Fine," I said. That's all I could manage.

As small a gesture as it was, it taxed me like labor and I felt unusually tired by the end of the day. That evening when Mudear passed me the newspaper, I intended only to skim and go to bed. But something on the community-affairs page—SCHOLARSHIPS FOR COLORED EDUCATION STUDENTS—shook me from my lethargy. A shortage of colored teachers had prompted the state, pushed along by a toe-in-the-butt from the feds, to invest a portion of its federal funding in Negro education. Teaching scholarships had become available for a dozen colored high-school graduates, one from each county in this section of the state. I showed it to Mudear. "Yeah, saw it. Must be Roosevelt leaning on 'em." Then she saw in my eyes that I'd seen a glimpse of grace. "You want to try for that, Lilian? You go ahead." She moved her chair closer to mine, took back the paper and read the column again, this time out loud. "Worthy applicants must have a secondary school record of a 'B' average or above." She looked at me and let out a superior-sounding "Hump." Her spectacles scooted farther down her nose as if even they wanted to get a better look. Suddenly the simple rattle of the paper became so auspicious it could have been the rustle of great sums of money. " 'May not be married and not otherwise personally engaged.' That means nobody with a baby grabbed onto her skirt tail." Some official moment had arrived in my life, akin to a soldier's family getting word of his coming home. Details emerged. Plans congealed.

A week later I placed a thin sheet of paper atop the mail-delivered application so that I could make a practice copy. With a typewriter borrowed through Mudear from Mrs. Patterson's niece who graduated from Ole Miss that year, I pounded out the first copy, making two mistakes I would skirt on the final one. The niece, via my mother, also gave some advice about drafting something called a resume. Mudear said I should list all my education and skills plus any raises and promotions. We'd all had a raise in salary a couple of years before. But the whole idea of a promotion was foggy. Did that automatically come with the raise? Promoted from what to what, anyway? People in Nadir worked under one title—field hand, housekeeper, janitor—all their lives and then moved on, it was thought, to heaven or hell.

I approached Mrs. Humphreys to ask her if I'd ever been given a promotion. Minnie—the maid who'd worked for the Humphreys the longest, and who'd been packed up with their other things and carted all the way from Connecticut—stared at me as if I were drunk. Mrs. Humphreys drew in her breath. Her eyes became serious and thoughtful, deepening the crow's feet daggers that menaced them. She smiled as if a stay in her underwear pinched and she was trying to be poised nevertheless. "Certainly, Lilian. I consider you a . . . senior maid like Minnie." Minnie's disbelieving stare turned into a nasty look. "You've been with us for what . . . eight years now?" The tone she used was one generally summoned to give comfort at a funeral.

Myraleen said I should add "tutor" too. "Well, that's what you did. Give yourself some credit."

Finally a direction had showed itself to me. Like those new traffic signs they were putting up in Hattiesburg, it was telling me to keep moving. Funny how a light in the future makes the present brighter, and I could better see the modest pleasures in each day.

Saturday I felt grateful to be off in the afternoon. Generous breezes whirled every few moments, rare this time of year. The cool, drifting air felt as if the wind were blowing a lullaby. It was as if it were gently pushing me to Mrs. Taylor's for a visit. I was in the kitchen helping her shuck peas when she said, "We can do this as well outside as in. Feels good today. Not many days Mississippi feels good."

Outside, with the two bowls on a stool, I bent over from a chair and continued to use my thumb to dislodge each pea from the shelter of its pod. A few yards away, the Germans worked. Both sat on the ground, their legs tucked beneath them, and strained their eyes for tiny pests homesteaded on the Taylors' cabbages. Each uncertified head was flicked and scrutinized until good enough to be shifted from a crate for the unapproved to one for the approved. Looking over, I exchanged nods with them. The one named Kellner was the Taylors' favorite. They thought he lit the sun and handmade the stars.

He was a doctor, they'd learned. After more questions, they found out he'd graduated from a college in England. One year he'd taught mathematics at a high school. He spoke French and a little Russian, too. So they started calling him Doctor Professor Strauss.

And he was a head doctor, a psychiatrist. That meant he wasn't conceited, they said. Because what person who thought a lot of himself would mess around with crazy people? "He may be white and on a genius level, but he's really just plain folks when you get to talking with him," Mr. Taylor said.

Plus, the German gave some advice on treating a sick cow and the cow got better. When the Taylors told me this, the light in their eyes made me think of Bible stories.

"Why, he's a people doctor. How'd he know anything about Sally?" Mr. Taylor said.

"Because Sally's a mammal and people are mammals. We have similar organs and our bodies work in some of the same ways."

"Yeah, that's right," Mrs. Taylor said. "I remember from school, mammals."

"Well, do Jesus," Mr. Taylor had said. "I've been looking at that cow for ten years and didn't know she was anything but a cow. See, having the Doctor Professor around is good, gets people to thinking and learning. We colored people can be too much to ourselves sometimes."

"How else we gonna be?" his wife had said. He didn't answer.

As I squeezed out peas, I sneaked a look at the German. He worked with such quick and serious movements that a person wouldn't dare get between him and those cabbages. Yet for someone so businesslike he tolerated being teased so easily. On breaks, Mr. Taylor conversed and laughed with him. The larger part of the conversation and the laughter always came from Mr. Taylor, though. On that cabbage day, he brought out lemonade and lunch, a job he'd taken over from his wife. He spread an old tablecloth on the ground for him and his two workers. They were going to have an abbreviated picnic in the dirt. Seeing Mr. Taylor so meticulously sociable, I got the feeling he was trying to show the German that he was a human being. Who knows? Maybe the German was doing the same thing.

"Y'all doing all right for yourselves out here, huh?" Mrs. Taylor said.

" 'Course we are," Mr. Taylor said. "You ain't the only one in the county who can squeeze a lemon."

"Sure you don't want anything, Lilian?" he hollered in my direction. I planned to eat inside with Mrs. Taylor after I finished with the peas.

"I heard something on the radio this morning about the big man in your navy—Dönitz." Mr. Taylor said this as if he were initiating an earnest discussion. "He's your boss, huh?"

"That could be said." The German held up his glass of lemonade. The soft sunlight made the ice cubes glitter like diamonds. He paused before drinking and pressed his lips into a slight smile as if he knew what was coming.

"To me it sounds like they're saying 'donuts.' You know what donuts are, Doctor Professor Strauss?"

"Pastry."

"Yeah, so when they called his name I couldn't help thinking of a donut frying in a skillet. So what does he look like?"

"Nothing unusual. Like any man."

"Like any man? Like me?" He laughed.

"No. He simply has no distinguished features. He's an older man, graying, balding. Not thin nor fat—ordinary, at least in the way he appears."

He turned to the man named Urs and said, "(Something, something, something) Dönitz."

At first, his friend looked startled. Then a hard chuckle and a tiny piece of bread burst from his lips. "And who's that other one with the funny-sounding name? A while ago, we saw a picture show with that Charlie Chaplin playing that Fury. It was a silly li'l old show supposed to be about Germany." Mr. Taylor put a hand on his chin and dropped his head for a second. "And . . . there was a fella playing the role of somebody important in the government. They kept misspeaking his name, calling him Garbage. Whenever anybody said something like, 'Come here, Garbage,' May and me, and Toby, we almost fell on the floor laughing. Tell me, this is a real man in Germany, isn't it? What fella were they talking about?"

The German man shook his head, still wearing that small indulgent grin. "No one in my country that I know of bears the family name Garbage."

"Now that's just how they called it. I bet you know who they were really talking about."

Again, the German started to shake his head but stopped and sighed with realization. "I think you are talking about Minister Goebbels, our Public Enlightenment and Propaganda Minister."

"Yeah, I'd bet a man that's it. All righty. Goebbels, gotta remember that." A few seconds passed before Mr. Taylor nudged his employee with his elbow. "But you don't mind me kidding you about all that stuff, do you? My daddy used to say, 'There are two sides to every coin, ten sides to every story.' We got our troubles here, too."

In a voice I could barely hear, the German said, "Between only you and me, my father knows him, Goebbels."

"Well, shut my mouth." Mr. Taylor said.

Mrs. Taylor and I packed our bowls of peas and went inside. "Passed your mama on the road yesterday," she said as we ate. "We didn't talk about anything but you."

"Things around here must be deader than Lincoln if I'm all there is to talk about."

"Now you know, girl, 'course she's gonna talk about her baby. Said you go to the white library. How do you do that?"

"The librarian gives me permission to go through the back door."

"Well, well. Your mama said you're studying your lessons for a college test."

"Yes, ma'am. Everything's coming back to me pretty easily. But I'm bad on mathematics. They didn't teach us trigonometry. And the niece of the lady Mudear works for said it would be on any college test. She went to Ole Miss, you know."

"But you'll just be going to a colored college. They're not going to be asking if you know some trick-athis and trick-athat. God'll take care of it, I'll pray for you." She looked down as if she were already beginning. She set her fork on her plate. Her hands, warm bread-crust brown, were thick and strong from lugging heavy pails of animal feed. "Know something?" she said. "You ought to let the Doctor Professor teach you your trigonometry lessons."

"Oh, no," I said. "I don't even know him."

"He won't do you anything. And I bet he can cipher numbers up, down and sideways. Now don't you be taking this the wrong way." She lowered her voice and brought her face closer to mine. "But you're a smart girl, Lilian, and you ought to go on back to school, so you can get to be a teacher, instead of working on the Humphreys' golden plantation for the rest of your days."

After we finished eating, she led me into her living room, normally cuckolded for life in the kitchen. "Sorry I don't have anything on trigonometry, but if you want to read anything you see, just say."

Mrs. Taylor was no less curious about the world than her husband. A squat bench with a shiny surface rose to knee height in front of the couch, token and ornamental. "They call it a coffee table, but you can't put coffee on it 'cause you'll scratch up the finish. Ain't that a mess?" she said. In the middle of it lay only the Bible. Just beyond, near the wall, stood a two-tier bookcase. *The Heart is a Lonely Hunter, The Member of the Wedding, Gone with the Wind, Tom Sawyer, The Sound and the Fury* and a couple of dozen others—almost all about the South—crowded the narrow shelves. I pointed to the one about the heart and she put it in my hands.

MYRALEEN

. . . a bus with no wheels . . .

AT FIRST I THOUGHT IT WAS FUNNY, BUT THEN IT WASN'T FUNNY worth a damn.

"Well, congratulations," Daddy said at dinner.

I thought he was talking about the chicken and dumplings. "Finally made 'em like Mama's?"

"You know what I'm talking about, girl. Mason told me, not long before you're going to be Mrs. Lewis."

I almost choked.

But the next morning, when I got to the bus stop, the first thing Lilian said was, "I didn't know you liked him that much."

"Liked who?"

"Mason! You're going to marry him, aren't you? That's what he told Mudear."

"He must have been talking about somebody else," I said. " 'Cause ain't nobody walking on these two bowlegs gonna marry that son-of-a-bitch."

Then I heard it again from Reverend Matthews on Sunday at church. Everybody was walking out the door, and he was shaking hands and giving blessings; then, he looked straight at me, and spit a curse: "Hope I can do the ceremony for you and Mason."

That son-of-a-bitch had told everyone I knew we were going to get married.

When he came by in the evening, I was waiting for him. This time I was "lying in wait" the way the machine-gun-blasting gangsters they wrote about in newspapers did.

"What have you been telling folks?" I asked him.

"Telling them about what?"

"About us getting married."

"Nothing, just that we going to . . ."

"FOO-OOL!" My teeth bit my lip trying to do his sorry ass justice. "Are you crazy?" I called him everything except a child of God. "You know damn well I never said I'd marry you."

He didn't raise his voice. "But you're going to. You know it. I know it. Now everybody know it. What else you got to do besides clean up after peckerwoods? You think you too good for me 'cause you look white? Well, close ain't close enough, sugar. Anybody put their eyes on you real good can tell there's a jigaboo in the woodpile somewhere."

I told Lilian about it in the kitchen at work. "Don't worry," she said. "You're grown now. It's not as if there's a chance of history repeating itself. You can absolutely say no this time."

" 'History . . . repeat' . . . ? Where do you come up with these done-up sayings? This ain't any history. This is some mess Mason's trying to pull me into. The only re—peating going on is somebody's trying to re—pee on me. And it took me years to dry off from the first time. I'll be damned if I'll be pissed on again!"

Minnie, dusting a chair, wiping and rubbing and wiping some more as if it were God's own throne, shot me a dirty look. A person would think nobody inside those pure holy walls had heard of pee until I brought it up.

I would just quit going out with the fool, that's all. But . . . I'd sure miss going to the show. Good God! Was my life so bad, I'd marry some coconut-head weasel just to make sure I had a ride to the picture show?

Over the next few days, I tried to close my eyes and see things the way most folks would see them. Mason wasn't really so bad, I got to thinking. Being sky-high picky when I was twenty-six didn't make sense.

He even gave me a ring. A real diamond on a gold band.

It's just that I never planned attaching myself to a man with Mississippi strapped to his feet. Thought that was the same as jumping on a bus with no wheels. But then again I hadn't made any plans. Not long after high school, Lilian started talking up New York like it was the garden spot of heaven. "Come on. Let's go to New York," she'd say, but I was ornery. I said, "You and 'Les' go on. I don't know anybody that far away. What if we got sick or lost our jobs? Who would help us?"

At least by marrying Mason I'd stop asking myself what's going to happen to me. Mason was going to happen to me. It could be worse. Wasn't as if I hated him or anything. He was just a man. Not one of the worst or best—just typical.

Sunday night the door rattled with his knock. If I knew the man enough to know his knock, maybe I knew him enough to marry him. He drove me to town. We went to see Bob Hope in *The Road to Singapore*. He cackled at a few cute parts. My mind skipped down a list of all the things I had to do.

After he pulled up to my house, I talked about the ceremony. That was my territory, he said. He'd be there and ready in a week. "Three weeks," I said. "I need to take care of details, get a dress. All that."

He pulled out a wad of green and placed it in my hand. "Anything you need, Puddin Pie." He winked at me and grinned. "You almost got away with it, didn't you?"

"What?"

"You were just going to keep to yourself and never get married, weren't you?" He aimed a righteous stare like a policeman who catches a hobo stealing a loaf of bread. And then, laughing, he gave me a quick hard squeeze around my arms and bosom. "But I gotcha!"

He'd talked as if I'd been doing something wrong by minding my own business and staying away from run-of-the-mill misery like him. Didn't I have a claim to my own life?

We swapped good nights. He started up his Ford as I walked to the door. And suddenly I ran back. My hand dove into my purse and scooped out his money. I yanked the ring off. "Here. I'm not gonna marry you," I said above the growl of the motor.

"You out of your mind, girl?"

"I'm going away," I said.

"Where!"

"I don't know. Anywhere. Singapore. I like the name."

"Has all your good sense gotten up and left you? I always heard you were crazy."

"Yep, I'm just as crazy as they come. That's why you should get to cuttin now and be happy for the head start."

He cursed and stopped the engine. "So that time we went to see *The Road to Zanzibar*, how come you didn't take a notion to go there, with your silly tail," he hollered. "Well, Miss Too-Good-for-Me, I hope they make a picture show called *The Road to Hell* and you have a front-row seat. 'Cause that'll give you the sho-nuf scoop on where you should go."

I walked into the house.

"YOU HINCTY WENCH. YOU CAN GO TO—" I closed the door.

LILIAN

. . . straight and true . . .

WE HAD THE USE OF THE KITCHEN TABLE, WHERE WE SAT
opposite each other. Draped in yellow and white gingham, it stood in
the middle of the room. The walls were a fresh, filmless yellow, renewed
since last Saturday. Mr. Taylor used paint like soap and water. A dime-
store picture of *The Last Supper,* featuring a Swedish-looking Jesus
Christ, hung above the German man's head.

How old is he? I wondered. Frail lines, the ones white people get early,
were beginning to gather at the edges of his eyes. His face was in the in-
fancy of Caucasian aging. He was about twenty-eight, twenty-nine.

He drew a right triangle. The skin on his hand was a motley marriage
of white and pink. "Do you know why mathematics is important?" he
said. "It is straight and true and it makes sense. It teaches us how to think
with logic." His tone addressed a child. It was the voice with which
people said, "Look both ways before you cross the road, now."

After more lollipop talk, he set up a basic problem, turned over the
page to me and said gently, "Can you answer this? Do not hurry yourself. It is allowed to make a mistake."

I jotted "c" to the second power and pushed the paper back to him.

Surprise widened his eyes. Another simple equation came my way. I scratched the answer.

"You have done this before at school?"

"No, I took out a couple of books from the library so I could be ready. Trigonometry, it seems like algebra and geometry put together, and I've studied both of those."

"I'm sorry. I did not know you knew anything."

"You couldn't have known."

"I should have asked first. That would have been logic."

He looked regretful. I felt bad. "That's all right, Dr. Strauss. I thank you kindly for helping me."

"It is not a problem. Show me what you know, and I will figure what you do not know."

During our sessions, Mrs. Taylor found work outside or took her inside work out into the sun. She'd mend the tattered seats of Toby's pants—"I do believe this boy's got razors in his butt"—while a rooster marched around her chair.

She shook her head when I'd suggested paying her and Mr. Taylor a little something for the hour of work they'd be losing. Each week she set out two pencils, several sheets of paper, two glasses and a pitcher of ice water.

Dr. Strauss drafted harder equations that took more time to figure out. The third week he said, "You are very smart." His voice relayed a sadness that mystified me. Do dumb people make you happy? I said to myself. But on the way home I realized something. He felt sorry for me because I was smart but buried in this place where it made no difference. Next time I would manage to mention that I did have plans to leave Nadir—twenty-year-old plans, but he didn't have to know that. Or maybe he thought I was buried inside my dark skin, and that would be my lifetime tomb.

So I said nothing unrelated to angles and figures and hypotenuses. We traded questions and answers and shuffled papers back and forth. He moved his chair to the side of the table so I wouldn't have to lean so far when he showed me something. I folded my arms as he wrote. When I could, I avoided putting my brown hands on the table near his white ones. The sight made me nervous.

"You are not feeling good today?" he said. "You seem that way."

"Oh, I feel fine," I muttered quickly.

"You are wearing a very pretty dress." He was trying to cheer me up.

I was wearing a cream-colored linen A-line dress with ripples of silk trim at the neckline and hemline. Mudear had scraped up the silk in the remnants bin at the dry-goods store. I took a quick look past my chin and felt as if I had seen the dress for the first time.

"Thank you."

He said I possessed sophisticated taste for a girl my age. Sixteen or seventeen, he said when I asked what age he thought that was. He assumed I had barely pushed a wing out of childhood's cocoon. I should have grabbed that reprieve and owned it.

"I'm twenty-six." He opened his mouth as if that were a great revelation. I, too, held membership in the grown-folks' club.

Dr. Strauss treated me differently from then on. When he explained why some long configuration of numbers and letters came to a particular conclusion, he'd look at me, not the paper, and hold my glance. We saw things on the same plane, he had discovered.

In the middle of the lesson he would weave conversation beginning with questions about me. Were my parents still alive? Did I get bored living in such a rural place? Did it feel strange for me, being in a room with a prisoner of war, a German?

The last one struck me silent. If I did, why would I be so mean or silly as to say so? I flashed back to what Myraleen had said: "How do you know that thang won't reach across the table and strangle you to death. He could get a knife from the drawer and stab you. It's their job to kill us. Miz Taylor means you well, but, girl, she's getting old; her mind's probably fuzzy. She'll get you torn up like chitlins and be crying at your funeral, wondering what happened."

"Why would he help me at the lake that day just so he could kill me in the Taylors' kitchen?"

"I don't know," she said. "People over there in that Germany are crazy, always shouting and marching and carrying on. They've even got their little children doing it. You know those folks can't be right in the head."

His gaze softened with concern. "Maybe not until I said that, no?"

"Does it feel strange to you? You're not supposed to like . . . people who aren't German."

"I am not political."

"But you went into the war."

"How could I not? It is my country. When Americans fight for their country, they claim they are patriotic. When other people fight for their nations, their mothers, sisters and neighbors, Americans say they are fascist. Your government says here people are brave and truthful; elsewhere people are evil or mistaken."

This was the moment Myraleen would expect him to strangle me. If she were here, she'd jump in the middle and reach for one of Mrs. Taylor's heavier pots.

He took a breath. "I didn't mean to sound angry. It is not your fault."

The only other people who'd spoken to me so directly, with their convictions naked for me to see, were Myraleen and Mudear. There were people in Nadir who'd known each other for fifty years and never had that many honest sentences between them.

KELLNER

. . . leave her alone . . .

IT TOOK HIM THREE SATURDAYS TO UNDERSTAND THAT THE
Taylors actually owned the farm. He kept expecting some person far
paler than they to come out and inspect their work and their management of the prisoners.

"You follow the fights, boxing and such?" Herr Taylor had asked the
last time.

"I hear about them," Kellner had answered.

"What'd you think about those Joe Louis and Max Schmeling bouts?
Gotta hand it to Schmeling." He gave a respectful low nod of his head.
"He beat Joe first match. But that second time—ump, ump, ump—Joe
rode that Schmeling hard and put him away wet."

"Who'd you root for?" Herr Taylor asked, tilting his head.

"Root for? If I saw a boxing competition, I would root for it to stop.
I am a physician. I do not see the great spectacle. I see the damage."

"Well, too bad you weren't there for the second fight. I bet that boy
Schmeling coulda used a doctor." He wore the smile of someone who
had just eaten something delicious. He stooped, bounced on the balls
of his feet and punched the air to the lower right side of Kellner with
his fists.

"What do you think of our Jesse Owens?"

"The American runner? He is good."

"Well, what did you think when the Fury snubbed him, didn't shake his hand after he won in the Olympics back in thirty-six?"

"It is said that he had an appointment and could not stay to greet Herr Owens."

"Ha! You believe that?"

"Perhaps so. Perhaps not. Tell me, before Herr Owens was a champion, did people here, white people, like to shake his hand?"

Herr Taylor leaned back on his heels and breathed out a hard breath. Kellner feared he had profoundly offended him.

"Humm," he had said. "You gotta point."

Turning from his side to his back, Kellner stretched his legs until they reached the cliff at the foot of the bed. He swept his arms from under the covers and extended them until he no longer could. That felt better.

How lazy of him to just lie in bed for the next hour until reveille. The Japanese, he heard, worked prisoners until collapse and death. Here there was not enough to do. So imprecise. So stupid. He turned himself back on his shoulder so roughly that it hurt.

It surprised him that the girl needed trigonometry. But why did he keep clawing at her mind, asking her so many questions that had nothing to do with mathematics? It was rude. He should teach her as he promised and leave her alone. But she wore fresh fabrics with vital colors. He wanted to touch the material, or her or both. He knew not which. At home, war brought drabness. How did she manage such prettiness?

"Do you not have shortages here?" he had asked her without saying why.

"At my house, we've always had shortages," she said.

She made his eyes happy at a time when they knew little pleasure. He wondered if she knew. Was that why she did not allow her hands to be on the table with his? Unless he was pointing something out, she leaned back, stretching the distance between them.

He didn't blame her. Perhaps she should not only recoil, but flee to the next province.

She protected herself from him. Yet she was generous, trimming their time together with an abundance of niceties. Always she arrived with gifts: pastries, a grocery-store bag of oranges, a current newspaper after he mentioned he had been forbidden them.

"I surely do appreciate this," she would say. "Thank you a bushel," she would say as she left. "Don't work yourself too hard now, you hear?" Why should she care how hard he worked? If this is how she acted when she did not like him, what would she be like if she did?

Once he realized she was not what he had assumed, he wondered who she was. She had large, sad, determined eyes like a fragile person trying to be brave.

Leave her alone, he told himself.

LILIAN

. . . so embarrassing to be human . . .

"WHAT WAS YOUR CHILDHOOD LIKE?" HE ASKED ME. HOW
could I answer that? What childhood? Nadir had 'young'uns,' not shel-
tered vacationers from worldly worries.

"Pretty much like anybody's, I guess. What was yours like, Dr.
Strauss?" Some people would have taken offense at the questions he
asked. A lot would have twisted their noses and wrenched their mouths
as if disapproving a bad smell and said, 'Whachu talkin bout?' But I understood. He found himself here with all sorts of odd folks with their
odd ways. There were no colored people where he came from. From
what I had read, most white folks were not white enough to live in
Germany.

"You do not need to call me doctor. Herr Taylor does it because he
has fun with the fact that a physician sweeps his barn." He smiled as
if he could appreciate the joke even though it was on him. "My childhood, mine was good . . . except for moments. I suppose anyone can
say that. I remember once . . ." He told me his sister had seen a sprite
gray ball and tail racing around her room when she was about nine. It
returned each night, and she begged him to kill it. Circles of her hair

were scared off in patches, and her head looked like that of a diseased old woman.

"I did not understand then. She had a phobia. This mouse symbolized something to her."

He didn't want to harm the mouse, but he didn't want to fail his little sister. He caught the thing and put it in a cloth bag and placed it in the basket of his bike. He pedaled the dancing sack into town and out again and released it in the woods.

"I do not know why I thought of that time . . . Yes, I do. In the last two years—it is strange—I have worked on a warship killing hundreds of men."

He had gone from a man who wouldn't hurt a mouse to someone who killed people. "Does that make you feel bad?" I said.

"No, that makes me feel inconsistent."

He apologized for taking time from my lesson. Yet, each subsequent session reached a midway point when our words drifted away from numbers. I looked forward to it.

"You remind me of someone I knew," he said the fifth time we met. "She was feminine like you, with no pretense to exaggerate it. And she knew much about many things."

"A girl *at home* where you came from?" I said it as if a grocer had just asked me to believe beans had gone up to ten dollars a pound.

"Yes. But she is not there anymore. Her father became political. He got into trouble and the family had to go to England." He shook his head. "I do not know why some people have to make everything hard for themselves—writing petitions, all that. It is just egoism dressed up as righteousness." At some point his focus had left me; he was arguing with the past.

Then his eyes came back to mine. "How do I say it? There is a way to be who you are without showing who you are. You understand that, yes?"

That evening Mudear fried codfish and potatoes, high cooking for a Saturday. As I placed a proper configuration of plates and silverware on the table, Mudear's voice and Myraleen's mingled.

More and more, Saturdays meant social days: after work in the morning, some time with Mrs. Taylor, lessons with Kellner, and later dinner with Myraleen and Mudear. I suspected the pattern of my life stretched before me, unalterable. If I won a scholarship, I would come back here after school. My old classroom where Mrs. Marsh taught us to be the exception called me back to obey some secret rule that dictated I would take her place.

Kellner would be long gone to his own country. The war would be over. They would lose, of course, just as they had lost the first Great War. History was like a crazy old man telling a story he had forgotten that he told before.

I imagined only a few changes. Soldiers had passed through with the kisses of different places on their collars, stirring wanderlust. So the number of Nadirites going north would swell past the usual one or two a year.

"We didn't have all them bra-ssieres and girdles manhandling us when I was a young woman," Mudear said. "You know that?"

"Yes, ma'am."

Mudear had never worn a brassiere. Neither had Miz Herdie or most Nadir women. As schoolgirls, they had all been bound in leftover squares of fabric. After motherhood or past thirty, women let their breasts gather in a roll within the darts of their dresses, solid and still and harmless.

"Back then you just wrapped your bosom and put on your slip. I hope y'all don't end up deformed by the time you're my age."

"I stay away from those girdles, Mudear." At some point when I didn't notice Myraleen had started calling her Mudear. "So does Lily."

"But I see you be wearing them bra-ssieres."

"I take them off as soon as I get home from work." Around Mudear, Myraleen's voice hosted an obedience it shunned elsewhere.

"Yeah, Lily takes her time bout taking hers off. She thinks she's so grown. I just tell her, Okay, Miss Know-It-All, you going to be crying to Jesus if you need an operation one day 'cause you been wearing that lace-covered noose 'round your chest so much."

"Better listen to your mother, chile," Myraleen said. I'd heard them talk many times, but tonight their speech seemed slowed and amplified. So did their movements: Mudear was standing at the stove, leaning her weight on one foot with fatigue settled in her hips, her eyes smiling— something she seldom allowed her lips to do. "It's ready, Lily. Come and fix your plate."

"Got your plate here," she said turning to Myraleen.

"Naw, Mudear, that's yours."

"Take this plate, girl," she said in a quick command.

I passed Myraleen, our arms touching in the short space between the stove and the table. Happy, she held her plate of cornmealed fish, corn bread, crispy potatoes and last night's warmed-up mustard and collard greens. When Myraleen moved she flowed as naturally as air.

"Here," Mudear said to me. "Made yours, too. What are you grin-ning for?" Mudear said. "You know I'm right about them bra-ssieres. And you need to start eating more. Nobody wants a bone but a dog, and even he buries it."

"Amen." Myraleen laughed.

I gave my mother a swift kiss at the top of her cheekbone. She almost smiled, then said, "You don't have to be kissing on me; I ain't about to die."

After Mudear's bedtime, Myraleen and I sat on the porch beneath a thick slice of moonlight.

"Still getting lessons from that man?" she asked. How long does it

take to learn some figuring? Thought you were supposed to be smart."
I could hear her dress swish across the wood as she whirled her knees
around to let me see the look on her face that was somewhere between
bemusement and disgust.

"I tell you, girl, that fool's going reach over and strangle you."

"He's had five chances, Myraleen. Why hasn't he done it already?"

"Don't you be getting smart with me." She reached up and pinched
some loose fabric at my side, and examined me with a searching gaze as
if looking for damage in the form of German-made fingerprints and
scratches. "If he snatches you while you're up in that kitchen, you'd be
the type to lose your mind over it. Then Mudear and I would have to
visit you in the crazy house all because you had a hard head. You'll go
from having a hard head to being touched in the head."

"You ought to be ashamed. He wouldn't do that."

"How do you know? He's a soldier and a soldier will grab anything
with . . . titties," she said in a loud whisper.

"I bet he's got some woman at home he's missing, some chalk-faced
big old thang. Because you know they say those German women are
some husky heifers. Their own men call them '*frau*.' You know they
must be some ugly women, or why would they call them that? You're
the first gal he's seen ain't six feet tall. He's probably got some monster-
size wife over there he calls Frau Nazi."

She turned around and folded her arms. "It's my fault."

I laughed out loud at the way her mind decided to play such a serious
game of hopscotch tonight.

"You've been saying you want to leave for the longest," she went on.
"And I'm always discouraging it. Now you just don't know what to do
with yourself, so you're sitting up under some foreigner who might kill
you for bragging rights. Truth is we both need to catch a fast wind out
of here."

Had I told Myraleen that I had been in the world long enough to recognize evil, it would not have impressed her. And when I looked at Kellner, head bowed toward equations and triangles, mind on what I needed to know next, I saw displaced dedication.

"Now I will show you something new," he said. As his hand advanced across the paper, his pencil sketched a fresh challenge. He spoke with respect in his voice, not too slow or fast. He paused to let me think. His hands rested on the table, his white knuckles bent with forefinger and thumb touching, making patient circles.

As soon as I made the last number after the equal sign, he leaned over, his hands sliding toward the paper. "No," he said, startling all the bones, blood and flesh that composed my body. "You do not have to do that." His hands had stopped my hands as I started to move them away from the table. His fingers pressed down against mine and movement halted. We just looked at each other. His green eyes—which struck me as an odd color for any part of a person's flesh—searched mine for reaction.

"Don't be afraid of me," he said.

"I'm not," I lied, but he did not let go.

The white fingers curled around the sides of mine. "I like you. Seeing you is the best occasion in my week." He brought his face closer, his eyes still searching. "I think you like me too, no?"

Now I was very scared. My heart beat fast and hard as if it were trying to run away. "That's none of your business."

He released my hands and I felt as if he'd let me go as I dangled over a cliff, and now I was falling into some deep sorrow. Maybe he was, too. To stop it, I had to say something.

"I-I do like you, but you're probably just lonely."

He reached for my hands again and held them, slowly stroking the backs of them with his thumbs. "Not just lonely."

For the fifteen minutes left in the session, we held on to each other. And we revealed small secrets. "It's better for me here than on the *Un-*

terseeboot, the ship. I had no peace even in my sleep." Big battles exploded outside; small battles rattled within, he said. "I miss my mother and sister. I do not miss the war."

I had long felt a fight going on inside me too. For a moment, it stopped.

When two hands touched, did the temperature of one alter the temperature of the other? I wondered this as I walked home. I felt the warmth of his hands on mine long after it should have faded. Even after the tactile memory had left, my skin remained changed. Now, when I wrapped my fingers around the red-handled broom at the Humphreys', I noticed smoothness where the paint was less worn, nicks where it was chipped, and the tiny ragged welts that were splinters in the making. At home, as I turned on the Motorola to hear the news, I felt the ridges and followed the sharp rise and fall of their peaks and dips. Outside, the slightest breeze got beneath the fine, invisible hair on my arms and rolled across my flesh, and if the wind was at all hearty, it seemed to caress me.

A breeze like that was flowing the next time I saw him. Soft gusts of it blew through the screen door, inviting us outside. Toward the end of the hour, he said, "Let us go and walk a bit."

In the back of the house we saw Mr. Taylor, squatting beside a bucket of soapy water on the grass behind the house, cleaning the tools he used to work on the tractor. Toby was driving Mrs. Taylor on an errand in the truck. "You all finished up a little early today," Mr. Taylor said.

"We thought we'd walk for a few minutes," I answered.

"Is that good with you?" Kellner said.

"Oh indeedy, fine, fine," Mr. Taylor said, looking up. "What you learning, Lilian? He teaching you any of that German?

"Well, you better get him to teach you some, just in case," he said, laughing. "If the Mouth and the Fury gets his way, we might all be speaking German soon."

His face returned to his tools, and we walked past him at an angle to the wire fence that separated his property from his neighbor's. We strolled along the length of the taut, rusty line. "Even if you did teach me, my German could never be as good as your English," I said.

"My English is that way only because I spent four years at a boarding school in Scotland. When time came for university, I had Oxford—a British school—in my mind."

A huge poplar tree with shaggy lower branches that hung to the ground grew near the end of the gate. He took my hand and led me behind it where we stood in small private green space.

"If you weren't a prisoner here, do you think you'd like this country?"

He just looked at me for a couple of seconds. "Difficult to know," he finally said. "This part, this part they bring prisoners to, it is not the best part, right?"

I chuckled. "One crime Mississippi will never be accused of, and that's being the best."

"You should see where I live. It is the most beautiful place in the world. We have endless art, a wonderful river."

"Being here must be pretty miserable for you."

He brought my hands up with his and stretched his arms out, then he drew them in a couple of inches. "This much less because of you," he said and smiled.

The wind made the leaves dangle on their branches like beads on a string. He pressed his back against the bark and pulled me to his chest, too suddenly, too close. I looked away. It can be so embarrassing to be human.

With a hand on the side of my cheek, he drew my face to his. His fingers outlined my ears and flicked the single-pearl earrings on my lobes. He took my hands and pulled me out of the sweep of time and into the shelter of stillness. It was a place where reason and flesh had no argument, and one mind could flow into another. So when the kiss came, there was a world created for it, a world in which it made perfect sense.

KELLNER

. . . his duffel bag had been packed . . .

HE WAS IN THE MESS HALL, PICKING AT A SLICE OF LOAF MEAT
shaped like a house without a chimney when they came for him. Everyone at every table noticed them. They were the only civilian dress suits
at a convention of khaki and prison fatigues.

So they had figured it out.

"Officer Strauss?" one of them said. "Sorry to interrupt your meal.
Can you come with us, please?" They looked like twins. The older one,
with streams of white threaded through his dark hair had on a gray suit.
His slightly younger counterpart wore a darker suit. A riot of thoughts
clanged in Kellner's head as he followed them across the base to his barracks. What would they do? Would he be a bargaining chip or a special
hostage?

In the barracks, he found his duffel bag had been packed and placed
atop his bed. "Get your belongings, officer," the light gray suit said.

"Where am I going?"

The dark gray suit looked at the other, who shook his head. "You'll
know when you get there," the older man said.

If they beat him within a breath of his life and he needed to identify them later at a war-crimes trial, he was not sure he could. The dark gray suit was expressionless, his features completely uncompelling. One forgot his face the second one stopped looking at it.

LILIAN

. . . a shame . . .

MR. TAYLOR WAS UNDERNEATH THE KITCHEN TABLE TIGHTEN-
ing loose screws when I walked in that Saturday. Mrs. Taylor was at the
sink with the midday-meal dishes.

His "Hello, Lilian," always big, boomed. "Be out your way in a
minute here."

I assumed Kellner was still out in the field, though I had seen only
Urs. Mrs. Taylor turned around. "Oh, honey," she said, sighing. "I see
you brought your books. I'm sorry I ain't had the time today to get
down to your house and tell you that boy done gone. Toby went to pick
him up this morning and they just said he's not there anymore and
didn't say anything else."

"They probably done transferred him to another camp somewhere
out-state," came an explanation from under the table. "I figure Uncle
Sam might move them around from time to time to keep up confusion,
so they won't try to get away or anything. But you never know with the
government. Everything's a secret these days except what they want you
to find out, which usually goes along with what they want you to think."

I hugged my notebook so tightly to my breast that I could hardly
breathe. Now I knew what it felt like to be told someone close had died.

"But," I said. And I couldn't find any other word to go along with that one.

"A shame, ain't it?" Mrs. Taylor said. "And he was nice."

Then guilt cut through sadness. Because I had never been so relieved in my life.

THE REMAINDER of my thin social life stayed intact. Myraleen's falling out with Mason did not end our Sunday evenings at the movies. We got the Taylors interested. Mudear, Myraleen and I would squeeze into the rear of their truck and Mr. Taylor would drive, with Toby's head bobbing between his and his wife's. I sat in the back in the same spot where Kellner had sat every week. Mr. Taylor would come and open the door holding his hand out to assist each lady.

Toby grinned through installments of *Flash Gordon* and fell asleep partway through the grown-up features. *Stella Dallas* flickered as the second movie one evening. The story spun around a well-meaning but ne'er-do-well woman, who gives up her daughter to the girl's wealthy father. What I'll always remember about that movie is the ecstatic sparkle in the woman's eyes when she sees her child is going to have a better life. Everything was gone but more was gained.

"Well that must have been a show for you women," Mr. Taylor said, on the way back. "Far as I'm concerned she should have stayed married to that rich fella in the first place and raised the gal. That would have cut out all that weeping and suffering and carrying on."

"Aw, Joseph, now don't ruin it for us," Mrs. Taylor said.

At home Mudear didn't go to take off her Sunday clothes right away, but sat at the kitchen table nursing a glass of water in one hand before transferring it to the other. "Don't know what I'm doing," she said. "This'll just send me to the slop jar. My bladder's getting old. Here,

Lily-Flower you take this water. I ain't even put my lips on it. You got a young bladder."

I sat down beside her. Our elbows touched. She pushed the glass toward me. As my fingers reached it, she said, "You don't have to stay here with me for the rest of your life, Lily-Flower. I know you and Myraleen been talking about Philadelphia. I know there are things you want to do."

That grand consent, which earlier would have been a precious ticket outbound, now felt outdated. I had taken the examination for the scholarship and each day looked for the envelope with the results until the time I found it waiting on the kitchen table. I peeled it opened and saw the high score I'd expected and an invitation to be interviewed. On a cloudy Monday morning I went into town and entered the clapboard building that once served as a white Baptist church and now was town hall. On the way in, I passed Clarrisa Reed, eighteen, just graduated. Friendly nods and greetings got swapped. She had a reputation around church as a high-minded girl who wasn't too quick to mess with boys and bound to "make something of herself." That was a new phrase going around Nadir that seemingly hadn't been invented when I graduated.

Mr. Morganson, Feudale County comptroller, spread the application, resume, school records and test scores out on his desk as if they were playing cards. His lips spread across his face and made me want to grin, too. He looked like a creditor who'd expected a five-dollar payment, but got fifty. A small man, his face looked like three-quarters of one, and the lack of space made his every expression seem to leap out at you.

"My Lord, this is the best presentation so far. Know your mama. See her at the café. You did all right for a gal with no daddy." His eyebrows lifted as if to bolster the declaration.

Was this an insult? "He died, sir, some years after he and my mother married." *Married* suddenly became an important word.

"Oh, I know about that. See, I knew you before you knew you."
Those words made him freeze. Everything stopped. He shifted through the papers and stared at the upper right corner of the application.

He looked up at me. I could see my defeat in his history-gathering eyes. "I didn't realize it had been that long." He leaned over. "I had put you at eighteen. Look like a baby of a gal. But I'm afraid, Lilian, the cutoff age for this opportunity is twenty-five. You're missing it by a year. I'll be a monkey's uncle. Darn!

"Got to pick somebody else . . . You hear me?"

I must have looked as if he'd just shot me; so stricken did I appear that even this country white man came around his desk to aid me. Standing back at a sanitary distance, he extended a hand to wrap around my upper arm and help me up. "Look, Lilian, no reason to pout. You got a job with the Humphreys, I hear. That's ever so much better. You can pull down some pay every week. You don't need to be going all the way to Jackson to school. There, there, here are your records. You're a good girl. Now go on home to your mama, and tell Sally Mr. Winston Morganson said hello."

"THAT'S JUST one puny prize that slipped away from you," Mudear said. "And one monkey don't stop no show. Plenty things you can do that'll leave your footprints on earth before you get called on to glory. Lord'll make a way."

But those things I'd wanted to do had lost form and degraded into mere chunks of childhood flotsam. Like the bits of junk I cleaned out from beneath Eddie Humphreys' bed on Monday—bullets of old dried chewing gum, jagged yellow sticks from broken pencils, and a cartoon of L'il Abner doing something disgusting to Daisy Mae—it was time to throw them out. The fourteen-year-old lay in the master bedroom being nursed through influenza by the ministrations of his mother and intermittent checks by the family doctor. I dusted his wide dressers, two oak bookshelves and four tall bedposts. I wiped and buffed to the point of resplendence, polishing the boy's golden life to the shine that befit his diamond-studded birthright.

As Myraleen and I stood at the bus stop the next morning, it occurred to me that we must have looked as common as corn. Two colored gals, one light, one dark, oiled hair glinting against bright glare, dull dresses right for work, four hardworking Buster Browns tapping out restrained impatience until transportation arrived to take us to our place of penance. Two Negro maids. Nothing more. Did people on the outside really see me better than I did, like someone knowing if a man's tie is straight when the person wearing it finds the tether around his own neck hard to judge? Or was I making an elephant out of an ant? Was this life just a matter of the natural defeat that is normality?

That night I slipped into bed feeling as though ice chips and lit matches were flowing through my veins. My arms and legs were tired enough to fall away from my body and surrender. How could so much nothing be so goddamned tiring? I slept and slept and woke only to feel my faults and failures, one by one, young girls with merciless tongues, sitting at my bedside. I agreed with them all and slept some more.

I awoke and nodded to my regrets and resentments, old women in black gowns who live forever but bury many. They got in bed and spread through me.

Mudear and Myraleen bent over me. A spoonful of oatmeal tried to get past my teeth, but I wouldn't let it. Water pressed against my lips, but I didn't care. The gravelly voice of the colored doctor, often summoned after drawn-out financial pondering had rendered his visit useless, said, "Young lady, do you know your name?"

I didn't want to know my name. So I didn't answer.

He gave advice. Mudear snatched up his every word. "Yes, yes, Doctor, yes." He left.

A swamp grew in my throat and lungs, and gave my breath a voice, gravelly like the doctor's but without words. "Spit," Mudear kept saying, holding a wet towel to my face and trying to lift my heavy head.

"Spit," Myraleen said after Mudear got too tired. Fear coated their eyes. I'd have felt sorry for them, but my heart was locked away from me. "You've got to cough and spit, Lilian. Do like your Mudear says, now."

Weakness wouldn't let me. Death didn't want me to.

More sleep.

Later I was being shaken and shaken. Myraleen gripped me below the shoulders and kept pulling and pushing, pulling and pushing. "Wake up! Wake up! Lily-Flower, I swear, if you get better, we'll go anywhere you want—Atlanta, Chicago, New York—if I have to carry a hobo sack and hop a ride on a chicken wagon."

I started to cry. Why couldn't life leave me alone? I wanted to go back to the easy, soothing world where I was forgiven and forgotten. It hurt here.

Mudear's face appeared above me, her eyes soft and pleading. "You're the only thing I ever loved. You're good, Lily, and people need good," she said. "The whole world loves you, Lilian. It just doesn't know it."

"Now spit!" Myraleen said.

THREE

LILIAN

. . . dancing mermaids . . .

THE MORNING MYRALEEN AND I RODE TO HATTIESBURG TO
meet the northbound Greyhound, it was three o'clock. I'd never been up
so late or so early. She sat in the front seat with Mason. I was in the back
with Mudear. We were all bouncing and swaying because Mason's un-
tamed old Ford sedan galloped as much as it rolled. It was completely
black outside. We could see only the rocking beams of the headlights
against a gravel road. A chilly breeze traveled fast enough to blow the
animal smells into the distance, and all that remained was the spicy,
moist fragrance of dew-covered crops. I liked riding through Mississippi without having to see or smell it.

"Y'all gonna be back. Mark my word," Mason said. This had been
his sad song refrain since he learned Myraleen was definitely leaving.

"When dancing mermaids do the jig," Myraleen said, rising up to
smooth her skirt underneath her, "on top of igloos in hell."

Mudear leaned forward. "Will you, children, stop all that fussin?"

"Scuze my language, Miz Mayfield."

"Yes'um, Miz Mayfield," Mason said. But he was still making his case
as we pulled up to the depot.

"Y'all gonna starve to death. Ain't no work up there less you can do factory work, and y'all don't know nothing about that." He hauled our six suitcases, two by two, to the teenage luggage checker who, in the darkness, looked like a thin phantom. Mudear finally gave me the hatbox she'd been clutching to her chest since we left. I'd asked her earlier what was in it. She'd dismissed me with her favorite saying: "Lilos to catch meddlers."

Now I looked inside. It was her gold-rimmed porcelain cup. We looked at each other.

"It's gonna be cold as a witch's tit up there," Mason said as the boy took the last suitcase from him. Then he sighed and stepped closer to Myraleen, who was looking around to make sure we left nothing behind. Her bright face seemed to reflect the little available light: the bus headlights that had just been turned on, and the glow of the full moon. "Damn, you a hardheaded yella heifer! If you'd just stay here, we could have something together."

"Well, honey," Myraleen said, "if you want to be together with me, you better fold yourself up like a shirt, and jump in that suitcase right quick. 'Cause, I'm gone from here."

"I mean it," he said. "Stay here, and I'll make you Mrs. Mason Lewis."

"I'd rather bathe in vomit, Mason. But thank you so kindly for the ride, hear?"

"Yes, Mason. Thank you," I said.

"Damn," he said again.

We waved and smiled at Mudear and Mason as the bus pulled away. They waved back, but they didn't smile or lift their hands above their heads. From the back, we eyed a set of seats across from the door. If we sat there, we'd get a shy breeze every time the door opened. Since we were headed north, it wouldn't hurt to try.

Balancing her steps, Myraleen walked to the front and talked to the driver. I could see the pink-faced man turn his head toward her twice. He probably wondered why she would have to ask. He cocked his head back to take a look in his rearview mirror, and saw me. "Well, ladies, I know they's just us in here right now. But I've got many more stops to make before Raleigh. If it ain't too crowded after Memphis, you can come on down. How that sound to you? Right now I'll have to ask you to sit in the back."

In each town where the bus stopped, it collected more dust. "Souvenir dirt," Myraleen called it. By noontime in Chattanooga, our seats were sticky hot, and we were still in the back.

At a stop in Nashville, a stream of Marines poured in and advanced with rough movements. The noisiest pooled to the back. "Damn, it's as hot as a whore's ass in here," a tall, husky one said. The men all wore the same crop-mower haircuts and khaki brown jackets. They looked like brothers hatched among the same sticky mass of eggs from some giant tan fish.

"Watch your language," one said. "There's ladies aboard."

The one who'd filed the complaint craned his neck over the heads of the row of men sitting in front of him. We quickly shifted our eyes toward the window. "Aw shit," he said. "Ain't nothin but some nigger wenches." Myraleen rolled her eyes, and I tried to fight away the feeling that I had done something wrong.

In Richmond, Myraleen shook me by my left shoulder. "Lilian, wake up now. We got to change buses." It was eleven at night. Two hours would go by before the Philadelphia-bound bus was ready to board. We were too drowsy to hold much of a conversation, and sat nodding on a hard wooden row-seat made like a church pew. The Motorola behind the ticket counter was playing "Somewhere over the Rainbow." I felt dreamy, and the checkerboard floor tiles were slightly hypnotic. I started to sing softly along with the radio, but Myraleen's sleepy left eyebrow shot up and I stopped. When the bus boarded, we discreetly took the right-side seats in the second to the front row, and no one said a word.

At some point Myraleen gave me a look like a doctor eyeing a patient for jaundice. "How you holding up? You doing okay?"

"I'm fine."

"Don't want this to be too tiring for you."

The Pennsylvania sun rose as the bus ate the last stretch of highway toward Philly. I had slept the first hour out of Richmond, my face peacefully smashed against the window. Then my eyes opened and I was irrevocably awake. I could feel the weight of Myraleen's head. It had tumbled over onto my shoulder. In the seats behind us a couple spoke quietly in a language I guessed was Spanish. Up ahead, I could see a cluster of skyscrapers, anchored by a mammoth variety of shorter buildings, that seemed to stretch into forever. "Will you look at that!" I said to no one. Eyes that had never seen a dwelling more than four stories tall couldn't imagine anything more fantastic. Bigness and greatness were the same to me. Just hours ago I'd been drowning on some stale island, and now I was going to be a part of the world. And it wasn't one town or one nation or any one place or people. The world was just that—the world. I was going to be a part of something grand.

We took a jitney to an address on the north side. It was written beneath the name Mrs. Wells, on a piece of paper bag, and Myraleen had secured it in her bosom. Her father had given it to her; he'd gotten it from a cousin in Pittsburgh. The driver helped us lug our cardboard suitcases up the front stairs to the door of a brown brick building sandwiched between row houses. A little old walnut-colored woman with steel gray hair emerged. She grabbed a suitcase and said, "Y'all have to be real quiet now, 'cause it's still real early."

She opened a door marked with swirly gold letters that said 2A. Inside, she said, "A toilet's on every floor but you're lucky you've got one of the far-end rooms. You've got your own. Now I know I don't have to tell y'all this is a nice house, and I require my roomers to act like they got good sense." She gave us a quick up-and-down glance. "Y'all look like very nice young ladies. So I know y'all ain't the type to be layin up in here with no mens. Just don't surprise me."

"No, ma'am," I said.

"No, ma'am," Myraleen followed.

Mrs. Wells quietly closed the door as she left. Myraleen followed and turned the eye-level latch. Then she put her hand on her hip, and said toward the door, "Old bat. If all I wanted was to lay up with some fool, I could have stayed home 'cause I had one ripe for the layin."

My eyes flew around the room and landed on a white wooden box divided into shelves by three slats. "A bookcase," I said. Now I wouldn't have to keep the twelve books I owned on the floor.

"Well, that could be used for little knickknacks and pictures, too. But with you around I guess I better not try to turn it into anything that ain't a bookcase." Myraleen stepped into the kitchen. "Girl, this floor is too nice to put your feet on." It was the first time we had seen linoleum that wasn't in a white person's house. It was printed with happy black-eyed Susans. The wall above matched the flowers' bright yellow petals. "Good God, I'm almost afraid of cooking in here," Myraleen said.

A "furnished kitchenette" was what the place was called. It had a slither of a kitchen that was built like a short hallway. The larger room held a bed, a couch, a two-chair dining set, a four-drawer dresser, a lamp, "a bookcase." And that was it.

Myraleen kept looking out the window. She was trying to figure out where the outhouse might be.

"Look." I pointed at a narrow door. "The lady said we had a toilet."

"I thought she meant toilet paper."

"Come here, see."

"I thought that was the door to somebody else's room." Myraleen looked around at the sink and commode. "Well, I'll be! It flushes. We can even wash up in here too?"

"Yeah, but when we want to bathe, we have to use the tub in the hall bathroom."

I walked about the room unpacking, and examining every corner that might hold something new. We had three wall plugs, two lamps and an electric icebox.

"Door damn well better have a lock on it." Myraleen opened her luggage, undressed, put on her chenille robe, grabbed what she needed and went to take her first bath away from Nadir.

MYRALEEN

. . . the nicest folks in Creation . . .

FOLKS WALKED SO FAST IN PHILLY. IF YOUR LEGS MOVED THIS fast in Nadir, people would think the law was after you. The women always had on stockings, even though the war caused a shortage. Anyone like Lilian, darker than beige, dipped her stockings in coffee. Companies that made stockings were short on dye. But by hook or crook, nobody had enough nylons to wear every day. Then I found out how the city girls did it. So the day I went to look for a job, I stuck the tip of an eyebrow pencil under hot tap water and tried to draw false stocking seams. I planned to pat a bit of tan powder on them afterwards and I'd be set. But the lines came out crooked, and I had to wash them off. Finally, Lilian took a try at it—saying she wished she had big pretty legs like mine—and did it perfectly.

By the middle of the day, after hitting my high heels against that mean concrete a million times, my feet hurt. Every place I went, though, people were real nice. In fact, I couldn't wait to get home and tell Lilian these Philadelphia people are the nicest folks in Creation. Nobody said anything about my being colored. I tried a candy-making business, a milk-bottling company, and a spread-out bread bakery in two buildings.

The folks all said, "Nothing now but if you haven't found anything, try back in a month or so." The North really *was* better.

Downtown I almost passed by the sign tucked in the lower corner of L. L. Dunham's giant windows: SALESGIRL REQUIRED. I could do that. I could sell clothes. Knew all about them; I'd worn them all my life. Inside I felt less sassy. Everything was so bright and white, the floors, the walls, the salesgirls. The place looked like a bleach rainstorm had cleaned it.

"You want personnel. It's on the fifth floor," one of the clerks said. She gave me a wide smile, and I let it nudge me to keep going.

My first time on an elevator hadn't been until that morning back at the milk company. It made my stomach feel floaty and not right. A couple of yellow-headed women stepped in after I did. They wore padded-shoulder tailored suits and done-up hair and looked like they had just jumped out of a bandbox. The car moved up and my belly sank down. I swallowed hard, afraid I'd puke on the two sophisticated, citified ofays in front of me.

The door opened to solid ground again just in time, and a girl at the desk said I'd have to wait to see the lady who did the hiring. A wide spread of shiny magazines stretched across a low-built table in front of a row of chairs. The *Saturday Evening Post, Photoplay, Harper's Bazaar, Vogue* . . . They fanned out in a colorful circle with the left corners overlapping like bathing beauties in an Esther Williams swim movie. I wondered what they did with those magazines after they were finished with them. Toilet paper? No, in Philadelphia that was all store-bought. I wanted to take one home to Lilian. But better not. Who knows? Maybe they'd spread all those brand-new magazines out there to see how honest you were. So I didn't even pick one up to look at it.

Lilian ought to come by here! She likes all this ladies' magazine stuff and she'd be a real good salesgirl.

The lady in the office sat behind a kidney-shaped mahogany table three times the size of the girl's. Her hair, pulled back in a bun, was an unnatural, navy bluish shade of black that made her skin look like chalk. I'd say she fit in the kicking-the-hell-out-of-sixty bracket and was gray headed underneath all that dye.

The only time she peered straight at me was when I walked in. By the time I sat down, her eyes were busy elsewhere, staring at a paper on her desk and making marks on it with a fountain pen. When she asked questions she sounded flustered from reading and talking at the same time.

"Did you work back in Decatur . . . oh, uh, Nadir."

"I did day work for Mrs. Catherine Humphreys. She gave me a letter for reference."

"Day work?"

"I was a maid, ma'am."

The woman took the letter and leaned back in her chair to read it, handing it back with her plain expression unchanged. "No sales experience, huh?"

"No, ma'am."

She sighed and wrote some more on her paper and said nothing for a while.

"Well, Myra, you came to the right place at the right time. One of our girls just left because of a personal problem. I'll just say it. She got herself in trouble. These servicemen tell these girls anything and they believe it."

She ducked to reach into a drawer. Her hand rose to wave a yellow sheet of paper at me. "Fill this out at home and bring it back with you to this office tomorrow at eight on the dot. Only the employee entrance will be open. Just tell Leo at the door you're the new girl."

I wanted to run around that desk and hug that funny-looking woman.

Maybe I was shaking the fruit tree too hard but I said, "I got a friend who's looking for work, too. Do you think you might need somebody else?"

"These days, never know. If she doesn't find anything, send her by."

Before I turned to leave, she stared straight at me again. "A girl like you, you look too classy for domestic work. You say you did graduate from high school? Wasn't much work in that town for girls, I suppose? I can see why you left."

Going back to the main floor, my stomach outdipped the elevator as it dawned on me: Jesus, Lord, she thought I was white.

LILIAN

. . . Negro writers . . .

I LEFT AN HOUR AFTER MYRALEEN ON A MISSION NOT NEARLY
so practical as hers. My goal was to see as much of Philadelphia as a
streetcar ride downtown would allow. Then I'd have a long dime-store
lunch and look around. I put on gray-and-navy saddle shoes, argyle
socks of the same colors, an indigo sweater set and a matching wool skirt
with a kick pleat. All came from the Sears catalog, and were ordered to
make a country turnip look like a city girl.

Getting on the bus was like walking into a crowded roomful of
strangers. The seats were all taken and a half dozen male riders held on
to overhead metal hand loops. It was longer than the two buses back
home and had a rear door. Everyone was colored except the driver.
"Miss," a man said, rising from one of the aisle-side rows of the double
seats. "Thank you," I said sitting down in his place. He was not so much
a man really as a long, stretched-out boy. He held on to a loop with one
hand and clutched a stack of three books with the other. The girl on the
window side smiled up at him and giggled. "All right, just watch him
give his lecture today and see if what I say isn't so about how that man's
face twitches." She said this over my head. The boy made "tsk, tsk,"
noises and said, "Juanita, you're something else." Her skin was medium

brown and she wore her hair in a lively ponytail made of a thick collection of shiny curling-iron spirals. A strict coil of bangs, the diameter of a quarter, sat on top of her forehead. "You go to the university?" she asked me.

"No," I said, and didn't know what to say after that.

The boy's voice rolled over my embarrassment. "She looks like a college girl, doesn't she?"

"Yeah," said the girl.

They didn't realize I was an old woman, almost twenty-seven. "No, I'm finished with school." Looking at the books in his arms, I added, "I still keep up my reading, though," hoping to redeem myself in their eyes.

"Whom have you read?" he said.

I never thought before in terms of who, only what. But the only name in my suddenly threadbare mind was the writer who wrote the book Mrs. Taylor loaned me. I offered it up.

But he wanted to know if I had read Negro writers. "Richard Wright, Jean Toomer, Langston Hughes?" he fired off. I was frozen in the hell of not knowing what to say. There were Negro writers? I thought. I had never seen any of their books in the Nadir County Library.

"Mitchell is a race man," the girl said, a mixture of pride and apology in her voice. Out of this context, I would have thought that meant he was one of those worthless men who threw away their money at horse-racing tracks.

The crowd thinned as the bus got closer to downtown. "Excuse me," the girl said, squeezing by my knees. Mitchell, the race man, stepped to the side and let the girl get in front of him.

"And try Nella Larsen," she whipped around and said.

I repeated the names to myself until they wedged in my memory. Now where was the library?

"Which library?" asked the woman I approached on Broad Street.

Again I didn't know what to say.

"Main library is over that way on Logan Square," she said, pointing a long dark finger.

My first challenge in Philadelphia was to avoid getting hit by a car. The roads downtown were so wide and automobiles flew past by the hundreds. Most busy corners had traffic lights, but the signals didn't give people much time to cross. Here cars became a force they were not in Nadir. It was them against me and the red lights were on their side.

I had never seen so many signs before, some on freestanding billboards. One with bold black lettering on a white background said BUY BONDS. BUILD BOMBS. A few were advertisements for various brands of cigarettes, which needed no advertising really since they were rationed and in short supply. People who smoked were doing everything they could to get them.

The words THIS IS THE ENEMY were at the bottom of a sign near the post office. It showed a man's hand stabbing the Bible with a long dagger, a big red swastika shining from his sleeve.

Just inside the Philadelphia Free Library was a picture of a proud-looking woman in a military uniform. It read: BE A MARINE . . . FREE A MARINE TO FIGHT.

What a huge place! Card files alone took up the width of an entire wall. I looked under the names the couple had recited and jotted down the numbers and letters, and then I had a hunch and looked under "Negro" and found the category took up half a card box with all sorts of books about everything from history to poetry. In Nadir there were no "Negro" files—although you could find *Uncle Tom's Cabin* under "Slaves."

At the desk, the librarian, a blond lady, told me to fill out a little square form for every book I wanted. More than a few books would weigh me down, and I had an afternoon of walking and looking ahead of me. So I requested only *Native Son* and *Quicksand*. Those were the novelties I showed Myraleen when she walked in the door—two books about Negroes by Negro authors. But they and the description of the couple plus a few observations about downtown were nothing compared to her story.

A lady who thought she was white had given her a job. She sat at the foot of the bed. I sat at the head with my stocking feet tucked under me. "Everybody in the whole store thought it," she said. Straightening her back, she held out her legs at an angle in front of her and wriggled her feet to free them of high heels. "Probably in them other places I looked for work, too. Should have known," she said, shaking her head. "And I thought folks here were so nice I could almost see halos circling around their heads. Come to find out they got fork tails up their asses just like everybody else."

Wriggling was not enough, so she kicked her feet violently as if trying to extract them from crocodile jaws until the heels went flying into the air. It was hard to understand. Myraleen's skin was the color of thick cream. Whites had flesh so thinly transparent you could see the blood cascading behind their faces. Myraleen's whiteness was not a Caucasian kind. Waves ran through her hair, which was a shiny off-black that appeared wet in bright light. Her legs were a little fleshy like a white woman's, but her behind was rounder and her hips not as wide. Anyone back home could see that Myraleen had been "touched by a tar brush." Then again in Nadir everyone was presumed colored until proven innocent.

"We're not starving yet. No sense in dancing with the devil for a dollar," she said.

"I think you ought to go ahead with it."

"What if they find out?"

"Why would they? No one here knows you."

Never go to see Myraleen at that store for any reason, I thought to myself. Being seen with friends and kin—that was how people were caught. Mudear once told me about a woman who passed to get a job as a secretary at a Hattiesburg insurance office. One of the woman's children took sick, and another came to get her. The boy had a light brown complexion; the next day she was fired.

Myraleen sighed. "Well, it's a job and it pays better than the Humphreys."

"And who's to say you're not white, anyway? If you look white enough to fool white folks, and what race you are is based on what you look like . . . Myraleen, anybody with a colored relative is supposed to be colored. But having white ancestors—which most of us do—doesn't do a thing toward making you white."

"I don't want to be one of *them*," Myraleen said, folding her arms and sticking out her lips against the notion.

"That's not the point. If every time a white and a Negro have a child that child is shunted off to the Negro side, that keeps their club pure and ours an anybody-can-join club. But it's their side doing the mixing, too. And as long as they can claim purity, they can claim superiority."

"Did that boy on the bus tell you that? Sounds like he got too much time on his hands, thinking about all that mess. What I need to think on is simple: Should I take this job and let these people treat me like I'm white?"

"That boy didn't—" I got up to start dinner, feeling barefoot on glass-covered ground.

She heard only part of what I said, and she heard it as a challenge. "Look, Lilian, I'm just as much a colored woman as you are. Just because I'm not dark doesn't mean a thing. Colored people come in all colors."

"I'm not accusing you of anything Myraleen. You didn't choose to be light skinned."

"Then why are we even talking about this mess? Doesn't make any sense," she snapped and turned away from me. She stooped to drag the ironing board from under the bed to ready some clothes for tomorrow and occupy herself with another subject.

"You need help in there?" she said from her safe station at the ironing board.

"No, that's all right."

After a while, I put ham hocks and corn bread and smothered cabbage on the table and we had to be face-to-face again. Myraleen dropped a soft grenade. "I used to think I was better than you."

"I know, but you were a child," I said.

She kicked the unexploded grenade around. "I'd still be thinking it now if it weren't for that tangle with Cheevers."

My hands lost their enthusiasm for picking the meat off the ham hocks and settled by the sides of my plate.

"Taking this job would be nothing but being that way all over again. They wouldn't give it to *you*."

"No, they would not. I just think you should see what it's like to have a job that doesn't call for a dust rag."

"But it'll feel funny with those people treating me like I'm a white girl."

"They won't be treating you like you're a white person, Myraleen. They'll be treating you like you're a human being."

MYRALEEN

. . . up to date . . .

By 8:30 the next morning I was tagging behind a girl named Doris Eisen through the second-floor aisles of L. L. Dunham's. She had a fry-pan round face dotted with emerald eyes, and brown curly hair that rose into a little bun at the crown of her head. She walked as if somebody was chasing her. She talked so fast, you'd have thought she was in a contest for who could stuff the most words into a minute. I needed to listen hard. Everything she said seemed stuck together. "Keepyour registerclosed unlessasale is takingplace," she said.

"Yes, ma'am." In Nadir people wouldn't trust anybody who talked this fast, not that a lot of trust was swarming around there, anyway.

"Youdon't havetocall mema'am. We'reabout the sameage . . . clothes on racksmust alwaysappear crispandneat." The more I listened, the more easily I could pry Fast Doris's words apart.

"You're from the South, aren't you? If I were you, I'd just say call me Myra. You'll fit in better. If people have to think a second to pronounce your name, it might give them enough time to think of the things they don't like about you. See that girl over there in cosmetics, she used to be Jovanovich; now she's Jones. I used to be Eisenberg. That won't do around here.

"Anyway, Myra, I don't have to tell you this is a classy joint, which means you never let anyone hear you call it that. But you do keep an expression on your face that's sanctimonious enough to scare off the riffraff."

It made front-page news in my mind that anybody would buy these things at all. The price tags seemed like they'd been taken off fancy furniture and placed on dresses for a joke. But for Doris Eisen's consumption, I pretended nothing here was new to me.

"First rule—never get sore, fresh or frothy with a customer. Nothing will get you a pink sheet faster than one bad word from them. Even if you catch them lifting something, slipping it under their fur coats, and you will, 'cause some of them rich hens have too many squirrels in the tree, suggest politely that they've made an oversight, and steer them to the cash register to pay for it.

"If you have any questions, I'll be right over there. Remember there are no stupid questions, only stupid mistakes."

I smiled. You machine-gun-mouthed heifer, I thought. A couple of minutes later, the store opened for business. I could hear the high heels of skinny women making short clacks across the hard white tile floor. "The girl in fine dresses can help you," I heard Doris say. After the woman browsed but left without buying anything, my eyes sneaked a look at Doris. Was she on her way over to say I'd made some foolish mistake? But she stayed on her side. Customers came and went and bought and didn't buy. Doris turned up beside me without my having noticed her walking over. "It's time to break for lunch. You're doing swell," she said.

L. L. Dunham had an employee cafeteria. It stretched out over half the basement and appeared dreary and dimly lit compared to the sales floors. Those funny-styled, coin-operated sandwich machines were stacked along the wall opposite the counter. Who knows what could crawl over those sandwiches while they just sat there? I went to the counter and ordered chipped beef on toast from a colored girl in a hair net. "Hello, how ya doing today?" I said. She looked up from the beef she was fishing out with a ladle, surprised. She took a hard look at me, curved her mouth upward a bit and nodded.

I intended to sit alone and get my nerves straight, but two girls at a table motioned to me. They introduced themselves as Elma from Perfumes and Lois from Cosmetics. "You mean 'Fine Cosmetics,'" Elma said. "Better not let them hear you or you'll get the 'This is not Woolworth's' speech."

"Oh, let them! I'm free, white and twenty-one."

The two talked as if they were speaking through their noses; their words buzzed like flitting bees.

"So you replaced Miss Clumsy," Elma said.

"'Miss Clumsy'?" I said, for a second not knowing whether it was a real name or not, names here being so different and all.

"That's what we've been calling her," Lois said.

"Well, you'd think in these modern times a girl would know better," Elma said.

"Maybe she was trying to hook him," Lois said. "Either way, she got herself in Dutch."

Elma bit into a machine sandwich of dead bologna. "Why don't these girls make sure these clowns use rubbers?"

"*Sssh,*" Lois said, dipping her head low enough for her chin to almost touch the pile of tuna salad on her plate. "You don't want people to think we're floozies. This is L. L. Dunham, after all."

"Well, excuse me," Elma said in a fast hiss. "I mean she should have used a 'fine' rubber."

These girls weren't good for my nerves. "What's a rubber?" I asked. So what if they thought I was country? I was taking a lunch break from pretending, at least to some measure.

The girls smiled. They cocked their heads toward mine and told me all they knew about the things, and threw in some stuff about something called a diaphragm, and foam that wasn't the kind that sat on top of beer. "Stick with us," Elma said. "We'll bring you up-to-date."

My chipped beef was missing only a little crust by the end of the half hour. I'd never sat down to eat with white people before. "No appetite today?" Lois asked.

"Those girls don't know what they're talking about," Lilian said at home. "How can a rubber band keep anybody from having a baby?" Looked like I knew something Miss Book Bootie didn't. I guess I'd have to bring her up-to-date.

LILIAN

. . . like fighting Joe Louis . . .

LOOKING FOR WORK IN PHILADELPHIA WAS DIFFERENT FROM finding a job in Nadir, where word of mouth from a relative or friend led you to someone who was hiring. In Philadelphia you had to go from building to building, not knowing who took on colored and who did not.

I would wear either of two outfits: a man-tailored black suit with narrow red lapels and red faux pocket flaps beneath the hips of its skirt, or a belted navy blue dress with a navy-and-white checkerboard middy collar. I bought them with money I had saved back in Nadir, and paid too much to admit their prices to Myraleen without her saying, "Guess when you walked in the store, they saw a fool coming."

"We'll let you know if anything comes up," said a white girl with spit curls framing her face. I had filled in the blanks in two pages of forms, hearing my mind's voice say at every new line, *These people aren't going to hire you.*

In the office of a box-making company, I talked to a secretary in cat-eyed glasses. Her eyes, at once quizzical and knowing, told me I had definitely entered the wrong place. She wanted to show me something. I followed her down a hall with office doors on each side. She stopped at one and opened it. At a long row of file cabinets, a fawn-colored girl on her knees stuffing folders between other folders, shivered. Her head was down; her eyes, loyal to her task.

"See," the cat-eyed woman said. "We already have a Negro girl working here."

"You don't need another Negro here, do you, Sarah?" The girl glanced up furtively. Before I could say that's all right, she said, in a thin voice, "No."

I would stare at my reflection when I passed a store window, searching for something that was wrong with me, something terrible about me, a deep flaw those people detected. At a bus stop downtown, a dark-skinned man with mixed gray hair looked me up and down. He did not appear old but as if he had been in the world just long enough not to be afraid of it anymore. "Trying to find a job?" he asked. I nodded, embarrassed. "I figured you were, out here waiting on a bus in the middle of the day like this, all dressed up. I'm retired myself. Where've you been checking?"

I recited the list. He shook his head. "Oh, no, no, darling." I could tell he, too, was originally from the South. "Those places just use white folks. Why don't you give Andover Meats a try?"

Mudear would have claimed God sent that man. It didn't seem so at first. Nick O'Connor, the boss, sat at a desk troubled by scattered forms, a bloodstained rubber glove and stacks of three-ring notebooks choked with papers. His scalp was as hairless as air in front, but from the middle of his head to his neck, short thick red curls clung as if they had staked a claim and refused to leave.

He looked at the letter of recommendation from Mrs. Humphreys, the character reference from Reverend Matthews and my diploma. He chuckled, and chuckled more as he went to the next paper and the next. He leaned back in his chair and folded his arms. "So you graduated from high school, did ya? I didn't. Why'd you bother? Were you going to college or something? Well, you should have, cause you don't belong here.

This is not like *school*"—he scrunched up his face and used a girly voice—"back in Needy, where you drew on the blackboard and flirted with Billy. Then you got a little job sweeping up for some little lady and she gave you a little note. Now I'm supposed to hire you 'cause you were such a nice girl when you lived in Never?"

I got up to leave. "Where are you going?" he said. "Nervous or something?

"Look, this is real work. If a twenty-year-old clocks in in the morning and she doesn't look as old as somebody's grandma by evening, I don't want her to come back the next morning. Can you be here between six and three? You got some heavy dungarees? We supply just a rubber apron and boots. And this is no place to be all dolled up unless you want to go home with your fancy dress splashed with mud and blood."

F ROM THE OUTSIDE, Andover looked like a giant cement barn. "Go with them," O'Connor said at dawn the following day. He pointed to other women who were arriving. I trotted behind them like a pesky little sister through half-lit doorways and long stairwells until I knew I couldn't find my way back without help.

We stopped at a gang of wall lockers. I seemed to be the only soul who did not know which one was hers. Just as I was about to speak up, I heard someone say "Mayfield?" Behind me stood Gladys, who said she was my supervisor and pointed out a locker. She handed me a big rubber sheath with ties that looked as if it could have been made from leftover yellow raincoat material.

"What size shoe do you wear?"

Gladys moved with impatience and her voice held a gruffness that sounded like hostility, but wasn't. She was a big white woman in her mid-fifties with dyed dark red hair styled in tight curls that could have passed for ripe, stemless cherries from a distance. She stopped for a second and pulled a scarf from her pocket. With a quick maneuver, she wrapped it and tied it around her head.

Squeaking, I trailed her, the rubber apron slapping my dungarees and the black galoshes, which fanned out above the ankles, slapping each other if my feet traveled too closely together. What stretched before me beyond that final door was a shock. Block-long rows of gargantuan cow carcasses dripped blood and water onto a puddle-splashed concrete floor. O'Connor said I'd be washing meat. I'd imagined cleaning manageable chunks, like washing dishes. I'd never before seen cows in this netherworld between the pasture and the kitchen table.

Gladys shoved a hose into my hand. "Make sure you get this crap and this crap and this," she said, pointing to red, brown and mucouslike debris on a carcass. "Ninety percent of these go to the Army in Europe. We don't want the food to kill them before the Nazis do."

I pointed the hard stream of water, and spikes rebounded on my face until I stepped back a bit. I didn't know precisely what I was washing off the cows besides blood. I could guess but tried not to.

Three other colored girls stood on a line of about two dozen women. One standing near eased toward me after Gladys moved her attention up the row. "Your hair's going to go back," she said, glancing at my straightening-ironed French roll and bangs. I already could feel moisture crinkle the hair at my temples.

"Do like I do," she said, her eyes lilting toward the paisley fabric on her head. "I put two scarves on with a square of raincoat fabric in between. Now don't put the rubber next to your hair. Your head'll sweat and that'll make things worse. 'Cause you know tangling with our hair is like fighting Joe Louis."

All the women at Andover, Negro and white, wore scarves tied mammy-style to protect their hair. I started using Saran Wrap as Nadine suggested. She'd come from Arkansas a few years ago, her husband driving their tired car, fueled on gas bought with their next-to-last dollars, and their two-year-old girl in the backseat sleeping.

Nadine was surprised I grew up in Mississippi. "You talk so proper and sophisticated," she constantly teased.

"I'm not so sophisticated," I told her. "This is almost twice as much money as I was making back home."

"This is more money than any of these girls were making before the war. Even the white ones," she whispered. "When mens do it, they make even more."

"Men had these jobs?"

"Yeah, naturally. And honey, don't you go putting a down payment on a Cadillac. 'Cause when the war's over, mens gonna have these jobs again."

MYRALEEN

gold wings

WALKING DOWN THE STREET IN PHILADELPHIA WAS LIKE watching a movie picture. All sorts of people marched down the sidewalk as if some big stage show had come to town. Rich folks brushed by ragged folks. White ones walked past colored ones. Fur coats and thin cloth coats, the tails of housedresses under wool jackets, the cuffs of fancy tailored trousers under Brooks Brothers trench coats—they all came together like everybody's clothes on laundry day.

Nadir had smelled like billy goats. Philadelphia smelled of smoke from high chimneys and cigarettes.

I started spending my lunch breaks out of the store watching the moving picture. In a white paper bakery sack, I'd carry a sandwich and an apple or an orange, a small carton of chocolate milk and a paper napkin. Hairy white men, dark strands crawling from their coat sleeves and onto the backs of their hands, stood on corners selling sausages and hot dogs from steam-belching wagons. None of that for me, thank you.

One Saturday I was downtown coming from Woolworth's with Lilian and she pulled a quarter out of her pocket and walked toward one of those peddlers. But I quick-like grabbed a fistful of material on the waist of her coat and pulled her back. "What's the matter with you, girl?" I said. "You don't know how many rat tails and whatnot they use to make that mess."

The diners were all too crowded to risk at lunchtime. With so many folks out working, stores were packed as people did rush shopping at noon. Doris Eisen told me my break had to be at eleven or one. I took one and that meant being back at a quarter to two.

Cafeteria grub at L. L. Dunham wasn't for me; it tended to percolate in my stomach later on, so a week after I started, I looked for other places. A little diner off Broadway posted not-bad prices. But a dozen set of feet pushed into every square yard of the place. It took a half hour to get waited on. You knew not to complain. One man did and a waitress said nothing until she slapped the day's *Philadelphia Inquirer* down on his table. "I guess you haven't read the paper in three years. So you don't know there's a war on, huh, fella?"

A few blocks from the store stood a scattering of trees and benches in a square-block patch of grass separated from the bustle by a wide boulevard. I ate there every day the weather would let me.

One afternoon a colored man in a crisp Army uniform said, "Miss, care if I sit here?" and settled at the other end of my bench. He gripped one of those big hot dogs decorated with relish and lemon-colored mustard and wrapped in peeled-back wax paper and held it up to his mouth. Fool. Guess he doesn't care about getting sick, I thought.

As if he were reading my mind, he pushed that wax-paper boatload of junk in my direction. "Have a bite?" he asked.

I looked at him, pursed my lips and shook my head. "No, thank you." He threw his head back and let a long laugh shoot through the air. He definitely ain't got all his marbles, I thought.

"I'm just teasing you, miss. Where are you from?"

"Mississippi."

"So I was close. I guessed Louisiana." He shifted the hot dog to his left hand and pushed his right one toward me. "I'm August Brown." He held his hand out. I shook it like it was a rattlesnake. His grin was wide and made bright by the darkness of his skin. His pants were pressed so sharply they could have walked off on their own. Gold wings rode the space between his jacket lapel and breast pocket. "You like to go out much?" he asked.

"I get to the picture show sometimes."

"How'd you like to do something with me?"

"Excuse me, Mr. Brown, but I don't really know you."

"Come on now, but you can get to know me."

"We haven't been introduced by anybody. I don't trot off with strangers on the street."

He wiped a paper napkin across his mouth and stood up. "Wait here," he said and crossed the boulevard disappearing somewhere in the middle of the next busy block. A few minutes later he appeared again, crossing the street arm in arm with a small, white-haired, walnut-toned lady. He took small steps to match hers. From the distance I could see her lips moving fast, and her head bobbing slightly, as if she were fussing at him. Then she started laughing. She was small but hearty and looked old enough to have been born during slavery times. They stopped in front of me and she said, "Young lady, I'd like to introduce Lieutenant August Brown, a nice unmarried gentleman who'd like to make your acquaintance."

Well, my mouth fell open for at least two seconds before anything sensible came out. "All . . . all right." August presented his hand again and shook mine again. The lady turned to go and he said, "Ma'am, let me get you back across." She waved him away. "I been crossing streets since the day before Creation."

We watched her make her slow way back across the boulevard. "That lady was something else," August said, a laugh in his voice. "She was really giving me what-for. First she said, 'You ain't married, is you, 'cause I ain't havin' no part of that kinda goings-on.' I said, 'Oh no, ma'am.' Then turns out she can't see well. Halfway across the street, she goes, 'That ain't a white girl, is it?' I go, 'Oh, no ma'am. She's one of us. Ask if you can check behind her ears, you don't believe me.' See, I went through a lot to be rightfully introduced to you."

"No less than you should have."

"Ha!" he said. His eyes sparkled and he grinned. "No less, you're right."

He was on leave for a week and staying with his cousin, he said. He was from Mobile, Alabama, had graduated from Tuskegee Institute and then trained there to fly. The Army wouldn't let him say where, but he'd flown in "dogfights," people shooting at each other in the air.

"You trying to impress me?"

"Sure, I'm trying to impress you."

"Yeah, and then you're going to get around to telling me I should give you something special 'cause of all the dangerous work you doing in the war."

"I said 'impress you.' I do believe you misunderstood and heard another word before the 'you.' Either that or where you come from, 'impress' means something entirely different than it does to most folks."

"Why'd you waltz this way, anyway?"

"'Cause I saw the way you took out your sandwich and unwrapped it daintylike. Then you started eating small bites, carefully and slow. So I figured you weren't the type to run off with a man's money too fast."

I looked straight in his face and could see his teeth were as white as stars. "Humm. Naw, last man I had, a good man too, I didn't run off with his money. I ran off with his daddy, but his daddy stole his money before we left, and everything worked out just fine."

He laughed. His hand flew to his thigh. "You can tell a lie as well as anybody I ever met—better."

"And if I'd just grabbed my sandwich, gobbled it right up. Was that supposed to mean anything except I was hungry?"

"I'd have passed you up. It would mean you were poorly brought up and probably a man-eater."

"I *was* poorly brought up, and I *am* a man-eater. Y'all just so easy to chew up. You substantial in the flesh, but flimsy in the soul."

"Hey now, the last time I weighed it, my soul didn't seem so flimsy."

"Sure you didn't press your thumb on the scale?"

HERE IN PHILADELPHIA things went on after dark. Cars honked even at two in the morning. Voices floated from far away. I could hear them in my bed. I wanted to be out there, see what was going on. But back in Mississippi a woman who showed too much interest in the night was tagged a slut. People figured if you wanted to do something you couldn't do in broad open daylight, it must be something you shouldn't be doing.

August came to pick me up the day after we met and escorted me into the night. He drove me in his cousin's Chrysler to a colored USO club, an old lodge meeting hall lit with bald ceiling bulbs and stocked with fold-up tables and chairs. Volunteers had tried to make it nice with plastic flowers in glass vases and pictures of Negro soldiers on the side of the wall where the American flag was draped.

We sat at a back table, the only empty one. Everybody seemed to know August.

"Slide me a one, buddy," one soldier said to him. "I'm broke." He shook his head wearily. "Been playing craps. I pay you back."

"How you know I got a one, man? I'm just a poor boy from Alabama."

The man chuckled. "Come on, Augie. You know you're a nice cat. And you air boys got more money than a Dago going to Italy." August gave him two ones.

"I've told him about gambling," he said when the man was out of earshot.

"Why did he call you Cat? Is that your nickname?"

He smiled and pinched my cheek, then paused a second to see if I'd get mad because he'd touched me. "It's just an expression. He calls every fellow that."

Three couples spun on the dance floor to a tune on the Victrola. The music had lots of drums and the women's hips knew every beat. I felt like I had no business here, almost as if I'd catch hell for it when I got home. Mercy wasn't dead, just less trouble. It was going to take awhile for me to really feel like a grown woman.

Suddenly, one man threw his partner in the air, and I gasped. For a split second I thought he was trying to kill her. But she landed with her feet splayed apart like she was coming down from a jumping jack in a schoolyard.

"You've never seen the jitterbug before?" August said.

"Where I come from they don't allow us to dance."

"Say it's a sin, huh? What do you think about that?"

I shrugged. "Folks interpret the Bible any way they want, and part of the time just be making up stuff as they go along."

He put his mouth near my ear. "I'll tell you something. I'm not too good at keeping up with the latest dances and the latest expressions and all that either. By the time I learn a slang word, it's so common, they're using it in the Sunday paper."

We watched as more couples hit the floor. Another soldier walked up to our table. He was a pretty man with a medium mustache, black diamond eyes and dark smooth skin like the browned top of a pound cake.

"Skeet Magee!" August said. "How you be!" He stood up and shook the man's hand and introduced him.

"Same company," Skeet told me.

"Philadelphia being good to you?" August asked.

"Except for my woman. She left me."

"That's unfortunate, but how did you know?" August said. "You took a head count and found one missing?"

"You coldhearted sucker."

Skeet asked us why we weren't dancing. We said we were waiting for something slow that we could handle.

He jumped up and grabbed my hand. "Come on, I can teach you," he said, pulling me toward the dance floor. I pulled back.

"Come on now, come on," he said.

At first it shamed me, being out there. But no one paid much attention to us. They were busy with their own twirling and twisting. Skeet held my hands above our hips and tugged my arms back and forth.

"Follow my feet," he said, moving his hands to my waist.

The music was full of trumpets and drums and saxophones. It started slow at some points as if it were sneaking up on you. Then the trumpets got louder, the drums crazier, and the saxophones—sassier. Soon I was rotating and gyrating and spinning into somebody I never knew I was. Skeet spun me out and reeled me in. He dipped me on one arm and pulled me up with the other. With one hand, he cupped my shoulder and pushed me until I slid between his legs; with the other, he whipped me back up. His arms made a circle that was my own little stomping and swaying ground.

The music was so good I could have eaten it. I was either happy or going out of my mind. Skeet grabbed my waist and with a quick jerk heaved me up in the air. For what seemed a long time, I was flying and fearful that I'd gone too far and breaking my stupid neck would be the punishment for it. I went up, up and my head bounced against air. And I was falling. Then he caught me.

"Thought you couldn't jitterbug," he said later.

I shrugged. "You thought right."

A tamer tune played while August and I danced a basic two-step. After Skeet, it seemed like a bashful shuffle.

When we pulled up past midnight outside the row house, I extended my hand. "Thank you so much for the very nice time," I said, reaching to unlatch the passenger-side door.

"Wait. You don't have to rush off. I'm nothing but a harmless mama's boy."

"Well, your mama's not here to vouch for that, so I'll say good night."

"She passed away."

What a jackass I felt like! "I'm sorry."

"You didn't know. All is forgiven. Just hold still for two seconds." He leaned over and put his lips to my cheek without the sound that a kiss usually makes. "All right. You're dismissed. Just let me get out and open the door for you."

He had four more days of leave time. "What do you want to do?" he asked the next day. He'd found me at lunchtime at my usual bench. I didn't know if I should balk or fuss a little. A lady, as I understood it, was supposed to show some resistance to a man. It shouldn't be "Can we go out?" "That sounds fine—let's get going." The truth was it did seem fine to me. Going out with August again sounded "swell," and I had never used that word before. I wanted to say it now but wouldn't. It was one of those radio-story and movie-show words that I knew had no tie to real life. Anyway, it was a white folks' word. No reason came up for colored folks to use it. Because for us, things weren't so swell.

I swept through the door as if it were a feather in my path. Lilian, home from the meat place, pulled her head up from a book to say hi. "Going out again tonight with that soldier?"

When I said yep, her voice took on a slow smart-ass tone. "Now, I somehow remember your saying something about soldiers grabbing anything with . . . a bosom. Now, let me know if I'm lying. Maybe I only imagined it."

"I was talking about that crazy Kraut."

Suddenly all my dresses seemed country looking. "Lilian, can I wear your blue dress, the one with the checkered collar?"

She mumbled as she walked to the closet. "How can you diagnose people as crazy when you don't know them from French toast?"

"You liked that man, didn't you?"

"What do you mean by 'liked'?"

"Never mind."

August, doggone him, showed up a couple of minutes early. Since our old-crow landlady didn't allow men inside rooms, Lilian, bless her, stood outside the door and made friendly talk with him. When I was dressed, squeezed into a pair of high heels and polished with a little lipstick, I stuck my head out. "Be out in a minute," I said.

"Shake a leg. It's a long drive," August said.

Perfume. But not too much. Didn't want to smell like a whorehouse. Earrings. Not the big ones. Didn't want my ears to look like a donkey's.

I grabbed my purse. "Oh, Lilian, could you please come here?" I tried to sound all ladylike. She appeared inside the door and I motioned her to close it.

"How do I look?" I whispered, but August must have heard.

"YOU LOOK JUST FINE! BUT YOU'D LOOK EVEN FINER OUT HERE ON THE DOUBLE AND IN THE CAR!"

Lilian busted out laughing. I rolled my eyes but got going. Two hours on the road and the meek shine of starlight replaced the streetlights. The car zoomed through New Jersey, a new state to me, but it was too dark to get a good look and nothing but highway to squint at, anyway.

"We're in the Holland Tunnel now," August said. On the other side, I could see the lights of New York City—more lights than I'd ever seen in my life. "Doesn't it look like God took the Milky Way and set it down on earth?" he said.

The people shimmered, too. At the nightclub, rhinestones decorated the lapels of satin dresses so tight I'd be scared to belch in them. Diamonds, real and fake, dangled from women's ears. Slicked and lacquered hair was pinned tight and high on their heads to a place at the crown where glistening curls bugled out. The singer on the stage wore a wide white flower in her hair that glowed in the spotlight. Any other time I'd have thought some gal who slapped a big gardenia upside her head was begging to be called a fool. But it complemented her white dress, a glittery sheer thing with a fluted hemline, and her whole body twinkled in the light as if she were a part of it. Her singing, though, pulled me down into some sad place where I didn't want to go. No matter what she sang about, money or love or men, her voice sounded like the moan of a hurt baby. As she walked off the stage, the crowd banged their hands together wildlike. Some whistled. Some stood.

As we made it out the door, inching against shoulder-to-shoulder people, we heard someone shout out, "Hey, Brown!" The man, whose name was Guy, was an old Tuskegee classmate. He pulled his girlfriend over to us, a short girl, looking even shorter next to his lanky, uniformed frame, with a row of dime-sized spit curls across her forehead.

"A rent party going on at One Hundred and Twelfth. Y'all wanna go?" he said.

Our car trailed his down streets I'd never seen. I felt excited, though I didn't know where I was going and what I was going to.

"What kinda thing is this?"

"People charge fifty cents or so at the door to get together their rent money."

We trooped up four flights of drearily lit stairs in a time-battled building where walls on every floor screamed for a lick of paint. I never found out whose apartment we packed into, but the tenant should have had enough money to sit pretty in that ugly place for at least a couple of months. August went to scout a beer for us, and it took him fifteen minutes to make it back to me through the tangle of folks. We laughed for the fun of it without knowing what we were laughing at. August was bigger than most men in the bunch. His shoulders fanned out hefty inches from his chest. His eyes were big and lively, and it always looked like someone was home behind that face, which was the shade of medium toast. In an hour, the folks thinned out, and we made use of the extra space by slow-dancing to cozy music playing over a radio. He didn't step loosely enough to be a good dancer. His legs moved a little faster than the beat, as if they were more inclined to march than follow violins. No matter how playful he seemed, he had a springlike readiness to get to business that never went away.

By the time we walked back to the car, I could see shy sunlight peeping through the buildings. I'd been out all night! In Nadir mothers told their courting daughters, 'If you come back in the morning, you better come back married.'

"Back home, people would say I'm going straight to hell." Underneath my seat, I quietly slipped off those biting high heels, hoping he wouldn't notice.

"And what would you say to that?"

"I'd say I've already been through hell, so I'm used to it."

"Life hasn't been that bad for you, has it?"

"It's hard to measure." I thought of that shimmery woman singing with a baby's moan. "I didn't have it any worse than anybody else I know." The sun mapped out the highway, and we whizzed by all sorts of signs pointing in a slew of different directions.

"People need a plan, Myraleen. When you follow a plan, you may not get everything you want, but at least you'll get some of it."

"So what's your plan?"

"Fly. Avoid being a good grade on some Kraut's report card. Make it through the war. Every hour I fly counts toward a professional license. Things are opening up. Get on as a pilot for one of the commercial airlines."

"Like TWA or one of those?"

"Yep."

"Well, maybe it's just my evil mind, but when those white folks find out a Negro is flying the plane, they gonna parachute out of there whether they got parachutes on or not."

August breathed out hard and sucked his breath back through his teeth.

"That's the crack in my plan."

He'd plugged up cracks before. "How'd you start to fly, anyway?"

"Canadians taught me."

"Cana—whody taught you?"

"The Canadians. In the country up north." He took one hand off the steering wheel and pointed straight up. "Border's right above New York."

"Oh, now I know what you mean. In Nadir, we never give any mind to folks that far up north. To us, the people in Chicago are Canadians."

He'd applied to a flight school in Michigan. But he could tell by the way they looked at him they'd never get over his being colored, he said.

"And it's dangerous to go up with some instructor who can't see the sky because he's too busy trying to hold somebody down."

A school not far from Niagara Falls in Ontario, Canada, let him in, he said. They acted like they had some sense and treated him like any-body else. A chain-link fence wound around the airstrip. Every couple of days he'd see a colored woman walking by, a grocery sack in her arms and a little boy tagging behind. "I didn't know there were any black people in Canada. Slaves crossed over, I knew, but after Emanci-pation, I thought they all came back."

He got a notion to go to the fence and tell them hello. "Nice lady. She spoke so well. Really friendly. Her great-grandfather beat back cold old Lake Erie, swimming from Buffalo to Canada, to get away from slave catchers. She was married, unfortunately, or so I felt back then."

Maybe August should get together with Lilian, I thought. He was proper talking. In Nadir nobody used the word *unfortunately*, though you might figure they'd be using it all the time.

"The boy was her son. I'd put his age at about six. He begged his mother to let me take him up. He used to jump up in the air, saying 'please, Mama.' It looked as if he were trying to fly on his own. She gave in. On the last day, when I had my certificate, I took him up. I've never seen such a look on a kid's face. He was in paradise."

At about fifteen thousand feet up, the boy craned his neck so far out, it seemed it would pop off his shoulders, August said. "Where are all the people, Mr. Brown?" he asked.

"What people?"

"Where are God and all the people?"

". . . Oh, oh, you mean folks who pass on and go to heaven?"

"Uh, huh."

"We're not high enough, son. God gave us this side of the sky so we can fly airplanes, feel the sun, see the stars sparkle. The other half is where God is, and His people. That means when you pass on, you can see the other half of the sky."

HE NUDGED ME with his elbow. "After the war, I'm going to take you up one day."

"Oh yeah, when the devil turns Catholic. When you see Catholic Devil Day roll around on the calendar, come get me."

"You afraid?"

"What else would I be? I don't see how you do it, how you can operate a plane with those crazy folks shooting at you. I'd just throw up my arms and scream."

"Oh, it's not so bad. Well, it is . . . but it's necessary."

"And I know you have to do it, but killing people . . . It's funny 'cause I swore I was going to kill some jackass many a time. But you, you've got to put your might where your mouth is."

"I don't kill people, Myraleen. I kill planes."

After I got home I told Lilian every detail. I'd have told her anyway, but I especially didn't want her to think "overnight" meant "in my drawers."

At work, my catching-on phase had ended, and I had caught on. Every dress dangling crooked from its hanger got jerked straight and smoothed out. Each lady received quick attention. "Are you being helped, madam?" I said to one with her back to me. She wore a beige cashmere coat with a tiny mink collar, and was checking the hem of a black dress for loose threads. She wouldn't find any here.

When she turned around, I stopped breathing. It was Mrs. Humphreys. "I think I'll try this on—" Her eyebrows rose a bit, as high as polite eyebrows dared rise. "Don't I know you? Didn't you work—" Her blue eyes darted a bit to see if anyone was near. Doris Eisen stood a few feet away. Mrs. Humphreys lowered her voice and smiled. "Small universe, running into an old friend here. You look well. I'm visiting family outside the city—a death, you know."

She strolled into a dressing room and returned to plop down $200 plus tax without blinking. "Good luck to you," she said. My heart felt like a racehorse that was headed through my chest.

"You ran into someone you know?" Doris Eisen said, walking over. I nodded.

"Good sale. Lucky you."

At lunchtime August sat at our bench with his left arm stretched out on the back of the unoccupied side. He watched me walking across the street. Not intending to, I met his big grin with a frown.

He crossed his hands over his face as if I were going to hit him. "What did I do?" he said.

I handed him a sandwich I'd made so he wouldn't have to eat those nasty hot dogs anymore. "Myraleen, there's nothing so terribly bad about what you're doing," he said. "What's bad is that you need to do it."

Then he lowered his chin and put on a solemn face. "My only concern is that I've been kissing an official white woman. Now I'm going to jump every time I see a tree."

"You ought to be ashamed."

August was the first person I'd known who'd graduated from college. Still, in most ways he was just plain folks. "You've got to let me take you to visit my cousin," he said when he picked me up that night. He was proud to have a girlfriend; he was even proud to have a cousin.

Leonard lived not too far from me in North Philly. When he opened the door, his head of knotty gray hair surprised me. I was expecting someone our age, but Leonard's mother was one of August's great-aunts. Inside, a kitchenette just like Lilian's and mine spread only a few yards long and a few wide. Negroes probably were boxed up as we were for miles in this city, packed up in a big storeroom behind all the better parts of Philadelphia.

"Pardon this place," he said, though the apartment was perfectly clean. We sat at his small table. I saw only one skinny bed, barely large enough for one grown man, definitely not two. I guessed while August was staying, one of them slept on the floor. Leonard stepped over to his icebox and returned with three bottles of orange pop bundled in the crook of his arm. He wasn't moving fast, but his breathing was labored. He wore round bifocals that magnified his cloudy brown eyes and made him look like a character from the funny papers.

"Now I'm going to tell you something about American Negroes and wars," he said. "I was in the Great War, so I know how the flimflam floats. The white man tells you, 'Join up, you colored fellows. Help us make the world safe, and when you come back—IF you come back—we got something for you.'"

August listened with his arms folded on his chest. He nodded respectfully every so often.

"So you make it back. In my case just barely cause that mustard gas squeezed my lungs till I thought I didn't have any. But the Lord sent me back ready for a new life and a good job now that I'd made the world safe. So I say, 'Mr. White Man, what you got for me?' And he says, 'This broom!' I've been a janitor ever since two days after discharge day, and that's been . . ." He gazed upward and counted in the air. "Twenty-four . . . twenty-five years."

August made a soft sucking noise with his teeth. He shifted in his chair. "Leonard, Roosevelt's in the White House now."

"The White House still ain't your house, boy! Why do you think they call it white? And that Franklin Houdini Roosevelt, able to pull a war out of a hat when the people didn't want one. He set them boys up at that Pearl Harbor and you know it. With all that radar equipment and whatnot, they couldn't see those Jap planes coming? I could have pegged them, and I'm almost blind. A day that will live in infamy, my black ass—pardon my French, Myraleen—he was probably writing that speech when those boys were getting their asses blown out of the water—excuse me again, Myraleen."

"Look, Leonard. You don't have to tell me the Allies aren't angels."

"No, you better not, boy. Not after you told me about how your squadron had to wait in Missouri while they put those German POWs on the train." Leonard shook his head. "Did he tell you about that, Myraleen? Then after they waited for those Germans to get in and comfortable, they had to get in the cars behind them." He'd rocked his head back and forth when he said the word *comfortable*. He let out a hard sniff as his nostrils flared like those of a disgusted bull. "White folks like Nazis better than they like Negroes."

"Nevertheless, Leonard, this is *my* country, no matter how they act. And I'm going to fight for it."

"How can you let somebody who hates you tell you who *you* should hate? And how do you really know what the hell you're fighting for? Those hoodoo demons with their lying asses—pardon, Myraleen. They'll tell you anything and do something else."

I sat in the middle. He leaned toward me as if he knew I'd understand. "I was over in France retrieving bodies on the battlefield. Much of the time, you didn't know who was who. They just pretended like they could identify them."

"Dog tags, Leonard, dog tags."

"HA HA HA! You think when a man's head comes off, his dog tag is going to stay on? Dog tag say to itself head's over there, but I'm going to do right and stay over here? You think I'm going to feel around in the dirt for a piece of metal and get shot to give a dead man a name? They played me for a fool, but I wasn't that big of a fool.

"Somebody would figure so-and-so went in, and he didn't come back. Guess that's him. Then they'd say, 'Mrs. Smith, here are your son's remains.'" Leonard held out his upturned palms. "But they don't know whose damn son it is. At the funeral, folks are crying over Joe, and any Tom, Dick or Harry could be in the casket."

Leonard wound down and they talked about Alabama and asked me about Mississippi before August got up to take me home. His cousin searched until he found paper to make sure he had my address and I his. "With this boy headed off tomorrow for God knows where"—he jabbed a thumb in August's direction—"we should keep in touch. If I find out something you don't know, I can tell you and vice versa."

"There's going to be nothing to find out," August said. We stood near the door, about to leave. "This thing is getting close to being over. I'll be back quicker than you can say Rumplestilskin," he said, giving my shoulders a quick squeeze.

We pulled up in front of my place before nine. August had to be on a five A.M. train. "Good-bye, friend," he said. "See you next time."

I got into bed and closed my eyes, but worries rolled around beneath them. Lilian was stretched out two inches away. We'd planned to get another bed as soon as we could save the money. What would that cost? A mattress? A frame? Maybe working it out would put me to sleep. I squeezed my eyes shut and nodded off until sometime in the middle of the night. It looked lighter outside. I walked to the window. Bales of tiny cotton balls blew against the pane. What? No, it was snow—the first time I'd seen it in my life. I held my watch near the window and could see it was ten to four.

When the light went on, Lilian sat up blinking. "I'm sorry," I said. "I tried to find everything in the dark, but I couldn't."

She watched me hopping around barefoot in my brassiere and half-slip. The floor was ice. Finally I could see where I'd left my shoes. I tugged my dress over my head and stepped into my black pumps at the same time.

"You've got to work this early?" Sleep rode her voice. "Are they having a special sale or something?"

"No, honey, go back to sleep." She put her head back down like a child minding her mother.

I grabbed my coat with one hand and the door with the other. Outside I wished I'd grabbed a hat. Fast spitballs of snow pelted my head with no rest. At the bus stop my teeth chattered as if they were tapping out a tune. The light wool coat I wore didn't help much when that freezing air smacked me. It felt as if the wind were saying, "I don't give a damn about you and your little coat, too."

A bus pulled up just as I was about to cry. The driver was a colored man with an oblong face and a long forehead that ended high in his hairline. After a big to-do, the city had finally started hiring Negroes. "That snow sure is cold," I said, dropping nickels into the coin box, my gloveless hands shaking.

"Not like that hot snow we usually get."

Old donkey-headed smart aleck. A man in coveralls, due at some job before daybreak, was the only other passenger. The bus stopped three blocks from the train station. I ran all the way. By the time I stepped in the door, my watch said five to five. What did I call myself doing, anyway? I flicked evil chunks of ice out of my hair, now plastered to my head. My bangs dripped into my face like tears. I ran out to the tracks to rows of trains hot to get moving. How was I going to even find him? Wall-to-wall servicemen packed the station. In a few seconds, I developed a method: Skip the sailors and the Marines. They were almost sure to be white. Look for Army. Army. And there he was, standing with two duffel bags at his feet, talking to Leonard. "Why, you'll be riding like a big shot," I could hear his cousin saying. "They let you sit up front all the way to D.C."

Leonard saw me first and didn't look a bit surprised. "Well, hey!" he hollered. August turned around. A smile grew on his face and in his eyes until he beamed. He opened his arms and stretched his fingers toward me, a shivering puddle of a person. I stumbled into his reach and he scooped me up inside his arms, pressing my head against his warm chin as if he were saving my life. He kissed my temple, my cheek and worked his way down.

"Oh, August, I'm going to get your nice uniform wet."

"Why, you just do that, baby," he said. "You just do that."

KELLNER

. . . Philadelphia . . .

IN A SHINY SEVERE BLACK CAR, THEY HAD DRIVEN HIM TO A
prison camp in Arkansas. "We're going to trade you for another high-
priority prisoner," the darker suit said. For fifteen days he ate generous
meals—eggs and sliced ham, turkey sandwiches, fried potatoes and
steak—alone in a puny room with a bed, sink and toilet. Then the two
figures appeared at the door. "Trade's off," the lighter suit said. That
ended the flow of information. They drove him back on a Wednesday.
He should have been disappointed, but his mind reached toward Saturday.

When Herr Taylor saw him climbing from the truck, the man took a
big step back, clutched his waist with his hands as if he were going to
flap his arms the way a bird beats its wings. "Why if it ain't good ol'
Doctor Professor Kellner!" he declared. "We thought you were gone for
good."

It occurred to Kellner that people in Mississippi moved their bodies
more than Germans, especially the blacks. It was as though they had
springs in their arms and legs.

"Surprise, ya?" Urs said. He'd learned a little English and was beginning to use it. "They bring back him."

"Where'd they drag you—and why?" Herr Taylor asked.

Kellner explained what little he himself knew.

"You're a special prisoner, huh? Gotta lot of rank on you?"

"It is not that. I think it has something to do with my father. He has much 'rank on him,' but it is government, not military."

Herr Taylor moved close to him, poking him lightly with an elbow. "You wouldn't happen to be related to the Mouth-and-the-Fury?"

Toby usually milked CoCo, whose teats had to be relieved every twelve hours. But his uncle was teaching him how to build an irrigation ditch. So Kellner ducked under the porch and chased the goat out to the barn. "Best milk in the world," Herr Taylor had said. "Goats should have put cows out of business a long time ago."

"Make yourself still," Kellner told the animal, but CoCo kicked the air with her hind feet. "You do speak English, don't you?"

It was rude work: grabbing a female's breasts and pulling. His grip kept slipping because the teats were slick and moist. At first, the milk didn't squirt at all, then it came in rhythmic streams. After the pour ceased, CoCo ran out of the barn and back under the porch. Kellner tossed grain to the chickens.

Frau Taylor came out exactly at noon with lunch. She was punctual like Berlin women. Kellner and Urs moved to the porch steps. "Joseph told me to let you all try some goat's milk," she said. With their sandwiches, she handed them two chilled glasses of CoCo's product.

"Is Lilian visiting today?" Kellner asked. "I will keep up lessons if she wants to."

"Guess you wouldn't know," she said. Her hand rose to her face, her fingers spread over her cheek. "Lilian left a few weeks after you stopped coming by."

"Oh?" He tried not to show the odd panic he was feeling.

"She moved north to Philadelphia. She passed the test you were helping her with, but found she was a year past age for the scholarship.

There's nothing for a girl to do around here except maid work, especially for our people. And Lilian could do better. She's a smart girl."

"Certainly," he said. "Good for her that she go."

Frau Taylor walked up the steps and returned with a piece of paper, ripped from a brown grocery bag, with Lilian's address penciled on it. "In case you'd want to write to her. I bet she'd like that."

Kellner stared at the numbers and the street name, his eyes searching them for comfort, until they were engraved in his memory. Then he joined Toby. Side by side, they attacked the earth with shovels. Mid-afternoon, Herr Taylor came over to mourn the weather. He wiped his forehead with this forearm.

"Who would believe this is October?" He looked at their holes. "Y'all doin just fine." He turned and walked away, calling over his shoulder, "Don't work yourself too hard now, Doctor Professor."

Kellner froze.

"Hit a rock, Doctor Professor?" Toby asked.

What a blunder he had made! He drove the shovel back into the dirt. It wasn't that women were so mysterious, he thought. It was that men were so stupid.

Four weeks later the gray suits returned. Pack, they said. Make it quick. "We're trading you." It was right before breakfast. He'd been brushing his teeth. Something about them made him want to scratch. They hustled him off into the stern, shiny car again. A third one drove. In short hair and business clothes, he looked like the others. The lighter gray suit sat in back with Kellner. An aged train depot came into view and the driver stopped. The gray suit stepped out first, carrying a dark briefcase. Kellner climbed out of the car, dragging a satchel marked U.S. ARMY that held the shaving kit, change of clothes, toothbrush and paste he'd been issued when he entered the camp. The lighter gray suit followed, carrying his own briefcase. It was warm out. Kellner took off his khaki army jacket and threw it over his arm.

They stood on a long splintery platform, brown with dirt, until a train pulled up and the driver nodded and turned to leave.

"Here," said the lighter suit after they boarded. He pointed to a seat on the aisle. Kellner sat on the inside next to him by the window. The other man settled in the aisle seat of the two chairs facing them. He imagined they would put him on a boat in New York Harbor destined for Europe or perhaps on a plane at a coastal airport.

He let the steady huff of the train lull him into a state resembling sleep and awoke thinking of Philadelphia. On the east coast of the United States, the cities hunched in a cluster like the countries in Europe. New York State bordered on Pennsylvania. He envisioned a hundred and fifty kilometers between New York City and Philadelphia. His mind floated into nothingness again, then somethingness, a condition in which he wished for a book to read or someone to talk to.

No black paper covered the windows on this journey. He watched the countryside float by—cotton, wheat and corn; wheat, corn and wheat; wheat and wheat and wheat—until he began to fiercely miss the black paper of the first trip. The train steamed into a big station. Kellner could see a pack of soldiers outside the window. Each one was black. The lighter suit glanced over his shoulder through the glass. It was the only time Kellner had heard him speak with any emotion. "Niggers," he said.

Kellner could hear the men boarding the car behind them. He heard the roll of their collective voices and their deep laughter. Sound was welcome to him; the two gray suits emitted mostly silence. Soon their sounds knuckled under the struggle of the train's engine as it growled out of the station. But the lighter suit summoned the conductor. "Aren't they supposed to be in the back?" he said.

"That's as far back as they can get, suh."

He pulled out his wallet, showed the porter a badge with Federal Bureau of Investigation emblazoned on it. "We're government men and we need quiet."

"Suh, the last two cars are full. Fraid there's nothing I can do." His caramel eyes blinked as if there was something in them. He was bald. Beneath his porter's hat, his baldness made his head and face, both the color and smoothness of a shelled peanut, appear as though they blended into each other.

"Damn shame," the lighter suit said. The porter stood until certain he no longer existed for the man and then hurried away. The gray suit turned to Kellner. "Comfortable?" he asked.

He nodded.

Kellner realized the silence of these men cloaked layers of knowledge about him. He stiffened in his seat and remained that way for a few minutes before settling again.

He wanted to beat the hell out of the sleeping lighter suit. He wanted to get off this damn train.

Daybreak didn't help. In Washington, a crowd of morning riders poured into the car which, by then, was sparsely occupied. A crush of riders stood for lack of seats. An awkward elbow knocked against his head. A blow of another kind came when the conductor bellowed, "PHILADELPHIA." He glanced at the gray suits. They were awake and alert.

He couldn't very well explain to them that he wanted to make a stop to say something important to someone. That nothing had ever felt as urgent. He couldn't get up and run through this impenetrable crowd, now absorbing more bodies and barricading the floor space beside him, pinning him to his seat.

The grayer suit bent his head toward his watch. "Two hours," he said to the other one. This confirmed Kellner's guess. They intended to get off in New York.

He tried not to wrinkle the bridge of his nose as he often did when figuring out a problem. As the train restarted, his head rocked to the side into the painful tree of elbows. He hoped, to the suits, his face looked as blank as theirs did.

"Grand Central Station. Last destination," the conductor called. Kellner gathered his satchel. "Wait," the lighter suit said. They sat until all the other passengers had struggled out of the car. "All right," he allowed. They moved out the door and down the three-step box onto the platform. They walked with Kellner in the middle, a tight parade of three. Inside the station, a thick assemblage of humanity maneuvered in every direction. Even Kellner, a fairly tall man, couldn't see above all the heads. The suits tried to step in unison and twice from behind the lighter suit gave a firm hand on the shoulder to keep Kellner in line. But the helter-skelter crowd didn't have room for a parade, however short. People came between the three: a young mother pulling a stubborn boy, a sailor with his arm around his girlfriend, a worker in a scarlet cap pushing a cart of luggage. Kellner began to step carelessly, too far to the right and then too far to the left. "All right, now. Let's stay together," the lighter suit said, tension stringing his tone. To the right, a wet-faced, elderly woman embraced a soldier, her son or grandson, and then swayed to the floor like a leaf from a tree. He stooped beside her. "Ma! Ma!" Flow in their direction stopped. A confusion of people clustered to stare. The woman created a tangled clump in the scheme of the crowd's movement, though most stepped around her. The lighter suit tried to direct Kellner to the left of it all. "Wait!" he said when his charge took a sharp leap to the right, crashing through the outer portion of the tangle. Dropping his satchel, Kellner moved swiftly, piercing the larger crowd. To them, his butting between them with his shoulders and plowing over feet meant no more than bad manners. "Hey, buddy!" "Jeez!" "Watch it, you!" He sprang through a cluster of three men, throwing one into another and both into the third.

"Hey get off my feet, you nut."

"Go to hell."

"I wasn't even talking to you; you're not the only nut in the world."

Kellner burst out into sunlight, unprepared. He should take a back street. He saw only a big boulevard stretching ahead, though. Must keep moving, he thought and began to run, grateful for another stream of people who would submerge him.

Hours passed and dark descended. He was walking about, shivering, looking for some inconspicuous shelter, when he heard a heavy, deep voice thundering in his direction. "Man, man. What's wrong with you, ain't got no coat? You gonna freeze yourself to death out here in that cotton jacket!"

Under a bridge, two men stood warming themselves by a garbage can fire. Both were about Lilian's color. The one who hollered at him was young with three or four days' growth of snarly beard, a thick, tattered jacket and oversized dusty pants. The tip of one of the crackling orange spirals touched his wriggling thumb and he hissed a brief curse.

"They gonna find you under one of these here bridges froze stiff, and they won't mind worth a bit 'cause some of these people they got in this man's New York City is colder than the weather." With a broad wave of his arm, he motioned for Kellner to come closer. "Ernest," he said to the older man on his right, whose hands were dancing over the fire. "You got something in your bag can help him out?" Ernest's bloodshot eyes examined Kellner before he turned away and reached into a big green shopping bag, with MACY's written on it. He dragged out a voluminous rag and held it up. It was a double-breasted wool coat, torn at the pockets and collar, eaten by moths or wear at the bottom.

"You better take it," the younger man said. Kellner walked over and reached up. The older man let the garment fall down into his hand. Kellner slowly cloaked it over his shoulders, feeling strange.

"Put that all the way on before you turn into an icicle," said the talkative one. "Ain't you got no sense?" The older one just stared. Kellner slipped his arms into the lining that felt alternately smooth and knobby. He folded the front flaps over each other and buttoned the few buttons that remained.

"Thank you."

"See you got some kina accent. You from overseas?"

"Yes, I came here when I was a little boy, with my parents."

"I'm from down south. Just got up here a week ago."

"South? Mississippi?"

"HELL NO. Georgia. You ain't one those folks think everybody from the South must be from Mississippi, is you?"

"No, it is only that I know people who live in Mississippi."

"How would you know folks in Mississippi?" that man said tilting his head, taking a harder look at the stranger.

Why had he told him that? Maybe all the prisoner-of-war camps were located in the states of Mississippi and Arkansas and he had just given himself away as a prisoner. But when he looked into the man's eyes, bright and innocently curious, he knew better.

"I spent time working on a farm."

"Work, now that's what I needs me, only not on a farm, but in this big old town someplace. A couple of times I done some spot work, helping people move furniture and things, but I needs something steady. It's cold out here."

Wearing the sad coat, Kellner stumbled down a sidewalk where the passing faces resembled the haggard ones of European peasants, and exhausted laundry hung from building railings. In front of a small grocery store, with the perfection of a still-life painting, a cart stood pregnant with oranges, tomatoes, bananas and apples. A wiry old man hovered behind it. Kellner pictured himself fleeing with two apples in each grubby hand. But he wasn't ready yet to be a desperate thief in a thread-bare coat. Perhaps in a few days. He wondered, in a few days, would he have the strength to run? He strolled by, dropping his head to glance at the fruit. "You want?" the old man said, holding out an orange. Kellner was startled by his voice. He stuck out a flat palm and shook his head.

"You pay next time. I get some good customers that way." He could hear a Polish accent.

"I don't live . . . here in this part of the city," Kellner said.

The man walked around the fruit stand. He took the hand Kellner used to say "no" with and placed the orange in it. "Take it anyway."

Kellner dug into the orange with his thumbnail and began to strip it of its skin. "I appreciate it."

He had deep dark eyes and full lips. His lined and battered complexion was olive.

"People call me Abe. What's your name?"

Kellner took advantage of his full mouth to remain silent. He would leave in a moment, but the man kept asking him questions. He did his best to mimic an American accent, to flatten his vowels, to make his consonants dumb and friendly. Still the man asked, "You from old country?"

Kellner nodded.

"Poland, maybe?"

He nodded again.

"I'm from Poland, too. You Jew?"

He shook his head. "Catholic," he lied. Atheist might make the man less friendly.

"We cannot all be so lucky as to be Jews," the man said and let out a meager chuckle. "What is your name?"

"Jan."

"John and Abraham—aren't we a pious pair?"

The man asked what kind of work he did, and after Kellner said he had none, he found himself sweeping the wooden planks of the store and eating more samples of fruit.

Kellner washed himself, his pants, shirt, and underwear in the storage room in a big cement basin used to rinse the produce. He spent the night in his khaki jacket under a blanket on a foldout cot amidst stacked crates and in the morning he unpacked crates and ate the breakfast that Abe's wife sent.

That evening, he spooned borscht to his lips at their dinner table. Spiced deliciously by his hunger, the soup tasted like a symphony. Three floors up and three streets down from the store, the flat was filled with pictures of four adult children and two infant grandchildren. They sat around a tiny table. White, knitted doilies the wife made herself cradled each bowl like pale fat spider webs. "You have any family here?" Abe's wife asked. Keller made up something about his relatives being in Chicago.

She smiled as he sucked in the fourth tablespoon of borscht. Then she slammed her fist down on the table and liquids spilled from their bowls. "WHO ARE YOU?"

"Elsie, what is the matter with you?"

She was deaf to her husband. The power of her ears and eyes poured toward Kellner.

He transferred his napkin from his lap to the table. "I am sorry to have upset you. I will leave."

"That's no good. That means nothing. You are working for my husband. I want to know who you are. You could be a thief, someone just out of prison. Why are you in such a bad position? It's obvious that you are educated. I've been around enough ignoramuses to know how to pick out the people who have something upstairs. What are you doing here, MISTER?"

"Elsie, shame!"

Kellner's eyes addressed hers. "You are right in your concern. All I can say, Mrs. Bruzda, is that I mean harm to no one."

"You have a wife?"

"After meeting you," Abe said, "he will know better than to ever have one."

"No, just mother, father, sister."

"We have many relations in Europe," she said. "No news from them in years. What is happening over there, we don't know. We hear horrible things."

"Elsie! How would he know?"

"Are you from Timbuktu? Listen to him. He is not so removed from Europe as he says."

"That is his business. You hear horrible things because you listen to old crones with nothing else to do but make up Hansel-and-Gretel stories."

Kellner worked in the store during the day and took dinner in the evening balanced with Abe's apparently uniform conviviality and Elsie's accusing stares. On the second Saturday, his host surprised him by slapping a bunch of dollar bills into his palm. Kellner thought meals and a bed at night were his pay for such trivial work as rinsing and stacking fruit and sweeping floors. "No," he said, trying to push back the bills.

"Don't be foolish. You must be paid."

Kellner poked the American dollars into his pants pocket, fingered them and asked, "How much does a bus ticket to Philadelphia cost?"

"Not a great sum. Less than half of what you have there." A quick shadow of understanding crossed Abe's face. "You are going to leave us, aren't you?"

That night under the glare of a bare lightbulb, Kellner scrubbed each piece of his clothing between his knuckles until his hands turned red and raw. He removed his undershirt and his shorts and stood naked until he finished. Then he wrapped himself in the blanket and eased into the cot.

When he woke up, only a toothbrush remained on the rim of the sink; the clothing he'd hung there and over empty crates was gone. He stood perplexed, dressed in the blanket.

Abe gently opened the storage-room door. "The wife said you would want to be nice for your trip. She tell me to get your clothes, but you'd already washed so she ironed. You like to be starched, no?"

Odd how a woman could render domestic services to a man she hated. Maybe it was a good-riddance gift. "Danke schön," he said through the blur of sleepiness before it hit him to turn on the English part of his brain.

"And so you are German."

Kellner nodded.

"I heard it in your voice many times. I understand. When war breaks out, you don't want to be unpopular. You say Polish, not German. Don't blame you. I wouldn't mind being like you, German, Polish, whatever you are. You are not tangled up with ties to strangle you. Being married is good, but it's bad too. Nobody wants to say it, but family is more obligation than pleasure. Me, I have a woman wailing and moaning about cousins in Poland we haven't seen in thirty years. 'Where are they?' In my hip pocket, I ask her. How am I supposed to know? If they are in trouble, what am I supposed to do—grow wings, fly to the old country, pluck them from the jaws of evil? I can barely get through a day here." Abe shook his head. "Savor being free, Jan. Take your time before you take on ghosts to ride your back."

As Kellner stood in line at Port Authority, he felt more exposed than he'd felt when he stood naked at the sink. He saw a man in a black uniform and cap, a policeman. Were pictures of him, the escaped German prisoner, passing from hand to hand in this gargantuan city? He had thought a bus station would offer more safety than any train depot. But he felt an echo of the racing heartbeat that had assaulted his chest when he ran through Grand Central Station, and boarding the bus did not calm him. He remembered the shock on her face when she realized he could speak English. Now another trick: suddenly appearing to her out of nowhere. What would he say? She might come to think of him as one of those people driven insane by war. Perhaps she would be right.

LILIAN

. . . an unrescued princess . . .

THE MAN WHO DELIVERED THE TELEGRAM WALKED WITH speedy, snappy steps. I could tell he'd delivered a lot and liked to be good and gone when people opened them. He was pale enough to be an albino and short enough to be a midget. During wartime, hardly anyone was happy to see a telegram man. Did he think they'd blame him for whatever the messages said, believe that his peculiar face and body had brought their bad luck? Maybe he just didn't like seeing people cry.

No tears escaped Myraleen, though. She just said, "Papa's dead. Got to get home."

Miz Herdie had sent the telegram. My mind's eye could see her dressing for trouble, pulling on her seldom-troubled shoes and getting out her little straw handbag and marching over to a neighbor's house to get him to drive her into town.

I wanted to take a few days off and go with Myraleen. But I couldn't afford to miss work. Mr. Chadham's funeral wouldn't have been my true reason for going. I wanted to assure myself that my own Mudear was still safe from the tide that eventually sweeps all parents—and children— away.

"Be sure to lock the door before you go to sleep," Myraleen said, dragging her suitcase down the stairs. "This ain't like back home where nobody'll do you nothing." I stepped carefully behind her, carrying her purse, feeling of little use. The suitcase was too big for a five-day stay, but it was the smallest piece of luggage either of us owned. We stood on the sidewalk waiting for a jitney to wave down. One finally stopped and Myraleen sped off in the back of some enterprising man's automobile.

This would be my first time alone, even for a week. I stroked the binding of an unread volume on the bookshelf and tipped it toward the crook of my thumb. Though the Sunday-afternoon half-light endured outside, I crawled into bed. In Nadir plopping onto a mattress during the day was thought to be an indulgence suitable only for the just lazy or near dead. If Myraleen were here, she would have had a fit of frenzied concern and asked a dozen "are-you-all-right's?" The recent past ran its fingernails across her nerves every time I got tired or blew my nose. For me, my "sick spell" had been a revelation. It had shown me that a door I assumed to be distant and unpredictable was close and amenable. I could draw the line of intolerability wherever I chose to, whether it was despair or a toothache. In Nadir, I had been expected to keep going toward what I couldn't imagine. Death, I suppose. But why a slow crawl instead of a decisive leap? Some people believed a person's life belonged to God. Whoever might own the deed to my existence the burden of it had been all mine. Now I knew I could lay that burden down anytime I wanted to and give it back.

I rolled over to Myraleen's side, then back to my own side, then back to hers. I hadn't done that since I was three and Mudear had said, "Quit playing in that bed before I beat your tail."

The sky was pouty and gray with cold air, but I kept a window open. A bright white tumbleweed cloud wheeled fast past the others. Dinnertime arrived purely by my own whim at nine in the evening. Everything flowed from one skillet where I poured batter for pancakes and fried bacon and eggs. I reached for the book again and my eyes glided through it until the meaning of paragraphs drifted from my mind as I read them. Then I turned out the light.

BEFORE LEAVING for work the next morning, I turned on the radio, twisting the knob back and forth until I came to a volume just high enough to be heard if someone stuck his head to the door. I didn't feel as secure without Myraleen and wanted to scare away the invisible bad people I'd heard about who skulked down the city streets.

Ten hours later I stepped off an evening bus, careful not to fall, hugging a too-big bag of groceries. Streetlights poked through the darkness, and as I approached my building, I could see a figure sitting on the steps. Someone was waiting for someone. Some tenant's boyfriend too afraid of Mrs. Wells to even stand outside his girl's apartment door. Closer, it looked like a white man—a housewares salesman or a bill collector. He had Kellner's long thin height and bread-crust hair. The man sitting there was just a pleasant thought of someone else until I raised my foot to climb the first step and looked in his face. He stood up. I almost fell back. The grocery bag rocked and the loaf of bread tumbled out. His mouth opened partly, giving a small gasp that echoed my own shock. His first words were "I'm sorry." He bent over to retrieve the bread. "I know this is a . . . horrible surprise."

"How?" That was all I could say, one word that seemed to remain in the air and drop away as we stood looking at each other. He reached out and for a second I thought he intended to wrap his arms around me. But instead he took the bag. I led him to the kitchenette, unmindful of Mrs. Wells. When we were upstairs, he said, "I know seeing me so out-of-place must be odd." He brought two fingers to his temple as if trying to give his brain help in explaining. "They let me out so that Germany would give back an important prisoner of the American side. I was sent to New York to catch a boat to Europe."

I nodded, barely hearing through the fog of disbelief.

"And I slipped away. I'm going back but first I had to say something to you." He looked down for a second. Our eyes came together and shifted apart and came together again. "I did not mean to disrespect you. I greatly misunderstood."

"Misunderstood how?"

"I thought you were interested in me—aside from as your tutor."

I didn't, couldn't say anything. Someone who was supposed to remain forever only a thought stood right in front of me and seemed to ask me to reveal things that were supposed to remain forever known only to me.

"I know I'm putting you into a dangerous spot with police," he said. "It is just that . . . if I insulted you, I am so very sorry. Now I should leave." He clasped my hand gently and then turned toward the door.

"No!" I said, feeling as if I'd stumbled down a flight of stairs and awoken during a sleep walk. "You came all this way. Don't go." I placed my hand on his arm and led him to the table. "At least sit down. Rest your feet. We call talk a while."

He didn't sit, which would have been a small relief to me. He stood there, a hundred and sixty pounds or so of life I couldn't fit anywhere.

"How did you get here?"

My question didn't interrupt his consuming stare. *"Windhund,"* he said softly and then he blinked. "Excuse me. I mean Grey . . . dog."

"Greyhound?"

"Yes."

"You must be hungry. I'll fix you dinner."

I walked four steps to the icebox and he followed.

"If you make dinner, I will help you. What can I do?" He stepped closer.

A green net bag containing three potatoes sat on top of the icebox. I reached and grabbed it—setting the hard balls into motion swinging inside the bag—almost hitting myself in the chin. "You can peel these," I told him, though I had no idea what for.

I felt as if I'd suddenly gone from being anonymous to being on a brightly lit stage. Every movement now felt amplified and scrutinized, not by Kellner, but by some great, glaring and disapproving audience in my mind. I dangled in the spotlight of an inexpressible fear.

He reached, I thought, for the bag, but grabbed my waist instead and pulled me to him. Three thuds pounded next to our feet as the potatoes hit the floor. He wrapped his arms around me and the gentle pressure of his hands was like life turned kind and accepting and pulling me toward it. My hands fell to the back of his shoulders. They lay there limply, afraid to move even when he hugged me closer.

"I cannot explain," he said in a low voice into my ear, "why I am here in a way to make it sensible. Because it is not."

He let me go then and bent over to pick up the potatoes.

A lady on the radio was singing an aria.

"You like opera?" he asked.

"No, I just use it to scare burglars away."

I got busy. Noise and motion becoming my refuge. Hopping from a boiling pot to a sizzling skillet and back and forth between table and stove created a circle of normality in a desperately odd situation. Here I was in the present cooking for a man with whom I shared a brief but secret past. We weren't supposed to kiss that day and he wasn't supposed to be here now. Nothing with Kellner had been as it was supposed to be.

Movement pushed away words, those we had already spoken and those we hadn't.

Together we composed a dinner of meat loaf, greens, and biscuits from a can and potatoes from the floor. I felt clumsy, feared that he thought I wasn't a competent cook. Perhaps that's why he helped—I had never heard of a man helping a woman cook before. But probably he was as nervous as I and wanted something to do with his hands.

We ate slowly—he, picking up each utensil delicately, chewing politely. I didn't taste anything. "You always were like an unrescued princess," he said. "I saw you sometimes when I did my work walking on the roadway to the farm, small, and brave, and alone."

"Brave, oh no. Me? I'd run a mile to get away from my own shadow."

"No, I am not talking about that sort of bravery. It's that you endure so and still remain so human."

"What choice do I have?"

"You could be not human, you could be hard. To be such a feeling person when so much of what is around you to feel is bad, that must be like being buried alive."

What had been true in Nadir was true here. Kellner's voice, though funneled through a foreign accent, was the clearest thing I'd ever heard.

"It bothered me that I could not do anything. Also it bothered me that I wanted to do anything at all," he said.

Then silence draped itself over us. I thought people talked honestly like this only on their deathbeds. Did he want me to say something?

"You see, you were a stranger in a foreign place, a country not like, for example, England, but very foreign—like the moon."

Before race was the elephant in the room we had ignored, but in ignoring it, it just became bigger and bigger. "And I'm colored."

He put down his fork, his eyes perfectly level with mine. "No, it was not mostly that you were 'colored.' I was in a place I didn't want to be, didn't belong. Added to this, I had come to entertain feelings for a woman that I was never meant to know. My mother did not teach me to stay away from one sort of person or another. But I know who is like me and who is not. Never have I had a friend who was different or who did not come from a good family . . ." He sharply inhaled. "Not that you don't come from a good family, this is not what I mean."

He shook his head when I said, "You mean money?" Into my mind jumped a cartoon picture of a bunch of Germans standing on bags of money.

"Not only money. I mean that never did I have a Jew for a friend or anyone too removed from my family's position.

"It is strange to me that American whites feel superior to anyone. To say the truth, they are only failed Europeans. America, I thought, would be where undistinguished people from all over could come, and where no one would be given any trouble. I see it is not that way."

I shook my head. "I don't think it's that way anywhere."

He shifted in his chair and leaned over his plate. "I am your enemy," he said. "In more than one way. It would be ordinary for you to hate me."

"No. You've been a friend to me."

"You let me kiss you that day, but we never had a chance to talk after that." He put down his fork. "Do you care for me?"

He sat there still, solemn, waiting as if the world's continued existence depended upon my answer. Now I understood why people in Nadir reserved all declarations of love for Jesus. Anchored to earth, love could be terrifying.

MYRALEEN

. . . a parting look . . .

NOW I WAS AN ORPHAN FREE AND CLEAR. A HEART ATTACK, from what the undertaker said. "Or something like that." In Nadir, these things weren't exactly exact. When Daddy hadn't been seen in a couple of days, a neighbor man went to check on him. Seemed he'd gone to bed one night and never saw morning, just like Mercy. Five years to the day she died, Mr. Hadley found Daddy.

"You've heard of hard-knot sinners," Reverend Matthews said. "Well, Luther Chadham was a hard-knot Christian. And he remained tied to the Lord as our Jesus led him into heaven."

At first I'd been alone in the front pew, but then Miz Herdie scooted, soft as a cat, beside me and Mrs. Mayfield came to sit on the other side. They might as well have heard my thoughts and felt sorry for me. The last of the Chadhams, I'd been thinking. Or as the left-behind old folks would put it, the last button of Gabrielle's coat.

On the way into the church, I'd gotten a good surprise and a bad one. I looked and there were Willamae's children: Vivian, Charles, Herman, Elbert and Leatrice coming up the new pavement in three rows. All were grown now and they walked toward me like the march of time. Amos and Louise had headed North to a steel plant. They'd all bettered their mother, who'd passed away suddenly just a month before.

Miz Herdie twisted her head around as boldly as her age let her be to see who else showed up. Her eyes followed the full pews but got stuck somewhere in a corner. I turned to see what she was looking at and noticed only a couple of boys in suits they hadn't grown into. "Well, do Jesus," she whispered to herself.

Time came for everyone to take a parting look at Daddy. I noticed in the circle weaving toward the casket there was a lady I'd never seen before. The two boys—about twelve and thirteen with bullet-shaped heads—following behind her had caught Miz Herdie's eye. Couldn't name them. Nadir had grown a new crop of babies, as if the war had somehow made men and women crazed and feverish for each other.

When it was my turn to pass by, people probably expected me to fall out, in front of the casket, the main most popular falling out location at a Nadir funeral. The second was the grave site. I'd disappoint them both times. The face I saw was a grayish brown mask of my father's real face. I'd dealt with the death on the bus, swallowed the hard thing down and felt my stomach turn, then accepted it.

Folks came to Miz Herdie's afterwards. There were church people and random relatives from Jackson and Biloxi. I give them all the same plain smile and respectful nod: cousin this one and great-uncle that one and some fool who said he was a second cousin once removed. Ma, Pa, and Grandma: that I understand. But what in the world was a second cousin once removed? Shouldn't the very fact that he's a second cousin hint that he's already pretty removed?

Women, kin and not, brought bails of corn bread and bread pudding and gallons of greens to be squeezed onto a crowded table. Mrs. Mayfield brought two sweet-potato pies and whispered for me to make sure I wrapped one up and took it home. I promised to spend some time with her before I left. "You can tell me all of Lily-Flower's secrets," she said, hugging my waist, trying to squeeze a cackle out of me. We both knew Lilian never did anything you couldn't do in church.

The men wanted to know, "How is it up there?" and pressed me for stories about Philadelphia. After, the last of the folks sidestepped out the door calling soon-to-be-forgotten forget-me-nots—"Don't be a stranger, Myraleen." But wasn't I always, I thought.

Miz Herdie reached for her apron and then started ladling the left-over food from pots and pans into bowls to be capped with plates and stored in the icebox. By and by, she'd return any cookware that didn't belong to her.

I tried to make myself useful and she said, "Gal, you better get you an apron. You gonna mess up your pretty Philadelphia dress. And I know you paid too much for dat."

My arms reached around my waist to make a big, sloppy bow with the apron strings. Something kept rolling over in my mind, and I couldn't get rid of it.

"Well, are you gonna wash that plate or rock it to sleep?" Miz Herdie said. She stepped back and gave me a long stare.

"Philadelphia ain't done you no harm. You lookin just fine. But don't seem like you gonna find yourself a husband," she said.

"I'm not looking for one, Miz Herdie."

She nodded. "Yeah, you got real good sense. Only a few decent men get born and now they tryin to kill *dem* off in dis war. Anyways, worth-a-damn ones always did seem to die fore the rest. They say a good man is hard to find, guess it's true—unless you got a hard-working shovel."

Sometime during the middle of the night, I sat up straight in bed.

In Daddy's room, I plowed through the top drawer of his nice and neat dresser, roughing up well-folded shirts and dignified ties. Then I went through the next drawer and the next. I remembered seeing an important-looking sheet of paper somewhere in that room when I was too little to read. Mercy had snatched it and when I asked what the letters said, she barked, "Tight-eye folks' language for none of your business!"

Underneath the rolled black and brown socks of the last one, I touched a piece of paper that had the thick feel of linen. I pulled it out and saw "Final Decree." It was my divorce from Mr. Cheevers. My eyes narrowed and I ripped it up. There was never any real marriage to that weasel, and there never needed to be any divorce. Nothing ever happened but some Mercy-whipped-up craziness.

I went through all the drawers. In the bottom one, I found another square of paper that felt as rich as money. It too said "Final Decree," but was the "marital dissolution of Mercy Annazette Turner from Watt Abraham Turner."

I just held it for a while, reading it over and over. Is this what drove Mercy crazy? Did she try to marry me off because that's what happened to her? Or maybe that wasn't exactly what happened to her. Maybe she had been trying to keep whatever that was from happening to me.

Scattered underneath were envelopes addressed in childish markings. "Dear Daddy," one letter read. "How are you? I am fine. For Christmas I would please like a spinning top . . ." All were to "Daddy"; and they weren't from me. At the bottoms were either the scratchy printing or the boxy cursive, depending upon the year, of a Herbert or Edward Chadham.

My memory shot back twenty years or so. Even when Daddy wasn't working, he wasn't home much. But that had always made sense, considering what was at home.

Those visions of evil and carrying on that Mercy was having had to do with Daddy and maybe even some jackass named Watt. I folded my arms and said to no one in particular, "Disgustin!"

It was terrible with Daddy freshly dead, but the word *bastard* crept into my mind. And I wasn't thinking about that Herbert and Edward, either.

All the time, Mercy and Luther Chadham had been in costume, I guess. If they liked playing make-believe, why didn't they make believe they were nicer folks? Then I would have had parents instead of people who tried to pimp me off on some tail-sniffing weasel when I was thirteen.

But I refused to feel ashamed. All this crap didn't have anything directly to do with me; I knew who I was. I'd just never known who they were, that's all.

Soon after daylight, I headed for Miz Herdie's.

"So you found out bout dem boys," she said. "Ump, ump, ump, your daddy and women in Gulfport. He was wrapped up in dose women like a knittin needle in a ball of wool. That man put a lotta money in the hairy banks of Gulfport."

Hairy banks? I had to think about that one for a second.

"Mercy was mad about it, but what could she do? Had a truce. He didn't say much about her shortcomings—and you sho know they could make a long, long list—and she wouldn't raise a lot of sand about his.

"She was seconds when she married your daddy. Did you know that, too?"

I nodded.

"She was young and goin over fool's mountain. Married a man named Watt from Hattiesburg. Nothin but a goodtimer, and he had the best times when he was beatin her upside the head. Good you know all dat now," she said. "You lucky. Most folks take dey licks in life and don't even know where de licks be really comin from."

A NOT-LONG married couple from church said they'd rent the house. I gave the clothes to Reverend Matthews to dole out to the poor. That still left mountains to sort through. Mrs. Mayfield showed up at the door faithfully each day after she got off from the diner. Between us we whittled at the job till we won.

All of it seemed good and finished when I rolled out of Nadir on that northbound Greyhound. From Hattiesburg to Cincinnati, I slept like a drunkard. By Pittsburgh sleep slipped away and left me thinking . . . Damn. Being born into this world was like walking along minding your own business when a big hand comes out of nowhere and drags you into a barroom like in the one in the Western picture shows. People you don't know, don't want to know, are cussing and punching and spitting. Women are dancing on tables. Gold coins are flying through the air. You get roughed up and patted on the back, kissed in the mouth and kicked in the ass. Then just as suddenly as it all began, you get flung out into the yonder and back into your own business.

LILIAN

. . . not unpleasurable . . .

FEAR IS THE DRAGON THAT PATROLS THE GATES OF PARADISE—
and it is the beast that guards the gates to hell. Which threshold was I on
exactly—both? Standing in that tiny kitchen part of the kitchenette, I
weighed the possibility of ruination against the probability of desola-
tion. If I opened myself to this man, I might regret it. If I didn't, I knew
that I would.

Nadir women used to say, "All any man really wants is for you to
raise yo' dress and drop yo' drawers." Would this man have gone to so
much trouble for that?

I felt his hand on the small of my back as I filled the sink with soapy
water for the dishes. "Truly, I can help," he said. "I once had kitchen
duty at sea." He whispered into my neck the promise, "I can wash well
and not break a dish."

Surely, German women have dresses to raise and drawers to drop.
Why didn't he go home, when he was allowed, to more familiar rations?

Something about the feel of warm water always calmed me. Beneath
the suds we reached for the same pan and his palm slid against the back
of my hand. I surrendered the handle and moved toward a plate. I could
have told him, "You dry, I'll wash," but I didn't. And my exacting mind

would not let me push that fact into its far corners. Awareness of my own pleasure in the sliding touches of our skin and the inevitable soft collisions of our bodies in this small space made me feel a hot shame, not unpleasurable in itself.

When we settled back at the table, we were different from when we'd sat there before. My back was no longer politely straight in my chair or my knees glued together beneath it. I stretched myself out, my back sliding diagonally across the corner of the seat, legs at ease and slightly parted as if I were lounging on the porch steps on a feverish Nadir night. He swung his chair around the corner of the table so that he was within reaching distance to my left.

A rare sense of mischief tugged at me. "My friend Myraleen, she's the one I live with here. But she's gone home because her father passed away."

"Oh, this is too bad."

I told him Myraleen said Germans shouldn't call their women 'frau' because it sounds like a woman who wears saggy dresses and has frighteningly big feet.

He laughed. " Ah, tell your friend Americans speak as if they are forever yawning."

"Oh," I said, waving a lazy hand. "That's just Mississippi."

"I have been to New York. They have honking-horn voices. I think each area of your republic is marked by a different speech impediment."

"So you think I sound funny, too?" Indignation allows the intimacy of confrontation, and I knew I was really saying, "What do you think of me? Tell me that you . . ."

"I like the way you speak."

"It's not that different from the way other people in Nadir sound."

"Does not matter. I simply like to hear your voice." He closed his eyes, sensing he'd made a mistake.

But about what?

"I don't want you to think that I am not honest. Or that I'm a man who says easy words to get easy results."

"No, I don't think that." My feet pressed the floor, pulling my chair closer to his. "But then again it's not hard to fool me." I shrugged. "I don't get around much."

We talked and talked until his accent flattened into familiarity and sounded like no accent at all. We did not want to stop, ever. But it got later and he offered to go. "Where?" I said. Eventually he'd have to turn himself in to authorities, and things would proceed as intended. "Not tonight. The government buildings are closed."

THERE WAS no couch for him to sleep on, and I apologized for the apartment's lack of furniture. With blankets and sheets, we made him a pallet beside the bed.

After I lay down, I felt a bit of remorse and scooted over to peer down at him. "You couldn't be comfortable down there."

"If I were to say I am not comfortable, then what would we do?"

"I could give you another pillow." I was too scared to offer more. "That's all right."

The disappointment in his voice tugged at me and I went down to him and, for what must have been an hour, we talked.

At seven before I left for work, I stooped to wake him and made him promise he'd remain another day. "When you get up, make yourself at home. Food's in the icebox. I've got books." I whispered these things as if they were carnal secrets. "And if you turn on the radio, maybe that no-singing lady'll scream another song." He blinked, reached up and put his hand around the back of my neck, smiled into my eyes—and I left.

That I loved him seemed simple; yet, I spent the morning worrying about the logistics. *Where do you get them?* Myraleen had told me about them, but not where to get them. She probably never imagined I'd need to know. "Something bothering you?" Honey asked. I'd almost splashed her, and though we got wet anyway, I'd soberly said I was sorry.

Quickly, before I lost my nerve, out of my mouth came the hardest thing I ever had to ask. I knew for the second time in hours what it was to surrender to blind trust.

When I asked, her dimples deepened as she laughed. "The way you looked, I thought you about to tell me somebody died. Girl, just tell your man to go to a drugstore and say, pack of Trojans. They're behind the counter. If he doesn't know that, he must be as shy as you. Good thing, though. You need the sweet type."

Last night when we'd spoken about it, he'd said, "I could stop in time, but that often does not work. I'm a doctor; I've seen things."

I'd seen things too, I thought and told him I'd get something.

Before I went to the drugstore, I picked up a bag of groceries. I didn't need to, but I didn't want the clerk to think all I ever bought were rubbers. I got off the bus two stops early and walked into a colored-owned apothecary. I set the heavy grocery bag on the counter, and the man behind it could see only the top half of my face. The bag walled off the bottom. "Pack of Trojans . . . please."

He craned his neck over my bag and said, "What? I didn't hear you."

WHEN I UNLOCKED the door, Kellner was sitting on the apartment's only stuffed chair, reading *Native Son*. He'd set the table. The spaces between utensils, plates and glasses appeared precise and consistent to the millimeter, almost as if he had used a ruler. He'd made the bed so tightly it seemed like the mattress was struggling to get out.

After dinner, we sat on the side of the bed, forearms interlocked, holding hands. He'd told me about his U-boat, how his friend died, how he was captured. He'd told me about his mother, his father, his sister, and all the stories of his life he thought I'd want to know. He planned to leave early in the morning and present himself at the downtown office of the Federal Bureau of Investigation. They'd ship him home, he said.

"Every day here is more risk for you."

"Believe me. No one's going to search for anyone here. You could stay until 1999."

"You cannot choose the rules you do not like and not obey them."

"But I have."

He stroked my cheek with the back of his hand. His lips moved over my forehead, softly kissing again and again as if bestowing a blessing and an apology. I was relieved when he got to my lips. He tugged the tail of my blouse from the waist of my skirt. I desperately hoped his hands would reach my breasts. They did, looping a finger into a brassiere strap to pull it down, fulfilling the first part of a long secret wish list. In Nadir, I'd hated the need to be touched like this. It felt like a bright awareness born in a coffin.

Now resurrected, it was roaring and reckless and wanting. When I'd imagined being with a man, it was as artful as a ballet and as light as oxygen. Of course, it actually was air I'd been with during those drowsy mornings in bed with my imagination. Now a real person, whose body was a shock and a solace to mine, occupied that space and moved against me, and into me. When we'd fulfilled almost the last of my secret aspirations, he hugged me to his chest, which was wet and felt tender that way. With his finger, he lifted my chin and parted my lips with his tongue, which pressed in deep as if it were searching for something final. I closed my eyes and sank into a state of peace in which I had no argument with the world and couldn't remember that I ever had.

Fatigue and sleepiness, wrought by a great adventure, hummed a drunken lullaby in my head. He started again, touching and pressing and penetrating. Those feelings rose again, this time stronger. They were giving all and taking all. They were crying and screaming. I put my hand over my mouth when I saw it was I who was screaming and shaking and ascending to a place where the greatest ache is met by the most generous resolution.

After the quake, silence. I curled up against him. "Are you . . . happy?" he asked.

"I could fly."

We gave up sleep and used the time to touch in every way we knew how. In bed together we'd wrapped our naked selves around each other like piebald stripes on a candy cane.

Early, we sat and waited the way people wait at a wake. He'd said six o'clock; he'd leave then. Ten minutes remained. Both of us were tired.

He sat on the other side of the table, looked at me with more longing, more apologies and more love. Then he reached out with an open palm. My fingers, knuckles and wrist burrowed into the cave his hand made. But there came a moment when my shelter moved away. He rose, walked over and motioned for me to stand and walk him to the door.

On the way, I stopped at the closet to get his coat. At the door, I tugged at the sides of the heavy black wrap to help him put it on, as much a subterfuge to run my hands across his shoulders as an act of politeness.

Suddenly, we were both wrapped in his coat and wrapped in each other. My robe fell to the floor and he said, "You are destroying my belief in punctuality."

He said, "After the war, I'll take you where I live, and you'll see how beautiful it is."

He said this as if it were actually a promise he could keep.

Before he walked out the door, I gave him a piece of paper with two telephone numbers. "When you can, leave a message for me," I said. I went to the window. He appeared at the bottom step and turned to wave before he walked onto the street. How had he known I'd be watching? My eyes followed him north and set his tall figure against the cement at his feet and the row houses at his head. Photographing him again and again to make him permanent. I did not know the moment when he disappeared and I was watching only the sidewalk.

MYRALEEN

. . . an ugly attitude . . .

"So you've got brothers then," Lilian said after I'd told her about all that buried mess back in Nadir. "Are you going to get in touch with them?"

She'd met me as soon as the jitney swung up to the curb, those big eyes of hers wide with well meaning. "So nobody packed you in a sack and stole off with you?" I had said, while the driver pulled my suitcase from his trunk.

"Guess nobody wanted me." She looked different; must have been relaxing not to have me and my mouth around.

"I don't have brothers; I have me," I told her. "And that right now is all I can handle."

I wasn't about to try to slap icing over my father's mess. "What happened is not the boys' fault, Myraleen. Somebody once said, 'There are no illegitimate children, only illegitimate parents.' It's not anything against those young'uns. It could have been the other way around and I was born outside the marriage bed and them born inside. It would still be the same. I'd still just have me. It's always been that way. Mercy and Luther were pretty il-legitimate, married or not."

"They still were your mother and father."

"I don't care whose mother and father they were. When people show their asses, I'm not about to break out into applause, kinfolks or not."

"Well, you've got friends. Me and August haven't showed our butts yet."

"And you bet' not."

"Yes, ma'am."

I dragged the suitcase into the closet, glad to be retiring it. "Guess Philadelphia is really home now," I said over my shoulder.

Being back at L. L. Dunham's on Monday eased my mind away from Nadir and Daddy. Work, it turned out, could be good for something other than money. I folded two undone cashmere sweaters and, with August in mind, tried to figure out whether I could afford to buy one with help from my employee discount. Nope.

Suddenly, a voice that sounded as if it had echoed all the way from Nadir drew my eyes away from the cashmere. "Dah-lin, can you help me?" Beside me stood a white woman who could have passed for, of all people, Red Briggs in a bobbed hairdo. Behind his mother stood the real Red Briggs in an Army uniform. His ugly, little rabbit eyes swelled in recognition, then narrowed in hate. "Where y'all keep y'all's perfume?" she said. He kept staring, saying nothing. I pointed her down the aisle and he followed. He turned around for a second to give me one last hard look. My stomach felt sick.

For lunch I ate nothing, just sat on the cold park bench where August used to meet me. Oh, that boy got better things to think about, I thought. "You're not doing anything wrong," I remembered August saying.

But when I returned to the floor and saw Red Briggs getting off the elevator, I knew that was that. I walked behind a cash register and faked sorting through some receipts. He walked straight over to me, though. "I told on you," he said. "Shoulda known you ain't had no business working here." His voice was ugly as if at first he intended to spit but spewed some spitty words instead. "I thought about it to myself, you know, and I said something ain't right. So I go up to the boss lady and . . ."

My eyes tore into his hard enough to blind him. But I smiled and used a nicey-nice tone as if giving tips about what gift he should buy for his girl. I spoke low enough that his head leaned over toward mine to hear. "Listen. You are going to die, Red Briggs. Boy, you're too damn stupid to make it cross a field of gopher holes. How you going to make it through anybody's war? Only thing keeps a fool's heart beating is luck. And the dirt you did just ended your luck. So mark my words with your last breath. You're going to *die*, you rattlesnake son-of-a bitch." Naturally, I didn't have a flint of knowledge about whether he'd get through the war. But he would die one day. Everybody did. Right then that was the only thing I was grateful for.

He took a couple of steps back. "See there, what'd I tell you? Black wench, you always did have an ugly attitude."

LILIAN

. . . sorry for me. Sorry for you . . .

IT ALL STARTED WITH MYRALEEN FLYING IN THE DOOR, TELL-
ing me she'd been called up to the office and let go. "They found out,"
she said.

I had only been home a few minutes myself and figured something
was wrong when I heard her key turn two hours early.

"How?"

She told me how she was working when poof! Red Briggs suddenly
appeared with his mother as if by evil magic. "I bought a Greyhound
ticket back home," she said.

"What in the world would he be doing in Pennsylvania?" I couldn't
imagine Red Briggs out of Mississippi any more than I could imagine
the Taylors' goat CoCo standing before the Philadelphia Philharmonic
with a baton, conducting Beethoven's Fifth Symphony. Suddenly,
everyone was in motion.

"Visiting his mama, I guess." She pulled her suitcase, which hardly
had a day of rest, out of the closet. With sharp clicks its mouth opened
wide in the middle of the floor. She started collecting beads and hair
clasps from the top drawer and dropping them into a satin suitcase

pocket. "People will ruin you if you let them!" She jerked the drawer out of the cabinet and emptied everything on the bed. "So you can't god-damn let 'em!"

"But, Myraleen, this all doesn't mean you have to go."

"If it's one thing Mercy and Daddy did, it's left me a house and a snatch of land. I know it'll be awhile before you can make the rent by yourself. So I'll send you my part every month. Got some money in Nadir National."

To Myraleen, making rent was comparable to being right with God.

"That's not what I'm talking about . . ."

She kept flying around grabbing things and flinging them into the suitcase as if she were having a fistfight with the air. It occurred to me that whether she left or not, she needed to go through the motions.

"I'm going," Myraleen said.

She had marched to the downtown terminal from L. L. Dunham to buy a ticket back to Nadir. Then she'd been too hopping mad to wait at a bus stop and had walked twenty blocks home. Soon her fuming and running caught up with her, and she plopped down in a dining chair. I put dinner on the table and we ate but didn't say much. The suitcase, with its various lumps of clothing and scattered belongings, still stood gaping in the middle of the floor when Myraleen crawled into bed. About an hour later a voice in the darkness woke me.

"Lilian? Lilian?" Her voice sounded soft and thin the way it did when she was a little girl fretting under the willow tree. "Why do people have to be that way? You read a lot. Why?"

"Myraleen, I could read all the books on earth, and I wouldn't un-derstand what makes people the way they are. All I know is that I'm so sorry about it. Sorry for me. Sorry for you."

That Saturday we were downtown to cash in her bus ticket. She planned to buy a dress with the money for the next time she went out with August—but not at L. L. Dunham's. When we passed the store's rambling glass windows that sealed in the Dunham mannequins, all bearing unwelcoming expressions on their faces, we walked faster. Just after we'd passed, we heard someone call "Myra!" We turned around to see a white girl running to catch up.

"This is Miss Eisen," Myraleen said.

"Doris," the girl said shaking my hand before turning back to Myraleen. "I wanted to tell you that I think they're heels. You poor kid. What difference should it make? Of course, they barely tolerate *me*. You find work yet?"

Myraleen shook her head. The girl's words sprayed from her mouth as if shot from a machine gun.

"What are you doing down here, just a little shopping, a little time killing? Let's go someplace and have a sandwich. I've got an idea."

Next thing, I saw a sign that said SID'S PLACE. When we walked in, I trailed behind Myraleen and her surprise friend. The man nodded hello to Doris and smiled at Myraleen, then stared at me as if I was an interruption in the flow of normal humanity.

"Get your eyes back in your head, Sid," Doris said. "They look better there."

We squeezed into a booth with red-cushioned seats and a wooden table scarred with cigarette burns. "When I heard about you, I said, I'll be a monkey's uncle. I knew there was something about you that I couldn't put my finger on. But secrets are A-OK. Knowledge is power. Anybody who tells everything—a woman especially—is a goofball. My secret was that I wasn't a virgin, but then I found out that wasn't a secret."

Myraleen and I just looked at her, speechless.

"Now your being a Negro . . ." She laughed. "That's a helluva secret. I have had a couple of doozies, but never one like that. Why, I almost got jealous when I heard. Most of the real goofs I've met wouldn't have had anything to do with me had I been a Negro. I could have saved a lot of time. Hell, I might just say that in a pinch."

Myraleen and I looked at each other. I couldn't tell whether I hated this shotgun-mouthed woman or kind of liked her.

"My sister Katie worked behind the counter at Rexall, and then she joined the WACs, you know, the ladies' part of the army. She's making more money and having a better time.

"Where did you girls say you were from? . . . I bet the folks back in Naked would stand up and salute if two local gals jumped aboard Uncle Sam's Army! And they take colored and white alike because the government said they'd better."

I felt the nudge of something familiar when this strange woman spoke. But I couldn't identify it.

Myraleen wore a barren smile of tolerance the half hour we were there, the sort the civilized flex at the insane. No matter how much Doris talked, Myraleen wasn't going to be any more than polite to this white woman. After we'd finished our Pepsi-Colas, she apologized and said we needed to go, while we still had time, before the stores closed. Outside, Myraleen's face unfroze and her shoulders loosened up. Then who Doris Eisen reminded me of hit me. I certainly wasn't going to tell Myraleen, though. She was already irritated.

"Well, that's an idea," I said.

"What! Who wants to go fight in some ladies' army! Those men probably beat the shit out of them. Crazy-ass white women. Never had no sense, never will."

"They don't fight, Myraleen. They do secretarial work, so the men don't have to do those things, and they can go into combat."

"Where'd you hear that?"

"Magazine article."

"So they all huddled up in some room typing—tap, tap, tap. And the men out getting shot—bang, bang, bang. That's kind of funny. But naw, old fast-yapping Doris was just trying to make me feel better."

So the idea receded like the alphabet in a page of newspaper print and didn't reemerge until days later. Myraleen was considering a job at a shirt factory where both colored and white strained their eyes above industrial sewing machines and risked their fingers beneath the rapid-fire staccato stabs of needles. We sat at the kitchen table, working pencils against sheets of paper, figuring the difference between our incomes and expenses, finding little difference. I didn't find this troubling in the least. To me, money was what you stuffed into the greedy spokes of the world as bribery so it wouldn't run you over. If you had enough to keep catastrophe safely parked at the curb for the week, plus extra for snacks and even a dress, that rated a big grin. But Myraleen's people were accustomed to putting two dollars—exactly—in the bank every other payday. During the last few years in Nadir, she had saved a bit herself, but it disappeared with the trip out here, the first month's rent, and the Greyhounds back and forth for her daddy's funeral. She had deemed the few hundred dollars her parents left her as insulation against sickness and life-death emergencies. Several lines of brutal subtraction revealed the salary she would make at the textile plant—less than at L. L. Dunham's—would leave next to nothing for a bank account.

I put the pencils and paper away and Myraleen cleared the table to make dinner. As she opened the cabinets searching for the night's meal, she said, "Those girls . . . humm."

"What girls?"

"Those girls in that army. I bet they get to save a lot 'cause Uncle Sam pays for room and board, and they get their paychecks to boot." A look came over her face that was a cross between envy and lust. "Why they must have just one big old saving-money good time."

I'd known Myraleen long enough to recognize determination in her eyes, and it startled me. I thought things were going fine. The rent was paid. She'd found another job. I'd slid into the rhythm at Andover like a foot into a shoe. Maybe I was meant for the meatpacking business. Myraleen had a boyfriend who flew jets, though she came from a place where only a handful of people had experienced a train ride. And I'd had a, well . . . a phantom romance, more than I'd had before. We'd grown to tall cotton here and I, the one who'd always agitated for progress, now was afraid that one move further might be a step astray.

But downtown that next Saturday, Myraleen and I stood before a man in a dark olive uniform seated at a reception desk with a pyramid-shaped sign that said RECRUITING.

"Sir, can you tell us anything about the Women's Army Corps? Are they still looking for ladies?"

The man frowned, said, "Wait" and disappeared into a room down the hall. A colored man in a dark olive uniform came out.

"Can I help you?"

Myraleen repeated her query.

He, too, frowned and shook his head. "We don't deal with girls here. Go to the main post office, to the recruiting station there." He wrote down the address on a pad and tore it off. He shook his head again. "A good-looking woman like you," he said handing the paper to Myraleen. "What a waste." I thanked him, turned to leave and realized Myraleen was still standing there.

"What the hell do you mean by *that?*"

"If you don't know, you should."

"Look, fool, I don't know you and don't want to know you. So get out of my damn business. The only 'waste' is the time you took to get out of bed this morning just to act stupid all day long."

Feeling things could get uglier, I pulled at her arm. "Let's go now." As she turned to follow me, he said, "Might have known." The urge to whip back around and have the last word at the expense of his mother or something was so strong I could feel it in her arm. But she heeded my second "let's go" in consideration of how easily I became embarrassed.

At the post office we went into a room plastered with posters, most of which showed a proud-looking woman in uniform, with the caption:

FREE A MAN FOR COMBAT. We talked to a woman in a jacket similar to the one the men wore. Her skirt didn't quite match. She wore cat-eyed glasses and had yellow hair bobbed to the level of her earlobes. Questions rushed from her mouth as soon as she saw us. Did we have any children? How much education? Ever got in any trouble? All our answers seemed to please her.

We left with our purses turned into libraries of leaflets. I took the pamphlets out of politeness. I had no intention of leaving Philadelphia.

When we got home, we spread the shiny booklets out on the bedspread. Most, we discovered, were about the army in general: veterans' benefits and the like. Two focused on the WACs. An outdated one called them Women's Auxiliary Army Corps.

We tossed our shoes off and ended up reading perched on our elbows like bobby-soxers with bodies prone, legs swaying and stockinged feet wriggling in the air. "You're the one who said it was a good idea," Myraleen said.

"I said it was *an* idea."

"Don't get sassy with me. You know who'd win in a tongue-dueling contest, so you might as well just put that little toy gun back in the holster."

"You're the one wants to save money."

"And you're the one who's rich, huh?"

"I'm just not as concerned. But you're right to go, they'll give you an old-age pension and all of that."

"How are you going to pay the rent?"

"I'll move someplace cheaper."

"I'm not going if you're not."

"Then I guess you're not going."

She knocked her leg against mine. "Told you about sassin me. You just got here in the city and started thinking you're so suchamuch, huh?"

It was partly true. In the last week, I'd certainly developed a stronger sense of who I was. "I'm not crazy about getting involved in a war. Violence is no one's friend but its own, Myraleen."

"Look I don't need to hear all that philosophizing shit that be lolly-gagging in your mind. Nobody's talking about any violence. I'm talking money, girl! You're the one who said ladies don't have to fight. I'm just trying to fight to keep from going to the poorhouse."

"Myraleen, they'll send us where they want to and we'll end up goodness knows where."

"I didn't say that when I got on that Greyhound to come here with you."

"Aw, Myraleen," I said and gave in. I resumed reading with new dedication. I needed to know all I could about my future.

FOUR

MYRALEEN

. . . zigzag . . .

MERCY COULD HAVE INVENTED THIS ARMY. IT'S A LOT LIKE her: giving orders and making you follow them to a half teaspoon, and asking questions while looking suspicious. "Are you pregnant?" he asked. I couldn't believe it, though I was looking in his mouth when he said it.

We'd stood in a dozen different lines, with bunches of women, colored and white, all morning at the big Army base just outside town. So many people were calling us every which way that we got separated. I continued on by myself, filling out long forms, talking to different folks, and then getting in another line. The whole time, the army people acted just like Mercy, scared something might sneak by them. Why did I want to join, one asked. Lilian had told me they might ask this. I'd told her I'd just say what the poster says: I want to send a man into combat. "No," she said. "Say you want to *free* a man for combat. That's what the poster says." Okay, I'd said. "But, same thing."

In a small room, a woman in nurse's cap told me to undress and gave me a sheet to cover myself with. I stood there. To tell the truth, I'd never been to a doctor in my life. No reason. In Nadir people went to get examined only when something was wrong. "Hurry up," she said. She looked me up and down as if I were trying to hide something. If I'd known I'd have to go through all this mess to get into the army, I would have just taken the job sewing shirts. I'd never been naked in front of anybody since I was a baby. Even Lilian and I took turns dressing in the bathroom.

"Would you please ma'am turn around?"

A mean-looking white woman, her eyes almost flew up into her head. "You don't have anything I don't have. Do you?"

When I got down to my slip, I arranged the sheet over the front of me as I undid my underwear. She stood shaking her head. And I thought that beat all, but then that doctor in the next little room asked me if I was pregnant. By that point I felt like cussing them all out. I looked at him square in his white face and said, "I wasn't before I met you." He turned red and proceeded to do his silly examination, pounding here, peeping there. While that went on, the questions came. "Are your monthlies regular?" This was disgusting. Did I hurt here or there? I would have stayed home had I been aching or hobbling. On and on he yacked, asking things that were too personal or too stupid. Finally, I said. "No disrespect intended, but I feel fine. The kinds of problems you're asking about don't affect me. Unless a hurricane takes me away or something, I will be on this earth longer than I want to. The first day I get sick will be the day I die."

The doctor and nurse traded a quick look. "Well, young lady," he said. He spoke with a Texas drawl. A too-skinny man, about forty, with weak blue eyes, he'd probably been a sickly child who'd become bookish because he had to stay inside. Him, I'd give another ten years. "I was going to recommend that they reject you because I didn't appreciate your attitude. But now I see you're just feisty. Maybe you'll be good for the Army and it'll be good for you. Just remember that feistiness when you're aboard a transport ship and a German torpedo sideswipes it."

Nine months later we were in the middle of the Atlantic Ocean, somewhere between home and hell, on the deck of some big boat called the *Ile de France*. I leaned over the railing and looked at the water, frothy and rippling like a boiling pot of salt pork, only cold. "Are you going to be sick?" Lilian asked.

EEL DUH FRAHNS, I thought. Ump, ump, ump. A boat with a name that sounded like a death rattle. Yeah, that was a real comfort. Who's got time for all this old hincty mess, anyway? Wish I were back in Ile de Philadelphia.

The ship was zigzagging all the way overseas to outsmart torpedoes. What if those things can zigzag too? If the Germans have sense enough to make bombs that fly by themselves, surely they could throw together a torpedo that could zigzag up this ship's ass.

"Why do you keep looking down there?" Lilian asked.

Poor Lilian. Following me, she might get blown sky-high. What kind of mess had I gotten us into? I could just hear Mercy cackling at me in hell. "Stupid-ass," she'd say. "If you have to zigzag to get somewhere, you ain't got no business going."

LILIAN

. . . measurements of a dream . . .

AFTER WE JOINED THE ARMY, THE CLOCK COUNTING MY
lifetime ceased to have hands, grew feet instead and ran faster and faster.
More had happened to us in the past few months than in a decade in
Nadir. Only a couple of weeks stood between the time the postman
brought our notification letters and the day we deboarded a train in Iowa.

Fort Des Moines was a campus of short, light-hued look-alike buildings. Hundreds of military personnel—male and female—worked and
lived on the base. We moved from one building to another turning in
paperwork, eating lunch, and getting our clothes and supplies. Everything came in olive or khaki; underpants, the latter. "I can't believe they
tell you what drawers to wear," Myraleen said. "Mercy, if you could
have only been one of the boss ladies here, you would have been one
happy . . ." Then she muttered something.

Myraleen and I had been assigned to the same company because the
rarity of colored ones narrowed the possibilities to few. We hadn't known
it initially, but we could have easily been separated. The Army, not the
recruit, picked the training center. So for once segregation served to our
advantage.

Though we ate at the same mess hall as whites, all the colored girls lived in the same barrack. We bunked three to a room. I got matched with Ruth from Atlanta and Hazel from Chicago. Myraleen was down the hall with two other recruits.

Only one mirror served a big bathroom of a dozen stalls and showers. Little room and little time were allotted to primping. In the morning I took a quick first glance at myself in uniform: a khaki skirt, blouse and tie beneath an olive jacket and a round box, duck-billed hat. The curling iron curls blooming out both sides of my cap didn't offset what to me was an uncomfortably masculine look. And even with the scarcity of stockings among civilians, the ones I wore couldn't be given away on a busy city street corner. The thick gauzy and, of course, khaki nylons were too light for my skin and gave the appearance that I'd borrowed someone else's legs. Yet, outside, in formation with the other women, everything came together. Brown oxfords marched in tandem. Shoulders aligned with shoulders. All eyes aimed forward. The Army derived its strength from multiplicity and unity. Sergeant Gable's steel voice both reassured and intimidated. A honey-hued woman, barely taller than the five-foot minimum, she embodied precision. We were to do likewise. "Discipline," she preached. "Learn to discipline yourself for your own good, or others will discipline you for their own good."

Over the course of basic training, Myraleen stole my skepticism and beat it into regret. She'd merely wanted a job. This was an entire way of life, and she hadn't understood that until too late. The Army was new to women, especially colored ones. She talked less and when she did, her voice was subdued, filled with quiet, compact distress.

Only when we went into town by ourselves or with a group to the picture show or to the diner, did she recapture her old identity. A small colored population existed in Des Moines. Often people spoke and smiled at us as we walked downtown. Sometimes they'd stop to talk, shake our hands and say they were proud of us, and Myraleen would talk to them, nodding and smiling, showing more animation than she did on base. I think she valued any contact with civilized civilian life now that she'd gone and gotten herself signed up for some kind of khaki-colored jungle. Occasionally, someone passing by shot us a peculiar look or didn't speak when we spoke. "Hump," Myraleen would say. "Those must be the rich, hincty ones. I don't see why they don't dress the part, though."

I'd figured out the odd stares. But Myraleen was happy in town, and I didn't want to ruin it. One Sunday morning, in the mess hall at breakfast, Hazel said she'd passed a teenage boy in town who called out, "Hobbyhorse." She had cinnamon skin that darkened when she became angry. Shirley Temple curls lazed about her head, a counterpoint to her adamant carriage. On duty, she kept the curls pinned behind her ears.

"I said, 'I'll hobby your horse.' Then he said, 'A bull dyke, huh?' I said, 'the only bull dyke around here is your mama.'"

Ruth squirmed in her seat. She hated trouble.

A mask of realization went over Myraleen's face. "Lord, what I've gotten myself into!"

"Aw, girl, that ain't nothing," said Clarice, one of Myraleen's roommates, from Chicago like Hazel. "A couple of boys cross the street started that mess when they knew I was joining. And what did they do that for? 'Cause I got three brothers. They caught them in the alley and say, 'We hear you talking about our sister. That must mean y'all looked in the mirror and decided y'all had too many teeth. Y'all's cheap-ass daddy said, I ain't got no money for the dentist. Better start bad-mouthing Clarice. Them Smith boys'll take some out for free. So that's what we gonna do.' And they beat the shit outa 'em."

Ruth squirmed again. *"Shhh."* To the left of us began the large expanse of tables where a great multitude of white WACs ate.

All that talk of scandalous rumors and revenge distracted me from worries about starting to work in Sergeant Gable's office that next morning. Oh nine hundred, I knew where I had to be. I had better stand there looking prepared before the line-thin second hand on her government-issue watch sneaked so much as a half notch past the twelve.

I had said I could type because Mrs. Lewis taught me in tenth grade. She brought in her old Royal manual after school for the smarter girls to practice on. "Lilian, get that finger where it belongs before I cut it off," she'd say. By the end of the semester, my hands had jerked along at fifty words a minute, tapping at the speed of my own nervous tension as Mrs. Lewis glared above. I'd imagined the power of her eyes united in one straight hot beam, like a ray gun in a Flash Gordon picture, shooting through the part in my hair that separated my underbraids, scrutinizing each letter that hit the page.

Sergeant Gable placed a pile of handwritten notations on my desk, indicating the clothing sizes, from bra cup to waist measurement, for every woman at the training camp. Many in our company and the others hadn't found the right sizes in available clothing allotments. Next to it, she placed a stack of empty forms. "Transcribe the information onto the proper boxes on the forms," she said. That meant numbers mixed with letters, typing onto a lined format and deciphering reckless handwriting. I prepared to be hollered at.

The sergeant walked over a few times, but no threats of amputations. "That was rather fast," she said suspiciously when I finished. She checked it, nodded and brought more work. At the end of the day, she said, "Very good job, Private." As I walked back to the barracks, I repressed the urge to skip. Mudear had the habit of softly saying "Yeah" to express approval for a task. In Nadir that was praise aplenty. Most folks mustered recognition only for mistakes, and depending upon the age of the offender, rewarded the oversight with a smack or a curse.

When I saw Myraleen, she scrunched up her nose, wriggled her fingers mockingly in the air and shook her hips to match the rhythm of her hands. This was a demonstration of what an easy trifling assignment typing constituted compared to her own kitchen police duty. Sergeant Gable had said that was a good place for her until "we can find something you're competent at besides rolling your eyes."

Each day I liked the Army more and more and felt guilty because Myraleen liked it less and less. In my mind, the war had shifted from suspect to essential.

On the cold, cold day before I left Philadelphia, I'd scurried about downtown tackling last minute errands in a frenzy. Abruptly, a gloved hand shoved a leaflet in my path. A dark-haired man in his early twenties stood to my left shivering and passing out flyers. His face was so red it looked sunburned. Bits of ice hung from his mustache.

I read it standing in line at the post office to get a box mailed. In big thick letters the heading said: DON'T LET NAZI HATRED TRIUMPH. In the right-hand corner: a sketch of the German chancellor, his face contorted in a brutal scowl that made him look capable of throwing the switch to rev up a million whipping machines. Beneath him, the paragraphs made claims of false imprisonment of millions, mass murders of children, loss of basic rights and on and on. People in the city were always handing out papers filled with various flavors of hysteria—Communists, anti-Communists, doomsayers, whoever felt the need for quick public attention. Mudear used to say: "Get your news from a newspaper. Don't just hitch a ride on somebody's wagging tongue." Leafleteers were just tongue waggers with mimeograph machines. Then it was my turn in line. I scooted my package onto the counter, a couple of flowered housedresses for Mudear from Woolworth's, which had no store in Nadir. "I've heard about that Woolworth's," Mudear had written. "I've wanted something from that place all my life."

I passed the man on the way back to the bus stop. He cocked his head in recognition like a hopeful puppy. Oddly, I stopped. "Where do you get your information?"

His ice-white lips crept into a smile. "You read it? Most people just throw it away."

Trying to put it politely, I asked how he knew these things were true.

"We get our information through refugee groups in Europe and letters sneaked out of Germany and occupied countries. The Nazis would kill off most of the world, if they had their way. They think your people are animals."

I felt a mixture of anger and embarrassment. "So, they think that here."

He lowered his head in thought, almost as if he were praying. He looked at me again. "You see, I know. But the Nazis go from hate to kill. Here they mostly go from hate to more hate."

THE QUESTION of whether my work at Des Moines actually boosted the war effort appeared as unclear as fog. Sergeant Gable had hinted at the possibility of Europe, but months passed with nothing else said about it. And all the WAC troops overseas, so far, were white. Newspaper pictures of people dancing and kissing in the streets, the Eiffel Tower in the background, announced the liberation of Paris. American and Allied soldiers were elbowing east. And I was still typing in Iowa.

Then came one of those days when everything happens at once, even though it's only two things. Sergeant Gable's announcement we'd be shipped to England in two weeks, which generated excitement at dinner that went around the table, leaped over Ruth's usual chair, for some reason empty. "I'm not going," she said, when we got back to the room. I assumed she was afraid. Her face, the color of weak tea, and her small dark eyes reflected continual caution. At night she slept in such a tight ball her knees almost touched her forehead. Even in sleep, she circled her wagons around herself.

Ruth's parents and two younger sisters died in a fire when she was fifteen. She'd gotten out a window, thinking everyone else was coming behind her. The neighborhood minister arranged for a middle-aged couple, well known in Atlanta for their mortuary business, to take her in. Their only son had packed for Morehouse, so they welcomed another young person, of a certain sort, who might serve as a minor distraction from his absence.

She stayed with them through junior college. After the son graduated, she said, he came home and they started going out. He got drafted right after they got engaged. Ruth didn't want to be back in Atlanta worrying all the time, so she joined up, too.

"Don't believe you, girl," Hazel said. "After going through all this crap, you're not going to stay to get the candy?" She plopped uninvited on Ruth's bed beside her. A nonregulation curl, shaped like a question mark, dangled from her forehead.

Ruth had received a letter that day from the lady who'd taken her in, she said. The woman had read a column in the newspaper by a reporter who claimed for a fact that Roosevelt commissioned the Army to recruit thousands of prostitutes to keep servicemen happy during the war. She'd written to her son about what she'd "found out," and considering the circumstances, he no longer wanted to marry Ruth.

"Somebody just ought to set them straight," Hazel said. "We could get Sergeant Gable to write them a letter."

Ruth's eyes were red, rubbed and washed with her troubles. She breathed out a weak, tired "No."

But word that Ruth planned to ask for a medical discharge did get to Sergeant Gable. As we lined up for a drill one morning, she asked Ruth why. Every sentence of Ruth's reply was coaxed out with "And?" By the time Sergeant Gable assailed with the last "and" to batter the last detail from Ruth, I was beginning to hate the woman. Why out here, in the open, in front of everybody? What had Ruth done to deserve two humiliations in one week? Then her questions took an even stranger turn.

"Private Daniels, are you promiscuous?"

"No, ma'am."

"Have you ever been an employee at a house of ill repute?"

"No, ma'am."

"Have you ever charged a man for having relations with you?"

"No, ma'am."

"Then why are you leaving?"

"I feel bad, ma'am."

"About what?"

"About myself, ma'am."

"Having answered the key questions in the negative, you have no reason to feel bad. When I discern a reason for you to feel bad, do not doubt, I will make you feel *very* bad. Understand?"

"Yes, ma'am."

"So, for now you will stay in this Army, correct?"

Ruth didn't reply.

"If you leave this Army before you are honorably discharged, I have no choice but to conclude it is due to justifiable shame. And that you are at that time, or at one time were working in a house of ill repute, having paid relations with sundry unwashed, excessively sweaty, parasite-ridden men. Understand?"

"Yes, ma'am."

ALMOST NONE of us had ever been on a ship before when we boarded *Ile de France.* Many women acted purposefully nonchalant. Others turned their heads slowly as they walked up the gangplank, trying to take in the full picture from stem to stern, as if they were surveying the vast measurements of a dream. Their eyes inspected portholes as their heads moved in a circle. They took the elevator to the top deck and leaned over the railing gasping at the number of decks beneath them. With their necks bent far back, they smiled at the signal and lookout tower. They asked to tour the engine room. Myraleen asked about life jackets.

At the base, thoughts of Kellner had filled every pause. Here, skimming the ocean, I thought about him more. There weren't many U-boats like the one he'd served on. If there was one and it detected us, it would torpedo us, but this was only a slight chance. That's what we were told. After all, the *Ile de France* harbored hundreds of U.S. military personnel, mostly battle-ready men, who sometime in the near future might take a German life. If time and circumstances were switched around, Kellner could have been on a U-boat, and he could have spotted this ship. He would never have met me and would have been in a position to kill me. And he would have. War was largely a matter not of what positions people took, but what positions they found themselves in.

The moderate danger of Myraleen's own situation made her think of August. Sometimes she would wonder aloud where he was.

"You think those German planes fly really fast?" she said one night before bedtime. There was no way that she would have left herself open to something like No, Myraleen, they hop around on crutches, unless she was truly afraid for August.

"Ours are far, far better," I said, not having the slightest idea of what I was talking about. But I said it with the certainty I had emanated when passing on school lessons under the hemlock tree those years ago. Visions of loss and grief left her eyes and relief lit up her face, and I felt thankful for the ability to lie.

We docked in Glasgow to a reception of coffee and donuts from the Red Cross. We all wore double-breasted winter uniform coats with wide lapels, but when the wet February cold blew off the ocean, we might as well have been clad in paper. A big schoolhouse became our short-term barracks. The temperature inside was the slightly warmer, domesticated companion to the weather outside. "Damn," Myraleen hissed.

The Army had designated us as the postal service for the European Theater of Operations. Mail was a mess because personnel moved constantly. In eight-hour, round-the-clock shifts we routed and rerouted letters that couldn't be delivered to the addresses on the envelopes. If a man was at the front, it might take three or four times of directing and redirecting his fiancée's letter for it to find him.

I saw this man in my mind's eye as I stuffed mail slots and filled out relocation cards. He tore open the letter with sore-ravaged, mud-plastered hands and shared the less personal parts with the other bedraggled soldiers, as hungry for hope as he. As he read, he became not just some ragged target but Tilden Williamson of Freeport, Illinois, whose mother used to heat his mittens in the oven on cold days to keep his hands warm on the way to school. He was the boy his brothers teased, talking of how big his ears were as code for how much they loved him. He was the young man Nancy Cunningham, whose letters have followed him to hell, kissed and maybe more. Those pieces of paper, getting dirt dotted and rain stained, drew him away from the world where he was a target and back into the one where he was loved. And later, when the bullet that took his life was delivered as surely as the letter, he knew he was not just some squalid bull's-eye, but a man.

Within a few weeks we were doing the same job in Birmingham, England. Myraleen acquired a comfortable dislike of the town when Hazel told her about the "tails" rumor. White servicemen had told citizens in the town that blacks had tails that came out at midnight. "One of them even had the nerve to ask me if it was true," said Hazel, who'd become the lightning rod for inhumane mythology.

"Sounds like some of Red Briggs's old devilment," Myraleen said.

"There are a lot more devils in the world than Red Briggs," I said.

Whenever I left the base with Myraleen, she did the same thing. We'd be walking down some commercial street, and invariably for some reason someone would stare at us. Myraleen would bend her head back to check an imaginary spot behind me. She'd start to frantically brush down the back of my coat. She'd go, "Lilian! Lilian! Your tail is showing! Hide it, quick. Don't let them find out!" She'd look up at the sky and start to moan. "Oh, Lord, why did you curse us with these tails? You know it makes it hard to find skirts that fit right. I'm tired of drawers I have to special order. Please give us normal behinds like white people, please!"

The staring eyes would bulge and Myraleen would laugh and the owners of those eyes scurried away like nuns who'd stumbled upon a peep show.

I'd be warm with embarrassment each time. But I couldn't begrudge her. It was the only thing about the Army I'd ever seen her enjoy.

Her only other pleasures were letters from August. With casualness so fake it almost squeaked, she'd tell me that she'd heard from him again. In the four-to-a room barracks we occupied in Birmingham, we'd arranged to room together and added Hazel and Ruth. "Humm, they haven't shot him down yet," she said one night not long before the lights went out, pulling from her purse the letter she'd been purposely slow to open. From our beds, all heads turned Myraleen's way.

"So, what does it say?" Hazel asked her.

Myraleen suddenly became stingy with words. "Oh . . . he's going to use his leave to come here."

"Goodgigglywiggly! All the way here just to see you?" Ruth said.

"He can't tell where he is. It might not be far at all," Myraleen said.

"But still," Hazel said.

In the free domain of darkness, each night I pretended there were grateful arms around me and a chest to rest my head against. I wondered if Myraleen did, too.

Two weekends later, cut loose by a two-day pass, Myraleen and I stood outside the high mesh gate at the entrance of the base. Only a minute passed before one of those big black London cabs pulled up and August got out. He stood with his arms open. Myraleen whipped up like a tornado, flew into his hug and gripped him with the sort of fierce, violent embrace that wills someone to stay in the world forever.

"Lilian," he said, when she let him go. "Don't act like you don't know me. Come here."

When he called, August had insisted that I come too. He grabbed me around the waist and gave a quick squeeze. He was a man with a lot of love and not just one kind. Inside the cab, he clapped his big hands and looked from side to side. "Good God, I'm so glad to see you all, I could tap-dance."

After the cab dropped us off, he looped his arm into Myraleen's and motioned for me to get on his other side, where he locked onto me, too. He said he was proud to walk down the street with "the two finest-looking women in London."

He led us into a pub on a side street off Kensington where his friends waved to show us where they were seated, though it wasn't necessary. Theirs was the only table of brown faces. All the men stood up except Harold, because he had an Englishwoman in his lap, and introductions were exchanged. Woodrow was the tallest. Alvin had doe eyes and long lashes wasted on a man. Harold had mustard skin and light eyes. Rising a bit, his Gracie extended her hand to us. She had a girlish face and blond hair that followed the shape of her face until it folded into a tunnel of curls at the end. "Oh, this is a dandy group, girls," she said. "These fellas, they're something. You're in for a great time." She talked to us as if we were from her local group of girlfriends. Myraleen nodded politely. I knew she was thinking, *Ump, another crazy white woman.*

I sat between Woodrow and August. Myraleen sat between him and Harold. In the symphony of their cackles and challenges and stories, the men urged us to order anything we wanted or thought we wanted. Harold pushed a piece of printed paper in front of me. "I don't know what a lot of this junk is, but I know the steak is good. Have that, Lilian."

Looking at Harold and Gracie, August lightly knocked his shoulder against Myraleen's.

"Why don't you sit on my lap?"

"I beg your pardon?" Myraleen said. I knew he'd said this only to see that exquisitely sarcastic expression, uniquely hers, flash from her face. It was fun to look at if your tastes ran that way.

The table filled with the men's offerings: plates of food, bottles of champagne, baskets of bread and pitchers of beer. When all of it had been sampled or exhausted, the busboy and waitress rushed over to clear it to prepare for more. Our table was the most popular. From it flowed the best tips, jokes and cheer. Plus, the men were in the business of possibly getting blown to unrecognizable bloody bits for England, America and the rest. Londoners appreciated that.

The proprietor turned the radio to the colored music program *Jubilee,* one of the broadcasts dedicated to overseas soldiers. Lena Horne was singing.

"Like that, lads?" the old man asked.

Everyone at our table clapped, and Harold stuffed some money into the man's apron pocket. Any request was honored. The men folded their pound notes in two and waved them in the air like magic wands in a champagne-soaked paradise where they were heroes and princes.

They had rented a cluster of rooms at a hotel down the street. Myraleen and I worried about air raids. "Not so much now," the desk clerk said. "You'll hear the sirens before anything happens."

We listened for pops and whistling sounds for a while and closed our eyes. I woke once when a timid, soft gray light streaked through the gap where a pair of curtains met. Myraleen's bed was empty. I went back to sleep.

"I'll never let you have half a beer again. Why, you'll sleep all day." She said she'd gotten up at dawn, fetched August and they'd had breakfast downstairs, walked in the park, and done a bit of sightseeing, taken a few pictures, kissed on bench in Hyde Park.

AUGUST SHOWED UP in London every couple of weeks. He'd hop a transport plane from the place he couldn't name and take us out. One or two of the fellows might be in town. Gracie always came along. When Harold didn't make it, she'd pair up with someone else. She was the sort of woman who could practically sit on a man's lap even when he was standing up. I could see how five years of being pelted with dynamite might have that effect.

Birmingham got more accustomed to us the longer we stayed. The townspeople had let go of the tail rumor. Still, we enlisted women bypassed the town on our passes. One Saturday in April, we boarded the train for London, military personnel packed into every compartment. Outside, tranquillity prevailed as rural pastures floated through a filter of morning mist. Inside the mood was robust and itchy. The landscape looked peaceful, but the country still was at war.

Back in the States, I'd imagined London as a charred nub. But it was more like a person who wore a big bump from being hit upside the head with a rock, but who otherwise was doing okay. Britain had been in a fight and all the pugilistic phrases applied. At first Germany had knocked her block off. Houses were missing chunks of brick from upper corners. But when I read about the firebombing of Hamburg or the hammering of Berlin, I thought, "You should see the other guy." I prayed that Kellner was nowhere near those places. Germany would be down for the count soon, and I must have been the only person in England not one hundred percent elated about it.

A block from the station, Ruth reached in her purse for a map. It was her first time here; she usually stayed close to the base, venturing only into Birmingham. We'd told her we'd grown familiar with the central pockets of the city. But she liked to carry totems to scare off disaster: a map, an umbrella, two discreetly wrapped Kotex, anything that confronted jeopardy. She'd diluted fear into caution and produced useful results. On duty, Ruth double-checked ambiguous addresses, found mistakes on information cards and did the most precise work in the company.

"All right, are we sure we're going in exactly the right direction?"

Before Myraleen cooked up some slightly nasty response, I spoke up and fingered a line on Ruth's map. "We're going directly here."

We passed seventeenth-century churches made exotic by age alone. To my untraveled eye, they appeared dreamy and unreal. Through the windblown dust, they laid out a life stretched thin and gauzy. Yet, there were rousing stretches of familiarity like the row houses that, excluding the bomb damage, looked like streets in Philadelphia. On a church was displayed a placard that made Myraleen laugh. Beneath a taped-on magazine photo of a little girl praying were written the words: IF YOUR HANDS ARE TREMBLING, TRY CLASPING THEM TOGETHER. Several lots were empty and cleared of rubble. Air swirled restlessly in those places, and I could feel a fine layer of dirt settling on my face. On every other street, we would pass an apartment house reduced to a ragged shell of glassless windows. Often beside it was a building intact, looking as if it stood in a different country from its neighbor. The shopping district was crowded and hummed with commerce. Many of the storefronts bore signs saying BUSINESS AS USUAL or WE'RE STILL HERE. Now and then we saw other American servicepeople. Some pretended not to see us; others nodded.

A man walking toward us halted in the middle of the sidewalk, even though several people had to make sharp turns to keep from running into him. Looking straight at Myraleen, he tipped his hat. He was thirtyish, white, likely English, in a black, wide-lapeled coat. Ruth adjusted the shoulder strap of her purse and folded her arms.

"Ump. Strange."

We stopped in front of a department store with huge display windows extending up and down half the block. "Let's look in here," Myraleen said. And we circled through the revolving doors.

It was almost as big as Gimbel's back in Philadelphia and modern enough to have escalators between the first and top floors. The mannequins wore short skirts and had confident smiles painted on their faces. Only the lighting was dimmer. English buildings were darker and cooler than the ones in the U.S.

We wouldn't be long. Buying new clothing required ration stamps, and they required British citizenship. Ruth wandered over toward the shoe department. We rode to the dress section on the second floor. Myraleen discreetly frisked a few shifts for price tags, her face looking pinched as she mentally converted pounds to dollars. "I wouldn't buy anything in here if I could," she said. She had not met a price she didn't frown at since we left Mississippi.

Midway back down the escalator, I spotted the man who had tipped his hat strolling by the cologne counters across the aisle from sweaters.

"Look, there's that man," I whispered. "Do you think he followed us? I think he likes you." Myraleen rolled her eyes.

I wanted to stop and look at sweaters before we left. The woman behind the counter was about our age with very straight posture. She wore a powder pink cardigan over a pleated gray skirt. Cases of sweaters were stacked on the shelves behind her in removable trays organized by colors. "You girls with the Army? Good for you!"

She showed me a cardigan not much unlike her own that was blue-green with pearl buttons.

"That's natty, isn't it? And it would look so pretty against your skin. Would you like to try it on?"

I shook my head.

"If you like it a lot and you have an English friend, you could slip her a bit of money and she'll get for you. So you'll have something to bring home besides a case of the nerves."

I thought of Gracie.

Then a frank, shrill wail sheared the air.

We heard air-raid-drill sirens all the time on the base. At first, they sounded like hell's reproach, but I got used to them. Standing here in a normal department store, with its festive and overpriced merchandise, the shriek felt eerily out of place.

"Don't worry. Probably nothing too close," the saleswoman said, leading me to a dressing room.

I took off my uniform jacket and blouse. What if it wasn't just a drill, and I had to run right then before the place collapsed? For a flash, I feared the indignity of being the first Negro WAC to run down the streets of London in her brassiere more than I feared being bombed. I stepped from the dressing room and called to Myraleen.

"Maybe I could get Gracie to get it for me."

Myraleen rolled her eyes at the very name. "How much?" she said and reached below the sleeve to look at the price. "Too high, let 'em keep it. Let's go someplace where they don't have their hand so deep in your pocket you think you got another leg."

The sirens continued. Then stopped. And continued. But no one was acting any differently from when we first entered the store. It had to be all right.

"Okay, but if I don't see anything I like, I'm coming back to get this."

When I got out of the dressing room, I didn't see Myraleen. Ruth stood there instead, out of breath from having run up the escalator stairs and circling to locate me.

"I thought this had stopped. I thought it only happened at night." She looked desperate.

"It could be a false alarm," I said.

"Then why does it keep going? Why are people running?"

I almost didn't recognize the woman behind the sweater counter. She now wore a metal helmet the shape of a salad bowl with a short rim around it and a thick band under her chin.

"COME ON." Ruth pulled my arm.

Suddenly, I saw two people running in the aisles toward the door. Dozens of others were stepping quickly in the same direction. The woman behind the counter moved closer to us. "We'd better push off." She cocked her head at the flow through the door. "Many are making a run for the underground, but that's two blocks away. Let's take the lift to the basement."

I felt a tight sickness in my stomach as if someone were wringing it out like a dishrag. "I've got to find my friend," I said, my head turning frantically, until I spotted Myraleen through columns of moving bodies, way over on the other side of the store in Ladies' Gloves, her head also turning.

I called her name, and we ran to her. "The lady says we should take the elevator down to the basement." Then I began to hear the distant barreling thunder of plane motors.

A man's polite voice came over the intercom: "All customers, please go calmly to the south and north lifts, which will take you to the lower level."

Something exploded not far away. It was a padded bang like a giant burlap sack of flour blowing up.

We got to the nearest elevator just as its white mesh gates drew together on a crowd of people too large for it to hold. I looked up at the floor indicator. A semicircle above the elevator door, it looked like a bottomless protractor with one clock hand. Its black arrow journeyed in twitchy movements from "1" toward "B," but in terminal beat got stuck in the middle.

If this had been Philadelphia, people would be stepping forward to stab the black elevator button with their thumbs repeatedly as if somehow that would make a difference. At least a minute passed before impatience flourished. "Better go to the other lift," one man said. "That's stuck too," a woman answered. The hefty group was thinning as some ran for the revolving doors. Myraleen and I looked at each other and decided silently to do the same when the door abruptly opened. The cubicle, about seven feet wide and nine deep, was empty with the exception of the middle-aged female operator. A stream of people swept Ruth and me in. I assumed Myraleen too, but I didn't see her above the heads or through the crevices in a mass of necks.

In the basement the group gushed out as if the elevator had been tipped forward. I took two steps out and realized I had lost Myraleen again. "You stay here, Ruth."

"No!"

We walked back in before the operator closed the door. She took her hand off the black lever. It looked like a small stationary billy club pointing at a forty-five-degree angle.

"Misses, this is the lowest level. Going back up."

"I got separated from my friend. She's still on the first floor."

"All right, "she said. "But I'm sure she knows enough to ride the lift without you."

The box we stood in squeaked back into motion. Then it rocked to a stop. According to the dial above my head, it was again stuck between "1" and "B." In a voice so quiet it seemed to seep out like an escaped thought, the operator said, "Blast."

She pulled the lever toward her with a strength that showed in her thin, stern mouth. Nothing. But I could hear a motorized drone above, from outside the building. It was getting closer . . . and closer.

Lifting my chin, though I knew how rude it was to holler, I screamed, "MYRALEEN!"

MYRALEEN

. . . a funny buzzing noise . . .

WHAT HAPPENED? ONE MINUTE LILIAN AND RUTH WERE
right in front of me and the next they'd disappeared quicker than a
fool's paycheck. I looked around and around and not one brown face.
Maybe she was on the elevator. When the gates opened, the folks to
the right of me, where Lilian was, all rushed in pushing me to the side,
out of reach of the door. By the time I got back to where I was, the thing
was full.

From the dial on the wall, I could tell it was in the basement. Now it
was coming back up . . . It was stuck again. Damn.

"Drat," said a man next to me. The way he said it—hot, dry and bitter—sounded as mad as any "Goddamn." That funny buzzing noise in
the air made people nervous. The crowd scattered toward the revolving
doors, leaving me there, waiting to find Lilian.

"Miss." I felt a hand around my arm. It was so cold I could feel its
chill through the fabric of my uniform. The man who'd tipped his hat to
me was staring into my face. He had a long, square chin and light and
sparkly eyes like a cat's.

"Better get cracking," he said. "Come along with me. There's a warehouse with a basement across the street. Shouldn't stay here. You'll get your pretty self hurt, love."

Was he being insulting? It was hard to tell with white men sometimes, but he fixed his eyes on me in the way people do when they're just trying to make you see the sense of something. Maybe I should go, I thought. Lilian was probably fine on the floor underneath me.

I walked a step toward him, but right then I heard a big-mouthed, unmistakable "Myraleen!" It was coming from the elevator shaft.

"I can't," I told him. "I've got to see about my friend."

He let go of my arm and a simple smile spread across his face. "Well, see you later, love." He turned through the revolving door with a spool of other people.

Every counter was vacant. Stacks and racks of fancy clothes spread out in all directions with no one touching or tending to them. The revolving door stopped revolving. Outside the buzzing got so loud it sounded as if it was headed straight inside. Just as we were taught to do in training, I lay down flat on my belly, letting my face touch that dirty, shoe-wiped floor, and crossed my arms over my head. But it didn't make me feel a wit better. The buzzing became like a bee in my ear, a bee that was turning into a lion, and I knew when it stopped buzzing, it would sting like hell.

When the explosion hit, I closed my eyes tighter and could hear things crashing and flying every which way. Something fell on me that felt like a long empty box or a big piece of wood, and a swatch of fabric swept over my legs. I opened one eye and peeped beneath the crack above my elbow. I saw a stiff beige hand with stretched-out fingers and no fingernails. One of the dummies had landed facedown, her head sticking out perpendicular to mine, inches from the floor. Out of the corner of my eye, I saw her grinning at me in a kind of nasty way, as if to say, "Foo-ool. If you'd stayed your tail at home, you wouldn't be about to die right now. See, a hard head makes for a hurt behind."

"The war is bout over," people had said. Over, my ass. Those Krauts were just over a thin slice of water from here. I'd come all this way and landed under their armpits where they could crush me when they felt like it. Maybe Mercy'd been right, and I really didn't have a nickel's worth of sense.

LILIAN

. . . face in the rubble . . .

T HE OPERATOR PAID NO ATTENTION TO ME. I STOOD FACING the closed white gate at the opposite end of where she struggled to pull the hand lever out of its stubbornness.

The buzzing suddenly clicked off and a wicked silence fell.

Every couple of seconds my eyes darted from the floor indicator to her hands around the lever. Her pink veiny fingers were the last focused sight I remember before the white gate rushed away from me. I was hurled to the back of the elevator by a roaring explosion so loud it seemed the world had blown apart and God, with giant feet, was coming down from heaven. Ruth screamed. Debris pouring from the elevator's ceiling glided about as if riding on waves of her terror. The elevator floor rocked and shook off the lightbulb covered by a wire mesh basket on a high wall. And the next shook it back on. I was on the floor in the back corner, curled up so my chin met my knees. It wasn't a willful position; it was as if my body were dice someone had thrown. I hoped Myraleen had found a way to get to the basement.

I could hear more buzzing, and I dreaded the quiet at the end of it. The next explosion traveled through me, and I vibrated from my teeth to my calves. It was not as close as the last one, but my body was completely limp, ready to yield all breath and life. If I died, I would not have to try to stand on legs probably broken, try to look at the wreckage around me with eyes too frightened of what I might see. I would not have to begin the first seconds of attempting to live with this, and then maybe be killed anyway by a blast in the next second.

Ruth sobbed a few feet away, as slapped around as I. I knew the urgency with which mothers listen for a baby's breath-affirming cry. Pain and survival could be one and the same.

I didn't want to look in the direction of the operator. I could feel her presence and guessed she too had been thrown back and was just a few feet away.

The first thing I saw when I began to focus again looked like snow. Without moving my head, I looked up. The elevator's ceiling was half gone. Floors above it, a round hole gaped open to the sky. My fingers bled.

"Are you all right, miss?" I called. Then I propped myself up with my elbow. Ruth wiped her face with her forearm and crawled over to the woman with the quick, determined movements of a bug with an instinctual destination. A big pile of rubble lay in the opposite back corner: a quandary of bricks, cable and broken wooden planks. I was staring at her shoeless legs for long seconds before I realized that's what they were, sticking from underneath the heap. Her nylons were torn, her flesh, streaked with blood. The brown, platform-heel shoes she had worn stood untilted beneath the immovable black lever, as if still on duty.

Ruth snatched chunks of plaster from the highest end of the pile, where the operator's face was buried. I started to do the same. "Hurry, she can't breathe underneath there," Ruth said.

In Philadelphia once, firemen found a tiny screaming baby tucked away in the corner of a burned-out building. You never know. She might still be alive.

I began moving away the pieces of brick and wood, working as fast as I could. She could be suffocating, and if she was conscious, she could feel messy and humiliated. I didn't know her, but I knew she was the type of woman whose brassiere strap never showed, even on hot Saturdays under blouses with skinny shoulder straps. She bought her clothes on sale, but she starched and ironed the cheapness out. Like Myraleen, she was as neat as a row of bank quarters and as proud as a flag.

I couldn't find her face.

The shallow hole I dug revealed a thin broad shoulder, bloodied and punctured by the jagged edges of broken brick. At the ridge, a bone jutted out like new teeth through the gums of an infant. I tore at the mound of debris above and saw her hair, no longer brown and gray but wet and scarlet as if soaking in some hairdresser's red solution. She'd been knocked on her side much as I had been, and now it was her right cheek that my hands touched. I reached around and pushed all the junk away from her nose. We tore away more and more chunks and shreds. Her face emerged like a white mask in sand.

I realized there was no nose, only red holes. It reminded me of those stories in the Bible about women being stoned to death. We unburied more of her. I put my ear to her chest.

Ruth grabbed my arm so tightly it hurt.

"She's dead, isn't she?"

She let go of my arm and gently placed the tips of her fingers on the white forehead. She grabbed my arm again and then went back to the broken face. She went back and forth like this again and again. She moved from life to death and death to life, attempting to understand the distance.

When I heard a voice scream "Lilian," it had no more meaning than a stranger's name called in the street. My mind was frozen on the wrecked face in the rubble.

"Lilian! Lilian!" It was Myraleen.

AN HOUR LATER, blue-uniformed civil-defense workers pried the gate open and threw a rope down to me. They lifted me up to the two-foot slit yawning through the bottom of the first floor and the top of the elevator. I crawled through.

Myraleen looked extremely put out. Her left hand was posted on her hip oblivious to the fact that a store hanger had installed itself in the shoulder loop of her uniform jacket. Her right hand was swollen to twice its size. Her cap was gone. Splinters and dust dripped from her undone hair. And her face conveyed the message that she wished only for the opportunity to stomp the SOB responsible.

A balding rescue worker with a taut face asked, "Do you require any care, miss?" Small cuts flecked my fingers, but that appeared to be all. I shook my head.

"Can you tell me about the other lady down there?"

"I think she passed away."

"Are you sure?"

I told him about her motionless chest, her noseless face, and the final stare of her pupils. Water pressed the back of my eyes, but I couldn't just fold into tears, surrendering to a luxury denied the man who stood before me.

The workers led us outside where they said we would be safer. Barrels of smoke choked the air, and the street was a torn-up alley. Through the haze, I could see a tongue of fire licking from the warehouse window across the street.

Another safety volunteer took a look at me. "You've got a fast pulse, clammy hands," he said. "Could be a shock case. This one over here, Ralph. Can we load her in the next ambulance?" he called to a man busy with someone else.

Ralph, a short, almost-elderly man, turned around and said, "She's with the Yanks. They'll be patrolling here soon."

Fifteen minutes later, Ruth and I were riding back to the base in a car with two MPs. Because there wasn't much room, Myraleen had said she'd catch the next one. They took us to the women's infirmary. Ruth had neither a bruise nor a symptom and was released. A nurse bandaged my fingers, and a doctor checked for broken bones. "Won't hurt to stay the night in case we've missed something," he said.

My bed was the only occupied one on the ward, and I warmed to the attention, the thoughtful prodding and checking. Kellner's hands had taught me the pleasure of touch. But in the evening I was alone between brutally starched sheets. Images and sounds of the elevator rolled by like pieces of a movie show. "Hurry, she can't breathe."

Every time I heard it, from the first instance, it made my soul shrink. It was not her death that distressed me. Millions of people who would have died anyway die in a war. It was the suffering when a human being's thin protection is shattered and her fragile humanity is ripped away and she weeps blood and bewilderment. I couldn't stand the idea of her under all that rubble, feeling so, so hurt.

I sank farther into the rough sheets and bleak memories until I heard the hard, lively footsteps of Myraleen against the infirmary floor. She brandished a startling plaster cast that turned her hand into a white club and went up two inches past her wrist. Like me, she wore a papery thin hospital robe to cover up the thinner, sparser gown beneath.

"Would you believe it? Broken in two places."

I reached out to touch it.

"What happened?"

"A dummy fell on me. Don't you laugh now, girl," she said as she did. "What they got you here for, anyway? Just got stuck in an elevator, that's all." She reached in her purse and brought out a lumpy paper bag. "Brought something for you."

It was peanut brittle. Even though I was never as crazy about it as Myraleen, I smiled with genuine gratitude. At dinnertime, an orderly brought me a meal of yellowed green peas and limp fruit salad that went mostly uneaten.

"How long did you wait before you got a ride?" I asked.

"Maybe about an hour. Long enough to see them bring out that lady who was on the elevator with you. Were you standing right next to her?"

"Probably five or six feet away."

"That's close. Girl, somebody must have been looking down on you today."

Now and then, Myraleen said churchly things like this, completely unanchored by logic, that I never agreed with or disputed. Why wasn't somebody looking down on the elevator operator, too?

I bit into the slab of peanut brittle, and it tasted like redemption. Just as almost dying does, hunger remedies finickiness.

"They have me on the other floor, but I'm staying down here with you," she said. "The heck with them. Got something to tell you." She'd found a chair and was sitting close to my bed. "You saved my life."

"How's that?"

"When you were in that elevator, nobody could get downstairs, so people started leaving the store, trying to get away from the bombing. Some people went across the street. Where a warehouse sits? A big old red brick building. You notice it?"

I shook my head, but thought again. "Wait . . . the one on fire?"

"That's the one," Myraleen said, her bottom rising briefly from the chair. "I would have gone there, too. But you called my name. They were still pulling bodies out of that building, Lilian, when I jumped in the MP car. Everybody up in there was dead."

She bent over and put her face close to mine. "If you hadn't called out my name, I'd be dead, too."

My tongue scraped peanut brittle off the roof of my mouth and I swallowed. I was desperately grateful Myraleen was okay. But so much credit equaled more responsibility than I could absorb. "Maybe your mother was looking over you."

Myraleen pushed herself back against the chair and blew out a breathy "Ha."

"Mercy ain't watching *over* anybody," she said. Then she gasped as if inhaling her words back in to avoid offending invisible forces. "I shouldn't talk that way about my mama. After all, she was my mother and I need to wish her a peaceful rest," she said. "Whether she's in hell or not," she said. Today God dumped somebody else on a mortician's stretcher instead of Myraleen. And she was going to be respectful, at least until morning.

MYRALEEN

. . . a foggy day in London town . . .

I T   W A S   M O R E   O F   A N   A N N O U N C E M E N T   T H A N   A   Q U E S T I O N
when August said, "So you'll marry me?" Damn, I thought, why does
everybody want to marry *me?* You'd think I had a million dollars stashed
up my butt.

Earlier when he saw my cast, August shook his head and laughed.
"Only you could manage to see combat in the *Women's* Army Corps."
He'd thought I was something else for joining the Army from the beginning. He said that it backed up his idea that I was special. The first
time I wrote him from Fort Des Moines and he wrote back, "I glory in
your spunk," I felt bad. I didn't have any spunk; just didn't want to be
kicking thirty without two nickels to keep each other company.

He wanted us to go out alone this visit. "Got to talk to you," he said,
his eyes shining with excitement. Maybe he'd flown his last mission, and
got to go home with his head still on his shoulders.

Everything had been fine. May lay on the horizon, and the dreary
wet season had dried up. We ate at that pub he liked so much. Then we
walked arm and arm, happy, kidding each other, giggling. Just like that
song said, in foggy London town, the sun was shining everywhere.
Should have known some crap was on its way.

After dark set, he asked me to come up to his room. "With no dishonorable intent," he said.

"Then why the heck should I bother?"

"I've got something for you," he said as we walked up the stairs.

"I thought you said you had no dishonorable intentions."

In the room, he went to the top drawer on the low dresser and pulled out a gold ring with a pretty diamond blooming from it. "That real?" I said. "For me?"

"Baby, who else?"

I hoped he hadn't gone broke for it, but it was the nicest present—though I hadn't even been given many—that I'd ever gotten. It fit loosely on my finger, but I knew I could get it fixed to fit just right. I put my arms around his neck and smacked his lips twice.

He lifted me against him, until my feet were off the ground, and kissed me twice in return. Why, he seemed as happy to give the ring as I was to get it. So doggoned sweet, I thought.

"So you'll marry me?"

"What?" Oh my goodness. It hadn't hit me that he was barking up that dead tree. In Nadir, married women whose husbands could afford it wore cheap little bands; nothing like this. Mercy never wore hers at all; it irritated her hand. "Naw, baby, we don't need to get married."

His pulled his head back and blinked hard a couple of times the way he might if I'd thrown sand in his eyes. I winced inside.

"Don't feel bad. I don't want to marry anybody, ever."

"I didn't think I was just anybody."

"Tell you what. When we get back home, we can get a place and stay together." I said this not sure if I'd do it. What about Lily?

"Don't be disgusting. You sound like a . . ."

"Like a what? I promised myself. Cheevers and Mercy and Mason—after tangling with them, that broke me from ever wanting to get married. You're the one who talks about sticking to your plans." I took off the ring and put it on the dresser.

"People'll think we're just shacking up."

"People can think we laid the bricks for the original sin. I don't care. People weren't there when Mercy was using my head for baseball practice, when I had to work the fields, when I got fired for not being as white as I looked. People weren't there when I was born and won't be there when I die. And I'll be damned if I'm going to let them tell me what to do in between. I am GROWN, August, and I worked hard to get grown."

"I know it's been hard. I'll take care of you." He took my hand, pulled me over to the love seat near the window.

"Why can't you care for me without marrying me?"

"Same reason a man can't get paid without doing work. To get something, you have to give something."

"Well, I don't want to give that, and you don't have to take care of me. Then we can call it even."

He dropped my hand and turned away from me. I went to get my purse; I'd dropped it on a chair. Then I scooted back onto the love seat. My good hand sifted through, digging past a compact, lipstick, comb, train schedule . . .

"Looking for a gun so you can add injury to insult?" August said.

Finally, a small box knocked against my fingers. I pulled it out, held it by my face and grinned, posed like one of those girls advertising toothpaste on a billboard. From the expression on August's face, it could have been a three-headed chicken I pulled out.

"How long have you been carrying those around?"

"How long you think? Since heck was a pup? Got them a couple of days ago."

"Just what do you plan on doing with them?"

I placed the box on the end table and stood up, motioning for him to stand. He shook his head and folded his arms. "Aw, come on, baby, just for a second." He stood. Quickly, before he could change his mind, I started to unzip his pants. Being right-handed made it hard. The cast kept punching him in the stomach.

"OW! What in the hell are you doing?"

"You don't have to marry me for us to—" I didn't know a nice word for it. "Do the do."

"So all you want is some cheap shack up?" He pulled away and walked toward the door, then turned around. "Myraleen, I'm going to get another room. I don't want to talk to you anymore, acting like this. I just want you to stay here and seriously contemplate just what sort of jackass you've made of yourself tonight."

I gave him a hard look straight into his eyes. As he turned away, he faced the door and sighed, and sighed again. Then he marched back over to me and spoke like a soldier.

"All right, if that's what you want. But I'll do all the work," he said, pointing to the cast. "You'll kill us both." First, tugging the knot loose gently, he untied my tie. His fingers weren't in agreement with his bossy voice. They moved lightly and carefully. I started to help with the buttons on my blouse. "No, baby," he said, his tone tender like his fingers. "I'll do it."

I'd never felt sheets on my bare butt before. In bed, I'd always worn nightgowns. In this bed I wore just the cast. *Whelp, it's a good thing to try something new every once in a while.* I pulled the top sheet to my chin.

August stood over me, his undershirt thin and tapered in, showing dark half-moons of his muscle-rimmed chest that moved against the ribbed cotton. Usually one to keep my hands to myself, I felt a notion to touch the shirt tracing the shapes beneath it. I wanted to go underneath the shirt to find the skin that filled it. He sat on the bed beside me and pulled the sheet so slowly, I hardly knew it had moved till it lay at my waist. He picked up my right arm and placed it away from my body till it made a V next to my side. "That's not uncomfortable, is it?" he asked. "So let's just make believe this cast isn't here, that it's out visiting, okay?"

Now right at this point, my plan, plotted for weeks in daydreams, took an unscheduled stop. I thought he'd get under the covers in bed with me, and then it would happen. But he sat, with his hip near mine, looking at me half naked. When I tried to pull the sheet back up, he tugged it down. "Are you cold?" he said. "Give me a little while. You'll think London's in the middle of a heat wave."

August put his hands on my breasts as matter-of-factly as he might have put them on a kitchen table. He pressed and fingered and flicked. He leaned down to kiss and suck and came back up to squeeze and stroke. His touch went from soft to firm, and he did the boldest things over and over again. The man worked as if it was his job.

Do tell, he had his own plan. He eased the sheet down to my thighs. His hands divided the work, with one up top rubbing and pinching and the other doing pure devilment below. The lower fingers burrowed with direction as if they were trying to meet the hand above, in the middle. I had what I at first thought was an epileptic fit like a lady in L. L. Dunham had when she rolled on the floor in Fine Dresses and needed an ambulance.

As his body butted against the length of mine and his breath came faster, mischief twinkled in my head. "Oh, I feel so bad."

"Am I hurting you?" he whispered. "I'll stop."

"Oh, no, go right ahead. I just feel bad about making you a party to a cheap shack up. I can tell you're upset and all worked up about it."

"Okay, you win."

In the morning I sank into a tub of hot water. It had been lukewarm before August went downstairs and asked for a pail of boiling water. I wriggled my toes and took my time. Coming up, I'd heard folks on the radio talking about some movie star, calling her the "It Girl." Well, this morning, I was "It," that and more.

"Enjoy your bath?" August asked. He'd pulled a chair up to the low dresser and was writing postcards. "Sit down." He'd placed another chair, facing him, on the side of the dresser.

He leaned over. Our uniforms were back on, and with this false desk between us, it felt like a meeting. "Now, you've gotten to know me better, and to enjoy that knowledge I might add, can we settle this marriage question?" He slipped the pen through his fore and middle fingers. The ring still lay on the dresser, out of place among the postcards.

"I thought it *was* settled."

"Not to my knowledge." This was the proper August talking. "You call yourself being slick. But I know what's right. This matter is going to go my way, or it's not going to go any way at all." He spoke with coolness and certainty.

"You said I won." I poked out my lips and folded my arms.

"Yes, *last night*. Any good soldier knows a battle is not a war. From where I sit, they should send you back to basic training."

"You can't make me marry you. Have you gone crazy?"

"No, I can't make you, but I can give you the opportunity to do what's right. You slept with me. I know you don't want to be the type of woman who sleeps with a man and thinks nothing of it. Those women come to no good. And what would Lilian think if she knew?"

"You were there same as me last night. Now you gonna throw it up in my face?"

"Look, Myraleen, I didn't write the Bible or make the rules. I worked hard to get to this point, too. If I get home alive, I want to live a respectable life among respectable people, not in sin among the wretches in low-life land. I want a good job, a nice house. I want a wife.

"If right and wrong are not important to you, I am sure there are all kinds of trifling no-counts willing to slide into bed with you. If you decide you want to live like decent folks, let me know. But don't wait too long."

"I can let you know right now! Kiss my butt." I was so mad, I was hollering. "'CAUSE ONE MONKEY DON'T STOP NO SHOW." I got up, grabbed my purse strap and whipped toward the door.

He went back to writing the postcard. "Good-bye, Myraleen."

KELLNER

. . . the fury of the whirlwind . . .

IN THIS SEASON OF DESPERATION, EVERY AGING MAN OR underdeveloped boy was healthy enough to die. If Kellner put his stethoscope to a chest and heard an unsound heart or a congested lung, it made no difference. He had permission only to certify, not to disqualify. With many, he had only to look. A fifty-year-old veteran of the previous war, with ten discolored bumps instead of fingers, did not get into the Navy. The Army got him.

Unterseebooten like *U.128* seldom came back anymore. Were Kellner to return to sea, his father had said, the possibility of his boomeranging back again was slight. So he gave physical examinations at a naval base. His being close pleased his mother and Kristel. And he was glad he didn't have to leave them again, at least not for a while. When he got a respite, he went home, as he would tonight.

His father served as a shield. The Reich asked for long hours but not his life. Jakob. Kellner thought he never should have asked Lilian a question he wasn't prepared to answer himself. What was his childhood like? He had ended up lying to her. The mouse incident was a limp stand-in for the times his father's belt came to life and gave him a man-sized thrashing for some childish transgression, beating a child for being a child. Boarding school had been Dorlisa's one way of protecting him. Now Jakob could be useful, at least.

Kellner had interrupted his loyalty to his bike to get a motorcycle, which expedited trips between the base and home. He started the ignition, hoping, though it would be late when he arrived, that his mother would be awake.

Checkpoints with their peering, weary faces slowed him. This was not the Germany he had grown up in. It had not been for some time. He had always known enough about the Reich to know he did not want to know more.

The hypnotic sameness of the road began to erase everything. Also, he smelled smoke. Mixed with the reek of manure, it was a faint acrid presence in his nose, probably the by-product of some activity in a farmer's day's work.

If Mother were awake tonight, he would tell her about Lilian. He had no idea how she would react, but he needed her to understand why he would be leaving Germany after the war. Lilian was only one reason, but that was the reason he would give her.

Kellner saw an odd light in the distance. He had heard there would be a carnival tonight. Perhaps he would stop momentarily just to see something that was happy.

He worried about Kristel. In the middle of the night, she sometimes sat straight up in bed and screamed. It was a long, loud, primitive shriek, as if her deepest inexpressible fears had risen and consumed her. She could never remember what she had dreamed.

The light. It was not the celebratory kind.

He heard the distinct growl of plane engines. He called his senses liars. The Allies would never bomb Dresden, any more than Germany would attack Oxford.

But he began to hear a constant, harsh whisper. At the edge of town, houses and streets reflected the glow of the massive torchlight two kilometers away. Fire made the hiss he had been hearing. The wind was unnaturally strong, blowing to the heat like a drunk careening toward a party.

Kellner's foot pressed the pedal when he saw a duck pond. He soaked himself to the neck before running back to the cycle and revving up the speed.

Flames raked the old central part of the city. The blaze jumped from house to house like a circus acrobat in a blinding red-orange suit. Big ovals of fire, with the appearance of fiendish balloons, broke away from a riotous scarlet cauldron. They jetted into the night, bringing hell's daylight to the darkness. Several people ran down the street, red and boiling in their own sweat. One, then another, appeared to spring into the blaze as if joining forces. He could see the firestorm wind was sucking people in.

His cycle sped faster. Fallen bricks and stray coils of metal made it buck and leap. A district lay ahead with rows of businesses on fire and crumbling. A mass of masonry crashed in front of him. Something popped beneath him and the wheels rolled to a halt, and so he ran. Houses were big flaming matchboxes that no one could get into or out of. He heard choruses of screams, the agony palpable.

A man two hand lengths away said, "I wish they would die more quickly so we would not have to hear them." Kellner noticed a few moments later that the man no longer struggled beside him, likely another kidnapped by the whirlwind.

The sweeping cyclone tore a baby in a pram from its mother's pleading grip. She swayed and sobbed in the lesser wind left behind.

From within the wind's wail emerged crackles and sizzles and long whistles that ended in big explosions like fireworks. The gale became a devil shoving at his back. Stinging heat sandwiched his body, and smoke plowed into his mouth tasting like dirt. Fire had swallowed the air and taken its place. His family must be in the cellar, he thought, huddled and horrified. He stooped and lowered his head to inhale the fresher air that swirled near the ground.

Outside the Dresden Zoo lay a great giraffe, her eyes closed and her ear to the ground as if listening to a secret. A man squatted near the animal's head with his face in his hands, weeping.

Kellner reached the bridge. Flames with skyscraper tongues licked it from below. Streams of burning people ran toward any relief. Two docked ships sat leaking petrol. All along the Elbe River, people on fire jumped into fire.

He found a park where a mass of people dotted the ground, most alive, avoiding the trees, fearing everything solid attracted flames. Many were displaced souls who had come from the east to flee the Russian advance. In the last weeks, they had doubled the population of the city. Now they had nothing but themselves and one another.

Kellner fell to his knees in the brown grass, warm though it was winter. He cradled his head in his elbow, let himself sink toward the ground and closed his eyes. Fires raged all around.

"Where are the firemen?" a voice groaned from the grass. Another voice answered, "Dead like us."

He began to wonder if he could navigate the flame-laced streets. He must get home, he thought. But the bragging engines of U.S. fighters reminded him he was still a bowling pin to be knocked down. Hundreds of them roared in, wing to wing, blotting out the sky. Some dove in a fatal swoon to let the gunners do their work. He covered his head. To all sides of him, people screamed and ran and fell and bled.

Kellner's rational mind broke from its civilized confines, and he began to hate. He hated the British, hated the Americans. He hated them all—except one.

After dawn, when the bombing had stopped and the fires had dimmed, getting around was still brutal. He made a misstep and crushed his foot against a hand. Rescue teams piled up corpses. Carbon-monoxide poisoning had turned many bodies bright colors. All over there were towers of torsos, arms, legs and heads that came in white, orange, blue and green.

He crossed the delicate, charred surface of the bridge and he walked until he saw the blackened skeleton of his family home. Outside something lay on the ground. Someone. Someone who opened her eyes when he cried her name.

Kristel's lips were two swollen welts and she no longer had eyelashes or brows. He kneeled beside her. Her rayon dress, where it remained, was stuck to her skin. Blisters covered her body. He could not hold her. It would be excruciating.

Kellner looked up into the smoke-plumed clouds and drew a huge breath.

"Kristel, I want you to listen to me," he made himself speak. "I want you to close your eyes. See the face of a clock, the big round white face of a clock. Do you see it?"

Her eyes alternately dulled with weakness and flared with pain.

"See it for me, please."

He placed his watch on the ground near her ear. "Twice every second it will tick . . . tick-tick . . . tick-tick. Follow the hand that counts the seconds as it moves—once—every—moment. Tick-tick. Tick-tick. Now it is on the three . . . and now on the four. See it. When it is again on the twelve, I want you to sleep. You will feel nothing except that I am here with you. And that I love you."

He sat with his eyes on her. Several minutes passed. He placed his index and forefinger on the side of her still neck.

Then he walked over to the house. He looked and looked, raking his hands through the hot rubble as abscesses formed on his fingers. He could not even find a piece of his mother's dress.

A POW work gang in their tatty U.K. uniforms was heading up

the hill. He approached one of the officers leading them. Kellner did not need anything except a shovel and some cloth. They produced the shovel quickly, but someone had to run to the truck and rifle through supplies to secure a large burlap bag. Kellner dug. The men waited for their shovel back. He hated to detain them, but he did not want her in some pile. A couple of English prisoners appeared by his side.

"No reason to go at it on your own," one said.

Kellner sat on the ground next to the markless grave. He placed his head in his hands until water dripped from between his fingers. Then he felt a tap on his shoulder. It was a small boy. His head bore a gash. Using two fistfuls of the stranger's scorched shirt as handles, he crawled into Kellner's arms. The child was shaking from his scarred bare feet to his hair-matted head. He looked like a large doll that had been dragged and pummeled. Kellner held him firmly.

"We must go and find water for you."

The child held on more tightly, his small weight more pressing, but did not stop trembling.

Three hospitals had been destroyed with their patients. By late afternoon Kellner and the boy found one merely damaged. He sutured wounds on a trauma ward that was part morgue, where dust floated in from the punched-in ceilings. He saw every kind of death, and was spared only the inconvenient individuals so carbonized they fell apart when anyone tried to move them.

Every space in the hospital was filled, and there was no place where he could sleep. He found a refugee tent. In the brown, dank confines of the canvas, people shriveled into miserable humpback elves. He talked to no one. He would not have known it if someone had not told him: in his sleep, he called for his mother.

The Russians finally broke through. They separated whom they would enslave from whom they would imprison from whom they would rape, rob and rule. They slated most for multiple categories.

LILIAN

. . . a part of history . . .

LIFE FILLED WITH ENDINGS. IN GERMANY, THE "FURY" SMASHED
a bullet into his strange brain after marrying Eva Braun, who poisoned
herself after the nuptuals. Both died in a Berlin bunker, a bombproof
basement made for hiding what couldn't be hidden.

Admiral Karl Dönitz, or "Donuts," took over as head of the Reich
and negotiated a cease-fire with the Allies. He would later spend ten
years in prison. The war Nazis had waged against civilians was judged a
crime. The minister of propaganda, Joseph Goebbels, known occasionally
as "Garbage," poisoned himself on the eve of his scheduled hanging.

An exact body count for the war was impossible to achieve, but
tens of millions perished. Russia alone lost twenty million fighting off
the Germans. Of the two million Japanese losses, about three hundred
and thirty thousand died because of the atom bombs dropped on Hi-
roshima and Nagasaki, at the final curtain call for the battle in the Pacific
Theater.

In America, a few months earlier, Franklin Delano Roosevelt had
suffered a fatal stroke. Mudear wrote me a letter on which she'd pressed
the pen down so hard the paper appeared engraved. "If it weren't for

Franklin and Eleanor Roosevelt, we'd still be scraping under the bed for pennies," she wrote.

Myraleen grieved, too. But not for Roosevelt and not admittedly. "August and I just couldn't agree on certain things," she said. "Nothing good lasts." That was all. She didn't say "son-of-a-bitch," "coconut-headed weasel," "piano-key-toothed mule" or "horse's ass." So I had no doubt she was crazy about him.

On V.E. Day, the whole of sedate England came undone in celebration. On the base, revelers let out shouts and cheers that came from their souls. I was on the night shift and felt left out.

Myraleen rechecked information about personnel who couldn't be reached after thirty days. That night she'd been standing, looking at one letter for a long time. From Mississippi, it had hopped around to four places with no success in locating the soldier. It came back with a cluster of smeared red "RETURN" stamps that from a distance could be mistaken for lipstick kisses. Myraleen poked through the files, her fingers moving urgently, until she found his card. "Garret Burgess Briggs" read the name at the top left-hand corner. "Place of Birth: Nadir, Mississippi."

"Well, do Jesus," Myraleen said. The card was stamped "Killed in action."

Hazel came over. "This is the man who lost me my job," Myraleen told her.

"Ooh, girl. You must have put a fix on his tail."

Myraleen shrugged. "All I know is I would have swum all the way over here to England just to see what it says on this."

Word spread. The card circulated as evidence. Our story about Red Briggs—from the lake to L. L. Dunham—spun from one mouth to the next. Many an "ooh" floated through the building that night. Getta, a private from Louisiana, walked up to Myraleen. "I never looked at you real close," she said. "Humm. Well, you do that hoodoo, girl." From then on Myraleen carried the nickname "Voodoo," but it was always used with respect.

We were bumped up to corporals that spring. An inspection had revealed a trio of lumpy, stuffed mailbags sitting idle, overlooked, and Sergeant Gable had received a dressing-down. Round-the-clock mail sorting became a mandate. Myraleen and I had quick eyes and long clocks. Sergeant Gable said the promotion rewarded "accuracy and distinction." Myraleen said, "Toil and trouble."

In those last days in Britain, before reassignment to France, many of us longed to get our own letters. Hazel hoped for some signal that a military romance had congealed enough to survive stateside. Myraleen didn't expect an apology from August, I believed, but wished for a written indication the argument could continue. And I hadn't received a message from Kellner through either of the numbers I'd given him. Each day the ghost of his touch filled the spaces of my dreams, from the comforting kiss on the forehead to the fusing of bodies that felt as if I were dying and being born at once. It could have been a mistake, maybe. But it could not have been a lie.

MAYBE NONE of it mattered. Months after the war ended, I still hadn't heard from him. Myraleen didn't get another letter from August. Hazel found out her fellow had a wife and child in the States. Ruth, though, brought a letter to work from her ex-fiancé. In exactingly formal handwriting, it said he'd changed his mind about WACs. After working with them on his base, he realized most were respectable women. She could disregard his previous letter; he was ready to resume their engagement. I handed it to Myraleen who gave it to the woman sorting mail next to her. "Well, woopdy-do!" the woman said. "Ain't that so nice of him." Myraleen recited her own version of the letter: "Dear Ruth: I don't think you a ho no mo'. All is forgiven. Come home soon. There are still parts of my butt you forgot to kiss—and Mama's too—Sincerely, Walter."

A huge canvas cart with a deep dark bottom waited at the end of the hall. We dumped letters in it when the addressees couldn't be found within thirty days. When everyone finished reading it, Ruth tossed Walter's letter in.

Minds turned toward home—or Paris—and bodies followed as WACs with seniority left Europe. After eleven months in France, Myraleen and I shipped out to Fort Bragg, North Carolina, for separation procedures. By the time Corporal Myraleen Tessie "Voodoo" Chadham and Corporal Lilian Joletta Mayfield received honorable discharges from the U.S. Army, they'd formed a sentimental attachment to the corps. One of them wouldn't admit it, though.

Ruth enrolled in nursing school. Hazel joined the NAACP and opened her own bakery.

"Now the Negro better sneak a few steps up the ladder," she said. "White folks are still talking about democracy. We can just play dumb and act like they're talking about us."

As our train to Philadelphia hummed into the station, something agitated passengers into squeals and dodging movements. They abandoned seats and clutched the tops of their heads. A fluttery flash of orange darted above. Even after the robin found its way out, some lifted an eye to the ceiling occasionally, just to make sure.

I remembered the times overseas when we'd watch takeoffs and landings at a nearby air base. We'd stand behind the mesh gate near the runway. American pilots ferried planes to different places for combat. Women flew some. Once a white girl, no bigger than I, climbed onto the gleaming, star-stamped body of a B-24 Liberator. She wore a bomber jacket and baggy pants, and a leather cap with her goggles strapped around it. Before she ducked into the cockpit, she waved at us.

The ceremonial rumble of the engine started. The B-24 rolled and accelerated until it lifted into the air. Without a thought, I clapped and jumped up and down. "What's the matter with you?" Myraleen said. "She's only taking it for somebody else to use. It's not as if she's on her way to kick a German's ass."

I could only say that sometimes being there made me feel a part of history.

"Don't know how you figure that," Myraleen said. "Nobody from Nadir was ever a part of anybody's history."

KELLNER

. . . brave daylight . . .

TIME LEAKED AWAY. YEARS BECAME BLOOD.

Still, to escape was to court life and death at once. Fence climbers, sneak runners, and barbed-wire vaulters reaped bullets, hangings or fatal beatings. That is, until a couple of men bolted together into midnight. They climbed the skyward mesh with the quick adeptness of primates in a favorite tree. They danced through the barbed wire as if it were nothing but a cluster of children's toy hoops. Desperate gunfire pelted behind them as if chasing robbers long vanished. In the cloudy eyes of the average prisoner, a weak glint of hope emerged. But after a few weeks, the two were dragged in from the forest frozen to thaw in the courtyard: wet, foul messengers of futility.

Nevertheless, the word *escape* had a way of insinuating itself into the dangerous, stifling air. Wilhelm's cautious eyes panned the dimness. But other men were resigned to the rows of bunks and asleep, or quietly masturbating beneath the bruising blankets or maybe quietly dying. In a far corner lit by a candle, their circle of insomniacs were the only ones talking and listening, keeping Franz company as he carved shoes from wood.

"We're not prisoners," Ivan hissed. "We're slaves."

"That wouldn't be so bad if you could do your punishment and then be freed," Franz said. "You know how it is when they finally let you go."

Kellner nodded. The only men who received humanitarian releases were the dying. Either the seeds of disease had been planted and grown, or the last bit of health and strength pulled up by its roots. He could feel malnutrition branching through his own limbs.

He had once been called dashing, a thought that would make Kellner laugh had his throat not become a nest of porcupine needles through some infection he guessed to be streptococcus. Kellner was unlikely to dash anywhere. He was on his way to developing the gait of the elderly. With each movement, he did a slow pantomime of his former self. Even the guards, Red Army sentinels, did not threaten or bellow about his work pace. They knew this stage came naturally at a certain point.

He needed real medical treatment, not some indifferent communist playacting with a stethoscope. And it would require a case more dramatically critical than his to merit even that. Escape was not reckless, but wise.

"If we could get to Tadzhik, I have people there, cousins. I know they would help," Ivan said, his words spoken so softly even those in the group could barely hear them. Niklay leaned in close. An eardrum was ruptured. A guard's fists had slammed into his cheeks like meteorites when he stumbled on a rock during a formation march.

"We'd have to double back," Kellner said. "Our only opening is north. To get to the town, we'll have to come back and go through the woods around the camp."

"If we can get help, it'll be worth it," Fritz said.

The plan was simple. They would run. But not at night with the fence as a potential crucifix, and the late-shift guards on the lookout for any activity among prisoners beyond sleep or meek walks to the latrine. They would do it in brave daylight. At the rails, where they worked, five thick guards stretched their elastic vigilance between supervising labor and restricting movement to the immediate area. They were in charge of fifty-nine prisoners. What if a number of men ran at once? Certainly some would be shot, but some would get away. It was Russian roulette on legs.

Kellner had thought of it the week he arrived. But the idea had to lie in wait, not only for a group willing to do it, but also for even the first person he could trust to hear it. "Any thoughts?" Ivan said to him during their late-night circle a week ago. It wasn't casual. He'd pegged Kellner as a person with a strategy.

Eight of them now were willing to try it out. Guards tended to stand to the east near the trucks being loaded to prevent theft and make sure everything was being stacked properly. A couple posted themselves to the west near the railway cars being unloaded. To the south lay the road to the prison. In the opposite direction, a black mass of forest sprawled beyond imagination.

"We'll fan out at different angles, spreading from northwest to northeast," Kellner said. He put his arms out with his stretched-out fingers separated as far as they would go. What he said in German, he repeated in Russian.

"They cannot shoot us all," Franz said.

"Who knows, we might all get away," Wilhelm added.

Ivan told them the names of his cousins and where to find them. "If I am shot," he said, "tell them and they will help you anyway."

In one week they would do it. "In the meantime eat," Kellner said. That meant boosting their daily allotment of bread and soup with all the frozen beetles, spiders and half-alive rats they could grab. "Work your legs; bend a lot. Play run in the air when you are in bed. And get as much rest as you can steal."

He put his mouth to Ivan's ear. "You are the youngest and strongest here, but do not run the fastest. They will naturally shoot at the fastest and the slowest first."

Ivan studied Kellner's face for motives. Then the eighteen-year-old smiled in a way that lifted every bone in his face. "You are right, comrade. But when I get going, I am going to run like hell."

Kellner was never quite like Ivan, but when the Russians captured him, he was still young enough to believe in his own central importance in the scheme of life. He remembered being determined to endure the freight car ride from Germany. It was pure defiance. With his mother and Kristel dead, he had wanted death, too. But letting oneself die is hard when every cell is made to strive toward life.

He recalled the daggers of light that sliced through the wood panels of the boxcar. He could see strips of faces, squinting eyes, trembling mouths, nostrils that leaked sweat and mucous until they were wiped with forearms. Thirty men stood in a space small for ten. When the doors opened and the car emptied, a few bodies lay conquered and scattered. In his car alone, three had wavered and slumped to the foul floor between eastern Germany and this final destination just outside Moscow. People falling like rain—he was used to it.

THE NIGHT before the escape, each man turned to the other and grabbed his hand. Work and hardship had turned flesh into sandpaper. As the gritty palms collided, soft scraping sounds and wishes of good luck echoed through the group.

"*Viel Glück!*" Wilhelm said.

"God be with you," Dalton said.

"Stay well, Fritz," Kellner said.

"They can't shoot us all," Franz said. Every man nodded.

On what was to be either Kellner's first day of freedom or the last day of his life, dawn brightened with an odd slowness. *Agile and fast*, he repeated to himself, the black bread heavy in his mouth.

At the rail track, Wilhelm and Ivan stacked apple-filled wooden crates hefty enough to quicken the breath. They worked together at one of several waiting trucks, sweating though it was cold. They placed each crate an inch off the edge of the one beneath it. One after the other, they stacked them to the canopy. They went from front to back until the truck was filled to the edge of the open back of its bed with green apples in shaky crates.

Though every prisoner had an assigned section in which to labor, the group slowly angled to the north, working near the trucks and out away from the boxcars. Less than a fifth of a kilometer of yellow-gray grass lay between them and the black woods. For even the fastest runner, the guards would have twenty seconds of clear shooting with their rifles. That is, if they spent the full ten or fifteen seconds estimated on the distraction.

The eyes of every man in Kellner's group discreetly followed the driver of the truck filled by Ivan and Wilhelm. He walked around the back of the truck, making sure it was full, and then strolled to the cab and hopped inside. Suspended seconds stretched into forever after the motor growled and the vehicle began to move slowly, then faster.

A jumble of crates flew out the back. Wood and fruit exploded on the ground as more crates kamikazied into the wet chunky chaos. Guards cursed and hollered.

Ivan shot off first. The other fourteen legs bounded in the next half second. Joy and fear mingled like lovers. Their bodies blurred and popped through the air like divergent streams erupting from an uncorked bottle of champagne.

Kellner's legs moved like bicycle spokes. But his back felt large and vulnerable, waiting for that inevitable bullet. And shots buzzed by them seconds sooner than anticipated. Bullets streaked past his head like jet-propelled bees.

Ahead of him on the right, Ivan ran as if on the wings of a condor. Then suddenly he froze seemingly in midair. He crumpled to the ground in a cascade of blood.

Kellner tried to block out everything and run. Yet, he knew the sound of bullets hitting bodies when he heard it. In the corner of his left eye, he could see Niklay, scared and confused, running within two feet of him, giving the guards twice the reason to shoot in that direction. And shoot, they did.

Kellner veered to the right.

The first bullet he took made Niklay run faster. The second came as part of a straight stream of lead that blew a hand off before his body fell.

The bullets that felled Franz made his arms fly up into the air, his gentle fingers stretching upward reaching for help.

Only two pairs of legs still ran: Kellner's and Wilhelm's.

The forest was close but not close enough. Kellner thought he could feel the fatal bullet already. He could hear Franz saying, "They can't kill us all," and he could see all the men, their eyes praying "Please," their heads nodding "Yes."

LILIAN

. . . in the land of the living . . .

A MAN AT THE NEXT TABLE SAT IN FRONT OF A HALF CUP OF
coffee so long, the faithful black aroma of the espresso abandoned it.
Loitering was tradition at cafés, but less so here on the Right Bank. I was
reading a book and kept ordering orangeades. The waiter approached
the man and asked him if he planned to order anything else. "I'm just
killing time, Mack," he said. The waiter winced as if something nasty
had flown into his face. As he walked off, he said, *"Stupide Américain,
vous ne tuez pas le temp; le temp vous tue."*

I wasn't that good yet, and it took me a second to understand that
he'd said, ". . . you don't kill time; time kills you."

In '45, the French had jumped up and down at the sight of a U.S.
serviceman. Now they saw an American and wanted to jump up and
down on his head. Yet, for me it was still more hospitable than home,
North or South. Here they didn't see me as an American but as a victim
of America. The biggest social discomfort was the unsolicited sympathy
they offered in the course of a normal conversation. Many were friendly
to me; yet, I had no friends.

The same waiter who'd been impatient with the man smiled widely at me as I left and said, "Please come again." I crossed Point Neuf to the Left Bank, heading for my apartment, feeling as if I were missing some Sunday activity in Philadelphia with Myraleen.

A painful longing for home attacked at least once a day. To me, Paris felt otherworldly, as if I'd died and come back to some former lifetime among medieval architecture, dirt-glazed statues and Gothic cathedrals. Paris was the Eiffel Tower rising out of nowhere, gargoyles everywhere and Notre Dame looming like death hardened into mortar. Walking down a cobblestone street as narrow as a double bed, between two old buildings that looked like they were going to cave in at any moment, I could just hear Mudear, her head turning every which way in disbelief, saying, "Why, this place don't look prosperous at all."

"These folks talk like they got a mouthful of grits," Myraleen had said when our company was stationed here. Then she'd inflate her cheeks and emit some incompressible parody of French.

Sidewalks jackknifed in twisty-turny directions, introducing a few too many abrupt corners and dead ends. I lived in a five-story walk-up that stood at the end of a boat-shaped street. When it was erected some time in the 1700s, only tepees stood in Nadir. Rust trimmed the outer door beneath a façade flagged with hanging laundry and dingy, open shutters ever threatening to drop off their hinges.

Still, the city projected the virtue of a personable stranger, when you don't know what's behind his smile. I didn't like Paris for what it was; I liked it for what it wasn't.

Our company had arrived at the Hôtel Sainte-Marie after the Normandy invasion. Some of the women were saying they couldn't wait to get home. But most of them knew this was something they'd one day tell their grandchildren about. And their awe didn't shrink because of the tiny drizzle offered by the showers that turned cold in fifteen seconds, or the room-temperature radiators, or the number of impotent light switches.

Negro servicemen strolled unmolested down wide-open boulevards holding the hands of Parisian girls. Myraleen had nudged me when we sighted our first mixed couple. "Back home, he'd be swinging from a tree." She said this as if it weren't a totally disagreeable idea. "I bet if somebody passed and said, 'Going to lunch?' he'd think they said, 'Going to lynch.' And he'd set out to running. Then that frog gal would have to catch up with him. She'd say, 'What's the matter?'" Myraleen puffed her cheeks for a grits-in-the-mouth imitation. "'. . . Mahn cherie? Dahn worree. There will be no hangeeg until we're certaah de Nazees wheel not come back and kick our scaredy-cat booteez again.'"

"You can't get a colored man to take you out here for the French women," complained some of the WACs. I empathized but also saw it as a sign the city might have a different attitude about race.

I'd asked Myraleen if she wanted to come back to Paris after the service. "We could take some classes at the American University through the GI Bill."

"Have you lost your damn mind over here in Europe?" she'd said. "All these old funny-style white folks running around. Nothing even works. This place so decrepit, it makes Nadir look like it's in good shape. And all these spooky-ass churches looking old and ghostly like they're the high headquarters for haints. Least the United States ain't spooky; scary maybe, but not spooky."

Back in Philadelphia after discharge in January '47, I brought it up again. She said, "You're crazy." We'd moved to an apartment, not far from our old one, with a bedroom, a living room and a kitchen. We could afford separate beds, a party line, and a four-tier oak bookcase. "Why do you want to hammer what ain't broke?"

Honey Whitcomb was right about Andover. "Can't use you, sweetheart," O'Connor had said.

"But I'm a veteran, too." My hand dipped into my purse for the discharge papers. O'Connor threw his head back in laughter. "You've always got some papers on you, don't you?" Mild affection warmed his laugh, like an adult chuckling at a child who's said some cute thing, pitifully incorrect, but naïve enough to be precious.

"You're something else, Mayfield. But unless you've got a dick in that pocketbook of yours, I can't help you. 'Sides, you can do better than this."

The honorable-discharge papers did grease the way into a downtown insurance firm. I pounded away in the typing pool for two and a half years where the only things dark were the keys on the Royal machines and me. For most girls, closer to twenty than thirty, it served as a way station until a man with a ring came along. When I gave two weeks' notice, my supervisor said, "Getting married, I bet. Just goes to show, it's never too late."

When it hit Myraleen that I was serious about Paris, she looked at me as if she didn't know me, her eyes straining to see the unseeable. Probably she wondered what bizarre mental process produced this odd whim.

"Be back before you can say Jack Sprat," I told her at the airport. We'd been alive now enough years to know what a stingy slice of time a couple of years represented. Still, her eyes pooled with water, something I'd never seen before. It was mostly because she thought the plane would crash. Myraleen, like Mudear, had a preconscious notion that airplanes never got where they were going; they all just exploded in the sky and stabbed the earth like flaming arrows. I reached around her shoulders and pulled her to me.

"I'll be praying for you," she said.

We also were old enough for jittery prayers in response to the precariousness of life. Myraleen had joined Mother Bethel, AME, where Philadelphia abolitionists used to agitate in the 1880s. God now left the confines of pews and perched on her shoulder when needed.

As I turned the lock to my flat, I knew I'd spend time tonight rereading her letters. The door was an arch-shaped obstruction of heavy dark wood that made me think of the opening to a dungeon. What lay beyond it was one room appointed with ancient appliances and furniture in various states of disrepair and brave endurance. The hard tiny oak chairs felt punitive, so I had made a couch of the bed. When I sat on it, the sharp point of a spring poked out to my left, as if to greet me, making a tiny tent in the bedspread.

Every flaw collectively served the purpose of low rent. That meant my post-tuition budget afforded me treats like weekly calls to Mudear. And I could send things like perfume, so she could make history as the first woman in Nadir with toilet water directly from Paris.

I punched a ragged pair of trousers some tenant had left behind into the mattress hole as emergency padding for the escaped spring. The bed was the platform where I lived, ate, studied and dreamed. I reached for my French textbook. With two emaciated pillows supporting my right elbow, I curled my body into a position that felt comfortable. After an hour, I repositioned in a U-turn toward the top of the bed. French was so much easier to understand on the page. When people spoke, their words all slid into one another, making specifics indiscernible. Paris would have been better if everyone just passed notes.

It would have been better still—best—if Kellner were there. Five years had passed since the war's end. For the first three, I had checked now and then with my South Street landlady for messages. Occasionally, during my weekly call to Mudear at the Taylors', I asked Mabel the same thing. Nothing.

After defeat, Germany was a ruin rife with starvation. People rose in the morning to find the vulnerable starved and frozen to death on the streets. I imagined they were gray like the rubble.

His name came up twice in Red Cross records, once on a list of the dead, another time on a list of the living. One man was from Munich and the other from Berlin. I'd found no record of a Kellner Strauss from Dresden. With a German dictionary in one hand and a pen in the other, I'd scratched out primitively worded letters to Displaced Persons registries all over Germany. No such person indexed, they responded.

Of course, it all might have been the calisthenics of naïveté. I'd told a neighbor about my search. Bibi was a civil servant, with a petite figure and cascading curls the color of dark chocolate, and known throughout the building as "the pretty girl."

"Could any of the city agencies help?" I asked her.

The city's bureaucracy never reached beyond Paris, she said. "What was this man to you?"

"A good friend."

She smiled. In French-accent-bloated English, she said, "Don't worry. It probably was not a big thing. If I looked for every man I was with during the war, I'd be wandering the earth for forty years. Like the Jews in the Sinai Desert."

Forty years sounded about right. If I didn't find him, and I likely wouldn't, for the rest of my life a piece of my mind would be adrift, distracted, looking. I shifted my body downstream again.

When it was late enough to excuse myself from further homework, I abandoned the hardcovers for the soft rattle of Myraleen's letters. Her chatter, whether traveling on paper or sound waves, had always been like a scythe chopping through high dense foliage, clearing the way.

I wondered if I could write to her about Kellner. We were both more mature, had been exposed to many different types of people. But she already thought me nuts for being here. Besides, she couldn't render practical aid if she wanted to. What would she know about tracking refugees? Who would know?

When I rummaged through the names of everyone I'd met overseas, Agatha Reilly's emerged. She was a girl I had met in the service and hadn't liked much. She was with the OSS code crackers who stayed at the Hôtel Sainte-Marie at the same time as my company. After Strategic Services disbanded, she had remained in Paris to work for the State Department. She was known to have friends in Army Intelligence.

I woke up the next morning with her name on my tongue, almost as if I'd been saying it in my sleep. In class, she kept intruding into my thoughts, and my teacher shot a sharp glance at me when I missed a question.

Maybe the desk at the Hôtel Sainte-Marie kept a forwarding address. It took just a seven-block walk from my apartment to find out. New silver brocade wallpaper covered the lobby, and a recently installed carpet covered the floor. The room smelled of the multiple vases of roses that lined a long mantel on the west wall. Perhaps management had tried to rid the establishment of every whiff of the Occupation.

I said Agatha Reilly's name, and before I could ask for a forwarding address, the clerk said he'd ring up. Unprepared, I blurted out, "Please tell her it is former Corporal Lilian Mayfield." Into the receiver, he merely said, "Lilian Mayfield." She wouldn't recognize the name. We'd only exchanged hellos in the hall a few times. Embarrassment descended like a cruel light that exposes you to the world when you're naked.

Agatha Reilly had hung out with a glamorous group. They walked and talked and looked as if they were the cream of their generation and the flash point of the future. They wore their military regulation uniforms as if Italian tailors had designed the suits for them. Not a man stood shorter than six feet; not a woman was less than pretty. Some of them were from Army Intelligence. Their voices always rose a little louder than most, allowing the less worthy of us to get nonclassified samples of their exciting lives.

Myraleen couldn't stand them. "They're just fools straining to look as important as they wish they were," she'd said. "I get sick of having to walk past those hincty-ass folks, every day posing as if somebody's going to take their pictures."

I stood up as soon as she emerged from the elevator so she wouldn't walk past me thinking a Negro caller could not possibly be for her. But she met my eyes immediately and called out my company's numbers as if I were still in uniform. Who could forget the WAC unit that was everything a WAC unit was supposed to be except white?

Still with the corps, she looked changed. In only a half decade her face had lowered slightly, probably along with her expectations. Her age couldn't have exceeded thirty.

We sat down on the lobby divan. It was much easier than I'd imagined. Aggie, as her friends called her, appeared grateful for any engaging event, even if just a visit by some colored girl she'd been generous enough to say "hello" to years ago. And the story intrigued her. I asked her if she could please help me find the whereabouts of a displaced person. My neighbors in Nadir, like a lot of people, had a POW working for them during the war. They were friendly folks and got to know him a bit. Now they wanted to hear if he was all right. Because I'd been in the Army, they expected me to be privy to such information.

"Oh, I imagine they must think you're a smart one coming from there and winding up here. They probably think you can call up the man on the moon if you get a mind to."

That colored farmers had German POWs working for them fascinated her. "But they were Nazis," she said. "Talk about the twain shall never meet!"

The twain did meet, I told her. The man we were talking about wasn't a Nazi. "He wasn't an ideologue."

"Ideologue?"

"He wasn't fanatical about the philosophy of the Reich or anything."

"Well, what the heck. I'll be a sport, give it a try. Not guaranteeing anything, though. There's always a chance some piece of information is classified. But this probably isn't. Just the whereabouts of some random missing person, why should that be a secret?"

Aggie was sure she would find the time to work on it between now and next week. "Come back Monday," she said.

Maybe encouragement enlivened my step or made my face look receptive. As I made my way down the street, one man after another tipped his hat. Three rims were offered in quick rises from their owners' heads—a porkpie hat, a sailor's cap and a beret—before I'd walked three blocks. Men paid more attention to me here. The previous week a man with intensely dark skin had approached me saying, "Nigeria?"

"No," I'd said. "United States."

His eyes widened. He looked closer. "I thought I had found one of my Nigerian sisters. But I've found one of my American sisters instead. Still, I am pleased."

Manfred Achebe was in the last meter of a medical degree paper chase at the University of Paris. He'd specialized in ophthalmology. "The eyes are the most important thing about anyone, and I want to take care of them." When he said this, his own black diamond eyes danced. What cafés did I frequent? he asked. I didn't know names, so I volunteered a couple of street corners.

I knew that the next time I went for tea and a cheese sandwich, this man would be sitting across from me. And though it was a few days later, I was right. "You're harder to catch than a shooting star," he said. "I've been here and at the other one, three or four times, and no American lady."

He likely interpreted my apology and congenial command to sit down as interest. It was empathy.

Another man tipped his hat as I stepped in my building's doorway. Sometimes, like Manfred, Frenchmen stopped to attempt to weave a conversation. I was polite but always announced a destination I had to hurry to. One had teased me, saying Americans always were "Rush, rush, rush; go, go, go." Others wasted their names and addresses scratched out on pieces of paper steadied by light posts, none of them knowing he was just the wrong man.

Monday at six my shoes made rapid clicks against the cobblestone walk leading to Hôtel Sainte-Marie. In the rhythm of my walk I could hear my panic. It is easy to pretend there is hope until minutes before the time when you may be confronted with proof there isn't.

Aggie smiled as we settled again on the red divan. A good sign? She clutched a piece of notebook paper scribbled on from top to bottom.

"This is great stuff, Mayfield. It was fun doing the trace."

"Did you find him?" I said. I sounded too urgent, though I tried not to.

"Now, hold your horses. Let me map the whole thing out, and you can give the folks back in Nada the whole scoop. They'll be real impressed with their smart little hometown girl. And this is the kind of stuff that's free-floating today but might be classified tomorrow because it has to do with the Russians."

"Russians?"

She looked at the paper she had brought. I wished I could just snatch it and read it and get it over with. "So this guy, Kellner Strauss, born 1915 in Dresden, Germany, a fellow I know found him in the back-room files at Intelligence. His folks had some clout, got him exchanged for an American prisoner. You said he wasn't a Nazi. I don't know about him, but his pop sure was.

"Russians captured Strauss, Jr., at the end of the war. That's all Intelligence could give me." She looked up from the paper and aligned her eyes with mine. "And my friend wanted to know why somebody like you would care about a German, anyway. I gave him the story you gave me. He didn't buy it."

I was a mystery to her, a colored girl who used words like *ideologue* and inquired about the welfare of a German. She was trying to unravel me with a good, hard look. If she could, she would have looked me up in the back files. Or she would have put me in the back files, so her tip-toey spy friends could keep an eye on me.

"He saved somebody's life. If you know people who farm, you know the dangers. My neighbors, their boy was almost hit by a tractor, but the German pushed him out of the way."

Her face softened. "Oh."

"So I thank you for finding out what you could, going to so much trouble."

"No. That's not all of it! My friend gives me the number of a girl in Berlin who works for a relief service. I give her a call . . ."

"I should reimburse you . . ."

"Nah. Made it at work, courtesy of Uncle Sam. Tell her I'm tracking a POW in the Soviet Union. Well, this is a hot topic over there. Lot of POWs have vanished, and the Germans are getting sick of the Russians' finders-keepers routine. The girl tells me she'll rummage around and call back with what she finds.

"Way I see it, the Krauts killed twenty million commies, raped their women and tried their damnedest to steal the whole country. That's not the sort of thing that puts people in a generous mood."

If I were lucky enough to die suddenly, I thought, I wouldn't have to hear the rest.

"Couple of days later, she calls back with something good. In fact it settles things. She found a paper that mentions a Wilhelm Haas. He dragged into Brandenburg with a bullet wound and an infection, saying he escaped from some deep backwoods gulag that quote—didn't release prisoners, only released corpses—unquote. Guess he could have gotten a job as a fortune-teller because he died a week later."

"But did he say anything about . . ."

"I'm getting to it. A few months later another prisoner who says he's from the same camp, one tubercular Gustav Klaus, is sent home by the

Russians for so-called humanitarian reasons. Of course, he's about to keel over too, but before he does, he talks about the attempted escapes. There were a few of them, but the one *we're* concerned about is that involving a Kellner Strauss."

I stopped breathing because the air seemed to stop flowing.

"This Klaus guy knew what he was talking about because he mentioned Wilhelm. He saw him trying to escape with several others, and that included Kellner Strauss. He said they were all shot dead, didn't know Wilhelm had lived for a while."

I tried not to let my face break like ice, thanked her again, and left.

Growing up, I had heard adults threaten to lose their minds if a particular irritant didn't cease or a specific horror came to pass. Just words. But now as I traversed some dark stone-paved street, I didn't know where I was. Dimly lit outlines of people and monuments gave the feeling of walking past skeletons. I'd turn to cross a street, but couldn't figure what the cars would do or what the traffic lights meant. So I walked around and around. Finally, I tumbled onto a bench.

I sat suspended in that endless moment when I heard the word *dead*. I was yet another Parisian statue, unmoved by hours gliding by in the wind. A voice said, *"Madame, est-ce que vous êtes perdue?"* I couldn't understand. Another voice: "Are you lost?" The two policemen wore Foreign Legion–type uniforms that roused me to the fact this was France. In English, I said I was a tourist and knew the right address, but had lost my way. They packed me into their car. I had been only two blocks from where I lived.

I huddled in my bed as if it had arms to comfort me. In generous doses, sleep was medicine. I'd get up only to go to the bathroom or get a glass of water. Afterwards, I'd slip back into the dark, blank portion of my brain. It was as if a sleeping potion had lain dormant in my blood, waiting for a time like this.

ONLY THE telepathic nudge of obligation interrupted the potion's work. I sat straight up, frightened. What day was it? My hair shifted and compressed to one side of my head, and the last dress I put on rumpled into a rag after days of scouring the bed. I raked my fingers through my hair and ran the palm of my hand over my dress. The decrepit shutters resisted but finally opened. Beneath the muted sun, blue-gray clouds hustled by, lumpy like full laundry bags. The sky was bright azure that suggested the flesh of electric angels. A boy in his teens padded down the street. *"Quel jour sommes-nous, sil-vous-plait?"* I called to him when he was beneath the window. He tilted his head up and gave me an odd glance. His eyes looked like bits of sky. I'd been sick, I said, and I just didn't remember. Sunday, he said.

My round desk clock said it was eleven-fifteen. I had fifteen minutes to compose myself. The black heavy machine with its round dial and numbered eyes, which once seemed like a luxury, now looked like a burden. Most of the tenants didn't have them. Occasionally, one would ask to use mine and afterward leave cigarette smoke in the air and a franc next to the telephone.

In Nadir, Mudear probably was taking a dish from Mabel's hands, circling a dishcloth over both sides till it gleamed, and reaching to stack it in the cabinet above the sink. Sunday stood out as the shiny day of her week, when she had dinner with the Taylors and anticipated my call coming at eight.

I traded my dress for a terry-cloth robe, walked down the hall to a closet-size room with a concrete floor and faced the sputtering spray. Mudear could probably *hear* dirt, I warned myself, so acute were her domestic senses.

A fresh cotton dress, with a pattern of tiny autumn leaves, washed over my body and pronounced it renewed. But it helped only minimally. "Your voice sounds like you're barely in the land of the living," she said. "Are you sick? You know your Mudear would go anyplace to see about you. Even get on one of them iron-winged angels of death."

"I'm all right, Mudear."

"Need money?"

"I'm okay for now."

"Ready to come home? People treating you all right?"

"Yes, they're nice. The gentlemen sometimes even tip their hats."

"What! White people tipping their hats to you. Gotta tell Mabel this."

I could hear her talking past the receiver. ". . . Ain't that something?" I heard Mabel say, "Well if that ain't the surprise in the Cracker Jack box."

Back to me, her voice was sterner. "But don't let your guard down. Men are men, don't care if they have ten hands so they can tip ten hats at once. . . . You seem to be doing good. Why is your voice like that?"

"It's just one thing."

"A big thing? You want to tell Mudear?"

"Oh, it's over now. Just something that went wrong."

"Well, Lily, if you're only one-want short, sounds like you ought to rejoice in what you have. You'll be fine, Lily. You'll be better than I could have ever dreamed you'd be, sleeping in a field of clover."

A knock on the door came as I placed the receiver back in the cradle. It was the building's pretty girl. She invited me to a get-together in her apartment that night. "Many interesting types," she said. "And people want to meet you. They've heard you are a pretty girl."

I went back to the shutters. A tiny child in a well-worn dress ran to keep up with another one. I asked myself: Was the hope that was unfulfilled the most important one, or was it the most important one because it was unfulfilled?

The whipped-cream clouds still tumbled as if hurrying to a destination. Spellbinding, sunlit, bright gray ones swirled above, following the rest.

The teenage boy walked back from wherever he'd been. *"Est-ce que vous vous souvienez, maintenant?"* he called. Do you remember, now?

I said yes.

MYRALEEN

. . . thought you knew . . .

EVERY WEEK, I'D WRITE LILIAN LETTERS ON A FUNNY SORT
of thin airmail paper that folded into an envelope. Mailing overseas cost
twice as much as mailing to anyplace in the States. Using regular-weight
paper to do it cost even more. The sheets were so flimsy they crackled
with threats to tear just going from the drawer to the table.

A jolt of meanness told me to rip them to pieces, anyway. Why the
hell did that heifer think she had to squat around for a year in Paris?
Why couldn't she just come back to Philadelphia like she had good
sense? She could have gotten a nice job, and we could have found a
pretty place together, satisfied old maids till heaven or hell called us in.
Damn, she made me mad.

Yet, the sting would leave as I laid out every bitsy thing that happened since the last letter and pictured her serious little face studying
each problem with concern and smiling every time something went
right. I'd use an entire second sheet if it were a big news week.

I told her she was wise beyond school smarts for pushing me toward
Uncle Sam. Now my bank account looked good enough to pass for
somebody else's. I was able to afford a one-bedroom in North Philly all

by myself without straining my head to match numbers that didn't get along.

At first, when I marched my honorable discharge papers from place to place to find work, people knocked their eyebrows together. One foreman at a pajama factory claimed there was no such thing as an army for women. Some looked at me hard, expecting to see a mannish woman or something they could talk about at dinner. It was finally Harriet Finer at a five-and-dime near downtown who said, "Well, well, and you finished high school too, an officer and a scholar."

I thought she was making fun and I was sliding my papers back in my purse when she said, "If you can defend democracy, do you think you can keep two little bobby-soxer clerks from chewing Juicy Fruit in my customers' faces and treating break time like the long good-bye?"

Managing, even managing teenagers, was more than I'd ever expected. Though it was none of her business, I said, "You know I'm colored, don't you?" I didn't want to have to look over my shoulder waiting for race to sneak up and say boo again.

She did. When I'd told her the company I'd served in, she remembered it to be an all-colored one. During the war, she'd ripped through newspapers reading every article about what all went on. She said, "My husband went. We've got two children. Otherwise I would have gone." A shamefaced sound pulled her voice down.

If the people back in Nadir could have seen me coming in every day totaling receipts and signing time cards, being called Miss Chadham by two girls—one colored and one even white—they'd think I'd become tall cotton.

I shouldn't have had any complaints. But suddenly I found myself in the world alone. The girls were too young to have much of a conversation with. Harriet Finer looked to be just a bit older than I. Pleasant and quick with a compliment, occasionally she'd mention something in the news, especially stories about some do-right Negro like Ralph Bunche or Jackie Robinson. After work she'd drive her Oldsmobile home to her family on another side of town, and I'd get on a streetcar headed to my one-bedroom.

Remembering the friendship Lilian struck up with that stray German, I wondered what she would do in my place. Would she keep Harriet company at lock-up time and maybe on a day off meet her to go shopping, and later they'd sit down together to a couple of White Castle hamburgers? I knew I would never in my life feel completely comfortable around ofays. I'd think they were watching to see if I did anything they thought colored people always did, whether it was eating a piece of watermelon or wearing a red dress. Then they'd say to themselves, "You see." With white people, under the friendliest circumstances, I'd be polite, so would they and we'd call it the best we could do.

Whenever Lilian wrote, she asked if I'd heard from August. After pitifully answering "No, I haven't" a couple of times, I finally wrote, "No, I don't want to." Thinking of him made me roll my lips in and breathe hard out of my nostrils like a bull. It was just an argument; there was no reason for him to disappear like Houdini. What kind of a man is that, anyway, can't stand a little disagreement?

I'd called his unit and they'd been stingy about information, but gave me an address in New York. I wrote to him giving him my phone number. It sounded friendly, not mushy, but got no answer. If he could fly a plane, couldn't he pick up the phone and say, "Hi, Myraleen, you still breathing?"

The answer came from an unexpected place. In the back of the store one Saturday afternoon, I was stamping prices on packets of perfumed bath crystals giving me a headache with their cheap scent. My not-young-anymore eyesight held a dull vision of a man who'd been standing at the cash register for much longer than it should take to spend the little bit of change anything in here cost. He was talking to Melinda, the colored cashier clerk, a nice high-school senior with good grades. I left the bath crystals to wait and walked to the front, and well, well!

"Skeet Magee!" He jumped back just as surprised to see me. He wore a trench coat and porkpie hat with a feather in the band. "Skeet, you're double that girl's age, and I bet her daddy keeps a double-barreled shotgun especially for hounds like you."

He laughed and winked Melinda's way, which made her look down at the counter. "Just trying to pass the day." He gave me a level-by-level inspection. "You look goo—ood! Your man is one lucky son-of-a-bitch."

"Don't use that kind of language in front of this child, and the only man in my life is the mailman." I sent Melinda back to the bath crystals to pick up where I'd left off. That was all she needed to know about Miss Chadham's social life.

Skeet didn't live far from me. He asked if I'd been to the old USO place. "It's still swinging every Saturday night," he said. And he promised to show up with bells on to take me dancing. He turned to leave, but before he reached the door, he whirled back around and said, "You look goo—ood!"

At least he gave me a reason to put on a pretty dress. But when I opened the door on his big old smile, it was still the wrong smile. At the club, he put a rum and Coca-Cola in front of me and said, "I can tell you need to loosen up, shake your hips a bit. Tell from looking at you, your hips don't get no action."

"Skeet, you're the devil."

"No, just the devil's black bastard brother."

The place had quieted down since the end of the war. Tables were empty except for those used by two other couples and us. He sat down across from me and wriggled his shoulders and swung them from side to side. I laughed. "Loose as a goose," he said.

On the dance floor, he spun me out like a top, pulled me in and stole a short squeeze. Each time my legs whirled sideways or into the air, for a second it felt like that night I first came to the club, the smell of after-shave, the way a breeze stirred by our movements sneaked up my dress, the dizziness that made things clear.

Back at the table and back in the present, I must have looked disap-pointed. "You miss August, don't you?"

"He's not the only person who can wear a pair of pants, Skeet. But to tell the truth, I'm not the going-out type, anyway. I'd just as soon be home ironing my work clothes for tomorrow than sitting somewhere with some man who's wondering how long he's got to talk to me before he can get in my drawers. No offense, Skeet. You're lovely company. Anyway," I said, "he's in New York."

"He's not in no New York!"

"Whaa?"

"Just saw Woodrow last week. You know, he and August were ace boon coons in the service. Wood kept up with him." It turned out Skeet was in the know and I was in the dark. He told me what was what and I just sat there, mouth open to the flies.

I got up from the table, a walking mummy and, apologizing for my impoliteness, said I'd catch a cab home. Skeet stood on the sidewalk looking sad, paid the cabby and said, "I'm sorry, Myraleen. I thought you knew."

GOING TO BED didn't mean going to sleep. I lay there, a mummy, for an hour before I got up, stood on a chair and dug through the closet shelf finding a box, then a piece of paper within it from years ago.

I dragged my satin dress back on. Out in the night, I didn't see a jit-ney. Walked fast for block after block until finally I saw the Chevrolet driver who'd dropped me off three hours ago rolling down the street with four passengers. I almost jumped in his path. "Kind of crowded," he said. One of the partygoers sat in front with the driver and freed up a couple of inches of space in the rear. The folks were drunk and happy and didn't care if it was a tight squeeze. "It's a more merrier . . . ?" the man next to me said, unleashing the smell of a pint of whiskey into the air.

"You mean the more, the merrier," the lady on his other side said.

The man swayed against her. "You so jazzy, you can read my mind." He slung his arm around her shoulder. "That's why I dig you."

By the time I got out, I wasn't sure if my thinking was any straighter than the drunks'. Still, I walked up the steps of that old tenement determined to do something, though I didn't know what.

A soft, gravely voice on the other side of the door asked, "Who is it?" Leonard, wearing a sad old gray robe, threw open the door and hugged me with the pure joy that didn't care if it was midnight. A black shower curtain strung on laundry rope divided the room and seemed to smother it. "That's so he can have some privacy. Don't worry. He just got to bed a few minutes ago. He don't sleep well, so he stays up long to get good and tired. But he's still awake."

"August, you awake, ain't you?"

"No, I am not awake and I am not prepared to receive visitors."

"Well, August," his cousin said, "since you're talking in your sleep, why don't you start walking in your sleep and come out here and entertain your guest like the gentleman we all know you are?"

Oh, the heck with him. I reached up and dragged the hooks against the rope. August sat on the side of a foldout bed inches from me.

"Go away, Myraleen." The look on his face was grim like death. My heart started beating faster. He sat up on his elbows, then his fists and with them locked onto the bedspread, he swung around to sit on the side of the bed. His bare left foot gripped the floor. No right foot came down with it. He stared me in the eye as if making a mean, wordless dare. The bottom half of the pajama leg was empty; the way it had waved when he spun toward me, it could have been a flag.

Oh, Lord, I thought. Skeet had warned me, but it was still a shock. For some seconds blank air passed through my mind as if I'd turned on a radio between the sponsor's message and the program. I had to find something to say—quicklike. "Looks like Uncle Sam gave you a way to cut what you spend for socks in half."

"You really are awful, Myraleen. Don't you have any respect for anything? I wish I'd known that about you."

Mad is better than sad, I thought.

"I'm going to have to ask you to leave."

"You can ask all you want," I said and laughed. "But this is your cousin's place. I don't have to go until he says so—and since he thinks I hung the moon and made it shine—that probably won't be for a while."

Tired of standing, I walked over and just plopped my butt down next to him. He had the nerve to turn his head away.

Ump! I could entertain myself. A newspaper or magazine would do until he got some sense. Before my eyes found anything to read, they set sight on a big wooden beige thing propped against the room's one chair. It looked like a broken-off piece of a giant doll. I went over, got it, came back and plopped down again. "This ain't your color. Why didn't you get one that matched?"

"I'm not even going to dignify that."

"Just asking." I balanced the leg in my lap. I stretched my right arm out, and put it side by side with it. "Well, what do you know! It's my color. Goes with me just fine." My shoulder snuggled against his. "Aw, you must have brought this back for me. Baby, you so sweet. You must have said, I'm going to treat my woman right. I'm going to bring her back a leg."

"Myraleen, I'm going to say something to you I never thought in my entire life I'd say to a woman. You go to hell."

"WHY DIDN'T YOU WRITE TO ME?" I hollered it straight into his face. "You take me for some fair-weather floozy who's only good for the good times?" He scooted farther up on the bed. I didn't know if he was afraid for his balance or just afraid.

"I didn't want the burden to be on both of us."

"Oh, don't give me that mess. Truth is you didn't want me to see you with one leg, with your silly self. Like it makes much difference. You're the same as the last time I saw you, only lazy."

"Look, Myraleen. You wouldn't marry me when I had two legs. How was I supposed to think you'd act if I had one?"

I let the leg slide to the floor. I folded my arms in disgust. He folded his arms in disgust. All the talking stopped for a full minute. My anger had worn itself out. My knee touched his empty right pajama leg. I unlocked my arms, slid down and put my head on his lap and said, "Baby, one missing leg don't stop no show."

After a while, I stood up and pulled my dress over my head. "I'm tired." In my slip, I climbed into his beanpole of a bed, trying not to take up more than half the space.

Soft jostling on the other side of the bed woke me after a while. I could feel the mattress bear down with the weight of another body. I felt his arm go around my waist. "I hope Leonard doesn't think I'm terrible for staying like this." He jerked slightly, startled by my being awake.

"The only thing he'll think is what I think, that I should thank God for you. I'm just so disappointed that I can't give you the life you deserve."

"Who knows? Every closed door ain't locked," I said, laying my arm atop his.

"And I know how you love to dance. I can't dance now, Myraleen."

"Baby, you never could."

LILIAN

. . . one perpetual moment . . .

During my second year in school, in the spring of '52, I still lived in the same Parisian flat. In Paris, I could finally be someplace without going someplace.

I'd been out to pick up breakfast food and a few other groceries before my first class and walked the pencil sidewalk that led home. Rain had washed the air clean, and the sky reached out in a popcorn explosion of white. Behind the clouds stretched a seamless blanket of baby blue.

But annoyance colored my mood. I'd had to search the city for insecticide because spiders with legs long enough to dance with the Rockettes had begun to march across my peeling windowsill. And the grocer had again tried to shove a naked loaf of bread in the sack among other goods, cans and cartons handled by numerous unwashed hands. So I tried to make him understand that, having a lower opinion of germs than he did, I needed a separate bag for my bread. I wasn't being a bossy American, just a hygienic one.

I saw a very tall figure in the doorway of my building as I approached. Probably some hopeful contender was waiting for Bibi to awake. Closer I could see his looking tall came as much from thinness as height. Several feet from him, I stopped. My groceries fell from my arms, the bread diving headfirst into a dirty puddle. I trembled so much, I felt I was dissolving.

Kellner's smile was scared and tentative. He walked up to me and took two circular steps around me to get a better look. I did the same. We were like ballet dancers making slow moves before decisive ones. Our eyes had a reintroductory conversation. His looked older and dispirited. He'd dragged through lifetimes of hardship to be here.

He stared at my left hand. "You did not marry." He wore a pale yellow shirt and black cotton pants, clothes that somehow said he wasn't their first owner.

"There was no reason to."

"Lilian, I lost everything. My world reversed. Things I thought would be problems are not. Things I thought would not be problems are. I have to start all over."

I nodded slowly. He might have thought I hardly understood anything he said when I understood it all and more. I was in shock about him. He was in shock about everything.

He shut his eyes against the hard slap of his own words. "Start all over. You see?"

I took a step toward him. I said, "Let's start now."

Kellner opened his eyes. He moved close enough to touch me. His reflexive politeness first drove him down toward my fallen vegetables and ruined bread. But then, suddenly, he straightened and pulled me to his chest. He made his life-weary feet do a celebratory spin in a movement so fast and free, my feet swirled above the cobblestones. And for one perpetual moment, I felt joy.

EPILOGUE

LILIAN

MYRALEEN SAYS SHE DOESN'T KNOW WHICH IS WORSE, *being old and tired or young and discontent. Either way, you're never at peace, she says.*

Maybe that is what death is for.

Our car moves down a highway that did not exist when we were girls in Nadir and exits at the heel of a mega-mall, a mass of bland mortar that, sixty years ago, would have seemed like a big outdoor air-raid shelter. It turns onto an off-ramp, then onto Town Street and glides past statuesque buildings made of glass, hard edges and money.

Myraleen's daddy bought four plots. Two for him and Mercy and the others for Myraleen and Mr. X, who he was sure would come along no matter what his daughter said.

We slow down, approaching the great stone entrance to Nadir Valley Cemetery, which looks like a monument from the Holy Roman Empire. Huge ornamental gates give the impression that the dead who clear this portal are preapproved for heaven. Myraleen nudges me, "Funny how you have to go through so much just to get to this point."

She's darker than she used to be—a faint tan now—I believe out of sheer contrariness. Her hair is gray dyed black. Time has left its fingerprint on her lightly lined face. She claims I aged better. I tell her that doesn't matter in the wild blue yonder of beyond eighty.

After many false alarms, I am actually old. The world is now a speeding train, too swift to hitch a ride on. My head is wracked with rushing numbers. Nineteen seventeen into 2000 feels like a long distance in a short time.

I stayed in Paris, pedaled through a few more years of university, and became a secondary-school language instructor. Myraleen lived with August in Philadelphia. They bought a house, and August's cousin Leonard lived with them until he died in 1968. She managed the dime store till it gave way to Wal-Marts and Kmarts. August counseled disabled vets at the V.A. hospital and was reenergized by the dazed influx of Vietnam casualties.

In 1969, he pronounced living with Myraleen so long without marriage "purely ridiculous." He was tired of living in "one crazy woman's personal asylum." Myraleen shrugged and said, "The doorknob works the same today as it did yesterday."

He married a woman named Vera, a divorced mother of two adult children. "Nice as pecan pie," said Myraleen, who bought an expensive wedding gift for them. "If I had to choose between her and me, I'd choose her, too." It lasted a year and then, as Myraleen put it, "went flat faster than cheap ginger ale." Within a month of the divorce, he moved back in with Myraleen. At first, the reunion was begrudging, but soon the household mood settled into the usual level of benevolent irritability.

August read a self-help book, I'm Okay, You're Okay. *Myraleen plucked the diamond ring from an old jewelry box and slid it on her finger again for the first time since 1945. People began to assume she and August were married, and she never told them otherwise.*

Mudear did make it to Paris. Despite her aversion to "flying coffins," she was on a Pan-American airliner, having prayed through its descent, when it roared into Orly in September of 1954. Even 4,500 miles of sky couldn't keep her from her grandbaby.

Myra's eyes, asleep, were two tight dashes when Mudear held her for the first time. "You sure her father isn't a Japanese? 'Cause you pretty partial to foreigners," she whispered and winked.

Mudear would get more comfortable with Kellner the longer she knew him, I figured. On that trip, though, she never knew quite what to say to him. Her one attempt at independent conversation went something like: "Do you ever go back to visit that place . . . uh, Dreadful?"

"Mudear," I'd said, "He can't. It's in the Russian zone now."

"Oh, yeah, that's right," she said, looking at him matter-of-factly. "And didn't you bust out of one of their jails?"

I had told her she didn't have to come, that I would bring the baby in a year. I ended up desperately grateful for her stubbornness. Days after her return to Nadir, the Taylors drove her to the hospital. She'd complained of savage head pains. Barely into a ward bed, she said, "Tell Lily . . . I . . ." before she was silent forever.

Miz Herdie passed the following winter. Nadir acquired its own county social-services division, and family-crisis hot line. Now along with fast food, it has flashy cars and flashy kids that get in drunken crashes on the weekends. Still, some folks who went north are moving back, saying Nadir is safer.

Mabel and Mr. Taylor left the farm to Toby, who nursed fickle crops and bashful dollars for forty years to keep it. Now, he is widowed and retired. His kids and grandkids run the farm these days.

Paris is changing. Pavement replaced cobblestones after students used them to pelt police in the '60s riots. McDonald's arrived in the '70s. Right-wing machinations and Third World immigration have strained the racial climate. Yet, the core city is much the same. It's a comfort to grow old in a place that's so much older, where even the light posts appear to understand. It must be so hard to age in America. A city block can be unrecognizable from one decade to the next, because the cheap plaster and plastic keep getting replaced by new cheap plastic and plaster.

Myraleen has had a good time, though. "We get so many senior-citizen discounts here, girl, you just don't know what you're missing," she'd said.

"August and I take advantage of everything . . . but the movies." Then she squinted as if trying to add numbers that just didn't come out right. "They're not like the ones we used to go to see with Mudear. People can't act, so instead, they make something explode or have sex."

A bugler plays "Taps." Two honor guard soldiers fire three times into the air. A young black airman steps up to Myraleen with an American flag folded in a layered triangle. His jaw is firm, his eyes directed straight ahead on some distant aspiration, his body arranged in a proud stance. He tries to reflect the spirit of the man he honors. "With thanks from a grateful nation, Ma'am," he says. She grants him a slight smile of approval. When he is back in line, she whispers to me, "Not grateful enough."

Before the casket is lowered, Myraleen walks over and puts her fingers to her lips and then on its shiny veneer. "Fly, baby," she whispers.

We will talk her into moving to Paris to live with us. After the requisite fussing, we think she will. She has no one left in Philadelphia. Only a couple of her casual friends continue to outrun death.

I have lived the last decades knowing two things: Up until the end, everything matters. After the end, nothing matters. Yet, I have never learned to reconcile the two.

For a blink of a second, it looks like Mr. Taylor is walking toward us. But it is Toby who comes over to hug us and to shake my husband's hand. Kellner stands, impressively straight for his age, waiting for us to scoot into the back of the funeral-home car ahead of him. I am in the middle. He holds my left hand. Myraleen squeezes the other.

"He did all right for a boy from Alabama, all things considered, didn't he?"

I squeeze back.

"We all did, Myraleen. We all did."

ACKNOWLEDGMENTS

Without the emotional and intellectual support of the following people, my writing this novel would have been much more difficult, if not impossible. I wish to profoundly thank Rose Marie Mayer, my close inspirational friend and Louisiana-born muse, and Beverly Jean Price, my lifelong buddy, occasional irritant and indispensable gift from God.

Thanks to the faithfully wonderful and keenly intelligent women of my writers group: Mary Brenneman, Tamara Chapman, Mary McArthur and Leslie Petrovski.

My appreciation also goes to Nneka Pitchford, who is always cheering me on, and Wuanda Walls, for her magnanimous enthusiasm about my work and my life.

I am grateful to Daria MonDesire for her generosity and literary camaraderie and to her husband, boundlessly kind Jim Torrisi, for his legal assistance.

And I am indebted to my great friend Molette Randle and her father, Clarence Randle, whose remembrance of his boyhood during the war pushed me to take my storyline in a risky and exciting direction.

Others whom I thank for sharing their recollections of World War II and the '40s are: Bettie Blair, Brian Kiernan, Fred Krueger, Ilsa Krueger (my gratitude to Holly Krueger for loaning me her parents), Manfred Scholermann and Freddie Washington.

Also, my appreciation goes to good friends: Dr. David Becker, Jan Bryant, Ethel Price, Hoover Price Sr., Alaxandar Josephs (with special thanks for her excellent publicity photos), Marty Josephs, Pat Raybon, Karen Stancer and Laurence Washington.

The following people lent their expertise in various areas: Boonie McCune, of the Colorado Department of Education, hypnotherapist and NLP trainer Katie Peercy, Professor Robert Pois of the University of Colorado–Boulder, Christine St-Pierre of Tourisme Montreal, Captain Jack Rogers of the Denver Fire Department and Sandy Schecter of St. Martin's Press.

In addition, a number of institutions provided valuable assistance: the African American Museum of Philadelphia, Bennington Writing Workshops, Bread Loaf Writers Conference, Colorado Council on the Arts (with special thanks to Daniel Salazar), French Government Tourist Office, Rocky Mountain Women's Institute and the Ucross Foundation (with special thanks to Elizabeth Guheen and Sharon Dynak).

Also, I thank Ontario Tourism and Monica Campbell-Hoppé of the Canadian Consulate.

I have the good fortune of coming from a family of women of exceptional intelligence. And I thank my mother, Jacqueline Singleton, who has staunchly encouraged my writing since I was big enough to pick up a pencil, and my late grandmother, Evelyn Henderson, who taught me the magic of language and the importance of history. Also, I am grateful to my beloved great aunts who shared their own war stories. They were Alice Johnson, former WAC Anna Lee Rogers and Lena Vasser, all of whom I miss so very much.

And I can't forget my grandfather Alonzo Vasser. He believed in my writing and my future from early on.

I am definitely indebted to Naomi Horii for pointing me in the direction of BlueHen Books, where Caitlin Hamilton and Kim Frederick-Law worked so hard to ensure the success of my novel.

Tremendous gratitude goes to my editor, Fred Ramey, who discovered my book and thus saved my life in the truest sense, for appreciating and nurturing my work and being so much fun to argue with.